Museum of Unheard (of) Things

[ANY 02]

Museum der unerhörten Dinge is
a "Literary Cabinet of Curiosities"
founded and curated by Roland Albrecht,
located between house numbers 5 and 6
on Crellestraße in Schöneberg, Berlin.

The museum displays unique things
and their unheard (of) stories,
all categorized according to weight,
and holds the record of being
the most visited museum in Berlin
(if one offsets the number of visitors
to the square meters of the exhibition space).

Museum of Unheard (of) Things is
the catalogue raisonné of the museum,
assembling its entire current inventory,
translated into English for the first time.

It intends to grow as the museum collection expands.
At the present moment (Fall 2015) it contains 78 items.

ANY 02 | Museum of Unheard (of) Things

Published by ALREADY NOT YET
ISBN: 978-0-996-94420-5

Book and cover design by You Nakai & Kay Festa

ALREADY NOT YET is a publisher run by members of No Collective, dedicated to consummating the age to come by making available unprecedented texts that question and/or traverse the boundaries of art, theory, fiction, and other curiosities, primarily via the medium of language.

http://alreadynotyet.org
http://nocollective.com

Send inquiries, requests, proposals and surprises to: info@alreadynotyet.org

Museum of Unheard (of) Things

Roland Albrecht

Translated by Alexander Booth and You Nakai

ALREADY NOT YET
Brooklyn, New York
2015

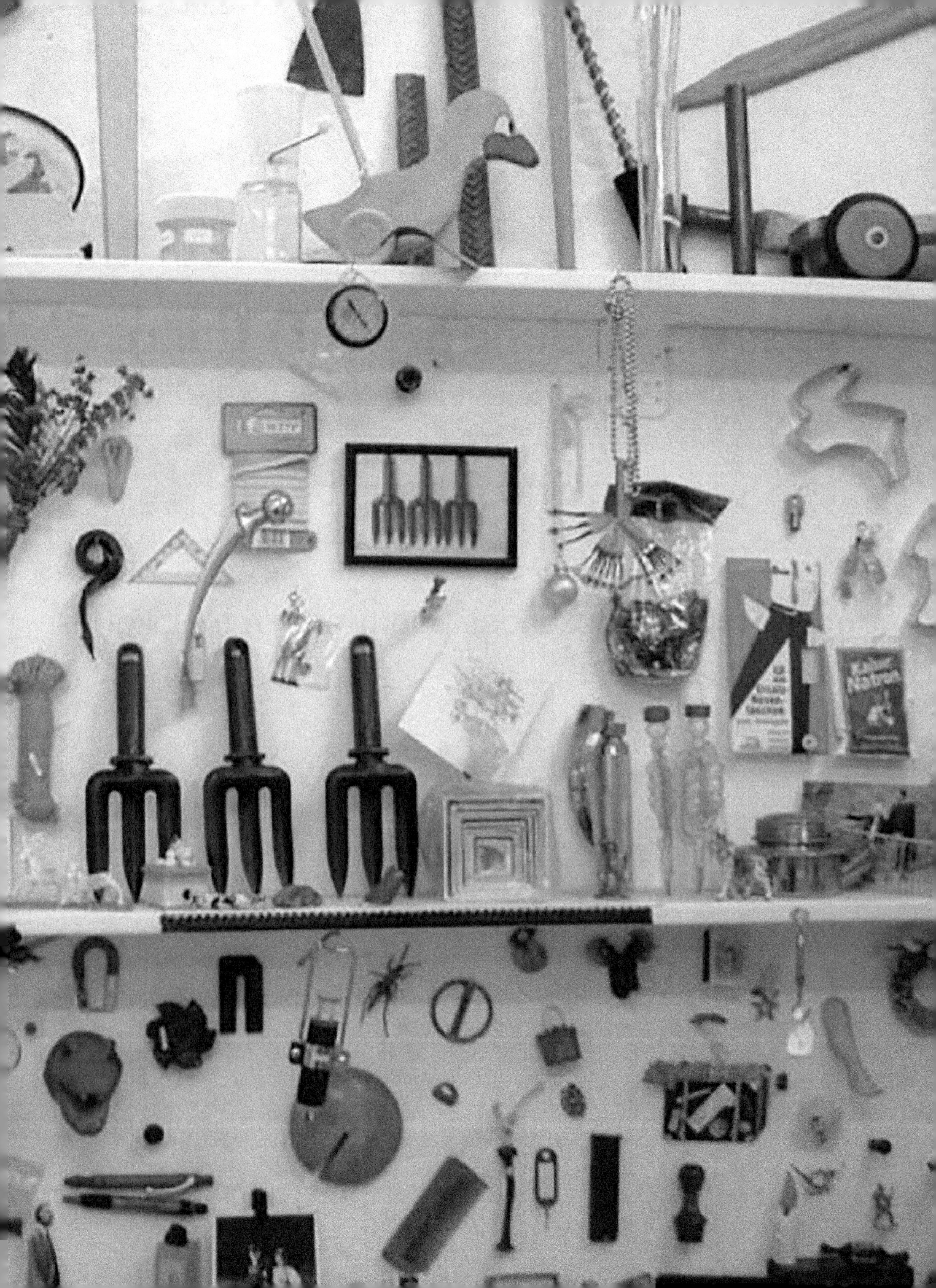

Inventory

<0.001g - 0.015g

0.016g - 0.050g

0.051g - 0.100g

0.101g - 0.170g

0.171g - 0.250g

0.251g - 1.000g

>1.001g

>0.000g

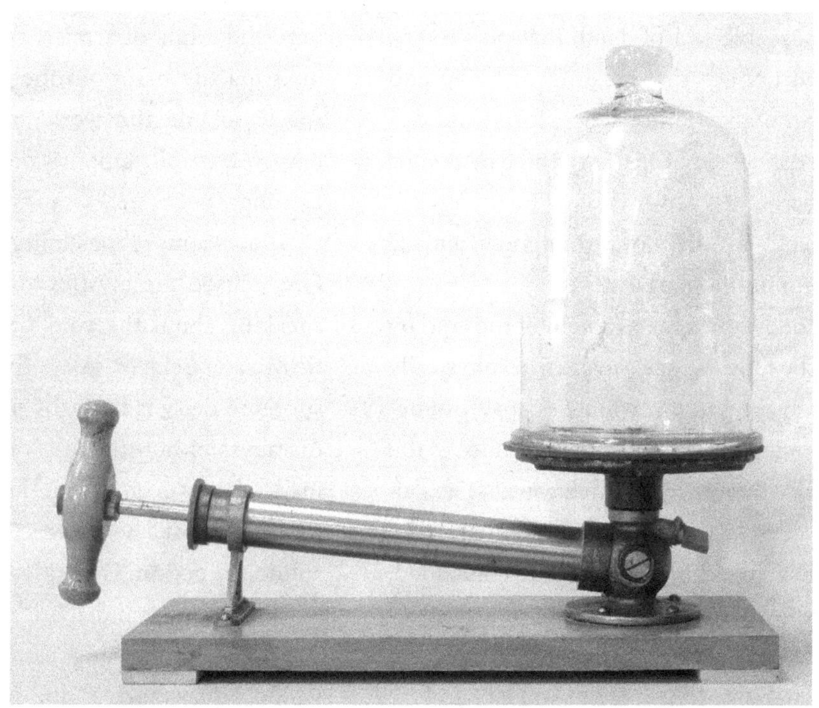

The Void and the Spontaneous Decay of the Vacuum or New Proofs of God

The question of the void has occupied humankind since time immemorial and indeed concerns the question "where do I come from, where am I going?" It is the question about our existence, about the inescapable fact of death that plagues us. The void implies the question of being and thereby the question of space, for a void can only be conceived of spatially and a being fills up a space.

The void is a place of nothingness, a place filled with nothingness.

Aristotle solved the problem of the void by saying the following: The void is a "physically unfilled space, but one which is capable of becoming filled." He rejected the presence of the void, since the space in which we exist was an already filled space where the void did not occur and could not be included. He concluded, "Since the void is not the cause of any effect in nature, the emptiness cannot be affixed." In short, what is not there is not and is therefore not worthy of concern.

This opinion was commonly supported by most philosophers from Thales to Plato, as Plutarch writes in Chapter 18 of the first book of *The Doctrines of the Philosophers*. Democritus, Demetrius, Epicurus, et al., recognized the void to be present in its infinite potential. The Stoics were convinced that the void existed not within the world, but within infinity outside the world. They argued: If there is a filled space, there must also be an unfilled one.

Christianity transferred the insights of the Greeks onto their worldview and, with them, the problem of the void and nothingness as well. Furthermore, nothingness was a place of limitlessness, and there was also the opinion that this question could not be posited to begin with. Christianity took over the unfathomable empty space of the Greeks, replaced their world of the gods with their world of God, filled it with angels and countless numbers and kinds of armies, and placed God in his tripartite nature in the middle. Thus the space outside the world of things was not empty, but full. Opposition was not long in coming.

The incomprehensibility of this world of God caused the mystics to once again begin speaking about the void. The medieval mystic Meister Eckhart said, "The sinking into the supreme deity is basically just a descent into the abyss of nothingness." The other opinion insisted, however, that nothingness was nothing, or at most a hell, a descent into a void, absolute extinction. God revealed himself in the world of things and therefore was not to be equated with nothingness, otherwise things would be themselves and not the revelation of God.

With the advent of the Enlightenment the question pragmatized itself and became increasingly materialized. The question became: what would happen if you could produce nothingness? As Descartes would say about emptiness, which he rejected as non-existent:

> *If someone asks what would happen if God were to take away every single body contained in a jar, without allowing any other body to take the place of what had been removed, the answer must be that the sides of the jar would in that case have to be in contact. For when there is nothing between two bodies they must necessarily touch each other.*

At the end of the sixteenth century the mayor of Magdeburg, Otto von Guericke, became interested in nothingness. He saw nothingness as a place of wonder and the absolute:

> *Everything that is, is within nothingness. And if God were to bring the fabric of the world, which he created, back to nothingness, nothing would remain but that nothingness, the uncreated, just as it was before the beginning of the world. For the uncreated is that which has no beginning, as nothingness is that which has no beginning. Nothingness encompasses all. It is more precious than gold. Strange is its growth and decay. It is more refreshing than the sight of the light, more noble than a king's blood, it is equal to the heavens, higher than all the stars, more powerful than a beam of lightning, it is complete in itself and thoroughly exhilarating. Nothingness is full of all wisdom. Where nothingness is, the power of kings fail. Nothingness alone knows no suffering.*

Otto von Guericke was a man captured by the Enlightenment Age: only that which existed was of interest to him, and that which was conceivable could also exist—if it did not, it was to be invented or discovered. If nothingness were conceivable, then it also had to be capable of being produced.He undertook experiments in which he pumped the air out of two compressed hemispheres and thereby invented the vacuum. At an imperial diet in Regensburg he demonstrated the force of vacuum at his own expense by having eight brewery horses each stretch one side of a vacuum ball, which proved that all the power from two-times-eight horses was not enough to separate an empty ball. Only when one freed the ball from the vacuum, the emptiness, and again filled it with air could it be separated by any children's hand.

Based on Guericke's experiments, and with his discovery of vacuum and air pressure, the motor could later be invented, and airplanes could be flown; and because of his calculations of nothingness, rockets can be shot into space today. The natural sciences split away from philosophical reflections and no longer considered the question of the void. The only thing they desired was practical application.

However, the philosophers and thinkers stuck to their question about nothingness and once again either put it on par with the Divine, with the absolute, or denied its existence outright. Johann Wolfgang von Goethe: "No living atom comes at last to naught! / Active in each is still the eternal Thought: / Hold fast to Being if thou wouldst be blest." G. W. F. Hegel: "...the Nothing, the first, from which all being and the multiplicity of the finite emerged." Franz Grillparzer: "One cannot conceive of nothingness, for thinking always remains and any idea about nothingness is then really just as an abstraction from the object." Pier Paolo Pasolini: "Whoever desires nothingness, desires power." Martin Heidegger: "Man is a placeholder of nothingness." Karl May: "You null, you nothing, you hole in nature."

In recent years, scientific research and philosophical reflections have once more engaged in a debate about nothingness. In physics there is the unexplained phenomenon of "the spontaneous decay of the neutral vacuum." This means that before an absolute vacuum can be attained, particles are formed in this near-vacuum and disintegrate right before the final one. For this very reason up until today no absolute vacuum has ever been produced. Where these particles come from is a complete mystery; it seems as if they do indeed come from out of nothingness.

There are two theories about this "spontaneous decay of the vacuum" and the origin of particles coming from out of nothingness.

The first theory: if an absolute vacuum could be produced, it would be an empty and godless space. But since a godless space can and must not exist, this space spontaneously disintegrates before it can emerge.

The second theory: if an absolute vacuum could be produced, this empty space would be the seat of God, or even God himself. Each and every person could install a vacuum pump at home and pump out God according to need, desire, and mood. God cannot allow this arbitrariness in his availability and therefore prevents his becoming through the decay of the vacuum into absolute nothingness.

And so the natural sciences, which stepped up to prove to God his limitations, through its efforts to produce a nothingness, in the end, point back to God.

Literature:

Gerhard Hummel, *God in Natural Science,* Regensburg, 2001.

Matthias Puhle, *The World in Empty Space: Otto von Guericke 1602-1686,* Munich, 2002.

Jonas Trobel, *The Not-Thinking,* Munich, 1987.

>0.000g - 0.015g

<0.001g

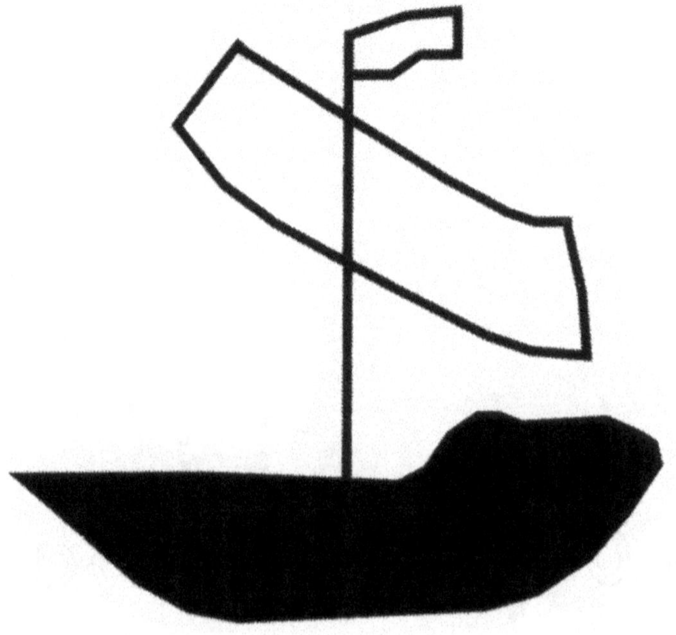

How the Ahoy Came to Seafaring

or

The Contribution of Sealess Bohemia to Sailing

In 1634 Igor Cleppr from the Bohemian town of Kutná Hora went to sea, and in no time at all his Bohemian greeting and farewell of "Ahoy" rapidly spread to become an independent word for invoking ships in the language of seafaring.

Even as a child Igor Cleppr had a great love for the sea. Again and again he secretly crept into the Baroque Catholic church of his native town to look at the painting of a large ship in distress being rescued by the gracious mother of God. Igor Cleppr's parents belonged to the Hussite faith, so it was not easy for him to go unnoticed in a Catholic church.

In the spring of 1634, just as the month turned into May and Igor Cleppr turned seventeen, he packed his sack, said his goodbyes, took his walking stick, and made his way to Hamburg to be hired on a ship.

Hoeg Dilsen, the captain of the Pride of Deventer, was just preparing the paperwork in order to set sail the following day with a favorable wind. They would be going to Antwerp. It was just a simple cargo trip, but he needed a few quiet, yet strong, hands. Igor Cleppr seemed the right boy for the job.

Igor Cleppr's incessant "Ahoy" quickly earned him the nickname "The Ahoy."

Already within half a year "Ahoy" was heard on other ships. Within three years "Ahoy" became the standard sailor's word for ship greetings and farewells. At the First Conference for the Unification of Civilian Ship Law in Antwerp in 1642, held on the occasion of the shipwreck at Glasgow in 1640, "Ahoy" became the official term for invoking ships.

Igor Cleppr returned to his beloved Kutná Hora in 1652, and everybody marveled at his whale tooth and tamed monkeys. After his death, the whale tooth was given to the Catholic church in Kutná Hora and can still be seen there today.

Literature:

Robert P. MacDowell, *Nautical Terms,* London, 1912.

Peter Moms, *Contributions of Countries to Ship Sailing,* Munich, 1898.

Rudolf Pilacik, *How a Whale Tooth Came to Kutná Hora,* Munich, 1988.

<0.001g

<0.001g

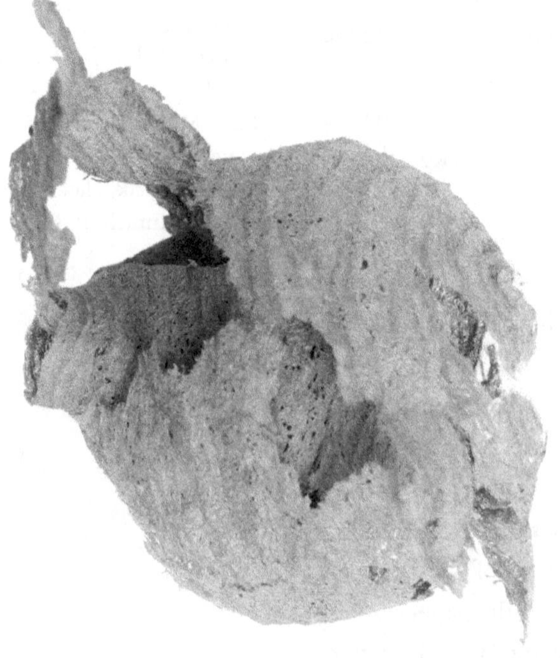

The Wasp Honeycomb Collection Point in Kröte

If you ask an art historian specializing in the Baroque about the town of Ludwigslust, first he will speak about the local papier-mâché sculptures, then describe the papier-mâché manufacturer, and finally begin to rave about the Ludwigslust Carton Company.

But very few indeed will know about Gottfried Keiser—Keiser spelled with an E.

Over 200 years ago Arthur Gottfried Keiser of Kröte was a key player in the refinement and transformation of waste paper into art and into sculpture. And, in fact, he is responsible for one of the most important contributions to improving and stabilizing the famous Ludwigslust cardboard: thanks to him, the sculptures could be weatherproofed for the first time.

Under the rule of the art-loving, educated, and god-fearing Frederick the Pious (1717-1785) Ludwigslust, 60 kilometers from Kröte, became a center for the production of papier-mâché sculptures.

Frederick the Pious, Duke of Mecklenburg, moved his residence from Schwerin to Ludwigslust eight years after the death of his father, Duke Christian Ludwig II, and immediately began to turn the old castle into a Baroque palace, to organize the village like a chessboard according to mathematical formulas, and to combine the palace with a magnificent Baroque garden in the French style with many water systems. It is no wonder that the whole castle is known as the "Versailles of Mecklenburg."

Frederick the Pious was engaged in a long-standing feud with Frederick II, King of Prussia. Prussian soldier recruiters regularly intruded into the ducal country to enlist young men, often by force. This angered Frederick the Pious so strongly that on the one hand he entered into an alliance with Sweden and let Swedish troops fighting against the Prussian king pass through Mecklenburg; and on the other he bought back the subjects the Prussian military had kidnapped for great sums of money and set them free again. Legend has it that he spent so much money on the ransom of his stolen subjects, that he had no money left for his castle's expansion nor its decoration with massive sculptures made out of marble or fine woods and metals. The only thing he could afford was papier-mâché sculptures, and thus he soon established his own carton manufacturer.

The papier-mâché sculptures of Ludwigslust quickly became very famous, world famous in fact, and the sculptures made out of old, recycled paper became a major export across Europe.

Early on the Ludwigslust carton was suitable only for indoor installation; however, people soon started using a refined, secret recipe and coating it in high gloss for outdoor installation thereby making it fit for parks and resistant to any kind of rain. To this day only specialists and connoisseurs know that the Ludwigslust sculptures installed in Baroque gardens throughout Europe are made out of cardboard.

This method of making the sculptures weather resistant remained a mystery until very recently, for the recipe had never been written down. In 1835 the demand for cardboard products declined so strongly that the factory was closed down and the knowledge of the papier-mâché recipe lost.

In the Prussian Secret State Archives there is a note mentioning that Kröte, which had six farmsteads in 1776, delivered large amounts of wasp nests to Ludwigslust. A citizen of Kröte named Arthur Gottfried Keiser, Keiser with an E, was responsible for this delivery and is said to have delivered up to 1,000 nests annually. Gottfried Keiser ran a "Wasp Honeycomb Collection Point" where, for a small payment, people could drop off their unwanted wasp nests. He had set up a special wasp-breeding apiary in his barn with around 100 nests. A marginal note in the document states, however, that the reason why the people of Ludwigslust used the wasp nests was unknown.

In 2008 an expert team of restorers from Holland led by the paper restorer Erik Fens succeeded in beginning to unravel the mystery of Ludwigslust carton. They showed that wasps' honeycomb was processed in every single layer of the cardboard sculptures. Which is to say that in each and every sample they examined they found high concentrations of different material from wasp nests.

That the writings on Ludwigslust can be found in the Secret State Archives in Berlin is due, on the one hand, to the aforementioned hostility between the two Fredericks, as one can easily see; but on the other hand it is also due to the secret that the recycled, printed paper concealed. The Prussians knew that the recycled paper used for the sculptures in Ludwigslust was not only bought from outside, but that it was also their own—in other words, the outdated files, documents, and notes from the ducal firms. The Berliners therefore repeatedly bought Ludwigslust sculptures not because they wanted to exhibit them—recourse to cardboard sculptures was unnecessary for the Prussians—but to take them apart and then reassemble the paper pieces in order to uncover Frederick the Pious's official secrets.

Thus we know more about the business of Frederick the Pious thanks to the restoration of old Ludwigslust papers in the Prussian Secret State Archives than from what is contained in the files of the royal archives in Ludwigslust itself. And we also know about the "Wasp Honeycomb Collection Point" in Kröte.

And where is Kröte exactly? In Wendland, 120 kilometers southeast of Hamburg, in the municipality of Waddeweitz, near the tiny villages of Dickfeitzen and Clenze.

Literature:

Peter Karl, *Paper Spies: On the Being of the Agent*, Hannover, 1961.

Robert Mayer, *Paper, Wasps*, Hamburg, 1957.

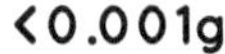

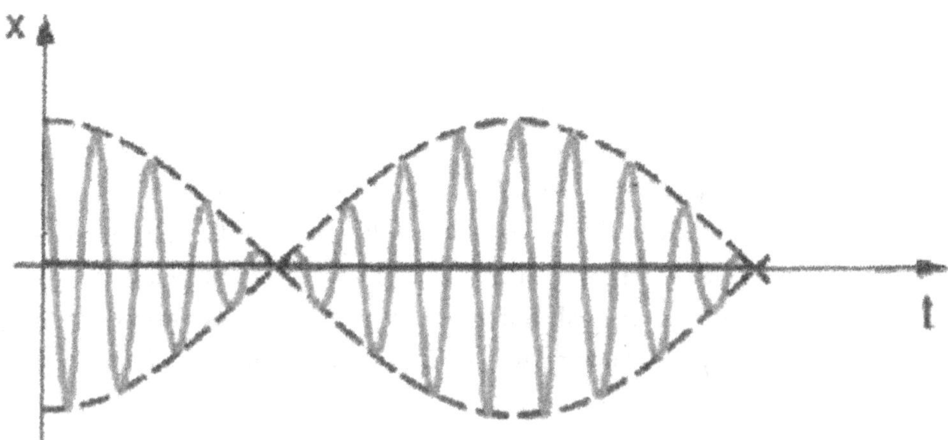

Bruno Retlau and His Tone-Neutralizer

or

The Audible Silence of Anti-Sound

Destructive interference, also called anti-noise, arises when a sound, tone, or noise—whether pleasant or disturbing—is eliminated. In other words, when a real existing tone or noise is rendered inaudible by another one. The original source of the tone, as well as that of the newly generated one, is not heard.

This physical phenomenon can be explained as follows. Each and every tone and sound is an oscillating wave the depth of which is called amplitude. Now, if an anti-amplitude—in other words, an identical counter oscillation—is applied to the first oscillation, both waves come into balance, are neutralized, and thus are no longer audible. The tones block each other so that no further sound waves can emerge. What is obtained is silence in the truest sense of the word—an audible silence, so to speak, for both the original tone as well as the newly created opposite one.

This audible silence, however, is fundamentally different from simple inaudible silence. In the latter there is no tone, sound, or noise—no amplitude deflection has been made. It is simply an absence of tone. In audible silence not only is a tone present, but it has been doubled, for a new sound, equal in strength and quality, has been set against the original one, albeit in negative form. A doubled sound is virtually present, although neither the original nor the newly emerged one can actually be heard.

Bruno Retlau (1900-1984) was the first person to show interest in this phenomenon. Retlau lived at Number 7 Methfesselstraße in the district of Kreuzberg in Berlin. His friend Konrad Zuse lived two houses away. Bruno Retlau did not live with his parents as Zuse did, however; he had a small independent apartment on the ground floor. But both were somewhat crazy, extremely self-confident, and stubborn engineers. The one wanted to build a general-purpose computer, the other a machine for pure, interference-free audio recording and playback. Zuse had abandoned his promising career in engineering at the Henschel Aircraft Factory where he had met Retlau, ten years his senior. Zuse's parents were skeptical of their son but nevertheless allowed him to tinker with his computer in their living room. Bruno Retlau, on the contrary, had a very small fortune with which he could live more poorly than well. He gave up his job at the Henschel Aircraft Factory a year after Zuse in order to devote himself entirely to the issue of sound recording and playback.

To this day the Methfesselstraße in Kreuzberg is a cobblestone street leading up to a slight, natural hill, which is a rarity in otherwise flat Berlin. Right at the top there stood the old Schultheiss Brewery, which has since been shut down. At one point a real estate agency wanted to convert the brewery site into outrageously expensive apartments and lofts, but they filed for bankruptcy during the first phase of construction so that only an unfinished building remains.

Be that as it may, today no beer carriages rattle up and down the Methfesselstraße as they did every day when Zuse and Bruno Retlau lived there. Many of these beer carriages had iron-banded wheels, which made a fair amount of noise, and the heavy horse-carts with their fittings clattered constantly. This racket annoyed Bruno Retlau to no end. He was highly sensitive to sounds, so he sent petitions to the district office of Kreuzberg to have the road tarred so that the biggest and fiercest vibrations might be absorbed. Nothing happened. His friend Zuse, who lived in Apartment 10 on the third floor, also resented the vibrations, which could be felt even in his flat. And so, both decided to take matters into their own hands. Zuse wanted to install a device in his apartment that would work against the vibrations. It would be a kind of a centrifugal gyro system oscillating in the opposite direction of the vibrations in the road. Today a similar technique is used for bridges and high-rise buildings. However, he was so busy with his computer that, in the end, his plan amounted to little more than a few drawings and calculations. Things were different for Bruno Retlau. The noise of the beer carriages was difficult to investigate and analyze. Following the theories of Paul Lueg (published in 1933), he undertook attempts to neutralize the noisy street sounds by countering the original sound oscillations with their opposites. These calculations were the first tasks Zuse gave his primordial computer to execute. After Zuse and Bruno Retlau compared the results of their handwritten calculations with great interest, they found out that both the computer as well as Retlau had made mistakes.

With time, however, Bruno Retlau got better at neutralizing sounds, and he sometimes even managed to produce a fairly concentrated and acceptable silence. He installed microphones on the Methfesselstraße, which decreased the sounds produced by the beer carriages. He directed these original tones in a kind of "anti-scope." This device measured the parameters—amplitude, phase, and frequency—of the real wave and generated a new wave with opposite values, which was then sent to large loudspeakers that projected the anti-wave at the coaches. The problem was that electrical impulses had to be processed faster than sound so that the artificial anti-wave could reach the original tone and eliminate it in time. At the trial stage the strangest things happened. At one point only high and painful sounds could be heard, at another the brewery vehicles sounded extremely wood-like. And sometimes the whole street squeaked obnoxiously or simply growled.

To this day some of the street's older residents tell stories of strange noises that could be heard in the Methfesselstraße as well as an almost frightening silence that would occur now and again where you couldn't even hear your own words, let alone the aircraft from the nearby airport of Tempelhof which provided the background noise that people had come to depend on.

During the war Bruno Retlau engaged in homeland service, as he was deemed unfit for service at the front. He came to the town of Grafenau in the Bavarian Forest, settled there, and married the daughter of a cinema owner. All of his equipment as well as the records of his Tone-Neutralizer were destroyed in the 1944 bombing of Berlin. Bruno Retlau enjoyed the silence of the forest where sounds were not as mixed together as they were in the big cities. He never returned to his hometown. He lived with his wife Judith at the Kino Delphi. He wrote to his friend Zuse in 1974:

> *...I enjoy the silence of the woods and congratulate you on your success and the belated, but well-deserved, recognition you are receiving to-*

> *day. I still fondly remember our attempts with my crazy calculations and your machine. I, for one, am glad to no longer have to concern myself with sounds...*

The inhabitants of Grafenau recall how the sounds and music in Kino Delphi were so intense that people always felt they were sitting right in the midst of actual events. That hissing one remembered from all other cinemas was missing.

Bruno Retlau died in 1984. His wife ran the cinema for the next three years. In 1987 the Kino Delphi was closed, and a branch of a chain drugstore moved in but not before selling all the cinema paraphernalia to a scrap dealer.

Literature:
Peter Kempin, *The Death of Origins*, Berlin, 2001.
—, *Anti-Noise and the Entertainers*, Berlin, 1982.
Hugo Mayer, *The History of Destructive Interference*, Munich, 2000.
Kreuzberg District Office, Commemorative Plaque in the Methfesselstraße

0.001g

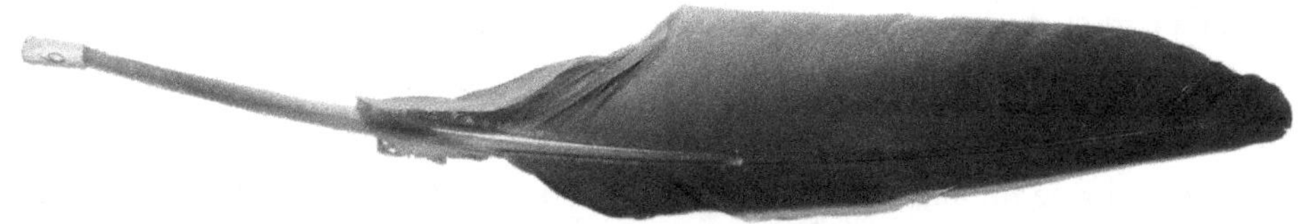

The Mystery of the Black Feather

or

The True Life of Artist Fellows in Wiepersdorf

Carl-Johann sat at his desk, nearly a skeleton, already ten pounds lighter than just a few days before. Around him lay empty low-fat cottage cheese boxes and beside him a black chicken feather. "Oh my," he said with fear and surprise, "it's you again. I'd forgotten that it was already Wednesday." At first the cleaning lady, grown patient through multiple insights into the private sphere of others, said nothing; in fact, she did not even look irritated for a second, but this in turn irritated Carl-Johann. How could she not have noticed that he was on the trail of the mystery of the black feather?

He had found the black rooster feather just a little while earlier during a tour of the village and shortly thereafter saw a whole flock of white chickens in a yard. He immediately remembered a shrine he had seen dozens of years before in a basilica high up on a mountain above a bend in the Danube River in Esztergom, Hungary. A black chicken feather embedded in silver, framed by precious stones. Carl-Johann had nothing to do with religion and did not understand it, having been raised as the only child of parents who were purely interested in the here and now. At the time he wondered how people could have ever come up with such an idea, embedding a chicken feather in silver. He later learned that the feather represented the impurity of creation but that impurity also belonged to the white of purity, of virginity, and that one could not exist without the other. The origin of such feather worship was that great Spanish pilgrimage route to the tomb of St. Jacob where a miracle had taken place.

From the moment he found the feather, he could not stop thinking about this. And so he immediately interrupted his work in the hopes of tracking down the feather's secret. He wanted to both know and to learn just what kind of feelings, and in what kind of ways, would make people worship a black chicken feather. The veneration of the black chicken feather had begun in Santo Domingo de la Calzada along the so-called "Camino." So that he could come closer to the pilgrims who were starving, praying, and hiking en route to Santiago de Compostela, Carl-Johann intended to enter into a state of deprivation by following the fast which had been developed by a certain Professor Müller. And thus, as a first step, he bought a lot of low-fat cottage cheese.

At the beginning of the fifteenth century the veneration of the black chicken feather spread throughout Europe. Chicken cages displaying white hens and roosters were set up in many cathedrals, and these hens and roosters were not allowed to have a single black feather. If they did, it was plucked, for only a white chicken symbolized the unity and virginity under which sign the miracle of Santo Domingo de la Calzada had taken place.

The plucked feathers were highly sought after by the faithful for symbolizing impurity and showing that purity first had to be plucked before it could become really pure, that even within purity sin had its place. At first people made fun of such devotion to plucked feathers, but when they became more prized than the white hens and roosters themselves, folks began to throw the black feathers away or to hide them. Very soon quick-minded businessmen began to profit from expensive, certified feathers as well as cheap, uncertified ones.

The whole thing became ever more unsettling to the clergy and so they slowly began to remove the chicken cages from the churches once again. The custom has survived until the present day only in Santo Domingo de la Calzada, for it was in this pilgrimage town that, with the active help of St. Domingo, the miracle originally occurred.

Seeing as that Carl-Johann could not make the pilgrimage himself (lacking all the prerequisites as he did—the faith, the devotion, the idea of redemption), he wanted to starve himself and thereby experience castigation. Prof. Müller's cottage cheese diet, which he'd heard warnings about on the radio, could put him in this state of hunger, and through that state of hunger he might get an idea of redemption, or at least redemption from starvation. The cottage cheese diet demanded that the fasting person eat only one container of cottage cheese per day, spread out over four times, and that they chew precisely twenty-four times for each spoonful. The salivary enzymes in the mouth would do most of the digestive work.

Carl-Johann strictly followed the specifications, counted the number of chews while eating, and consumed nothing other than cottage cheese and water. Day by day he felt hungrier. Soon he began to feel that he was focusing more and more on himself, and less and less on his environment. The only thing that found its way to the center of his attention was the shorter eating process and the lessening of intestinal activity. After four days he felt very close to the pilgrims indeed, sensed the consciousness of the starving, and the delivery of his very being. He often thought about the pilgrim couple Philips from Saities who had belonged to the diocese of Cologne.

This pilgrim couple had set out in 1465 in order to pay tribute to the great St. James, accompanied by their wonderful son Marcus. One July evening, they got a hostel in Santo Domingo de la Calzada. The maid of the hostel liked the handsome son so much that she repeatedly tried to get his attention. He, however, did not react; therefore the rejected girl retaliated by hiding a silver cup in his luggage and in the morning accused him of theft. The cup was discovered and the summoned judge sentenced the innocent boy to death by hanging. In sadness and despair his parents continued on their way to the Apostle's grave.

Upon their return, they passed by the executioner's place and saw that their son was still alive, healthy, and in good spirits even though he still was tied to the hangman's noose. What they did not and could not see was that St. Domingo was beneath him, supporting him on his shoulders. They immediately rushed to the judge who was sitting down to eat a roasted rooster and a roasted hen on the plate in front of him. When he heard the story of their son, he laughed out loud. "Your son is as dead as the chicken on my table! The hen will not cackle, nor the rooster crow." But at that very moment the two animals jumped up from his plate and immediately began to sprout feathers. The cock crowed loudly several times, and the hen scratched and cackled to herself. "In Santo Domingo de la Calzada the chicken crowed after being roasted"—the saying goes today. The boy was immediately released, and the maid was hanged in his place.

Ever since then a vaulted niche decorated in honor of this great miracle and known as

"El Gallinero" (the chicken coop) has stood in the Cathedral of Santo Domingo de la Calzada in the right wing of the transept. There, up to this very day, a white hen and a white rooster are kept. Every three weeks they are replaced, and each is thoroughly investigated to make sure it has neither black feather nor fluff to disturb its purity. Opposite the chicken coop hangs a piece of wood from the gallows with the sign: "Esta madera es de la horca del pelegrino" (This wood is from the gallows of the pilgrim). The miracle with the chickens became so popular that, by virtue of the event, the rooster was later named the national animal of Spain.

Carl-Johann was very close to attaining the feeling that such legends create when the cleaning lady came into his room, and, after a long silence, said to him clearly: "You look famished. Go to the kitchen. There's something left over from lunch today that you can warm up." Carl-Johann knew that he had to leave his room for two hours, and the cleaning woman's clear, contrary, and negative tone made him go into the kitchen. And indeed a wonderful and warm dish awaited him there, which he ate with great pleasure: marinated chicken with hoisin sauce, vegetables, and rice.

Literature:
E. Bingel, *The Miracle of the Black Feather*, Berlin/Santiago, 2003.
Nolte/Sossenheimer (eds.), *Wiepersdorf Castle*, Göttingen, 1997.

0.001g

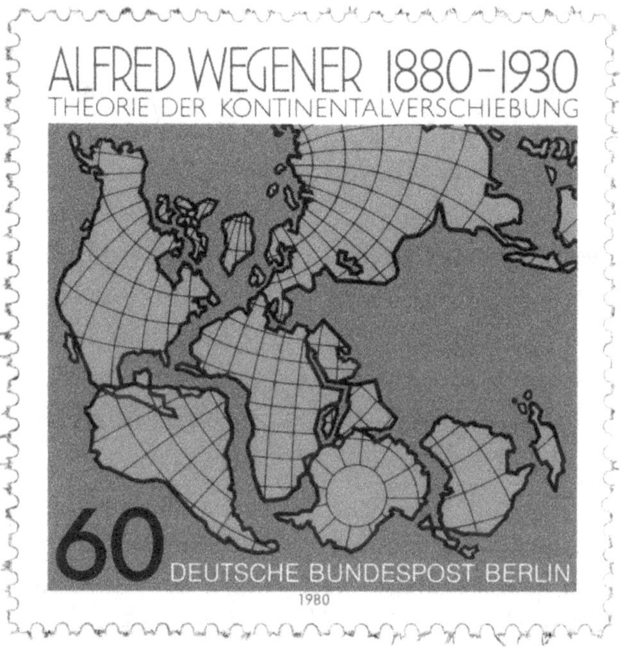

On the Beginning of Light

and

On the End of Vegetarianism

In 1969 the great Fluxus artist and engineer George Brecht (1926-2008) made the proposal to relocate England to the Caribbean for five years in order to democratize the average amount of sunlight exposure between continents. He made drawings to show how this could be done and also found a nice location for the UK to be anchored. The plan, however, was not carried out.

In his proposal George Brecht referred to Geo-Cadence research, a geospatial theory of harmony in which it is assumed that all nature strives toward harmony and balance. High-pressure strives toward low-pressure, alkaline strives toward acid, and so forth.

It was only with the establishment of Geo-Cadence research at the end of the twentieth century—to which, it must be stated, the Bielefeld sociologist Dietmar Badger contributed considerably—that the laws of Geo-Cadence were detected in almost all phenomena, and the tectonics of the Earth's crust became comprehensible.

The continental plates of the north strive for the warmer south, and the southern plates aim for a bit of the cooler northern regions. Already Alfred Wegener (1880-1930), the discoverer and pioneer of plate tectonics, had suspected that a goal-oriented force had to lie behind continental drift.

On the basis of this science of balancing, of harmony, which is very similar to the Asian idea of balancing forces, one can understand why Kröte, that quiet and resilient town in Wendland in the North German Lowlands, had remained on the equator for such a long time.

The small village of Kröte with its thirty inhabitants lay on the equator for almost 150 million years. From the Cambrian to the end of the Devonian Period, in fact, long before the supercontinent of Pangea arose, Kröte lay on the equator and intended to stay put. It belonged to the small but autonomous continent of Baltica and, even when all the earth's plates moved and the continent of Baltica gave up its independence to form the continent Laurussia with North America, Kröte continued to cling on to the equator.

Kröte was located on the southwestern continental shelf on a lagoon by the ocean. There the ocean would have been heard; if there had been fish, one would have seen them swimming in the waters; if there had been animals on the land, they would have peacefully come and gone along the beach. But, instead, it was a bare, sandy, rocky, and desolate place. No palm trees grew in Kröte, not a single plant greened its shores. Nothing at all existed in the whole dry world just then. The only plants that were there grew in the sun-flooded water.

And it just so happened that on the beach of Kröte some plants had to choose whether they would die out on account of the lagoon which was constantly drying up or adapt to the new waterless, arid, and airy way of life.

Kröte's decision was a long time in the making, a few million generations in fact, but then, suddenly, the earth was green, plants evolved out of the water, changed shape, and their stalks grew in size from small to huge. Horsetail forests emerged. Clubmoss forests.

But the greening of the world was not the only thing to emerge from the Bay of Kröte. Following the Geo-Cadence theory, the continent of Baltica would by that point have drifted to the north in order to cool off and to obtain harmony. But that did not happen. The expanded Geo-Cadence theory, however, holds that what becomes compensated is not only heat, but social affairs as well. Here from Kröte the greening of the world emanated in a wondrous manner. But something else was needed, something which could neutralize the beautiful and compensate for the harmony. Thus emerged the eye, with which radiation was converted into light, and with which sight was made possible.

Previously there had only been cell organisms plodding along, bacteria and micro-organisms that drew their power from exposure to the sun and from sediment being washed about hither and thither and occasionally, when in their blindness encountering other cells, snapping shut to eat them. But then the first creatures to be endowed with eyes arose, compound eyes, which are still common among insects today. The first known eye appeared in the trilobite.

At that point it was all over with coziness. It was now possible to see the splendor of the green earth, true, but sight also awakened greed. Potentially delicious others could be detected, were found to indeed be tasty, and, on top of it, very nutritious. Vegetarianism was thereby out. The tasty ones now had to quickly obtain eyes in order to be able to avoid the craving ones or at least to be able to flee. Some grew thick armor as protection, others grew large teeth to be able to crack the shells. A spiraling movement of rearmament was built and established. "Thou shalt not crave thy neighbor..."—that was a much, much later development.

Now a balance had been achieved, the beautiful green compensated for the mechanism of eat-or-be-eaten. Kröte had lain on the equator long enough and in all respects had imposed a lasting effect upon the Earth; it could now drift to the north.

It took another 300 million years for Kröte to get to the place where it is today.

Literature:

Volker Arzt, *When Germany was at the Equator*, Berlin, 2001.
Dietmar, *The Geo-Cadence Principle*, Bielefeld, 1997.
——, "Oceans and Continents," in *Spektrum der Wissenschaft*, Heidelberg, 1987.
Jürgen Jerusalem, *From Radiation to Light*, Berlin, 1998.
Peter Kempin, *Striving for Balance*, Berlin, 2001.
Günther Schmatz, *Eating and Being Eaten*, Munich, 1967.

0.001g

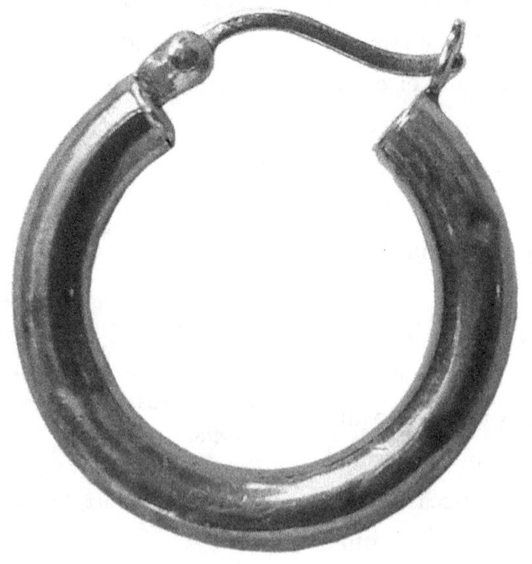

Why the Ear-Slitting Surgeon Mathias Gotthilf Lauphner Is Also Called the "Father of Plastic Surgery" or How the Correction of Ear-Slits Helped Middleclass Women to Attain a Second Beauty

During the first great imperial legal investigation in 1485 it was discovered that, after having expiated their deserved punishment in a particular region, many wrongdoers, rogues, and thieves would move on to other cities and areas where they were unknown in order to continue their dubious activities. For this reason people increasingly began to brand such riff-raff or to cut their earlobes with one or more slits. As a result, these people became marked and visible to all.

This method of ear-marking, however, already had a long and successful disciplinary history in Christian seafaring. Defiant, contentious, and peace-disturbing sailors would have their obligatory golden earring torn violently from their earlobes so that only a painful ear slit remained. In the case of the sailor's drowning, his ripped-away ring was originally worn to guarantee the body a Christian burial once it washed anonymously onto shore as, being made of gold, it would cover the funeral expenses. But without these earrings the drowned body would be buried on the beach where it was found. The prospect of such an un-Christian end terrified everyone. Furthermore, an earmarked man would no longer be hired on any ship. Even in civilian life people would quickly note a mark on the ear. When you encountered such a "slit-ear rascal" you immediately knew whom you were dealing with: a ne'er-do-well up to no good.

This successful method of punishment soon spread throughout the free cities of the north. Scammers, swindlers, and false preachers were punished in this way "so that they would immediately be recognized as such in other places too."

However, the further south one went, the more unusual this form of punishment became. There was, you might say, a sort of natural slit-ear border. Most often ear-slitting was imposed to the north of the Main River but rarely, if ever, to the south of it.

Opponents of this kind of punishment argued that such injuries could also occur from accidents at work—for instance, from woodcutting or horse-shoeing—or from diseases known to disfigure ears. One text from 1488 described fifty-six possible ways the ear could be disfigured through injury. How were people to be able to distinguish brave men from evil ones without mistreating the former? A pamphlet from 1510 demanded, "as, however, one cannot do an evil person wrong, for the sake of justice, it would be better to just hang him immediately..."

For all the rightly or wrongly marked people help, however, could be found in the small Swabian imperial city of Memmingen.

Mathias Gotthilf Lauphner, born in 1498 in Lindau, resident barber surgeon in Memmingen, specialized in skin lesions. His masterful art of stitching with fresh catgut and fixing with resin glue so that after healing no visible scar remained was unparalleled. In fact, he mastered this art so well that he was once accused of witchcraft; but, as it turned out, the plaintiff had simply not paid his own bills, and so the charges were dropped, the plaintiff convicted, and he himself was physically marked as a result.

Memmingen was proud of their famous barber surgeon, otherwise known as their slit-ear surgeon. Indeed, people came from all around to be treated by Mathias Gotthilf Lauphner.

It must be recalled that it was strictly forbidden to recompose an ear that had been slit by court order; however, fixing an ear that had been injured in a work accident was considered good and just as innocent citizens were to be protected from the inconveniences that a slit-ear would justifiably give them.

In order to register for ear-slit correction surgery with M.G. Lauphner the patient had to submit a notarized letter from two independent notaries proving that the ear had indeed been injured in an accident. Furthermore, the accident had to be described in detail and officially confirmed witnesses had to be named.

At that time Memmingen had the highest density of established notaries in all the southern German cities (and you could be sure that the most magnificent houses in town belonged to them).

M.G. Lauphner employed twelve assistants at a sufficient wage who were then allowed to start their own businesses after seven years of training.

The success of his art resulted in him being increasingly urged to apply the art of surgical correction to aging women in the city as well.

And this he did. After his first tentative trials on the neck, he greatly improved his method and began to venture into corrective operations on the visible areas of the face. When the mayor's wife proudly appeared one day at Sunday mass with near-unwrinkled face, M.G. Lauphner became swamped with new registrations.

This, however, resulted in the religious authorities' immediate objection, for they felt it was arrogant for man to change what God had created. Such vain embellishment was the expression of old beliefs, of the ostentatious Catholic, they said, and could not be reconciled with the new, pure, reformed faith.

M.G. Lauphner, who unfortunately did not record his art in writing, did nevertheless pass on his knowledge and skills to his disciples and apprentices and thus the art of fine skin corrections that emerged from Memmingen spread all throughout Europe. M.G. Lauphner died in 1576, highly regarded and respected—i.e., wealthy—in Memmingen.

In 1597, the surgeon Gaspare Tagliacozzi from Bologna described for the first time the technique of plastic and reconstructive surgery, referring expressly to the students of Master Lauphner from Memmingen. Dottor Tagliacozzi specialized in truncated noses, which he fixed through a complicated, and rather painful, process. At that time the punishment of truncating noses was applied to miserable adulterers and delinquent prostitutes.

Literature:

M. Hiller, *The Closure of the Wounds*, Berlin, 1999.

K. Joller, *Penalties and Physical Integrity*, Osnabrück, 1975.

N. Nigell, *From the Slit-Ear to Creation: On the Beginnings of Cosmetic Surgery*, Nuremberg, 2001.

D. De Pellegrini, *German-Italian Comparisons*, Padua/Memmingen, 2000.

U. Sach, *What City Names Say*, Ulm, 1973.

B. Wagner, *On the History of Fine Threads*, Olching, 1953.

0.002g

How Curt Friedrich Ernst von Watzdorf, the Hussar of Wiesenburg, Pulled His Belt so Tight That It Tore or How a Figure of Speech Became a Survival Strategy

At the beginning of the twentieth century two new phrases appeared in everyday German: "to tear one's belt" and "to be in a state of shock." Both terms come from the language of the military and both terms describe a psychological process. "To tear one's belt" means "to pull oneself together." The person in question is not to indulge his feelings, his momentary emotions, but is instead to overcome and orient himself towards what is "higher" rather than that which is fleeting. It is an appeal to oneself to deny one's own tenderness for the purpose of attaining something better.

The word "shock" describes a condition in which "tearing one's belt" does not help, where feelings and experiences can no longer be organized, where the "shocked" person can no longer orient himself, where all previous experiences and coping mechanisms have failed. It is a state of great mental upheaval that is often associated with somatic responses.

Not coincidentally both terms first appeared during the First World War. Traditional medicine could no longer deny the power of the psyche described by Sigmund Freud as it had managed to do so well previously. With the recognition of a psyche, however, for the first time progressive doctors could describe the state they had previously observed in railroad collisions: the sudden, total change of a person, without any external traumatization, following an accident. The doctors observed the same symptoms in soldiers during wartime and described the condition as "shock." They took the term from a battle formation of the Middle Ages. A "shock" was that living wall of spear-carriers that would walk toward the enemy in close formation. The impact of two shocks mutually protected by shields was often so great that the staggering soldiers fell over without having even been stung—and this condition began to be known as having been "shocked."

During the First World War for the first time soldiers were designated as unfit for battle due to a "state of shock" and returned to the home front. The condition, the notion itself, was filed for the first time, and in large numbers, under this name.

The phrase "tearing one's belt" became popular around the same time as the notion of "shock." Indeed, some medical historians see it as a reaction to "shock." "Tearing one's belt" was mostly used by doctors who thought little of "shock" and such things that appealed to the outlandish psychic life of the soldiers. They were of the opinion that the soldiers who suffered from so-called "shock" were only effeminate cowards. One simply had to "tear one's belt" and return to a usable shape, even if only to die to the glory of the German fatherland in one of the trenches. That end was preferable to the feminization that would doubtlessly occur in an asylum where that cowardly body would have opportunity to rest and live on dishonorably while the enemy grew stronger.

"Tear your belt" was first heard in Germany from fathers returning from the war. They introduced it so that for their families, and especially for their sons, the lost war would continue and—at least privately—be won. The phrase itself originated with a regiment of Prussian Hussar Guards who had in reality not played any role in the recent war at all, seeing as it had been the first industrially led one in which attrition warfare became more decisive than the Hussars' prowess.

The commander of the Prussian Hussar Guard Regiment during the Franco-German War of 1870-71, Curt Friedrich Ernst von Watzdorf, invented the process of "tearing one's belt," a method that he had employed quite successfully upon himself and later propagated to his subordinates. Curt Friedrich Ernst von Watzdorf was a person of subtle and delicate feelings. "Oh, if only I had just two souls within my breast," he liked to paraphrase Goethe repeatedly, but he was also a true warhorse when it came to leading his regiment.

One of his main passions was the Wiesenburg Castle he had inherited in the High Fläming region and, in particular, the gardens and the pheasantry he had begun there. His enthusiasm for plantings in his garden at Wiesenburg drove him across Europe on the search for new and increasingly rare seedlings, which he then handed over to his talented forester Carl Gebbers for cultivation in the English style. Today his garden is regarded as the most beautiful between Wörlitz and Potsdam. In fact, many connoisseurs prefer his garden to others due to its diversity, sophistication, and peculiarities.

A second—and life-defining—passion of von Watzdorf's was his love, albeit an unrequited one. His beloved, as is often the case, had been promised to a man of higher standing. Von Watzdorf had met the "Württemberg princess"—whose name to this day remains a mystery—at a young age in Kannstadt (known as "Bad Cannstatt" since 1030) where they promised each other eternal love and mutual fidelity. In fact, his decision to rebuild the Wiesenburg Castle was for her; to give her, the princess who would be marrying below her station out of love, an adequate home.

However, one day a secret letter arrived from the Württemberg court informing him that nothing could come of this love, for the princess was not free to decide whose wife she would be. She did not belong to herself, as had become customary amongst the lower classes, but to the well-being of her gender and, in any event, had been engaged for a long time. He was to refrain from any further feelings towards her. The letter had been written in the ordinary tone of command as befit the high nobility speaking to the lower and had been signed by one Walter Ulrich. Von Watzdorf destroyed the letter as instructed in the postscript.

0.002g

Franz Hardenburg, with whom von Watzdorf connected through his third passion, that of serving His Majesty as Hussar, wrote in his memoirs:

> *My friend Kurt [referring to Curt Friedrich Ernst von Watzdorf] was silent for three days, did not eat any food, and staggered upright as those fatally wounded in war occasionally do who then show no respect for the flag, only to honorably fall over shortly thereafter. The letter seemed to have hit him like a bullet in the field, or a sword blow in battle. It seems to me that it was then that his subsequent illness, which he hid from me for a long time, began...*

Fourteen days after von Watzdorf acknowledged having received the letter, he had to attend a scheduled military exercise at the nearby town of Jüterbog. He was worried and scared. How could he appear attentive and stand up straight before his regiment as their role model? How could he ask his subordinates to be powerful during the exercise when he himself could only stand there tottering, hunched over and dejected, sunk into himself and suffering?

He put on his uniform—he had lost weight over the previous two weeks—pulled his belt tight, ran the narrower strap across his upper body, and looked in the mirror. He looked flabby, and his belt hung forlornly down. There was no way he could show up like that. Reporting sick was not an option—a von Watzdorf had never called in sick. He palmed his belt smooth and pulled it tighter; then he suddenly became angry with himself and, in so doing, noticed that he had automatically straightened himself up, that he had come to attention as a reflex.

This was the first time a man had ever assumed correct military posture by tearing his belt and had felt better thereafter because of it; regaining control of himself again, overcoming his softness and effeminateness, once again becoming a man, strapping, upright, ready and tough, assertive with himself and with others.

Von Watzdorf overcame the subsequent four-week exercise rather well. Any time he felt depressed, every time his beloved inadvertently crept into his thoughts, each time his garden began to take shape in his mind, he pulled his belt tight and immediately found his mental and physical bearing change. This constantly reappearing, and unsettling, tenderness was set straight; he stood tall and once again became a Hussar, a master of the sword, and an exemplary leader of his soldiers.

He decided that what had helped him was also to help his soldiers. And so in due turn at morning roll call people soon began to hear his cry "tear your belts!" on a regular basis and all would stand straight as a pin.

Back in his castle he discussed the latest plantings with his botanically-minded forester, planned the latest modifications with his architect Hense, and rejoiced over an ever more prosperous pheasantry, which by 1875 could already boast more than 450 pheasants.

And yet, he suffered from his unrequited love and, for that very reason, vowed over and over again to transform his castle into something truly special, to make his garden magnificent. A place of love, beauty, and form as a testament of his affection for the princess of his heart. But every now and then, when he was overtaken by anxiety, overwhelmed by beauty, form, and love, he would put on his uniform and pull his belt tight in order to once again become his own master.

But then, one day, a slight tremor began. He was diagnosed with a neuralgic nerve disorder. His nervous trembling and subsequent sporadic paralysis of a nonspecific nature were considered incurable. One day it was the hand, the next it was the leg, then the thigh would suddenly begin to itch for days, or half of his face would go numb.

Before his fellow Hussars he would pull himself together at ever-shorter intervals. Nevertheless, he enthusiastically took part in the victorious war against the French between 1870-71 and was duly celebrated. What could not be seen from the outside, and what he himself did not even perceive, was a growing fatigue from the increasingly necessary pulling of his belt.

His nerve disorders grew steadily worse and more and more noticeable, so one day he received a bravery medal and bid his beloved Hussars farewell. Nonetheless he remained a consultant Hussar of the guard until his death. As his illness got worse, he took to using a cane. He repeatedly tried pulling the belt even more tightly, but it had ceased having the desired effect. He became very active in the renovations of his castle and the expansion of his garden, and even when he could no longer leave his bed, he still gave daily reports and managed to see the method of belt-tightening recorded in a textbook on modern military service.

He died, too young and too soon, in 1880 after a long illness. In his final, intense discussions with his priest, he is said to have spoken repeatedly about the advantages and disadvantages of belt pulling. When on his deathbed they wanted to give him his belt, however, he waved his hand and said: "Let it be, it has already been pulled enough" (which was followed by a long pause). "My belt is torn, alas, it was pulled too much, too much," and he fell asleep exhausted. His servant looked puzzledly at the belt and, sure enough, noticed that the leather patch that had long held its parts together was torn.

Literature:

Hans-Joachim Dreger, *Landscape Park*, Wiesenburg, Bonn, 2005.

Josefine Günschel, *Phrenology in the Garden*, Kreuzberg, 2007.

——, *On Love and Senses*, Kreuzberg, 2007.

Bernhard Mann, *Biographical Handbook for the Prussian House of Representatives*, Dusseldorf, 1988.

Lutz Röhrich, *Encyclopedia of Proverbial Sayings*, Freiburg, 1991.

Rosa Tinitas, *Princess of Hearts*, Rostock, 1959.

0.002g

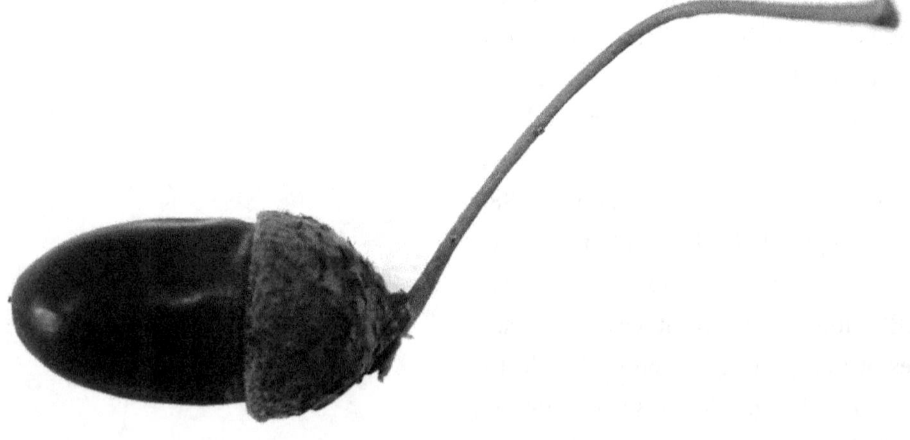

The Olive Oaks (Quercus Olivae) of Wiepersdorf

or

Were the Crossing Experiments of the Baron Achim von Arnim-Bärwalde Successful?

"It must work out!" This was the brief message that Achim von Arnim-Bärwalde (1848-1891) wrote on a postcard to Baron von Grudtwitz in the autumn of 1891, just four months before his own death. Von Grudtwitz immediately understood this short, almost desperate message full of defiant conviction. The two had met on a trip to Italy near Lake Como.

Achim von Arnim-Bärwalde, who died at a young age, was the grandson of the poet-couple Bettina and Achim von Arnim. He took over the management of their familial estate in Wiepersdorf in Berlin after completing law school in 1870. As a young man he had already felt attracted to the fine arts, and so he decided to study art history in Berlin that same year. After being admitted to the course of studies, he felt that he not only wanted to deal with art, but to create it and to be called a painter. And so he went to Munich, the then capital of academic painting, to study historical paintings. In the early summer of 1872 the twenty-four-year-old painter traveled to Italy for the first time and immediately fell in uncompromising love with the beautiful country and its treasures of art. During this first trip to Italy, he decided to convert his estate in Wiepersdorf into a very modern neo-Baroque style and to devote his garden to Italian sculptures.

He brought back three Italian vases from this trip. In 1877, after the expansion and cultivation of his triaxial studios on the north side of the manor in Wiepersdorf, while on a new journey to Italy (now already his fourth) he purchased a statue of Jupiter and several more vases. In order to give his sculptures a worthy environment, he built a sweeping terrace, lowering the front of the structure, and created a middle bed so that his existing and still expanding sculptural decoration might find a dignified, staged, and prestigious frame.

Inspired by the great landscape gardener Fürst Pückler, whom he both knew and worshipped as a teenager, he began to plant trees, paying particular attention to the visual axes in his Wiepersdorf Park. He was especially enthusiastic about oaks and in particular those that existed in Italy: the evergreen oak (*Quercus ilex*) and the sessile oak (*Quercus petraea*).

Between the years 1888 and 1889 Achim von Arnim-Bärwalde built a one-story orangery on the southern side of his park to grow olive trees of the varieties Cerignola, Ligurine, and Kugano. But he desired not only to breed olive trees but to cross them with the native oak. The newly created tree would be named the Olive Oak (*Quercus olivae*). The aforementioned letter to Baron von Grudwitz refers to this very endeavor, and it was thus that Achim von Arnim-Bärwalde spread his convergence theory to his followers.

This theory maintains that, in order for us to recognize their significance, plants must be observed by their outer appearance because a close examination of plants and the precise detection of the inner value systems would result in having to take into account the traditional historical significance, accordance, lineages, and relationship of plant species. This theory arose in opposition to the scientific exploration of nature which had by then established itself and condemned it as cold, dissecting, and ahistorical rather than analytical.

Achim von Arnim-Bärwalde recognized great similarities between oaks and olives. Not only were the fruits amazingly similar, but he also found that both trees were well over a thousand years old, and that they both were known for their great mythological significance. The Germanic tribes had consecrated the oak to the thunder god Thor and in Greece it was sacred to the lightening tosser Zeus. The branches of the olive tree have been used as a symbol of peace since time immemorial and the oak branch as a symbol of mourning for fallen heroes. Both trees are revered as trees of life and the world.

Furthermore, the fruits of both trees are sought after as food, one for humans and the other for pigs. A tasty oil can be made from the fruit of the olive while from the fruit of the oak a tasty, coffee-like drink. Because of these and other clear and unequivocal accordances, Achim von Arnim-Bärwalde was certain that crossbreeding, though difficult, would indeed be possible. He considered the sessile oak and Liguria olive as appropriate candidates for such experiments.

He began his first experiments by trying different parallel crossing methods. He crossbred through the pollination of flower pollen, root grafting, truncal spreading, and, most promising of all, fruit integration. The first seedlings he feverishly awaited arose from truncal spreading and pollination and looked like any normal oak seedlings. He cherished and cared for five of the most seemingly robust before putting them in open land in the fall of 1890. In February 1891, Achim, the baron of Arnim-Bärwalde, died without any heirs. His eldest cousin Erwin von Arnim (1862-1928) took over the property and brought the garden to completion in accordance with the existing plans.

Erwin von Arnim, who continued to live at his castle in Zernikow, allowed the villagers of Wiepersdorf to collect the acorns and feed them to their pigs. This unwritten law turned into a common law and has remained so until today. The five seedlings of the crossbreeding experiment grew into large oaks that survived many storms, some very cold and frosty winters, poverty, hunger, and, last but not least, the Russian occupation of the castle and the expropriation of the manor.

Nevertheless, the peasants of Wiepersdorf continued to collect the acorns in the garden no matter who happened to be in the castle or what kind of weather there was in order to feed them to their pigs. In 1956 an agricultural cooperative to breed pigs was created more or less voluntarily.

The local pigs continued to devour the acorns from the garden, which, however, was now officially called "The Recreational Area of the Intelligentsia." The pork of the agricultural cooperative of Wiepersdorf, which from the outset was particularly tasty, was considered the best in East Germany and designated as being above average in all socialist gourmet guides. The meat was described as mild, spicy, pleasantly salty, not too dry, and was thus honored repeatedly with medals and other awards. At state receptions in Berlin, pigs from Wiepersdorf were requested regularly.

The cooperative pig farm was liquidated in 1992 and discontinued in 1995. In the neighboring village of Werbig, Hybrid-Pig-Breeding Ltd. has since been trying to revive Wiepersdorf's tradition but, to date, has not come anywhere close to reaching the quality of the Wiepersdorf pigs.

In the autumn of 2003, as part of a cataloguing of oak trees in Brandenburg, the oaks of Wiepersdorf Castle (today an artist residency) were examined. Professor Bengas of the Institute of Digital Plant Systematology in Potsdam noticed that some of the mature acorns of the sessile oak there were surprisingly black. The investigations could not detect any deviation from already known sessile oaks. Only once a DNA analysis had been arranged did it emerge that the doublehelix DNA structure of these black acorns had a purine that was foreign to the sessile oak. Through data matching, this purine was detected in the "Liguria" type of olives. Since then an argument has erupted among experts as to whether Achim von Arnim–Bärwalde's attempts at crossbreeding were successful or whether these small changes in DNA should even be considered a crossbreed at all. Furthermore, should the five oak trees in Wiepersdorf now be referred to as a new species, that is, as olive oaks (*Quercus olivae*)? Or was it all an accident, a whim of nature that cannot be repeated?

Every autumn the acorns of the Wiepersdorf oaks continue to grow in the castle garden but are seldomly collected by the villagers anymore. Only now and again one of the artists staying at the castle, lost in his or her thoughts, will slip or roll on one of them and so arrive head over heels to other thoughts.

Literature:
B. Albrecht/D. Sossenheimer, *How to Please Everyone*, Munich, 1995.
M. Behm/D. Döping, *Botanical Discoveries in Fleming*, Luckenwalde, 2003.
V.Dathe/K. Dietrich / R. Schallhammer, *Culinary Services*, Berlin, 1988.
M. Fabisch/K. Hauptvogel, *From Art to Cultivating Gardens*, Dahme, 1999.
R. Karbaum, *Knowledge of Wiepersdorf*, Berlin, 1996.
Karbaum/K. Kummer, *Intimate Glimpses of Artists*, Jüterbog, 2000.
Richter, *On Patience and Kindness*, Luckenwalde, 1997.
Schiemann, *The Bank and The Artists*, Wiepersdorf, 1994.

0.002g

0.003g

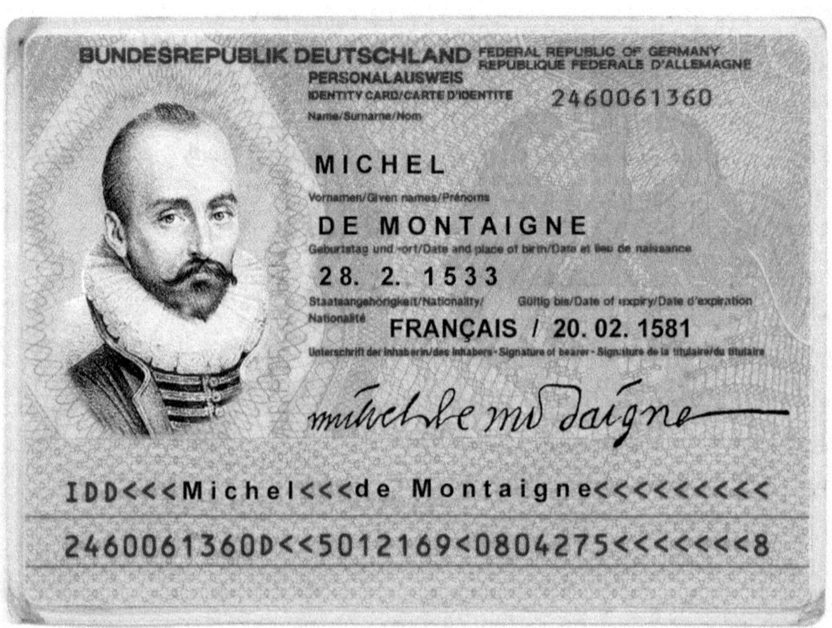

From the Gift-Portrait to the Passport Photo

or

Mssr. Michel de Montaigné's Modern ID Card

"The Germans are very fond of coats of arms; in every inn you will find hundreds that gentlemen who have lodged there have had painted on the walls; and all the windows are decorated with these emblazonments."

This remark was penned by the great French philosopher, humanist, skeptic, and founder of the literary art form of the essay Michel de Montaigne (1533-1592) on the occasion of his stopping in Augsburg en route to Italy.

For any inn such coats of arms were the greatest honor and ornament. In those days it was customary for a gentleman who had been satisfied with his accommodation to leave behind his coat of arms in painted form. These then were proudly displayed as a means of showing future guests who before them had gladly spent time there.

At that time a person's identity was determined by a coat of arms and by their clothing. The blacksmith from Celle was recognized in Brunswick as a blacksmith from Celle because of his typically Cellian clothes as well as their being marked with the insignia of his profession. Even the person's name was of only limited importance in terms of how he was addressed—the blacksmith from Celle was usually only addressed as "blacksmith from Celle." The coats of arms of the higher classes were rather clear and showed that the person came from a higher class and that they belonged to a particular gender. Those who had to go on trips exhibited certified letters on their coats of arms and on their clothes so that people would recognize their persons. For the most part, such signs of identity were issued by border officials and cost a fee.

As travel began to increase in Europe in the sixteenth century, roads got increasingly better, coaches more convenient, and attacks on travelers less frequent. People everywhere grew curious about traveling, not only for business, but to get to learn about things outside of their own surroundings.

This increasing desire to travel in turn resulted in an increasing number of coats of arms presented in inns, as described by Montaigne above.

In order to stand out, however, certain very wealthy gentlemen began to leave behind gift-portraits. These gift-portraits would depict them next to their personal coats of arms. Since the preparation of one's own portrait was an expensive and time consuming task, only the wealthy and influential could leave behind such images in appreciation.

Indeed, we owe our current knowledge as to the appearance of many important contemporaries of the time to the existence of such gift-portraits.

On September 5, 1580, Michel de Montaigne departed with a large travel group from Beaumont, in the north of Paris, en route to Rome. His intention was to kneel before the Pope, to have his bladder trouble treated in Lucca, and then to return home to his tower in order to withdraw back into writing.

Throughout the trip the group repeatedly suffered long delays related to the preparation of the required documents. This harassment was conducted for many reasons. At one point, because of plague prevention, they were informed that a health certificate had to be prepared right then and there, and that the officer in charge was ready at the checkpoint.

Another time, in order to make it easier to track down a group of criminals, complicated ID papers had to be prepared that by that very evening would, however, no longer be valid. Censuses were also very popular, and accurate information regarding the reasons for the trip had to be presented as well as officially confirmed. All in all, however, Montaigne observed that these measures seemed to serve only one purpose: to get money out of the traveler's pocket.

Michel de Montaigne began his journey with fifteen gift-portraits, which he would leave as additional gifts in those inns he had found particularly comfortable. Today, two of these portraits remain in the old German imperial city of Augsburg. One was left behind at the Zum Morgenstern Hotel, the second entrusted to the engraver Julius H. Greiderle.

At a dinner honoring Montaigne and his fellow travelers, served by seven uniformed waiters and consisting of at least fourteen types of local wine, Montaigne learned what was being planned and discussed in the city. This appealed to him very much. He heard, among other things, that thanks to the initiative of Augsburg, the free cities of the German states were considering making travel easier by means of a unique personal identification card that was to be recognized in all cities. This card was to be richly and abundantly decorated and thus difficult to imitate and was to list the person's most important data so that they could be distinguished from all others.

This important document was also to include a portrait of the designated person that was to correspond to reality as much as possible and thus also be done without any of the usual attempts at beautification. This personal-document was to be issued and authenticated by the cities themselves and thereafter to be recognized in all the German states while providing free transit and obligatory protection.

Montaigne immediately requested such a pass, and the councilors referred him to the engraver Julius H. Greiderle who was just then designing a pattern. Montaigne's secretary gave the engraver one of the former's gift-portraits so that the so-called "passport picture" of Mssr. de Montaigne could then be applied to the card.

Shortly before his departure on October 19, 1580, the City Council handed Montaigne his card, complete with his full name and a very lifelike portrait. Montaigne thanked and congratulated the councilors of Augsburg for this Personal ID. He was filled with pride to be the first person with just such an ID card because, he knew, the future was to belong to them.

As usual, however, the imperial cities could not agree on a single ID card. Each city wanted their own, and the princes boycotted the idea altogether. So, after four rounds of negotiations, the whole thing was shelved.

It was not until over 300 years later, in the wake of World War I, that such an ID card was introduced. People were given a piece of paper describing them in every possible way and upon which had been placed an image of their faces using the new technology of photography.

Michel de Montaigne's German ID card was heavily damaged in a devastating housefire in 1885 but was reconstructed in 2005 by the restorer Meike Mentjes in Berlin.

Literature:
V. Groebner, *The Appearance of the Person: Characteristics, Identification and Control in the Middle Ages,* Munich, 2004.
G. Häberlein, *The Gift-Portrait in Transition,* Stuttgart, 1991.
M. de Montaigne, *Diary of the Trip to Italy via Switzerland and Germany from 1580 to 1581,* Frankfurt, 2002.
——, *Essays Volume I, II, III,* Frankfurt, 1998
U. Schulz, *Montaigne,* Reinbek, 1989.
W. Weigand, *Michel de Montaigne,* Zurich, 1985.

0.003g

0.003g

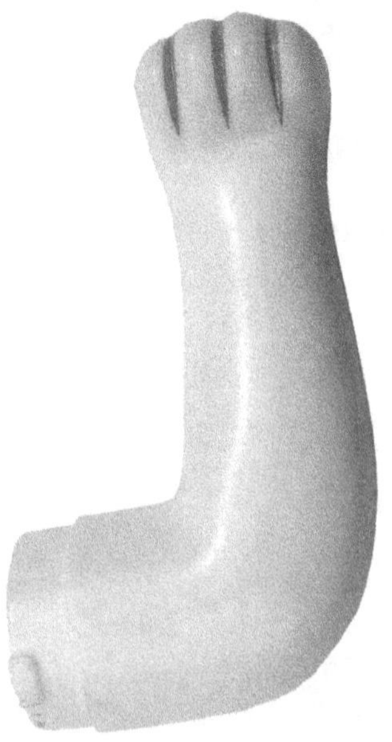

How a Waving Cat Lost Her Body but Her Arm Did Not Lose Its Effect

Effect

Haru Yamada strolled through the early afternoon street feeling dejected and withdrawn. It was the third job he had lost in the last six months. Before that he had been a clerk in a shipping company for seven years until the company was sold. The new owner had only kept the driver.

Sunk into his empty thoughts and feeling rather hopeless and useless, he kicked anything that got in his way to the side. What was he supposed to say to his wife, how would his son look at a father who could not find any work, how was he supposed to go on? He kicked whatever was in his way to the side, not out of the aggressive need to make something else atone for his predicament and give him a clear path, but so that at least his feet would have something to do, so that they would not be like him: jobless, depressed, a good for nothing. How would he ever find a job?

Once again he felt like kicking something, carelessly, blindly, and it was then that he caught a glimpse of the single waving arm of a cat—*maneki-neko*—a bodiless arm lying in the dirt road. Yamada stood there mechanically and abruptly, without thinking or paying attention, and not very perceptive about what it was he was looking at. "Ah," he thought, "who threw away this waving cat's arm here? How lonely it must be." He bent down and put it into his pocket. It was not a beautiful arm; it was scratched, broken, dirty, and bitten. No doubt it had remained unnoticed for days, if not weeks, there on the road. Very faintly, in the far corner of his eye, Haru Yamada saw a Persian cat slowly turn a corner and disappear.

A few days later, once he had told everything to his wife and hinted to his son that he had no job and that he no longer knew how to proceed, he received a call from a vegetable wholesaler who inquired whether he could help them out. They wanted to know if he would have the time to assist with bookkeeping for five weeks.

His wife found the arm of the waving cat in her husband's jacket pocket and, smiling with amusement, placed it in the living room closet behind a glass door.

Yamada's new job at the vegetable wholesaler was so satisfactory that, after the initial five weeks, he got a permanent position and after a year and half became a senior buyer. Mr. Yuto Hatake, the owner of "Shinsen Yasai"—which simply means "Fresh Vegetables"—was not so young anymore; as he was very happy with Haru Yamada, he entrusted him with more and more work. In his sixth year Yamada became Mr. Hatake's assistant, and the latter increasingly withdrew into retirement. Over the following years, Haru Yamada singlehandedly led the company with great success. He introduced new operating structures that allowed the company to grow even more. When the company already had over one hundred employees, supplying the whole area with fresh vegetables, the old Mr. Yuto Hatake summoned his employee Haru Yamada to talk to him about the future. Mr. Hatake said: "Yamada-san, I am now too old for the business. I have no children, and I have taken you on as a son. I want you to take over the company now."

The first thing Mr. Haru Yamada placed on his new boss's desk was the arm of the wav-

0.003g

ing cat. It had been lying under a glass case on a yellow cushion. He was convinced that he owed all of his happiness and wealth to this waving cat arm alone.

On his 70th birthday he handed the company over to his son and worked together with one of the leading architects in Japan to design the plans for the buiding of a large Shinto shrine in honor of the arm. Today, many years later, this shrine attracts thousands of people annually who bring their devotion to the auspicious, disembodied arm of the waving cat, and ask for happiness and prosperity.

Events

Hayato had already been locked in his room for half a year, refusing to go to school, refusing to even go to the door of his parents' house. One day, however, when no one was at home, he slipped out to a nearby park. Hayato was not thinking about his fifteen-year life; he would soon be sixteen, but that didn't matter to him, because nothing did. He sat on a bench and stared of into space, but could not do anything. He did not even feel bored; even that was too exhausting. He just sat there and sometimes held his head in his hands. If someone had come over and seen him, they would have thought that the young man was thinking about something, mulling over something—homework, maybe. As he sat there, disinterested, a cat crept to him, slipped around his legs, rubbed against him, and squeezed itself between his feet. Still Hayato did not respond.

Suddenly the cat began to talk. "You're Hayato. I see you often from the tree outside your window as you sit in your room. You seem not to understand the world of humans in the same way I don't understand the world of cats. Are you here in the park every day now?" Hayato did not answer. The cat waited a moment then said "See you later." She rubbed against his left leg one more time, and left.

Over the next few days Hayato avoided looking out his window, even slightly. After seven days, when once again no one was at home, he went back to the park and sat down on the bench. It was not long before the cat snuggled up to his legs and began to speak. "I don't understand cats. I've travelled far and wide in my life and have met cats from all continents. I've observed the Japanese ones here very closely, but have understood them the least. I'm a Persian cat and am always left alone—they don't even notice me, even though they meddle in everything else, including the affairs of humans. At some point I'll tell you what I've been through." She rubbed Hayato's left leg again, went behind his back, and disappeared into the bushes.

Three days later, as Hayato sat down on the bench, the cat dashed up to his legs and told him about her cat life. Hayato came now almost every day. He never said anything, but the Persian cat did not seem to mind. She never introduced herself to him, just as he never uttered a single word. She told him about cats from all over the world, how they were all self-willed, self-contradictory, solitary, and yet, at the same time, how they wanted to be together with others but how they never cared about anything. How they could not endure changes and, being pedantic, rejected everything new just to jump immediately onto something new.

One day the Persian cat talked about Japanese cats. She said that normal cats could suddenly change into cat monsters, into *bakenekos*, and steal dead people, occupying their spirits and directing them like zombies. She spoke about *nekomatas*, cats that had a split tail, walked on two legs, and were very, very evil. And about how the fire-cat *kasha* stole human corpses before they were buried, then dragged them down into hell. Above all, she told him just how much *kasha* hated *maneki-neko*, the waving cat who brings luck and prosperity—and especially its eternally waving arm.

Then one day the Persian cat told Hayato about a fight she had seen. Two evil monster cats, a *bakeneko* and a *nekomata*, instigated by *kasha*—who never leaves her fiery chariot—ambushed and attacked a *maneki-neko*, the bearer of luck. They cursed the *maneki-neko* for being arrogant and insinuating, and demanded that she stop waving her paw. Incited by their own speeches they became increasingly violent until, with a roar, they pounced and tackled her. During the fight *bakeneko* and *nekomata* became even wilder as kasha egged them angrily on from her car. They tore the *maneki-neko*'s fur and, in a frenzy, began to shred the auspicious cat to pieces. When they stopped, only the ever-waving arm lay on the ground. But they were not finished: they proceeded to scratch, bite, spit, and pee on it, they smothered it with dirt, and tried to maltreat it as much as possible without breaking it completely. They were afraid of destroying the luck-bringing arm, for were they to do so, they would suddenly revert back to being the normal cats they once had been.

Once they had calmed down and *kasha* had driven off in her chariot of fire, the two monster cats also went their separate ways. The arm, however, remained lying alone in the street. The last thing the Persian cat said was that it was then that she saw a sad man come along, pick up the hand, and take it away with him. After rubbing against Hayato's feet, as always, she disappeared into the bushes behind him.

That evening after the Persian cat had told him this story, for the first time Hayato sat at the dinner table with his parents again. The next day he went back to school, and continued to go throughout the entire year.

Now and again he would sit down on the park bench for a moment while on his way to school, but the Persian cat never appeared again. The other cats he met did not speak with him, or, if they did, he did not understand them.

Literature:
Susanne Gross, *The Maneki-Neko App*, Berlin, 2014.
Michael Olbricht, *Cats in Myth*, Berlin, 2001.
Robert Rinck, *Cats of the World*, Hamburg, 1976.
Margot Tauchert, *The Laces of Cats*, Nürnberg, 2010.

0.004g

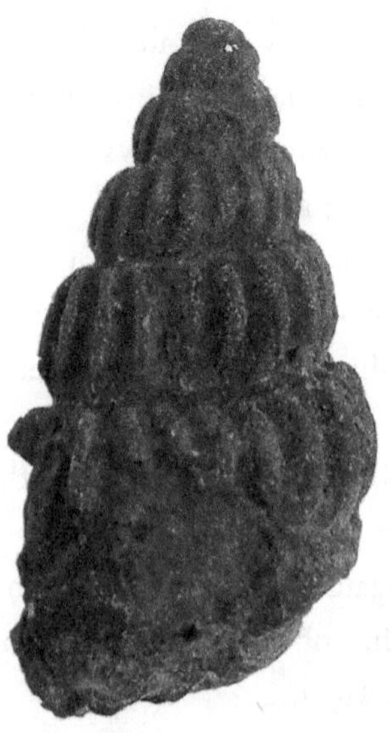

Inner-Snails (Gastropodes Interiores)
Genus: Early Acidic Water Snails
(Protogastropodes Aquacidophiles)
23-136 Million Years Old

Inner Snails lived from the Jurassic through the Cretaceous Period in a fateful symbiosis with dinosaurs. Their precursors are suspected to have existed in large selachiis, and their presence in the first Coelacanth and amphibians has been proven.

It was originally believed that the fossilized snails inside the bellies of fish and Coelacanth had accidentally been swallowed while eating. It was only when the same snails were also found in increasing numbers in land animals, for example in the Melanosaurus, that closer attention was paid to them, and thus the amazing symbiosis between the dinosaur and the inner-snail was discovered.

Today inner-snails are divided into the following categories:

1. Inner-snails with vegetarian hosts (a hard and very calcareous shell);
2. Inner-snails with carnivorous hosts (a tough though flexible-cartilaginous shell);
3. Inner-snails with flying hosts (a thin, porous, and extremely lightweight shell);
4. Inner-snails with swimming hosts (a jelly-like, almost transparent, but fixed shell).

It is assumed that all of the over 600 different types of dinosaurs hosted inner snails. One can imagine the function of these inner snails from the size of the dinosaur's stomach.

The stomach size of a Brachiosaurus or Apatosaurus is huge: 4-6 square meters and filled with enormous amounts of gastric juice. The dentures and masticatory organs of dinosaurs, however, were not particularly well built, not even among the carnivorous dinosaurs (they could tear meat, but could not chew), and so they simply swallowed their food or, more accurately, gulped it down in a more or less un-chewed state. The aforementioned giant amounts of gastric juice allowed for the decomposition of their food and ensured the dinosaurs' diet.

The primary disadvantage of this huge amount of gastric fluid was the algae that would form in the constantly full stomachs (gastro-acid algae). The algae easily proliferated in these climatically warm and unlit spaces and thereby prevented the dinosaurs from ever feeling hungry or properly digesting the small amount of food that did come into their stomachs. Enter the inner-snails which settled in the dinosaurs' stomachs, fed on the algae growing there, prevented their overpopulation, and enabled the dinosaurs to feel hungry and to feed themselves.

This mechanism was discovered in those dinosaurs which did not grow old and died young; one could observe that they had suffered from diarrhea and vomiting and hence lost their snails. Unrestrained, the algae proliferated at a rapid speed. Each and every species of these dinosaurs that died young was without exception skinny to the bone, which leads one to conclude that they all starved to death due to an absence of inner-snails.

Some experts even believe that in the wake of the general shift of vegetation that occurred during the Cretaceous Period there was a change in the acid balance of the dinosaur's stomach, which led to the extinction of inner-snails and, consequently, to that of the dinosaurs themselves.

0.004g

Literature:
David Norman, *Dinosaurs*, Munich, 1991.
Alfred Sherwood Romer, *Osteology of the Reptiles*, Chicago, 1956.
Dong Zhiming, *Dinosaurian Faunas of China*, Beijing, 1992.

0.004g

0.005g

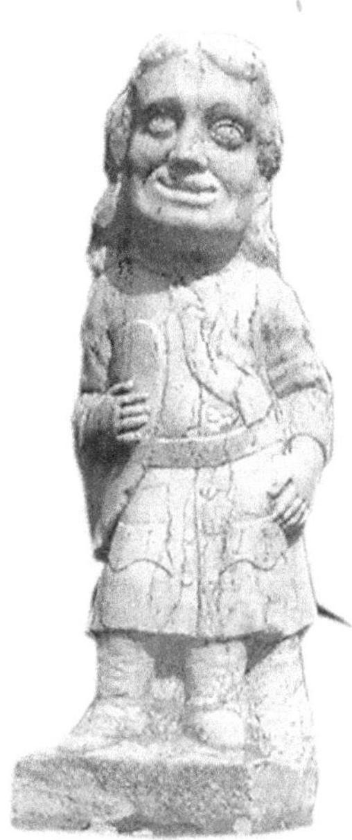

The History of the Callot Figures of Wiepersdorf

The essence of a castle lies in its mysteries, legends, and ghosts, for every castle conceals a secret. In addition to the many accessible rooms, there are always the inaccessible ones, not to mention the parks, the castle ponds in which there are always corpses, the large dusty floors beneath the roofs, their shelves containing frightening mummies, the inaccessible, confusing corners, from which a groaning can often be heard. These all contribute to what is hidden, and what is hidden is the bearer of secrets. One secret of the castle at Wiepersdorf is its five Callot figures.

Each and every visitor to the castle garden at Wiepersdorf at some point stumbles across the five figures of the crooked, dwarf-like people—two females and three males—standing in a semicircle. The origin of these figures remains a complete mystery to this day. The only thing that is known is that the painter Achim von Arnim-Bärwalde—to whom the castle owes its present appearance, and who was not only a historical painter, but also a collector of sculptures—erected these five Callot figures alongside a number of Italian Baroque figures, and this fact has been proven by numerous letters.

Callot figures are named after the great French draftsman and printmaker Jacques Callot (1592-1635). Jacques Callot revolutionized etching through newly developed techniques and turned it into an art form. He was the first person to depict the atrocities of war—the Thirty Years War to be precise—in impressive, realistic, and shocking ways. In 1616, during a stay at the Tuscan court of Cosimo II where he worked as a court artist, Callot created the famous twenty engravings "Varie figure gobbi" which depicted dwarfish cripples blowing bagpipes, fencing, scuffling, etc.

One hundred years later, as the Baroque approached the Rococo and became more and more sophisticated, these engravings of crooked, grotesque dwarfs were used as templates for producing sculptures and were implemented in three dimensions. These figures, which people always referred to as Callot figures, became a trendy phenomenon. Every castle that considered, or wanted to consider, itself of any worth had to have these figures erected in their gardens. For example, Weikersheim Castle in Franconia has more than twenty characters, each of them representing an allegorical virtue. There are also counterfeit Callot figures in Kremsmünster, Gleink, St. Pölten, Griellenstein, Castle Neuwaldegg, and Neustadt on the Mettau, just to name a few. Some of today's most famous figures are the twenty-eight, approximately 1.30 meter large figures that Archbishop Franz Anton von Harrach (1665-1727), born in Milan, had erected in Salzburg's Mirabell Gardens. They are assumed to be the first figures of this kind.

The tale of these figures is very similar to that of the kidney-shaped tables developed approximately 200 years later: no one knows who designed them, nor where they first appeared. Suddenly they were simply there, spread throughout all the apartments, and then they were gone. In a similar fashion the Callot figures emerged, enjoyed great popularity, and then disappeared after a period of disuse, so that one can regard them as having been made only by the prevailing taste of the times.

Over time the Callot figures grew ever smaller, and this led to the emergence of simple dwarf statuettes. In 1744 the first porcelain gnomes were made in a Viennese porcelain manufactory. Fifty years later, the first garden gnome series was being manufactured by the Derba Company in England. And just ten years after that, the dwarves with the phallically pointed caps that are so popular today appeared.

In any event, the most famous collection of Baroque Callot figures stood at Kuks or Kukus Castle in Bohemia. More than forty dwarf figures were assembled on the local racetrack by the riverbank and accompanied visitors on their way up to the hospital where the figures were replaced by large, Roman allegorical sculptures on the likes of virtue, frivolity, despair, affectionate fornication, and so forth.

Kuks Hospital had been established in 1692 by Franz Anton Graf von Sporck (1662-1738), one of the earliest philosophers of the Enlightenment. This hospital specialized in the increasingly widespread "French disease" or "Galante disease" as Casanova referred to it. In fact, Casanova twice stayed in this special clinic for several months in order to have himself cured.

The Callot figures of Kuks were talked about throughout all the European courts, not only for being midgets, but for the obscene emphasis and display of their genitals. Dwarves with oversized penises and women with exuberant breasts posed in tempting, explicit positions next to other figures with their buttocks exposed. These representations demonstrated the joys and voluptuousness of sensuality but also served to admonish viewers of how unbridled devotion to bodily pleasures could lead to diseases that were, in fact, the very reason for having to stay at the hospital in the first place.

In August 1740 the Elbe River flooded to an unprecedented degree. Fifteen houses in the village and the entire racetrack were washed away, and the castle was so badly damaged that all subsequent attempts to repair and renovate it came to naught. In 1901 the castle was completely demolished. As for the Callot figures, only two that had been standing in the vicinity of the hospital remained; the others disappeared into the rushing waters of the Elbe.

In all the courts of Europe people spoke at length about the disaster and in particular regretted the disappearance of the small, picturesque dwarfs. The cleanup took years.

In 1755 a dubious Bohemian sculpture dealer named Luthwer Webker (1712-1764) began to sell Callot figures in secret. Those who heard the description of these illegally sold figures immediately realized that they had to be the lost figures of Kuks. This sculpture dealer had paid a fair sum of money to farmers and fishermen along the Elbe River ensuring that they pass on the figures to him once they washed ashore.

The problem for the dealer, however, was that only courtiers were viable as purchasers, and they were familiar with the figures and considered it not just criminal but inelegant to make such illegal purchases. If the origin of the sculptures had been Italy or Greece, it would not have been a problem, but something stolen or illegally obtained from a Central European court was considered undesirable and was frowned upon, so people were anxious about having them installed at their homes. Bavarian Prince Elector Maximilian III Joseph (1727-1777), known as "the Good" and the person responsible for introducing compulsory education in Bavaria in 1771—the first Germanic state to do so—, came under suspicion of having erected an illegitimate amorous sculpture taken from Schönbrunn Castle in Vienna in his Nymphenburg Palace in Munich. Although experts immediately refuted this suspicion, and only a vague resemblance was actually attested, the rumor remained attached to him so that he was excluded from the most illustrious balls for a number of years. If even one as good as Prince Elector "the Good" felt a great craving for such a dishonest gem and succumbed to it, then there was no choice but to store the piece in secret so that the public would not be able to see it.

And thus Saxon Elector and King of Poland Augustus II (1676-1763), who was known as "the Strong," instructed his architect Friedrich Borm to secretly and anonymously purchase the Callot figures so that no whisper could ever arise suggesting the figures were in Saxony. Through intermediaries and strictly concealed operations seven perfectly preserved figures were brought to Pillnitz Castle and installed in a difficult-to-access basement dungeon. Two figures were from the group of "Frivolous." In his many visits to Pillnitz Castle Elector Augustus II "the Strong" allowed himself to be led to the figures and, when it was time to leave the room again, he always said goodbye to the female figure standing next to the door, grabbing her by the nose. On one of these visits the nose broke off, and he put it in his pocket. This nose must have become his constant companion. It is reported that during difficult negotiations the Elector took the stone nose out of his pocket, put it in front of him, and said, "To make this decision, one must have a good nose." Over the course of time this phrase "having a good nose" became an idiom in German. And today this stone nose can be seen at the Electoral Estate inside the National Archives of Saxony in Dresden.

As the growing bourgeoisie began to spread and construct even cuter dwarf figures, interest in the Callot figures within the Central European courts decreased—they were now regarded merely as an amusing variety of past-time.

In 1870 Pillnitz Castle was expanded and the jousting building was remodeled into an orangery. In 1876 the shelved and forgotten Callot figures from Kuks Castle were rediscovered. People quickly recalled the origin of the figures and under no circumstances wanted them set up in Pillnitz as their origin could still potentially cast a shadow over the Saxon court. People were afraid of destroying them or once again returning them to the Elbe, so they looked for a decent buyer.

It was discovered that Achim von Arnim-Bärwalde had received a considerable inheritance from his stepmother, a wealthy Brentano, and that he wanted to turn Wiepersdorf into a proper castle. A learned history painter, he traveled through Italy and bought vases and statues to give his palace a Baroque appearance. Achim von Arnim-Bärwalde purchased this group of figures, but on the strict condition that he would never disclose their origin. As no written contract was involved, he was able to buy the figures at an especially low price. For safety reasons, the sellers allowed the figures to be slightly altered in Saxony by a local stonemason.

In 1881 these seven figures were delivered to Wiepersdorf. Baron Achim von Arnim-Bärwalde placed them in front of his studio window in order to always have them in sight. He immediately had the broken nose repaired, but it snapped off several times, for, afraid that it might not be holding, he had adopted the habit of repeatedly checking the figure and shaking it.

Achim von Arnim-Bärwalde was determined to keep the origin of the figures a secret, so whenever he was asked where he had purchased the flashy dwarfs, he said that they were bought on one of his many trips to Italy; or, at other times, in Upper Austria. And it is precisely these two false variations on the origin of the Callot figures in Wiepersdorf that have whizzed through literature ever since.

There is no doubt at all that these figures were of great significance to Achim von Arnim-Bärwalde. In a letter to Mrs. von Gudengut written on December 5, 1884, he explained:

> *Now I have them, my seven. My grandmother Bettina told me many times as a child that her husband, my grandfather, from whom I got my name, grew up with similar figures at Zernikow Castle, but that they always gave him the creeps. And the fact that there are just seven of the dwarfs reminds me of how close our family once was with Jacob and Wilhelm Grimm. I only just recently was able to visit their grave at the cemetery of St. Matthew. The new street there is also undergoing a fierce amount of construction.*

In 1883 Achim von Arnim-Bärwalde commissioned Reinhold Begas (1831-1911), the highly revered and patronized Prussian court sculptor who had been the last pupil of Christian Daniel Rauch (1777-1857), to create 24 centimeter miniatures of his seven dwarfs. Reinhold Begas seemed the most appropriate person for this job as, under his watch, the revival of the Baroque soared to unimagined heights. Achim von Arnim-Bärwalde wanted his figures "naked," for he intended to paint them himself.

In a letter to Baroness von Brüttel he wrote, "Prof. Begas breathed so much life into each of the little ones that they do not appear to be copies—they are self-standing, small beings." And later in the same letter, "From the estate of the ingenious chemical researcher Friedhelm Ferdinand Runge of Oranienburg (1794-1867) I was able to procure artificially produced colors that seem suitable for my seven dwarfs..."

The first figures were painted in July 1874. The Frivolous was the first figure to lose its "nakedness." The painted figures are described emphatically in the letters of many visitors to Wiepersdorf Castle.

After the death of Achim von Arnim-Bärwalde in 1891, his cousin Erwin von Arnim took over Wiepersdorf. The first thing he did was have the "salacious" figures, as he called them, disassembled and removed. It bothered him that such obscene figures stood so close to the church. Where the "salacious" ones were thrown away is not entirely clear. There was credible evidence that it was into the castle pond. In 1912, during a search for a missing child, people poked the pond with long poles, and it is reported that at one point they pushed against a hard object quite deep in the mud. The search operation, however, was called off when the child, a twelve-year-old girl, was found safe—she had been with an aunt in the neighboring village of Merz.

The seven small Callot figures remained. Up until 1945 they stood in a studio, which was used as a reception and banquet hall. Frau. T., who worked as a maid in Wiepersdorf Castle from 1939 to 1989, revealed the following in a 1992 interview with Vera Nolte:

> *I always found the small figures in the hall to be very cute; the big ones in the garden I liked less. There were formerly six, and later five, of the big ones; the small ones were always seven in number. I often set the little one with the naked breast to the side when we had visitors. I once heard a conversation between Clara von Arnim and her husband Friedemund, who was lord of the castle, in which it was mentioned that the figures be entirely disposed of. Frau von Arnim, however, insisted that all the figures remain together, and that if they received a visit of a sensitive nature, the figures could be set aside as they had always been. The other figure with the naked bottom stood in front of a curtain, so you could not see it from behind anyway. The figure that was put away always went into the big duck terrine standing in a large glass cabinet. Since this terrine had many cloth layers, nothing inside was ever damaged.*

In 1945 the castle was plundered badly and after serving temporarily as the Russian headquarters, was cleared for demolition. Shortly before the scheduled demolition in 1946, "Poet Foundation e.V." became the newly established owner and plans to destroy the building were dropped. During a reconnaissance of the building, among other things, it was discovered that not only had many manuscripts disappeared, but that the seven small figures had also been lost. The big ones were found overturned in the park.

The seven small figures stood in the officer's casino of the Red Army in Jüterbog until 1957, and in 1964 were transferred to the House of Officers in Wünsdorf, where they stood in a room for art works until 1994. With the departure of the Red Army from Wünsdorf, these figures were brought to Serov at the outer eastern edge of the Urals, where they now enjoy great popularity in the local military museum. Since military art treasures are specifically excluded from the negotiations on looted art, their return is impossible.

The remaining six large Callot figures have long inspired those writers seeking relaxation and tranquility for their work within the castle. The line in Sarah Kirsch's poem *Wiepersdorf*, for example—"The stone images smile—I go"—refers directly to the Callot figures. Anna Seghers, who enjoyed a permanently reserved room in the castle, states in her 1975 novella *Stone Age*, "Six stone dwarves stood. One uglier than the other. One even had its pants down—what a ridiculous sight." Even if the story takes place in South America, this passage clearly refers to the Wiepersdorf dwarf with the naked buttocks.

In the general renovation of the castle that took place between 1974 and 1980 all the figures, including those of the dwarfs, were brought to Berlin for restoration. The foreign trade imperium of Schalck-Golodkowski was aware of this and, during an inspection, confiscated the aforementioned dwarf of the bare buttocks. They were certain they would get a particularly good price, as it was a rarity. It was sold in 1978 in the west, and from 1980 to 1992 could be seen in the front yard of a bungalow in Böblingen. Since 1992 it has been on view at the privately funded BESM (Böblinger Erotic Sculpture Museum). The remaining five figures were brought back to their original location and now stand, as they did during Achim von Arnim's time, below the studio window, inspiring many a contemporary scholar and visitor to wonder just where they are from.

The female dwarf, however, likely located in the castle pond, still awaits rescue.

Literature:

W. Andik, *Together with the Red Army*, Jüterbog, 1989.

M. Feitag, *Runge*, Berlin, 2003.

G. B. Hanke, *Theatrum Fagi*, Náchod, 2002.

M. Heibner, *Time Lapse: Lectures and Essays*, Wolfsburg, 1995.

G. Kahan, *Jacques Callot: Artist of the Theatre*, Athens, 1976.

Sarah Kirsch, *Cobblestones: Poems*, Munich, 1978.

P. Loeffler, *Jacques Callot: Attempt at an Interpretation*, Winterthur, 1958.

J. Petty, *Gnomes on the Rise*, Marburg, 1987.

H. Petzold, *The Secret Wiepersdorf*, Magdeburg, 2004.

H. Rademacher, *Acute Literature*, Berlin, 2003.

Anna Seghers, *Narratives: 1963-1977*, Berlin/Weimar, 1977.

D. Sossenheimer (ed.), *Wiepersdorf Castle*, Göttingen, 1997.

The Saxon State Archive News, Dresden, 2000.

0.006g

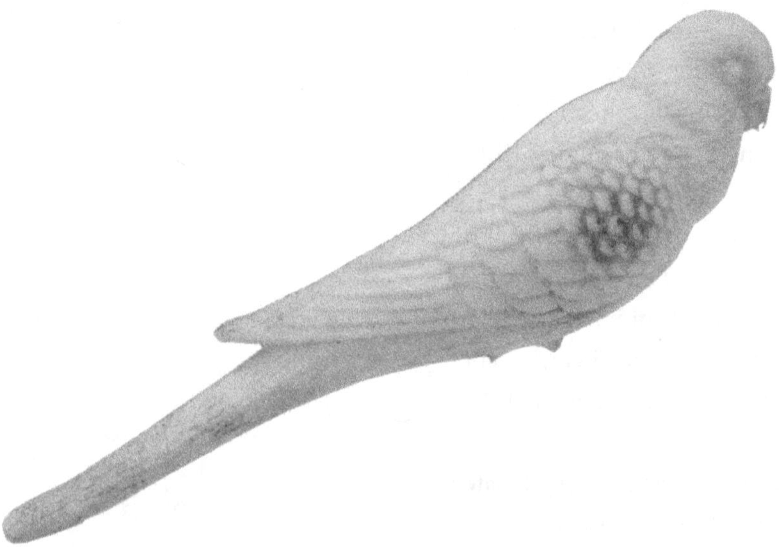

The Canary Birds of Fraxern

or

How the Harzer Roller Found Its Voice

At the World Championship of Songbirds held in Riebelhausen in the area of the Ruhr in August 2002 the bird Klausi won first prize with 90 points. Klausi belonged to the genus of mountain scooters and had made his way through the various disciplines of singing—hollow rolling, gnarling, water rolling, and swaying—just as brilliantly as he had clucking and whistling. In spite of the ever growing popularity of ring tones, they were not assessed due to the fact that many breeding clubs do not recognize them. The Ü-O and the GLK-BLK consonant clusters of Klausi's cluck were particularly impressive, but even there he could not be given more than a top score. There was a bird was who almost handled the consonants W-G-D-L-H-R and B better than Klausi, but he fell short in all other disciplines. The newly crowned world champion belonged, like all the other canaries involved in the championship, to the approximately one-hundred-and-fifty-fifth generation of canaries kept in captivity.

When Isabella I of Castile married Ferdinand II of Aragon following a jointly won battle against the Moors on October 19, 1469, her kingdom became united with her husband's. She remained the ruler of Castile, however, and played a decisive role in the expulsion of the Moors from the Iberian Peninsula, while her husband—also known as "the Catholic"—more through chance and to all intents and purposes unaware, let Christopher Columbus discover America. One of their wedding presents turned out to be a number of these beautifully chirping, cute-looking, little birds. Indeed, the ladies of the court liked these merry birds very much and even fell downright in love with them.

These birds were named Canary Birds after their place of origin; they were also known as Sugar Birds and in Latin were called Serinus Canarius. A warship brought the first bird from the strongly contested archipelago in 1402. It was only in 1496 that the last of the islands, Tenerife, was finally conquered by the Spaniards, in the process so thoroughly destroying the culture of Guances that only a very small part of it—whatever the destruction happened by chance to spare—can be seen today.

In their home on the Canary Islands one can find the 12-13 centimeter sized birds with their 6 centimeter long tails and 7 centimeter long wings living in freedom in the shady forests up to a height of 1,500 meters. Like the finches of the Galapagos Islands they have developed into a unique, special species of bird thanks to the remoteness of the islands and pertain to the order of sparrows, the finch family, and the subfamily of gimpels.

In no time at all in the European courts it became fashionable to own a canary. There they were considered more valuable than silver or gold and through their vividness also demonstrated the transience of wealth as well as the mortality of possessions. Many men had their women portrayed in paintings with a canary on their finger as their only jewelry. Over the following decades, this motif of "Woman with Canary" developed into a commercial painting genre in its own right.

The chirping birds were kept in golden cages, and aviaries in landscape gardens were decorated with precious ornaments. In fact, the great royal garden architect Buyeau de la

Baraudeerie even considered the canary aviaries to be the chief ornament of any landscape garden.

The breeding of these prestigious canaries lay in the hands of Spanish monks, and they sold only males. The male birds also chirped in the most beautiful and delightful way, thus marking their territory as well as their presence to females. As the monks only sold males, they enjoyed an absolute monopoly on breeding for almost two hundred years, which made any breeding outside of the monastery walls impossible. They kept the sales figures very tight in order to maintain a high price for these much sought-after birds. All attempts to cross the birds with other finches and gimpels failed, so the ordinary shares were dominant.

0.006g

The canary trade was an important economic resource not only for the monks but for the whole of Spain. And thus the Spanish court, enjoying a rich supply of birds, had an immense interest in maintaining its monopoly.

The greed of the European courts grew infinitely in the seventeenth century, and increasingly more people wanted to participate in the business. Some princes from north of the Alps set high rewards for the transfer of one or more canary chicks. Far-sighted contemporary economists issued urgent warnings about developments like that in Holland where on February 5, 1637, with the abrupt end of the so-called "tulip mania," many respectable and wealthy merchants lost all their assets from one day to the next and ended up beggars. All attempts to obtain female canaries were unsuccessful, and so the compartmentalization of the singing canary breed seemed perfect. In some writings from that time it is often reported that the monasteries of the "Bird Cowls," as people called the monks, resembled besieged castles, as there were always strangers hanging around in the hopes of catching an escaped female canary.

Abbot Anton "the Good," who built a Capuchin monastery in 1679 with generous donations from Haller councilor Peter Tasch and other benefactors, was so bothered by the monopoly of his fellow believers that for years he did everything he could to disrupt their monopoly of canary breeding. After all his efforts of obtaining a female canary in a friendly manner proved unsuccessful, in 1699 he sent five young, daredevil lads—Johann Rupert from Matrei in West Tyrol; the brothers Conrad and Joseph Streiter, and George Kammerlander, all from Imst; and Christopherus Kathan from Vorarlberg—to procure one. Before they headed out, he instructed them in the art of aviculture and bird transport.

The five crossed the Alps with a letter of recommendation from the abbot in their luggage. They identified themselves as pious Tyroleans from Imst wishing to enter a Spanish monastery because they found the northern ones too cold. They were firmly determined to immediately head back once they had a female canary. The first monasteries rejected them, but at the fifth, where they appeared in person, two were allowed to start working as servants immediately; the other three were employed part-time in a nearby monastery as handymen.

After a year they were ready. They secretly kidnapped some male and female birds and took off. They crossed the Pyrenees, travelled up the Rhone Valley, passed Lake Constance, and the first stop they made back in their homeland was at Vorarlberg in Fraxern, where Christopherus had come from. All along the way they were afraid that Spanish monks would follow them and seek revenge or at least destroy their canaries.

To prevent this from happening, they left some canaries at Flaxern, had Christopherus' parents swear to never tell anybody about the birds, and continued on to Imst.

What the boys did not know was that the Spanish monks were not pursuing them; they did not realize how many servants had been disappearing from one day to the next, nor that the monopoly had already been broken for some time, and on a large scale. English traders had secretly imported wild birds from the Canary Islands and in Southern Italy a whole load had escaped from a ship in distress at sea so that the birds were now living in the wild. Some of these birds had even ended up in breeding cages. The ever-increasing availability of canaries caused their price to fall rapidly.

In England and Italy a distinct form of breeding developed. In Italy they put a lot of emphasis on the shape of birds and their posture, especially the head position, while in England they bred the birds to have highly colored feathers, and in Imst it was always about what the birds could do, especially in terms of song. This differentiation of breeding goals has remained up until today, so that one can still distinguish between signing, posing, and colored canaries.

In Imst the miners from the local iron mines adopted the birds and kept breeding them to use as early warning systems for gas influx and as a source of entertainment in the pits. Imst became the center of singing canary breeding and the birds became a significant trade factor.

The canaries in the small, remote mountain village of Fraxern also continued to multiply so that soon almost every farm had its own chirping bird. For their part, however, the farmers did not place much importance on any particular differences or peculiarities. One could therefore consider these birds as the only natural, pristine birds in captivity. Be that as it may, what the farmers noticed was that the birds felt very comfortable and at home at an altitude of over 1,000 meters.

A particular feature about the sunny mountain village of Fraxern was, and still is, that they grow about twenty different kinds of cherries, an absolute specialty for that altitude, and that those cherries are very tasty indeed. To this day, when it is cherry season, people come from all around to taste and buy them.

These cherries were placed in the birds' cages, and they pecked at them with such pleasure that, when in season, they became their exclusive diet. At other times they often received softened cardoon-seeds from the so-called safflower. This artichoke-related thistle, which was once a popular staple, is now known almost exclusively in western Switzerland or among hard-nosed, organically-inclined folks.

When ore exploitation in Imst decreased considerably at the end of the eighteenth century and new unexploited ore veins were found in the region of the Harz, many miners moved to the new mining areas and took their birds with them. A small group of miners from Vorarlberg remembered the canaries in Fraxern and took the birds with them to the German low mountains, settling near the newly excavated Catharina Mine in Saint Andreasberg.

What the miners quickly heard was that the birds they had brought from Fraxern had a clearer and purer singing voice than the ones they knew back in Imst. In the nineteenth century, the Andreasberg canaries from Fraxern were so trained in their singing that people gave them a special name: the Harzer Roller.

A professional Harzer Roller breeding business developed in St. Andreasberg so that, at times, more than one-hundred-thousand birds were exported annually around the world—especially to the United States, but to Australia and South America as well.

In the US a large-scale study of the singing canary was conducted in 1998, and it was discovered that the glottal of all Harzer Rollers was characterized by exceptional flexibility. It is thought that this could have been caused by a unilateral diet over tens of generations containing food rich with organic acids, sugars, and pectines—in other words, cherries and cardoon seeds.

Today, canary breeding no longer plays a significant economic role anywhere, and there are no longer any professional canary breeders. Instead, breeding takes place at the level of small animal breeding clubs. In the Andreas Mountains there is a beautiful Harzer Roller Museum with gorgeous singing mountain scooters. In Fraxern the last natural canaries died during a cold winter in the mid-nineteenth century so that the chirping canaries displayed there today are actually re-imported ones.

One final word. Before you think there might be a roasted canary wrapped up in bacon hidden somewhere when you hear the name of Harzer Roller in a culinary context, remember that it is only a certain type of cheese belonging to the genus of stinky cheese and is in reality quite suitable for marinating:

* 2 packages of Harzer Roller
* 4 garlic cloves
* 1 red chili
* 2 bay leaves
* 1 sprig rosemary
* 1 sprig thyme
* Extra virgin olive oil for refilling

Cut the peeled garlic in slices, cut the chili in half and remove the seeds. In a glass container, alternate the individual Harzer Roller rollfills with layers of bay leaves, thyme, and rosemary leaves, garlic and chili peppers. Fill it up with olive oil. Leave it in a cool, dark place for at least four days. The cheese tastes especially delicious when it is drizzled (before eating) with a few drops of good wine vinegar and garnished with some onion rings. The cool, picked Harzer Roller will be ready in approximately two weeks.

Literature:

Rolf Gessner, *Plant and Animal Health in Mines Convention From the Example of the Harz Region*, Braunlage, 2002.

Otto Wendt, *Family Lexicon*, Leipzig, 1863.

Meyers Conversation Encyclopedia Vol. 9, Leipzig/Vienna, 1890.

"The Cherry Miracle of Fraxern," in *Heimatblätter* Vol. 28, Bregenz, 1952.

"Harzer Roller Canary Museum," Students of the Glückauf School, Saint Andreas Mountain, 2004. http://geschichtsatlas.de/~gc7/index

0.008g

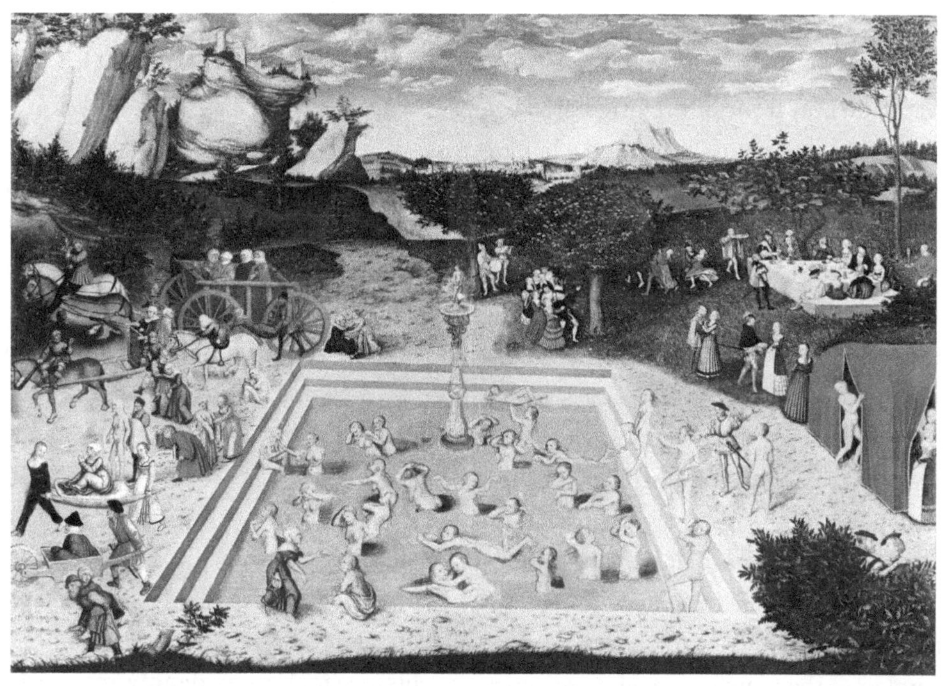

"The Fountain of Life": On the Newly Decoded Sub-Image (Pentimento) of the Highly Acclaimed and Famous Painting "The Fountain of Youth" by Lucas Cranach the Elder

At twelve o'clock noon on February 26, 2011, the latest results of research on a sub-image of the famous painting *The Fountain of Youth* were presented to the amazement of the expert audience. For the very first time the previously invisible sub-image was shown in front of the original image in the Gemäldegalerie in Berlin, and a lecture was given on its history and discovery.

The sub-image of the painting *The Fountain of Youth* was studied at the radiation department of the Charité Hospital complex using various imaging procedures like computer tomography, mass spectrometry, O2 decay analysis, etc., and shown to be an accurate, sharp, colored picture beneath the overpainted image.

The hidden sub-image shows the exact opposite of the visible image: it depicts the process of aging. In this picture there are no longer any old women rejuvenating themselves in the fountain—the young ones who are entering from the right instead emerge as mature, old women from the left.

The narrative of the painting moves from left to right and demonstrates the growth and decay of life. Since going from left to right aligns with our habits of seeing, the aging of the young can be perceived, but the rejuvenation of the old, which proceeds from the right to left and is thus diametrically opposite to our habits of seeing, cannot. The old, at the left, thanks to their many years of lived experience, can see how their former selves, on the right, once were; but, on the contrary, when we are young, we do not know what we will be like at an old age. Thus one can only look backwards and never forward. Looking into the future, there on the left, is forever obstructed.

The structure of the sub-image shows how Cranach the Elder dealt with life and aging in those years. And the inscription on the back of the painting can be understood from this perspective:

Fresh bread shall quickly turn you red,
Ripe bread alone will make you full.
Old bread waves from the land of the dead.

The master's sayings from those years that have been handed down to us by his assistants now can also be understood in a new light: "He no longer wants to paint the nude, he only wants to paint the image of the old"; "Life begins young and ends wrinkled, no doubt about it"; or "I want to try and paint the process of aging, a very important life-path."

His personal data suggest a confrontation with aging and death. His wife, with whom he had five children, died a few years before the creation of the painting. In 1544 he tendered his resignation as deputy mayor; his friend, the reformer Martin Luther, whose best man he had been, had died earlier in the year. It is understandable therefore that the year 1546 found Cranach pondering life, the process of aging, and death more than just a little and that he thus painted a corresponding image.

At the first presentation of the painting Elector and Duke Johann Friedrich I of Saxony rebuked Cranach the Elder, thundering, "He should re-paint this ugly image, I do not want to see it ever again. Away with him." Now even this comment, which had remained enigmatic until the present day, is explainable.

And so Cranach the Elder had to paint over the image, turning it into a true *Pentimento*, a real image of repentance. He painted *The Fountain of Youth* over *The Fountain of Life.*

0.008g

Cranach the Elder was accustomed to painting images to fit the liking of his clients as well as to re-painting them. And yet, his anger must have been extreme, for he never painted a profane theme again. After *The Fountain of Youth* only altarpieces emerged from his workshop.

In *The Fountain of Youth,* however, Cranach the Elder left some indications that have only been understood today with the discovery of the sub-image. Venus and Cupid in the center of the image are not only gods of love: Venus is also the administrator of the list of death and Cupid the god of an infantile self-love and the idea of eternal life. The woman fleeing from the rejuvenation process in the upper right-hand part of the pool and turning away in disgust can also be understood better, as can the woman who must be persuaded to stay in the pool.

Thanks to the discovery of *The Fountain of Life*—as the sub-image is now called—a whole new era of research on Cranach the Elder has begun.

Literature:
Hiltrud Himbeer, *Infantile Desire, Eternal Life,* Stuttgart, 1996.
Sandra Kuttner, *The Importance of* The Fountain of Youth *in the Course of Life,* Berlin, 2011.
Meike Mentjes, *Layer by Layer: The Beauty of Discovery,* Berlin, 2009.
Robert Smutje, *The Cognitive Power of Steel,* Stuttgart, 2009.
Georg Simmel, *What Fountains Reveal to Us,* Munich, 1978.
Timor Tinglan, *The Sensation of Cranach the Elder, Newspaper Supplement,* Frankfurt, 2011.
Friederike Thomas, *Pentimento: Forever Unknown Beneath the Layers,* Stralsund, 2010.

0.011g

How Sigmund Freud Distanced Himself from the Basilisk

or

On Basiliskmus and Narcissism

On December 16, 1908, Sigmund Freud wrote to his Berlin proconsul and chairman of the Berlin Psychoanalytic Association, Karl Abraham, "in regard to the treatment," i.e. psychoanalysis, "of a person suffering narcissistic withdrawal, one must make sure that he is not all of a sudden mirrored too much. A simple reflection can have fatal consequences for these people; not only will the patient immediately terminate treatment, no, he will also often feel himself disintegrate. Diligence and the highest degree of caution are required. [...] The mirror method must be used in very sparingly in order to avoid an MM-effect..." The wildest rumors have surrounded these lines ever since. Different interpretations and conjectures twine around the "MM-effect."

A newly discovered letter of Freud's dated June 4, 1903, and addressed to the folklorist Braun in Memmingen (MM) now reveals the secret:

> *Vienna IX, Berggasse 19, June 4, 1903*
> *Dear Mr. Braun,*
>
> *I have read with admiration the amount of in-depth knowledge you have on the basilisk. Your "draconic warrior behind the angel" is the piece of the puzzle that was missing for me to describe a repeatedly observed medical condition in my patients. I am considering calling the appearance of this neurosis, if it can be seen as an independent condition, as "Basiliskmus." Your description of the liberating effect of the mirroring of your Memmingen basilisk on the delinquent who, due to a prenatal life disappointment, lives alone in seclusion so as not to ever be hurt again (though he is himself not capable of contributing to this goal) was a revelation. This pathogenic characteristic of an encounter with mirroring seems to me highly suitable for healing the fears of self-chosen solitude. The uninhibited aggressiveness of driving forces belonging to this perversion seems to me truer of the Basilisk than Narcissus gently contemplating himself in the watery mirror image. I thank you again for your great help in the search for the essence of the basilisk. I would love to accept your kind invitation to visit your certainly very beautiful and venerable former imperial city of Memmingen. I will allow myself the opportunity in the near future to travel to this area, though my work in Vienna regrettably claims my constant presence.*
>
> *In the highest esteem and gratitude,*
> *Your devoted Freud*

0.011g

But just what—or who—is this basilisk that so fascinated Freud? The basilisk appeared for the first time in documents 600 years before our present time. The oldest descriptions refer to events in North Africa. There is evidence that it has to do with the drops of blood that fell from Medusa's head as Perseus flew over the desert of Libya with that severed head in his hand, his own head covered by the helmet of invisibility he had received from the Stygian nymphs. The basilisk is there described as being a particularly toxic creature, one that could kill with its glance and was depicted as a snake with a crown on its head.

The Crusaders were responsible for bringing the basilisk to Central Europe. Here its appearance and doings were adjusted to the customs and habits of the local people. The size of the basilisk is between 15 and 50 centimeters, and its weight between 1.5 and 10 kilograms. It is not so large and certainly is not a dragon as so often assumed. And yet, though small, it is powerful. In Europe it has a serpent's tail, a rooster's head, legs, and wings with which it cannot fly. Overall, it is rather immobile.

The mystic Hildegard von Bingen thought a lot about basilisks, and her description of the creature has become a standard:

> *An old rooster lays an egg.*
> *A toad feels fertilized and sees the egg.*
> *She will fiercely love and care for it,*
> *and will now incubate it with her own eggs.*
> *Then her eggs will die next to those of the basilisk's.*
> *Now, with only one egg, the toad's love for the rooster's egg increases.*
> *She loves this leftover egg like she never loved her own.*
> *Then, when the time comes, she recognizes her unjust passion*
> *and flees before the brood hatches.*

What a sad fate. Madly loved before being born but then abandoned, lonely, without a partner. Abandoned and anxious it now sits alone in holes, wet basements, and cisterns, always careful not to be seen but with the desire to be both marveled at and admired by all, forever on guard that the disappointment never happen again, the abandonment never again be repeated.

The real tragedy of the basilisk is that it does not, it cannot, ever know the reason for its drama. It knows nothing about it, for it never learned anything from either its father, the old rooster, nor its stepmother, the toad. It senses its lonely despair deep in its unconscious and acts from those deep abysses. Anyone who comes too close will receive a look so poisonous that they will immediately be fatally wounded and sink to the ground. Here, similarities to narcissists are very strong, indeed almost identical. The narcissist also suffered early childhood disappointment and subsequently withdrew into his or herself; the focus of their love is always themselves alone, they avoid the treasured object, hurt those who come too close, and suffer alone in their relationship-anxiety. The similarities in speech regarding the two are also many—people are often accused of "the evil eye," "the poisonous gaze," of "looking evil"; we have also heard "if looks could kill," and of someone with "a deadly expression."

It is certain that, as a Viennese man, Sigmund Freud knew the basilisk, for the story of the basilisk is rather well known in that city. In Vienna, at 7 Schönlaterngasse, today a house plaque commemorates an incident that occurred on June 26, 1212, when a basilisk robbed the consciousness of young Hans, apprentice to the master baker and landlord Martin Garbibi. Hans, however, did not die, which was extremely unusual, and which is also why for a long time people doubted the veracity of his story. But the reports he made in front of a venerable investigation committee were convincing. Thanks to him we have a detailed account of the appearance of a basilisk. Almost every old European city has a similar story.

Even today in Basel every August 4 people think about August 4, 1474, when an eleven-year-old rooster was executed by court order because he had laid an egg. The autopsy that followed revealed another two basilisk eggs inside of him. And so he was burnt together with his eggs. Basel derives its very name from the term "basilisk," and its coat of arms is carried by a basilisk known to have caused mischief in that area around the time of the city's foundation.

Naturally what interested Freud most was how to get rid of basilisks; in other words, how a person plagued by narcissism could be treated. A common and rather effective method was holding up a mirror to the basilisk, which, upon seeing itself, would then commit suicide. It is said that Alexander the Great and his soldiers once had to cross a valley overrun with basilisks. Alexander ordered their shields to be so shiny that they would reflect everything. And so huddled together, secured from all sides by the mirrors, they safely made their way through.

In Memmingen one convict who had been sentenced to be hanged got his freedom because he risked his life when expelling a basilisk. It was a trade. He completely surrounded himself with mirrors and went into the basement inhabited by a basilisk. The basilisk infected himself with his own gaze and died on the spot, and the convict became a free man. Similar mirror-based basilisk killings have been reported from many cities like Warsaw, Zwickau, Vienna, Magdeburg, and Basel. Freud mentions these "mirrorings" in his letter to Karl Abraham.

Just why Freud became so interested in the legend of the Memmingen basilisk remains unknown; we have only the recently discovered letter. The reasons for which Freud retained the concept of Narcissism without introducing that of Basiliskmus are also unknown. It is, however, very likely due to the fact that he was a great friend of the world of Greek myth and saw many things anticipated there; though it is equally likely that the theory of Narcissism was simply far too advanced to be easily replaced by Basiliskmus.

Literature:

Gerhard Dahl, "Primary Narcissism and Internal Object," in *PSYCHE 55*, Stuttgart, 2001.

M. Ernhart, *From the Finding of Letters*, Berlin, 2009.

Sigmund Freud, *The Introduction of Narcissism*, Leipzig, 1924.

Freud/Abraham, *The Complete Correspondence 1907-1925*, Frankfurt, 2002.

L. Hammer, "Reassessment of Freud's Concept of Narcissism," in *Motion 67*, Hamburg, 2003.

H. Himmel, *Self-love in the Animal Kingdom*, Stuttgart, 1957.

M. Sammer, *The Basilisk: The Story of Nature and Importance of a Mythical Animal in the West*, Munich, 1998.

0.015g

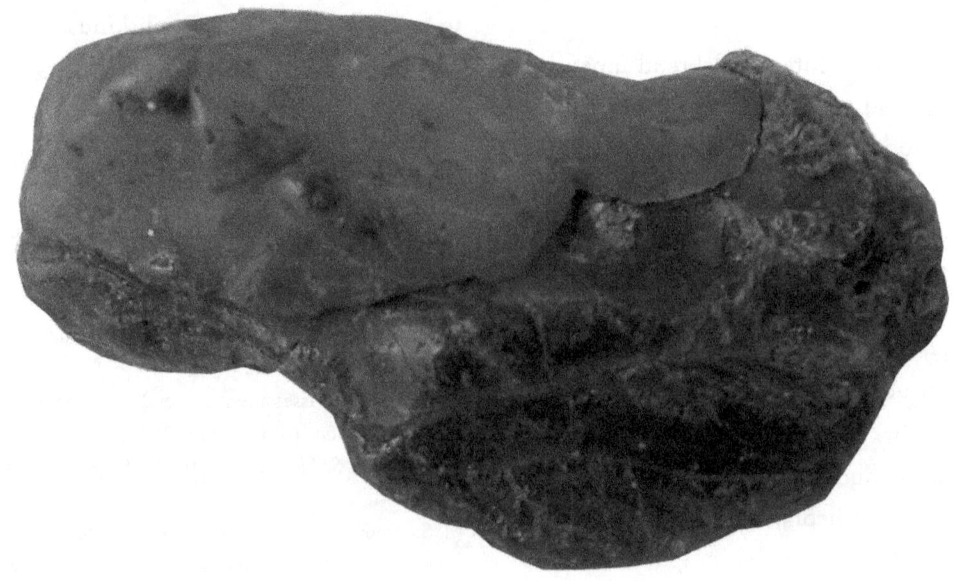

The Only Remaining Piece of Amber from the Legendary Amber Room in Königsberg Castle

Mika Lotowosch (*1) recalls: "Yes, back in 1975 the building (*2) was not yet completed, and it remains unfinished to this day. (*3)

"No one knows why. It might be related to the excavations that I participated in from 1975 to '76. According to one rumor, the foundation would not hold. Back then, between 1975 and '76, we dug up the all the subsoil just to find the legendary Amber Room. If we could've found the whole thing, or even just a part, undamaged, that would've been a real triumph. And we did find real amber during the excavation. Tons of it. But, unfortunately, it was all unusable. I know now that it was melted amber. The resin had become soft and liquid-like again, like it had been before. Today it looks like any normal, inferior, impure piece of amber that you can find anywhere along the coast. Our bosses didn't believe that that could be the Amber Room we'd been looking for, but today I know without any doubt that it was. But back then nothing could be what they didn't think it was.

"Without any particular plan in mind we dug up the site, really turned it back and forth, over and under. We had only one condition: everything had to be kept top secret, we had to leave the room undamaged, and prevent the building from collapsing.

"Two years later, once we had ransacked everything, the last bits of the salvaged amber, together with the building debris, were removed and dumped into the Baltic Sea off the Curonian Spit. They dumped it far off the coast and it got strewn along the entire shoreline. You can't see the castle or the discovered amber anymore. If you could find some amber, it would probably just look like any other kind. But I think that some high officials knew darn well what'd we found, they just didn't want to admit it.

"When everything was gone they ceased excavations, and no one talked about it anymore. I did research on my own. At first secretly, then later "behind dark glass," as they say in Russia. To this day no one wants to know about it officially. I was interested in what I was doing back then, and I found out that there, right there where we had discovered all those pieces of inferior-quality raw amber, that was the place where the complete Amber Room had been installed.

"The then head of the municipal ministry slipped me some documents which were in German. Now, old Kulsowitsch, a professor of German who—as he can't live on his official salary—looks after German tourists who have come to have a gander at their old home, translated these texts for me. These documents make clear that the room was not taken apart and reconstructed elsewhere but simply undone and stored in the basement. The former German city administration had officially announced that the room had been removed and several other versions of the story went around suggesting that it had been sunk in a mountain lake somewhere in southern Germany.

"Near the kitchen you could go down into a dark cellar where they used to store excellent wines, wines that were a hundred years old and more, wines that weren't intended for everyday use. And down there there was a door that opened to another cellar even further below with a barrel vault. Very few people knew about its existence. And that was where they had brought the disassembled, boxed-up Amber Room. The plans of the city castles available to me revealed that, in addition to the large entrance door, this basement room had a small door which led to a spiral staircase that wound through the entire castle. And this was to become the tragedy of the hiding place.

"In mid-March 1945 the fifth firestorm that raged over the fortress city of Königsberg engulfed the entire castle. In this fire, which almost completely destroyed it, the basement functioned just like a vent in an oven, and the cellar vaults were scorched accordingly. Professor Ilian Karpv believes that some kind of highly combustible material like rolls of film, heavy oil, or something, must have been stored in the kitchen because the vaults flamed like a blast furnace and the barrel vault was like firebrick. The cellar itself did not burn, nor did the amber, but the temperatures must have been so hellish that the amber, as well as the iron, melted. The amber flowed like honey across the shelves, clumped onto the floor, then softened again, dripped into the cracks, melted...the plaster exploded and mixed with the softened amber mass, the stones burst, the clay floor exploded and turned to dust, in turn swallowing the flowing amber and becoming one with it. In the end the vault must've collapsed.

"There are reports of soldiers who testified that, even fourteen days after the fire, they could not enter some parts of the castle, the temperature was just too high.

"And that's precisely the part of the cellar where we found huge amounts of amber with dirty inlays, which, as I already said, were just thrown away like garbage. I sorted out a whole bag of these at the time. I think that every single one of us who participated in the excavations did the same thing. We thought to ourselves: 'Why dig around the Baltic Sea for the same thing we can take from here?' At the same time, I was inclined to believe that this could perhaps be the Amber Room we'd been looking for...why else would so many pieces of amber be in a single place? While only inferior pieces of amber showed up in all the excavations, why so many in a pile, and together with the debris of the castle? 'That can't be a coincidence,' I thought to myself, and so I collected a whole bag full of it."

Here the statement of Mika Lotowosch ends.

Notes:

(1) Mika Lotowosch is one of the few "real Kaliningradians." Born in 1955 in Kaliningrad to parents who had been relocated from the borderlands of the eastern Urals by their own free will. He is now inquiring about the city's history, a process which was previously illegal.

(2) In 1971 they began to construct "The House of the Soviets" upon the remains of the city castle, which was detonated in 1969. It remains unfinished to this day.

(3) 1999.

Literature:

Paul Enke, *Amber Room Report*, Berlin, 1986.

Guido Knopp, *The Amber Room: The Myth on the Trail*, Hamburg, 2003.

Gert Dieter Schmidt, *Hidden Treasures on the Trail: The Endless Search for the Amber Room*, Zella-Mehlis, 2014.

Bernhard Rund, *Amber, Amber, Amber*, Berlin, 2010.

0.016g - 0.050g

0.017g

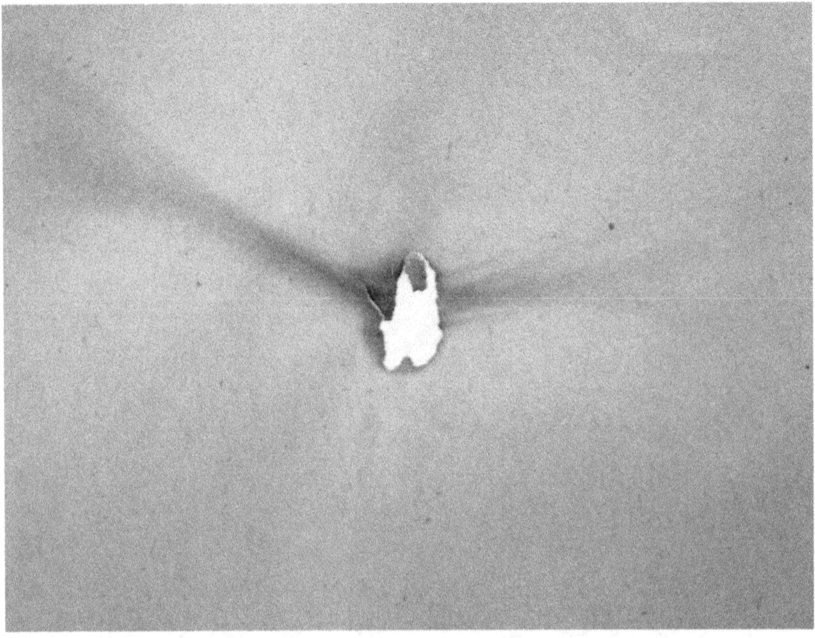

The Impact of a Flash of Thought

One day the Cologne neurologist Dr. Helmut Dröf began to notice himself wincing at sudden thoughts. Thereafter he also observed this phenomenon in his patients and therefore decided to study it in detail.

He assumed that it had to have something to do with electric charges that were so strong that they caused the body to twitch.

And so he set about developing equipment that would catch, measure, and identify this twitching. The result was the electromagnetic graph for the flash of thought.

With this equipment he was finally able to successfully capture these flashes. This cage functioned like an inverted Faraday cage—a cage, that is, from which no electric charge escaped. The electrical impulse was derived using an iron wire and brought to discharge at the end. Based on the impact of the flash Dr. Helmut Dröf could study how strong the flash of thought had been and from the form of this impact he could even understand what its content had been.

In 1889 he registered his device as a medical patent.

However, as of today, the thought-flash electromagnetic graph still has not been accepted within the field of neurology.

0.017g

Literature:
Wolfgang Maier, *Early Electrography*, Berlin, 1982.
Wilhelm Reich, *The School of Orgasm*, Berlin, 1932.
———, *The Orgone*, Rangeley, 1952.

0.018g

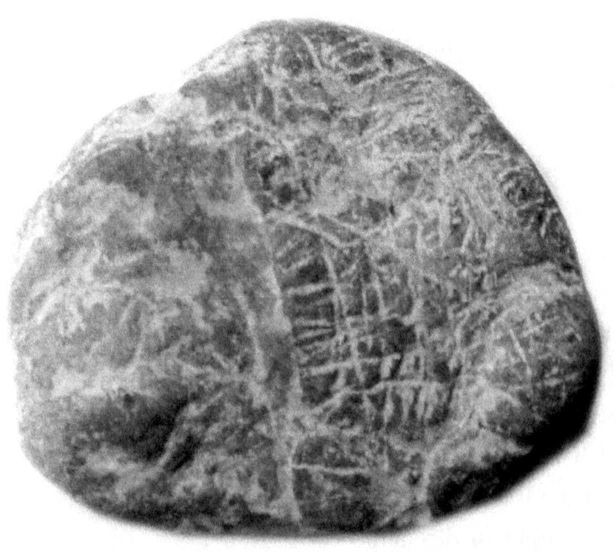

The Mystery of Time-Stones and Their Significance in the Lives of Herdsmen

To date, the mystery of the significance, the essence, of so-called Time-Stones has not been solved. These enigmatically carved stones can be found all over the world with the exception of the American continent. This lack of Time-Stones in America is one of the great, unsolved scientific mysteries in the study of our early history. These fine, cleanly carved stones emerge en masse in cultures older than the colonization of America. But the reason why the ability to deal with Time-Stones was not brought to that continent remains both completely unclear and puzzling in its singularity.

The Time-Stones point to semi-nomadic herdsman. They have not been found in either purely nomadic cultures or in urban, city-dwelling, craft cultures. These rocks have not emerged, nor have carvings of this type been discovered, at the sites of the Egyptian pharaohs or at the excavations of the centers of civilization in Mesopotamia, the Tigris and Euphrates, or even in Central Asian Transoxiana by the rivers of Amu Darya (Oxus) and Syr Darya (Jakates).

One can find Time-Stones at the edges of these civilizations, which suggests that they were native to mixed cultures. This rather unspecific term of "mixed cultures" refers, for example, mainly to settled nomads, often herdsmen with a fixed location, who valued their own cultures and for a long time could not be assimilated by so-called civilization.

Linguistic archeology has not yet succeeded in recognizing the carvings as writing or something similar to writing, for they are missing a uniform structure. That stated, it is certain that they were used to report information, for they have been found in residential towns, in houses, outlets, and stables. They are, however, completely absent from places of worship, so it can be assumed that they contained messages of everyday life. Some researchers, such as the research team of Central Asian specialists Christel Gernhard and Ernst Rössler, believe the Time-Stones to be pre-writing communication-stones whose application continued parallel to the development of writing and that they were used by herdsmen up until the nineteenth century.

According to Gernhard and Rössler the carvings display the positions of herding flocks. That is, they are a type of drawing, or recording, of flocks—for example, sheep—in the countryside. The stones were given to herdsmen so that they knew which areas had been grazed and which had not.

From the various and different forms of the sharp carvings we understand that the stones were used and inscribed by different people.

The stones are known as Time-Stones because it was once believed that the carvings were a kind of pastime for the herdsman, a kind of time-recording whereby they would carve out their guard time. Today this interpretation, however, is mainly held only by those outside of the scientific community, as in the case of esoterics who often refer to the Time-Stones as power stones even though, in spite of intensive research, they have not been found to harbor any peculiar abilities.

0.018g

Literature:

Werner Linster, *From Time-Stones to Rogue Times*, Berlin, 2005.

Ernst Rössler/Christel Gernhard, *Writings Along the Silk Road*, Berlin, 2007.

——, *Shepherds of Mongolia*, Berlin, 2005.

Cloria R. Gessner, *Records Before Writing*, Lohra/Marburg, 2008.

Frank Ratzhüber, *Herdsmen, Signs, Breeding*, Munich, 1999.

0.018g

0.018g

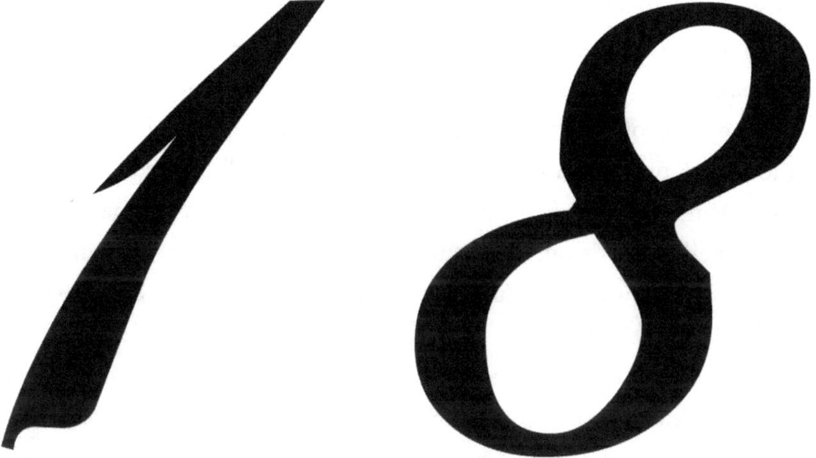

How Balthasar Rihnwalde Explained the World With the Number 18 in 1599 and Then Disappeared

In 1599 the book *The World of Numbers on Their Own Terms as Explained by Balthasar Rihnwalde* was published in Basel. It was published by the Petri Press, which was the same press to have released *The Cosmographia* by Sebastian Münster (1488-1552) to great acclaim in 1544. *The Cosmographia* had just reached its twentieth edition when the "Number Explaining Work," as it was called in short, was released. The Petri Press still exists today under the name of Schwabe AG, and is probably the oldest printing house in the world. Sebastian Münster's portrait adorned the 100-German-mark note from 1962 to 1991, while Balthazar Rihnwalde, for his part, became lost in the tides of history.

It was no coincidence that the publisher of *The Cosmographia* released Balthazar Rihnwalde's book. In *The Cosmographia* the entirety of the known world was explained in terms of its appearance, comprehensively described through its exteriority, and made intelligible through illustrations and detailed reports. Despite all its wonder for the curiosities of the world, however, the book already carried the Enlightenment's disenchantment and objectification of the world within itself. In contrast, or in a complementary manner perhaps, Balthasar Rihnwalde explained the world from its interior; he described its internal logic as well as the interactions and interdependencies of phenomena and events. Exteriority did not interest him, so he conducted research on rules that were hidden inside.

People were continuously making new discoveries, the world was continuously growing larger, new countries were continuously emerging, and the number of inventions and explorations was continuously increasing. What was true yesterday was outdated today, and what was today seen as correct was annulled and unusable tomorrow. Religion, keeping its distance from all the explanations, failed miserably with its views and different factions managed to stay at war with one another. Understanding the world became a great vacuum.

Balthasar Rihnwalde found a pattern in the number eighteen with which he was able to explain with "what holds the width in the interior together," as he stated in the introduction to his major work. Approximately 200 years later his phrase was used by an admirer of numerology, though this admirer failed to specify the source.

Balthasar Rihnwalde was born in Annaberg in 1547. The great arithmetician Adam Ries (1492-1559) often visited the boy's familial home, bringing with himself new calculations that Balthasar's father immediately employed in his thriving trade business. It is known that Balthasar received his Master's Degree in Latin and Astronomy at Wittenberg when he was only seventeen years old. According to the chroniclers, even at that time he was already very concerned with numbers, numerical values, and the mapping of numbers to each other. He fought for the general introduction of Arabic numerals, published writings on the disgracefulness of Roman numerals, refined line calculation, practiced the algebra that had been discovered by Ries, and lauded new views on root extraction. The few testimonies we have of him describe him as a number-zealot and as a man committed to his work of explaining the world through, unsurprisingly, numbers.

Because of his writings, which were praised on the one hand but suspected of heresy on the other, he had to defend himself in court numerous times. He was accused of belonging to the Templars and, furthermore, of having contact with Rosicrucians, of being involved with Jewish occult sciences, of dedicating himself to black magic, and much else besides.

In 1580 he settled in liberal Basel for fear of having to face other trouble. And it was there that he worked feverishly on his "explanation of the world through numbers." For him, the number eighteen was the number of highest perfection. This number consisted of "one"—signifying perennial beginnings, uniqueness, singularity, the number of God, and the foundation of all numbers—and "eight"—the number of the material world, but also of justice and infinity. In the number eighteen all the affairs of the world would come together, the world could be recognized in its true essence, and all its internal mechanisms be described and calculated. Even God could be recognized and calculated from this figure.

Starting from this "eighteen"—which he worked upon with all known arithmetic, compared and calculated it with all other numbers—he was able to explain all the phenomena of the world: he calculated the date of Adam and Eve's birth, the depth of the water in the Flood, compared all events in the Bible to historical data and presented it along with his calculations, finally claiming that there was no such thing as coincidence and that everything was determined and specified by the number eighteen.

When the 567-page work in folio format was presented in 1599, it caused great confusion as no one could understand what was being calculated. No image adorned the book; there were only tables and formulas. Concepts of world history were incorporated into the numbers and treated as numbers. Arithmetic that had been completely unknown until then appeared along with results that no one understood. Rihnwald calculated the zero in its own terms and proved its correctness. The book begins with eighteen and, after 567 pages of calculations, ends with eighteen.

A small circle of initiates praised the book as a work of genius, as a book that made all other books superfluous. On the part of the general public, however, the book was simply met with bewilderment. Many orders were canceled, and in some cities it was even placed on the *Index Libroum Prohibitorum*.

The Emperor Rudolf II (1552-1612), who had just relocated his imperial court to Prague, summoned Rihnwald to his court. Rudolf II, who was considered by his relatives to be mentally ill, gathered the most famous minds of Europe at his court, including the astrologer Johannes Kepler and Tycho Brahe. Balthasar Rihnwalde accepted the Emperor's generous offer and settled in Prague.

Then, something strange happens. The up-to-that-point traceable life of Balthasar Rihnwalde abruptly breaks off. The only thing that is known is that he arrived in Prague with eighteen disciples on July 18, 1601, and that he was provided with a study room at the imperial court. Any further knowledge about him ends there. We do not know what he wrote in Prague, if at all, or when and where he died.

The first edition of his book, published in 1599, could not sell. It disappeared from people's memories, only a few libraries preserved it, for the most part unknowingly in their cellars, and it remained unavailable to the public.

Later there was a person who referred to Balthasar Rihnwalde. Quirinus Kuhlmann (1631-1689), the crude, great and, to this day, still puzzling Baroque poet, was very interested in the inner essence of numbers. All his poetry is based on numerology, and he makes several explicit references to Rihnwalde's work *The World of Numbers on Their Own Terms as Explained by Balthasar Rihnwalde.*

Literature:
Pietro Bongo, *Numerorum Mysteria*, Bergamo, 1599.
G. Melchor, *18 and Nothing Else*, Munich, 1957.
Th. Ruf, *The Number of Numerology*, Hamburg, 1952.
M. Toller, *Eighteen: An Orientation*, Berlin, 1931.

0.022g

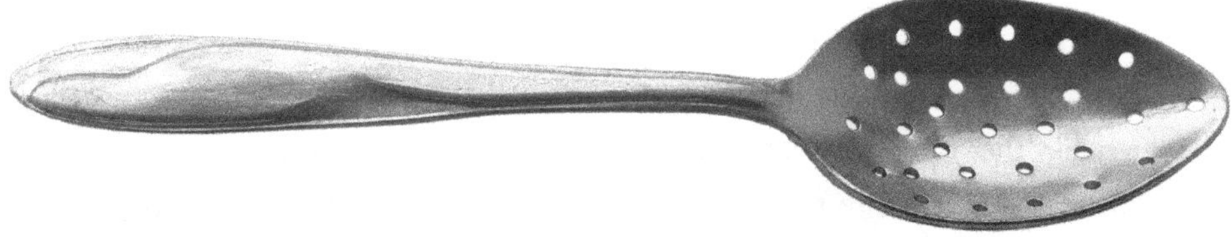

On the Attempt to Make Children More Comfortable with Reading through the Instilling of Letters

In an archive within the cultural center Artenne, which is located in Nenzing in the Austrian part of Vorarlberg, there is a spoon whose bowl is perforated with twenty holes. The spoon is perplexing at first glance, of course, for one naturally wonders: How could you ever successfully eat a soup with such a thing?

This spoon is not a real soup spoon used to spoon soups but a pedagogical one. A typical alphabet soup spoon from the second half of the nineteenth century, to be precise. And it is referred to as such in the archive.

When the Brothers Grimm invented alphabet soup at the end of the first half of the nineteenth century in order to carry out phonetic shift experiments, alphabet pasta was soon adopted by teachers of pedagogical institutions in the belief that it would help children to learn how to read and write more quickly and efficiently.

At that time the case of Kaspar Hauser was still being discussed everywhere. What happens when a human being grows up without any exterior influences? In Leipzig experiments were being made with foundlings. They were being raised without language and with music only in the hopes of creating humans who would then be able to use music as language. Around this same time Daniel Gottlob Moritz Schreber was developing orthopedic educational equipment to which children could be firmly tied so that they might develop a healthy mind.

It was a time of educational methods which held that children could be shaped like masses of dough and that a good upbringing consisted of training and dressage. Sitting still, rote learning, and obedience were the ideals of a true education.

The thinker and educator Johann Georg Sulzer wrote about the "Experiment on the Upbringing and Instruction of Children" as follows:

> *Among other things, these first years have the advantage that one can use force and coercion. Children forget everything. One can take away their will, and thereafter they will no longer remember that they ever even possessed one.*

In 1977 the Berlin sociologist Katharina Rutschky designated these methods of upbringing "poisonous pedagogy." In 1980 the term "poisonous pedagogy" was adopted by Alice Miller in her bestseller *For Your Own Good* and has since become the term for a form of upbringing that breaks a child's will.

Based on the nutritional science from the middle of 1900s by the fashionable doctor Christoph Wilhelm Hufeland, the founder of macrobiotics, a special diet for children was developed, for "you are what you eat." Infants in the crawling stage were not to eat meat in order to prevent them from remaining at the developmental level of four-legged animals; when they could walk upright, on the contrary, they were to be given less vegetables so that they would not succumb to a sedentary lifestyle like that of plants and vegetables.

Children were always to be nourished in a goal-oriented fashion. For children who would later exercise a sedentary profession, a more vegetarian-based diet was appropriate; whereas children who would later exercise a profession with movement—for example, as postmen, policemen, chimneysweeps, etc.—were preferably to be fed meat, if possible horse or beef. Pork was warned against on principle, as it was believed to lead to a warping of morals as well as to obesity. For future sailors, the early consumption of fish was heartily recommended.

In the same spirit, children who would later be engaged in reading, writing, or commercial vocations were given alphabet soup. The belief was that, with the incorporation of letters, these children would have better, faster, and more sustainable access to reading and writing. It was soon discovered, however, that children who still did not recognize letters before beginning school simply ate their soup and paid no attention to the letters at all. This form of unconscious alphabet-consumption no doubt also worked, but it was assumed that a conscious perception of the letters before their incorporation, i.e., before putting them in the mouth, would have a deeper, more engrained, and more permanent effect.

With this insight in mind, pedagogues developed a perforated spoon which would allow the broth to pass through while leaving the letters visible: the alphabet spoon. Children could now catch hold of the letters clearly and distinctly without any soup to distract them. Once they had eaten all the letters with their alphabet spoon, they would be given a simple soup spoon so that they could spoon up the remaining broth. And thus, in addition to learning how to recognize letters, children would learn how to distinguish the aqueous from the solid, the essential from the inessential, the writing from the paper.

In some very ambitious educational institutions the children ate solely alphabet pasta. This, however, soon led to malnutrition and the children's subsequent removal, their aberrations explained by the fact that the juices for reading and writing were only slightly present in their gastric juices, and that they therefore could simply not tolerate the alphabet soup.

Since the beginning of the twentieth century, however, alphabet soup has been put to less and less of a pedagogical use.

The traces of the attitude that the stomach and digestion have a major impact on the nature of a human being are still present in today's language—one speaks of "gut feeling," or says, "I listen to my gut," "my gut tells me," etc.

Today alphabet soup is popular with children who can read and write and is treated almost like Scrabble. With the addition of broth, of course.

0.022g

Literature:

Mechthild Liebreiz, "On the 'False Self' by Donald Winnicott," in *Anthology*, Essen, 2003.

Anton Michel, *Manipulative Food*, Berlin, 2011.

Alice Miller, *Thou Shalt Not Be Aware*, Frankfurt, 1981.

——, *For Your Own Good*, Frankfurt, 1980.

Catherine Rutschky, *Poisonous Pedagogy*, Munich, 1977.

Johann Georg Sulzer, *Some Reasonable Ideas on the Upbringing and Instruction of Children*, Berlin, 1745.

Gerburg Wolf, *On Child Dressage*, Berlin ,2013

0.022g

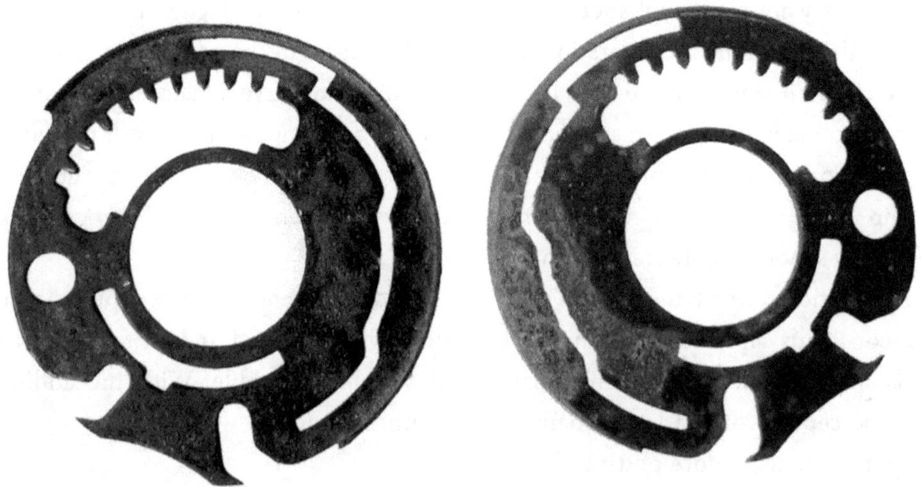

Two Parts of a Typewriter on Which Walter Benjamin Wrote His Famous Essay "The Work of Art in the Age of Mechanical Reproduction"

[These parts were discovered on June 10, 1994, at 33 Böhmischen Straße in Dresden. They were identified with the assistance of Mr. K. Britschka, a former typewriter repair master (now retired)]

Benjamin's typewriter, a portable one, jammed and broke down while on a short visit to Dresden. He had quartered himself for four days at the Neustädter Hof Hotel. During this intermediate stop in Dresden on his way to Vienna to meet Karl Kraus, on his first night Benjamin visited Mary Wigman to learn about dance. On the second night he met with her once again and was introduced to Ernst Ludwig Kirchner who was visiting Mary Wigman for several days. Inspired by his visit, Kirchner later painted a picture of the wonderfully beautiful and dynamic dancer when back at home on his Swiss Alp.

During the daytime Benjamin looked at the usual tourist attractions of the city and continued to work on his essay "The Work of Art in the Age of Mechanical Reproduction." In the middle of a sentence in Chapter VIII, the typewriter stopped at the letter "a" inside the letter sequence "Ka" when the ribbon jammed.

As we now know the word he was trying to write was "Kamera."

He brought his typewriter to a quick repair shop at 33 Böhmischen Straße in Dresden's new town. Benjamin, however, forgot to roll out the page he was working on.

When he went to pick it up two days later he was told that the repairs would take longer. Benjamin had an English model (a Remington Portable) but the spare parts, the nuts for fastening the ribbon, had to be ordered. But for an extra charge of 25 marks he could get a refurbished Adler Transport typewriter. He agreed to this offer and took the new typewriter along with the manuscript page that had been missing.

He continued to write on the same paper with the new typewriter. In the Benjamin Archive in Berlin one can see in the original manuscripts that a new and different typeface starts precisely from the word "Kamera"—the letters are slightly larger, and the line also slips. The first syllable "Ka" is emphasized.

For the son of the owner of the typewriter shop, who was just sixteen years old at the time, it was a great event to have met a real writer. He read the manuscript, memorized the name and the line, and later bought Benjamin's books and writings to recall this experience from his youth.

0.022g

The typewriter for its part was never repaired. It stood as a display piece in the shop, and slowly fell into disrepair. Later, a typewriter factory was set up in the same house. Mr. Britschka was no longer active there but continued to live on in the Böhmischen Straße, the road he had grown up in.

In 1979 the factory closed down, and the house was exposed to decay and vandalism.

Shortly before being demolished in 1995, the site was opened to the public through a beautiful installation by the artist Lubisc. Mr. Britschka visited the building and identified the findings as the typewriter that had indeed belonged to Benjamin, for, up until today, no German typewriter has had the same shift locks as English ones due to "th" and the lack of umlauts. Those are the typical prongs of an old Remington portable.

Literature:

Walter Benjamin, "Die Transaktion des Griffels zur Maschine,"
unpublished and lost manuscript written for F. Pfemfert's *Die Aktion.*
——, *The Work of Art in the Age of Mechanical Reproduction*, Frankfurt, 1963.
Friedrich Kittler, *Gramophone, Film, Typewriter*, Berlin, 1986.
Freiherr v. Rast, *The Musical Beauty of Tones: The Typewriter as a Musical Instrument*, Leipzig, 1919.

0.022g

0.023g

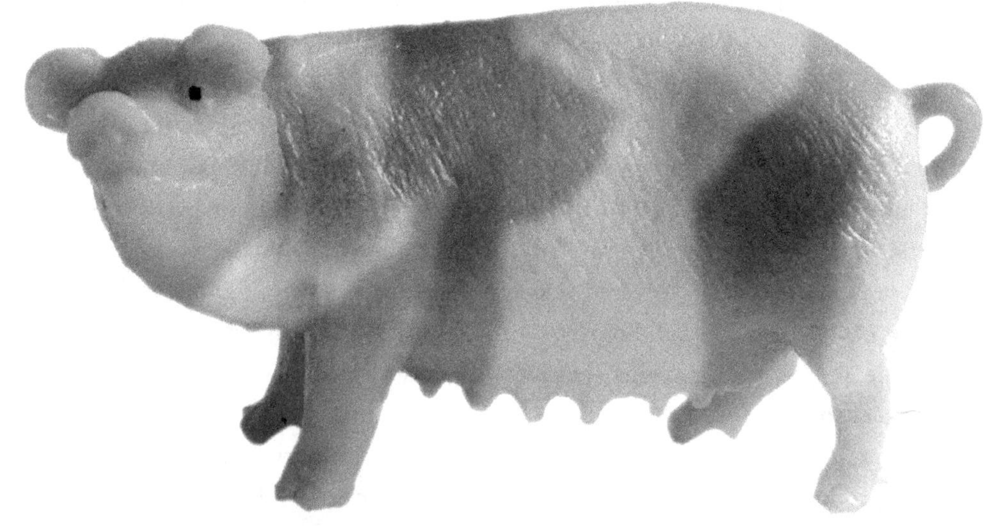

How the Husum Protest Pig in Austria Became a Political Symbol and Nearly Replaced the Double-Headed Eagle

Between 1910 and 1912 a curious discussion from today's perspective took place in Austria: a debate on the introduction and dissemination of a patriotic pig, which was also known as the "Austrian Emperor's Pig." To understand this debate and the concerns of the debaters, it is necessary to try and bring those times back to life, or at least to mind.

The Austrian Emperor Franz Joseph I (1830-1916) was battered by many personal tragedies, and, quite probably due to these private catastrophes, was very well loved by his subjects. Almost mystically revered and affectionately called the "Eternal Emperor" by many, while simply referred to as "Franz Joseph" by everybody else, he had been Emperor of Austria since 1848.

In Vienna proposals for how to celebrate the seventieth anniversary of the Emperor (which was coming up in 1918) had been circulating for a long time. In salons, clubs, and backrooms, in civil organizations, at balls—discussions were being held everywhere on how people could celebrate this great festival in the most appropriate manner. The sixty-fifth anniversary in 1913 was to be a kind of a rehearsal, an introduction of what was to come. However, the unspoken, underlying concern was that both festivities would stand in obvious contrast to the meager, inexperienced, twenty-five or thirty-year reign of the German Emperor, Wilhelm II.

Memorials were erected, strips of land and rivers were to be rechristened, even constellations were to given Franz Joseph's name. That fireworks would be set off across the entire country was a given, and music commissions had already been made. Everywhere discussions ensued, preparations were made, and new ideas appeared, were discarded, and replaced by new, even grander ones.

One group led by the Viennese court official Rüdiger von Schittmacher came up with the idea for a pig with a red, white and red stripe; that is, a pig in the colors of the monarchy, the colors of the triband state emblem, the colors of the military. This pig would be declared a national pig and most importantly be recognized as a specifically *Austrian* pig, and all the farmers of the monarchy would be encouraged to switch their pig farming to producing this national pig.

In Rüdiger von Schittmacher's view the advantage of this plan was that such a pig would have, in many ways, great and highly respected characteristics. Such a plan and such a pig would incarnate all levels of homage and appreciation, as well as have a very persistent, lasting effect for decades to come; in addition, it would embrace the Austro-Hungarian dual monarchy in its entirety, like no other project on the occasion of the great celebrations ever could or would be capable of.

This national Austrian pig-to-be was bred for the first time in 1880 in Schleswig-Holstein. It was a frugal, fleshy, sturdy pig, which had not yet received any official recognition or appreciation, so that it was still entirely free to be named and recognized—clearly it was just waiting to be discovered.

Why such a pig was bred, and why the Austrians felt an affinity for it, can be explained by the following story.

On February 18, 1864, Austrian and Prussian troops crossed the border into the Kingdom of Denmark and conquered the dukedoms of Schleswig, Holstein, and Lauenburg. On October 30 of the same year, in the so-called Treaty of Vienna, the three dukedoms were ceded to the joint administration of Prussia and Austria. Holstein would be administered by Austria, Schleswig by Prussia, and Lauenburg completely incorporated into Prussia. The Austrians immediately abolished the Torsperre—the nightly closing of all gates—in Lübeck, and the Prussians declared Kiel a Prussian naval port.

A fierce and heated debate immediately flared up between Prussia and Austria as to whether displaying the Danish flag and colors was to be tolerated. Austria, with its experience of multiethnic mixture in the Dual Monarchy, largely tolerated this while Prussia prohibited it outright with threats of severe punishment. In the end it was agreed that things would be handled differently in each administrated territory.

Two years later on June 6, 1866, Prussian troops occupied Austrian Holstein. On July 3 of the same year Austrian troops were devastatingly defeated by the Prussian army at Königgrätz (Hradec Králové), which is located in today's Czech Republic. This resulted in Holstein being passed over to Prussia in the Treaty of Prague. Prussia immediately proceeded to ban the showing of the Danish Red and White in Holstein.

Fifteen years later, in 1881, a Prussian police station in Husum reported to the government in Berlin that they had recently observed farmers with red and white striped pigs—clearly the forbidden red and white colors of Denmark. When questioned, the grumpy, uncommunicative, and secretive people answered: "We've always had them." Some farmers claimed it did not mean anything; some claimed it was just a sun tan—that the pigs had taken a nap under a German oak by mistake. They were immediately reprimanded for their insolent reply.

An inquiry committee subsequently set up in Berlin created a dossier. After extensive interviews with farmers, they discovered that this red-and-white striped pig was derived from the widespread marsh pig. However, it could not be ascertained whether the specific colors had been brought about by deliberate breeding in order to decorate pigs with the prohibited colors. This kind of provocation would be considered treason, and all these pigs would then fall under the law concerning epidemics and immediately be killed, the farmers severely punished. And yet, it was difficult to argue against a random, spontaneous trend, and one could not abolish or prohibit colors as such. According to the report, the spread of the pigs had already progressed to such a degree that one could speak of their having become domesticated.

The secret report concluded further that the farmers were well aware of the fact that this pig constituted an insult to the Prussians, but because this insult could not be verified, and the pig was now so widespread, a ban and a culling would likely cause a rebellion. For the time being it was recommended that the government not intervene and simply ignore the pig. However, by no means was this nameless pig to be officially recognized, nor entered into the Prussian Domestic Animal Registry as a new breed, for only that which could be named was capable of becoming a danger. As long as the pig remained nameless, it would remain non-existent.

0.023g

These connections spurred the imagination of court councilor Rüdiger von Schittmacher. This as of yet nameless pig was a provocation against Prussia, true, but if one were to show it off in all its beautiful colors, convince people that the red, white and red indicated the Austrian court, declare it the Austrian National Pig and officially recognize it as an Austrian breed, then these pigs would suddenly be transformed into a symbol of patriotism, an honor for Austria, an homage to the emperor, and a humiliation for Prussia.

If the pig were to be officially declared an Austrian pig in 1913 on the occasion of the 65th diamond jubilee, registered in the list of national farm animal species, and thereby recognized internationally, this Austrian national pig could be recommended by the monarchy to all farmers with a premium notice, and five years later, at the seventieth anniversary, seventy-thousand, or rather, seven-hundred-thousand Austrian pigs would be disseminated throughout the Dual Monarchy, each and every one a tribute to Franz Joseph. It would be the most beautiful, grandiose, and impressive gift that had ever been offered an Emperor.

In his secret dreams Rüdiger von Schittmacher already saw a double pig's head instead of the double eagle in the Austrian coat of arms.

When discussions about the national pig reached their peak in 1911, the legend concerning the origins of the Austrian monarchy's colors of red, white and red marked its 730th anniversary.

Indeed, during the third crusade to liberate the Holy Land in 1191, the Austrian Babenberg Duke Leopold V came back after the conquest of Acre victorious, his jacket blood-soaked from battle, and when he took off his gun belt, a white stripe was visible. He then made this victorious Red-White-Red the ducal colors of Babenberg. Ever since these colors have been the colors of all the dukes, kings, and emperors of Austria.

And this legend could now be improved by the presence of the pig. The allusion to being warlike would be refined by peaceful farming and the farmers' pragmatism, and, in addition, the colors would represent valor as well as the peacefulness of the monarchy.

The other important aspect would be that of obliterating one thing belonging to the Prussians—to recognize the pig in Austria would be tantamount to condemning Prussia to perpetual shame and would be a kind of revenge for Königgrätz.

There were fierce discussions throughout the salons. In Hollabrun in Lower Austria some of these red, white and red heffers were already grunting. Leisure trips were excitedly organized to go and inspect the local Kaiser pigs. By all appearances, the pigs felt pretty good in Austria, all of them weighing in at more than 300 kilograms and glowing red, white and red like the many flags pinned up around the pigsties. From a distance you could barely tell the difference between the flags and the pigs.

But not everyone was thrilled. There were dissenting votes, as always when something big is being planned. Frau Diotima's influential salon could not decide which position to take. Both opponents and supporters of the Kaiser pig came together there for discussions. General Stam, for example, objected, "What people should fear is that the complicated balance of the K&K monarchy is at risk. The mere fact that our Muslims of the south, not to speak of our Jews, do not think much about tasty pork, but, on the contrary, see this animal as unclean—this makes me doubt the potential success of the plan." The bank director Fischle agreed with him with an approving nod.

In the spring of 1912, once the supporters of the pig had agreed on the name "Austrian-Pig" and the application for recognition was about to be submitted, an anti-imperial diatribe appeared in Vienna that immediately ended all discussion.The anonymously written pamphlet stated: "The whole Hofburg is a giant pigsty, and what stands out most is the main pig himself, a red, white and red striped Kaiser." The whole piece was an insult to the monarchy, a call for its overthrow, and an invitation to anarchy. It stated that the farmers were the only ones who truly belonged to the pigsty and that slaughterhouse workers should be proud as they had the honorable task of killing the red, white and red. The anonymous pamphlet ended by calling on both farmers and workers to stop serving the pigs, to take charge of the pigsty, and to once and for all remove all the manure.

By secret decree the Kaiser-pigs of Hollabrunn were immediately slaughtered and their carcasses burned. Not a single one was left alive. The authorities avoided public prosecution of the pamphlet in order not to bring disrepute to the clubs and salons which had dealt with the question of the pig. They simply dissolved themselves abruptly, renamed themselves, and went on to pursue other goals. Not a word was spoken about the whole anecdote involving the pig, and it was agreed on all levels not to disclose it. This silencing was so well organized that hardly anyone knows the story, and it is still denied by officials even today.

Robert Musil, who used discussions about the Diamond Jubilee to provide the background for his observations of society in his greatest novel *The Man Without Qualities*, knew the story about the introduction of the Red, White and Red Kaiser-pig, and even briefly contemplated including it in his novel. Nevertheless, in the end he rejected the idea, finding it too grotesque and silly, as he remarked in a letter from 1928.

The pig for its part was officially recognized in 1954 and named the "Bright Red Husumer Protest Pig." It was believed to have emerged from the crossbreeding of the black and white spotted Holstein and Jutland marsh pig with the English Tamworth pig as well as a bright red split of the Angeln Saddleback pig. It had been widely bred as a symbol of protest and the farmers' independence in the face of the Prussian occupation.

Today the protest pig is included on the list of endangered domestic species. This easy-to-care for, good-natured pig has the normal number of ribs and is therefore no longer of interest for spare-rib production. Only a few farms still breed the tasty animal, which is indeed very popular among gourmets.

0.023g

Literature:

B. and M. Flegel, *Pig Breeding*, Lüchow, 1987.
Norbert Kimele, *National Colors and Their Legends*, Möhrs, 1954.
Müller and Funk, *Flags, Legends, Streaks*, Drosendorf, 2000.
Robert Musil, *The Man Without Qualities*, Frankfurt, 1930.
———, *Unpublished Notes*, Klagenfurt, 1967.

0.027g

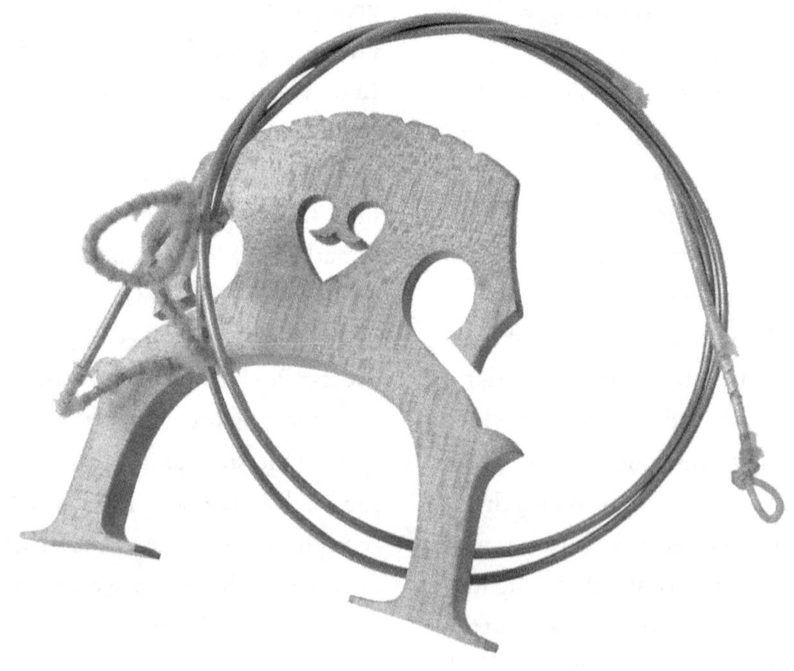

On Marin Marais' Torments with the Seventh String and Why the Flute Was the Solution

France, 1701, spring. Marin Marais, the solo viol (viola da gamba) player of the Royal Chamber of Music and director of the Royal Opera Orchestra for six years, causes a scandal. It is the high Baroque: powdered faces, wigs, formalities that define formalities, a thoroughly mathematical and mechanical worldview—everything is solidified in rules, a life in classification. It was here that Marin Marais, much admired at the court, shocked all of society. His name stood for the viol, the seven-stringed viol to be precise, and when this gifted viol player presented his latest piece all the listeners froze. Diplomatic circles were afraid the piece could irritate the Spanish court. Marin Marais, who had always refined music—adding more color to tones, testing new grip techniques, creating more and new sounds—suddenly reduced himself to only four notes: A, B, G, and F-sharp. However, the biggest scandal was that Marin, who hated the flute and referred to the instrument as an over-toneless, flat, silly wooden pipe, played a flute in all the thirty-two variations constituting his new piece—yes, the piece had been composed for the flute. And the name of this meagre piece composed of only four tones was *Les Folies d'Espagne*—the Spanish Romp.

1284. In the small trading town of Vito at the Spanish-Portuguese border, after being admitted by a secret knock thirty-five people of both sexes meet nightly to dance *La Folia*. They are mostly in disguise, but later, during the romps, will drop their masks. The bagpipe is inflated, the whistle set to the lips. Everything is ready.

For five years now this dance has once again been banned, denounced as both Islamic and as the work of the devil (though it is well known that the very same dance, *La Folia*, has also been banned by the Muslims). For centuries people had danced this dance here, and it was from here that it spread. It is reported that the dance is performed under a variety of names and forms, even in the cold regions of Brittany and by peoples as distant as the Danes and the Saxons. Nevertheless, it has also been persecuted and banned wherever it has appeared and is similarly an eyesore to all the authorities.

Having no rules, it was claimed that this dance led to debauchery, that the music *La Folia* was too wild, that it could be improvised too freely, that it lacked any sort of order or organization whatsoever. But what frightened the authorities most was the fact that the song always had new texts, very often with frivolous and seditious content. Again and again there is talk of it celebrating all sorts of romps, sexual debaucheries, frenzies, even falsely attached heads—in short, utter licentiousness.

Indeed, it was considered such a threat that a few centuries later a committee was set up in Seville in 1512 to halt the nuisance of *La Folia*. However, its chairman, Antonio Gonzales, was caught in the act of dancing the same dance a year later and summarily executed. In his repentant and extensive confession, he said that he had only danced it once out of curiosity, but that thereafter he could not stop, his will having been taken away. At his execution, he pleaded for redemption and for the mercy of the Almighty. The first request was granted; we know nothing about fulfillment of the second.

0.027g

In any event, Marin Marais was aware of the reports concerning this music that supposedly broke the will. His intention, however, was to create music that led to ecstasy. His motto was, "The only thing that matters is music which forces the interior of beings to vibrate." But what were the conditions for such music, how could it be listened to, and how could one cause or produce such a thing?

In order to discover the intensity and unconditional nature of this music Marin Marais focused on the seventh string of the viol—a coiled gut-string in A. It was only in 1650 that the first string of this kind was made, and it served as a low bass string. The conical, stretched-out sheep intestine was wrapped with a thin silver wire in order to create a denser string and thereby a better sound. This seventh string was tuned to A. Now, this A was a revolutionary thing to Marais and the odd number of seven already concealed a secret. As he saw it, this A, being the first letter of the alphabet, and coupled with the number seven, could signify a new beginning, the key to a new dimension in music. Marin Marais concentrated harder and harder. If only this seventh string could resonate continuously, like the drone of a bagpipe…if only the A could resonate that intensely, then those vibrations would also dominate the other pitches—B, C, D, and so on—and the totality of vibrations would jump, as it were, onto the listener, inevitably carrying him or her away while, as an added effect, rendering them will-less.

Marin Marais began to compose and perform pieces for this viol with the seventh string exclusively. In fact, he had special viols made that would support the permanent sound in particular; but, alas, the string vibrations did not jump on to the audience. The listeners who heard it continued to behave in a rather disciplined fashion. And so he tried a specifically developed fingering technique that placed emphasis on the seventh string, but even that did not help him achieve his goal; namely, to transform the audience from being a group of mere listeners into becoming one with the sound itself.

The chronicler Pièrre Renault recounts that following a court concert on Holy Thursday, 1701, Marin Maris was approached by a marquis he did not know and was invited to a secret meeting of "subtle music lovers." Marais assumed that it would be just one of the many secret meetings which were commonly held at the court. Anyone who thought highly of himself, was important, or wanted to be or feel important, held secret meetings, had hidden conversations, wore false wigs, and used dumb waiters. Marais was about to decline the offer, but curiosity overcame irritation. Blindfolded, he was driven in a carriage to an unknown palace. His blindfold was only taken off once he was in a hall. Standing upon a balustrade he saw that it was made of many pillars. Suddenly he heard music—a flute. Very quietly in the background he thought he also heard a viol as well as a bagpipe. But Marin Marais could not see where the music was coming from, he could only hear and feel it—and was paralyzed. The only thing he could discern were a few, very limited number of tones that the flute produced over and over again in small variations. There were no repetitions. The moment he thought he recognized something familiar, it instead became something he had never heard before, the strangest of melodies. He wanted to write down the basic sequence but could not find his notebook, he wanted to make a score, to memorize it, but he could only hear—he simply became the act of hearing, he became one with the music, nothing else was possible. He was completely caught in the moment. Every now and then he saw a hand emerge from behind a pillar, then a foot making the rhythmic movements of a dance. These never-ending variations of a small number of sounds made him forget everything and the diversity of the variations was similarly endless. "So this must be eternity," he thought, though he did not know whether it was heaven or hell.

And then all of a sudden Marin Marais was in a coach again, the strange marquis sitting next to him. "That's enough," said the unknown marquis. Marais looked blank, overwhelmed. "Sir, what music, what a sound, and what a flute!" The stranger replied, "My dear Marais, you have always wanted to hear it, and now you have." Marais, "Sir, who are you and whence this music?" The stranger laughed, "It is known as *Les Folies d'Espagne,* The Spanish Romp." And then he was gone.

The next day Marin Marais cancelled all his appointments. He sat in his room and composed a piece he called *Les Folies d' Espagne* or *The Spanish Romp*. It consisted of only four notes: G, F-sharp, A, and B. Marin Marais wrote thirty-two variations with these notes, and then, with the exception of one time only, never touched any of his seven-stringed viols again.

Les Folies d'Espagne, a.k.a. *The Spanish Romp,* went on to become the most improvised and varied music piece in European music history. Carl Philipp Emanuel Bach made a version of it for the harpsichord; Antonio Salieri made an orchestral version; Vivaldi and Corelli composed pieces for violin and basso continuo; Geminiani a piece for string orchestra; with Beethoven one can hear the sudden G, A, B, F-sharp at the end of the *Symphony No. 3, 'Eroica'*; Wagner in *Tannhäuser*; Satie varied it countless times; Rachmaninoff wrote a large orchestra and piano piece around it; Schönberg created his own versions; Kagel experimented on his own; and Stockhausen composed a counterpoint.

The only time Marin Marais composed another piece for the seven-stringed viol was three years before his death. In 1735 the sixty-nine year-old composer wrote the work *The Operation of the Bladder Stone for Harpsichord and Viola da Gamba.** In his comment on this piece Marin Marais wrote: "This seventh string is as superfluous and painful as a bladder stone, but thanks to the Lord, I now am free."

0.027g

* In 1965, Professor Ernst Ludwig Hammer (viola da gamba) and Helmut Heinz (harpsichord) performed and recorded an outstanding album, which includes this piece dedicated to the bladder stone.

Literature:

E. Bingel, *The Flute as Enchantment,* Berlin, 2000.

A. Corneau, *All the Mornings of the World,* Film, France, 1991.

A. Nägele, *Marin Marais as Language,* Vaduz, 2000.

J. Savall, *La Folia, 1490-1701,* CD, 2003.

Scherzi Musicali, *Le Tableau de l'Operation de la Taille,* CD, 1999.

0.029g

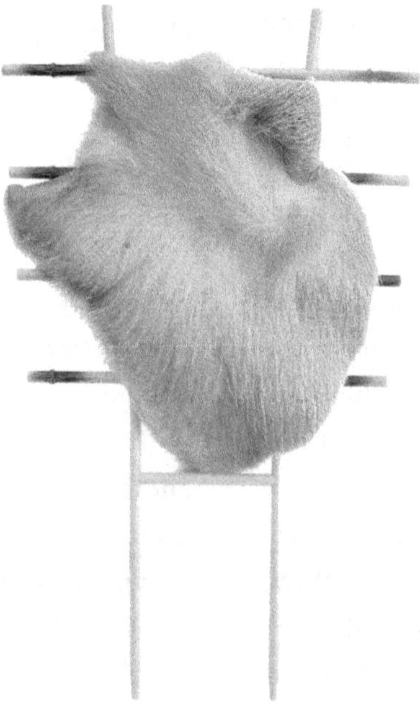

The Fur of One of the Last Bonsai Deer from Eiho-ji Temple, Dated circa 1819

Once Japanese Zen monks had succeeded in breeding small versions of large trees such as oaks, lindens, maples, etc., to reify and worship the ideal of a plant in miniature, they also began breeding small animals, especially deer and roe deer, according to the same principles and rules.

The heyday of such small breeding was the years between 1710 and 1790. Thereafter, interest in small animals disappeared. The extinction of bonsai-animal-breeding is believed to have been due to its extremely time-consuming methodology and the difficulty of breeding as such. The Art of Bonsai-trees, however, has remained preserved until today.

Between 1752 and 1764 one could see re-enactments of mountain landscapes in the Eiho-ji Temple at Tajimi in Gifu Prefecture, at the foot of Kokei-zan Mountain, as well as in the Kinsho-ji Temple at Kooriyama, in Fukushima Prefecture. Between a collection of particularly beautiful Bonsai trees, scaled-down stags, roe, and wild boar roamed freely, grazing on open areas and engaging in courtship. The general public was only allowed to witness this great miniature-sized miracle once a year on the anniversary of the founding of the temples.

The deer measured only 7-12 centimeters. Today it is no longer understood how the monks managed to breed these animals so small. In order to prevent counterfeiting they avoided writing down any of their techniques. Only monks of the highest rank were allowed to intervene so deeply in nature, and they alone would be capable of knowing how not to abuse the technique.

Only a few pictures and records of the bonsai deer remain. Each animal had to be bred anew as propagation between them only produced large animals. They were not genetically modified. Everything had to do with the method of breeding.

The lifespan of these miniature animals is believed to have been about half that of normal-sized ones.

Literature:

Hiroshi Oshikawa, *The Art of Bonsai Cultivation*, Tokyo, 1934.

Keiko Hitomi, *Farmed Dwarfism*, Tokyo, 1958.

Henry J. Smith, *On Shrunken Heads and Shrunken Animals*, New York, 1947.

Thomas W. Glenn, *The Secret of the Monks of Eiho-ji Temple*, London, 1988.

0.029g

0.032g

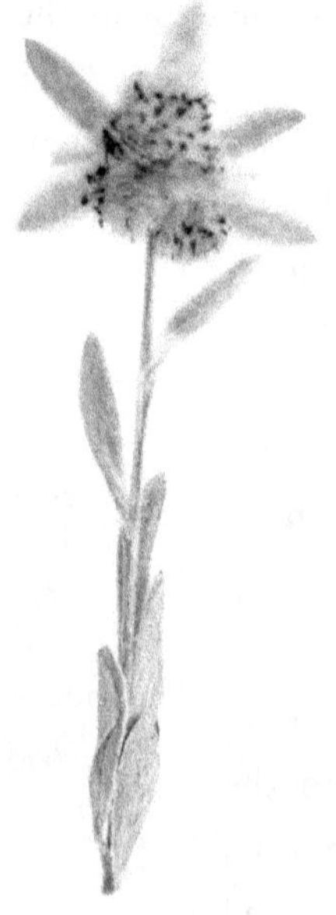

How the Edelweiss Became Famous

or

The Flower of Countess Maria Franziska of Dornbirn

In the summer of 1717 Countess Maria Franziska of Dornbirn, who was only eighteen years old at the time, visited the small farming town of Matrei, which belonged to the bishopric of Salzburg in today's East Tyrol. Matrei, sandwiched between Grossvenediger Peak and Grossglockner Mountain at the southern foot of the Hohe Tauern, was already inhabited in the Roman era. Weißenstein Castle was built on the foundation of a castello located near Matrei. The young Countess of Dornbirn stopped at the nearby castle of Lienz Hof. She really did not care for such representational trips and wanted to get back to Vienna to the receptions, theaters, concerts, and, of course, countless balls at which she was always wooed. But now here she was in Lienz and every time she looked into the dark valley of Matrei, she dreaded her visit even more.

The farmers in Matrei also saw the upcoming visit with a mixture of anxiety and nerves. A fortnight ago they had learned that their rulers would be paying a visit. "Alas, the French speakers are coming again with their elaborate dress," thought the peasants. "For God's sake, we have been put in this situation again!" A vanguard court messenger explained to them sternly that the countess wished to see their buildings and that she would speak in German with them, which was explicitly desired by the new and modern Imperial Highness. All were allowed to come, but asked to kindly spruce themselves up, to put on their best clothes, and not to forget a gift. The messenger knew that the mountaineers were a bit naive, clumsy, stubborn, and often as rugged as the mountains that surrounded them; thus, he reiterated that they not forget the gift of tribute for the Countess.

And now the dreaded day had finally come. The Countess appeared with her accompanying coaches. Everyone looked rather the worse for wear, as they had had to cross the badly swollen river several times on their way to Matrei. Lord Chamberlain August Friedrich Khevenhüller, from the family of Khevenhüller at Riegerburg, directed the protocol.

A prayer meeting was held in the parish church, and they solemnly declared that they would have it remodeled (construction was completed only in 1783). This was followed by a trip to the nearby St. Nicholas Church and a subsequent luncheon in a tent. After that, homages from the people were to be accepted. Up until that point everything had gone well. The village was reasonably clean, the dung heap somewhat ordered, the church cleaned, and even the peasants one had seen thus far had all put on their Sunday best.

0.032g

Countess Maria Franziska of Dornbirn sat down with her entire retinue outside the tent; people would now be admitted and introduced. A standard, and somewhat boring, cheer was given, but not one that caused complaint. Now the gift from the upper-class farmers was to be presented. However, thanks to all the excitement surrouding the visit, they had somehow managed to forget it. Being a sympathetic and insightful man Lord Chamberlain Khevenhüller simply changed the protocol. The petitions and claims were now going to be heard first, and in the meantime, the farmers could come up with a gift. The chief farmer, as he usually did when things got difficult, handed the task over to his wife, knelt before the Countess and told her about the farmers' exploitation at the hands of their rulers, the severity of the peasants' work, and thanked her submissively for the fact that they only had to fulfill a part of the taxes in consideration of their hard labor in the harsh Alpine valley. He told her about the mountains: the accidents, the avalanches, the pious nature of everyone there in the village.

Throughout his humble speech he was constantly hoping that his wife would show up with the gift. At the same time she took counsel with the other women folk. They decided on one thing, then rejected it, became enthralled with something else, then remained unconvinced. This went back and forth until the Lord Chamberlain sent the message that it was time to bring out the gift.

Just at that moment, Alois Rupert, the sixteen-year-old boy from the Hochbauer house passed by. He was coming from the uppermost pasture where he had been keeping his goats for four weeks. He therefore knew nothing about the distinguished visitor and was only surprised by the sudden cleanliness of Matrei. He had a big bouquet of edelweiss with him, a flower that grew abundantly on the upper Gamswies. The bouquet was for his mother so that she could put it in the family altar in the living room. Edelweiss was very popular for this purpose since it was easy to clean, did not wilt, and did not need to be watered very often. In their desperation the farmers came up with an idea: they would send the boy to the Countess and have him hand his precious white bouquet to her.

And so Rupert Alois appeared before her, dropped to his knees and gave her his handpicked bouquet of edelweiss. The Lord Chamberlain whispered to the Countess that the boy had just returned from the very top of the mountains. Up there, he pointed to the glaciers, this humble boy had risked his life to pick this bouquet. He had just come running down, which explained his shoddy, but forgivable attire. Though the Lord Chamberlain told her everything in a whisper, the boy heard every word.

The Countess took the edelweiss bouquet and, in accordance with the new protocol, said a few words in German to the bearer of the gift: "Your flowers sure are beautiful, boy." Rupert Alois, who had always been bright, in spite of his great excitement said, "I picked 'em for your excellency. Every boy needs to pick edelweiss from the top of the mountain for his beloved." Growing bolder through his own talking, he went even further, "The edelweiss grows at the very top, where it's most dangerous. There're eagles up there. Many folks who go there to pick a nosegay, fall and are never seen again. For love they need to go get'em, cos' everybody likes to go up there, up high, where the snow and the jackdaws mate, and where the edelweiss grows on the exposed rocky peaks. That's where the edelweiss lives, protected by steep, rugged rock...only the bravest and most daring can get it, others just keep away. Only he who carries his love in his pure heart comes back alive." Being quite moved by his own words and not as of yet having been interrupted, he continued, "And the bouquet I've picked here is for my love, since we all love the Countess, who I carry in my heart, and for whom I fetched the flowers today."

The gentlemen were all petrified by the boy's impudent words but were at the same time moved. Now the Countess sprinkled the protocol by once again addressing the boy, "That's beautiful of you to say," and pressing the edelweiss to her chest. The courtiers applauded and the Lord Chamberlain's cough brought the scene to an end.

Then they got in their coaches and went back to Vienna. Throughout the entire journey home the young Countess held the edelweiss to her breast, and smelled the white, mossy, odorless flower again and again.

Days later she arrived back in Vienna and put the flowers on her dressing table, telling all the ladies the story of the edelweiss and the importance of the flower for the Alpine residents. One maid told another and invented several other details. Soon the entire courtyard was speaking only about this edelweiss, the flower of the Alps. It was said that there were separate cemeteries in the Alps reserved only for the young men who died for their beloveds. The rumor that the edelweiss was the only flower to survive the Flood—since it grew in great altitudes—was not denied by the clergy. More and more pharmacies introduced an elixir of edelweiss, which was said to strengthen manhood. And many other stories and oddities began to circulate, which cannot all be listed here in this short story.

Two years later, the Countess Maria Franziska of Dornbirn married the twenty-three-year-old Prince of Parma. It was a diplomatic marriage that was reasonable in those times and appropriate to both of their stations. However, she kept the edelweiss bouquet her entire life. If you happen to take a tour of the princess wing of the town castle in Parma, you can still see her bouquet on a dresser, protected by a glass dome.

Literature:

I. Maria Mallers, *The History of Matrei in Image and Text*, Berlin, 1999.
Sandor Marai, *Die Gräfin von Parma*, Munich, 2002.
S. Müller-Funk, *Clarifying the Language in the Alpine Region*, Vienna, 1993.
J. Maria Wölters, *Nurture and Shapes of the Alpine Garden*, Hohenlohe, 1965.

0.032g

0.034g

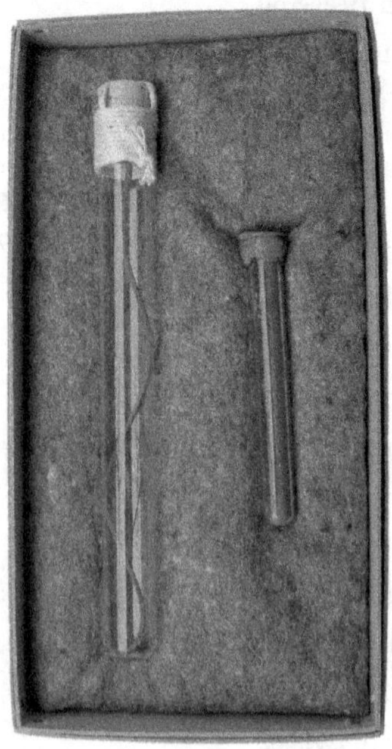

The Red Thread That Ran through the Life of the Marquis of Maillets and Some of the Red Powder That Remained

Between 1792 and 1796 at his castle in St. Fargeau, 120 kilometers south of Paris, the Marquis de Maillet conducted experiments designed to extract the essence of life. At first he tried with the elixir of life, and was lucky enough to find something. It was a red substance he was unable to preserve, as it would not solidify but, instead, immediately dissolve again.

Due to the fleeting nature of the substance (and as principles are often forgotten), the Marquis assumed that he had found the principle of life. He tried to solidify it, but did not succeed. To understand what that red mist was, he tried to imagine something that could completely penetrate it and proceeded to experiment. At the end of 1796, he succeeded in making a breakthrough.

In his experiments the Marquis of Maillet tried to understand the red substance he had found as a comprehensive, fleeting material, and subsequently was able to extract, with no real difficulties at all, a firm, thin, red thread.

It was the red thread that ran through his life.

With the thread now outside of him, he suddenly felt a great deal of uncertainty and confusion, and instantly realized what it was he had extracted. And so he set to work undoing the thread so that he could once again regain his sense of well-being. However, in his panic he poured too little of the disintegrating liquid into the test tube, and therefore a small amount of powder from this thread remained.

At the beginning of 1796, he described the experiment, kept the test tube with the powder, and built a model of the red thread he had extracted.

Greatly upset by the results, he gave his research up completely.

He died alone and impoverished in 1808 at sixty-eight years of age in his castle in St. Fargeau.

Literature:
Gunther Baile, *The Color Red*, Ulm, 1999.
Rudolf Mayer, *From the Life of the Marquis de Maillet*, Munich, 1924.
Erich Rummel, *From Thread to Life*, Göttingen, 1957.

0.034g

0.051g - 0.100g

0.055g

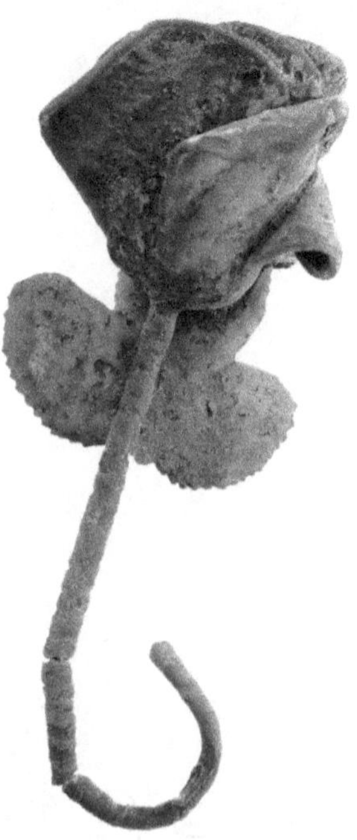

The Goethe-Rose

Do you know the land where the lemon-trees grow,
In darkened leaves the gold-oranges glow,
A soft wind blows from the pure blue sky,
The myrtle stands mute, and the bay tree high?
Do you know it well?
It's there I'd be gone,
To be there with you, O, my beloved one!

Johann Wolfgang Goethe wrote this dreamy poem in *Wilhelm Meister's Apprenticeship* in 1780 before his first trip to Italy. Ever since childhood, he had longed to visit that country. His mother Catharina Elisabeth Goethe wrote to him in Rome: "Dear son...I am overcome with joy that that desire, which has lain in your soul from your earliest days, has finally come true..."

By September 3, 1786, the time had come. Under the pseudonym of Johann Philipp Möller, a businessman from Leipzig, Goethe slipped secretly away from the bathing resort of Karlsbad in the wee hours of the night. "At three o'clock in the morning I snuck out of Karlsbad because they otherwise would not have let me go." The false name was to protect him from the always-quick surveillance of his Duke Carl August, but also from prying eyes, for his *Werther* had made him famous throughout Europe. Furthermore, to act under an assumed name no doubt gave him a feeling of freedom. Goethe had been uncomfortable in his skin for quite a long time by then. Nothing seemed to come about, nothing seemed right. Working for the Duke Carl August had become stale after ten years and his relationship with Charlotte von Stein was not developing at all. It only grew more complicated, he only felt ever more "controlled" by it and somehow "blamed" for the way things had gone. Everything around him seemed to be tough, stale, dark, and petrified; he felt stuck, tied down, and closed in.

He felt like the petrified roses from Karlsbad, which then, as now, were sold at that high-class health resort. After being placed in Karlsbad's hot mineral water for two weeks, paper roses deposited bubble stone and took on a petrified appearance: "...in those Karlsbad roses, which I have observed a lot, I recognized myself..."

Johann Wolfgang Goethe as Johann Philipp Möller took one of these petrified roses and put it in his luggage; henceforth it would serve as a reminder of how dead he had felt in Germany.

No sooner had he crossed the Alps' main ridge at the Brenner Pass than he began to recite: "Light, light, the light here so much clearer and brighter..."

In Padua he found himself enchanted by the Botanical Gardens where he sought the archetypal plant and received two related leaves from the local gardener. These remained a great treasure to him up until his death. But he went on, never once looking at his petrified rose. Goethe felt free, full of curiosity and thirst for knowledge, imbued with joy and openness. His petrification had dissolved—why did he still need a fossilized rose? He forgot it.

Once in Palermo he wrote enthusiastically in his diary: "I spent the happiest hours in the stillness of the public garden, which lies directly on the roads. It is the most wonderful place in the world. Though laid out quite regularly, to us it still seems enchanted..." He felt his archetypal plant near. He remembered his petrified rose from Karlsbad with astonishment and could not believe he had ever felt so rigid and immobile. He gave his petrified rose to a gar-

0.055g

dener, while secretly hoping for a gift in return, a tip to finding the archetypal plant perhaps. Alas, he did not receive the hoped-for hint and soon realized that what he was looking for, this archetypal plant, was to be understood as a principle and not a real, living thing.

After his return from Italy he ended his relationship with Charlotte von Stein and met a worker from an artificial flower factory, Christiane Vulpius. After his first encounter with his future wife, he thought about the abandoned petrified rose in Palermo and was childishly happy that it, the rose, could once again live in the presence of a simple worker and finally come back to life.

His petrified rose from Karlsbad can still be seen in Palermo today in the collection of the Botanical Gardens. There it is called "La Rosa Petrificata del Signor Goethe" (Mr. Goethe's Petrified Rose), or more simply "La Rosa del Goethe" (the Goethe-Rose).

0.055g

Literature:
Ilse Jentsch, *Botanical Fossils in Italy and Spain*, Leverkusen, 2002.
Dagmar von Gersdorff, *Goethe's Mother*, Frankfurt, 2001.
JW von Goethe, *Wilhelm Meister's Apprenticeship*, Project Gutenberg, Internet 1998.
——, *Travels in Italy*, Project Gutenberg, Internet, 1998.
——, *Letters*, Stuttgart, 1928.
Wolfgang Huber, *A Rose Wanders*, Munich, 1934.

0.058g

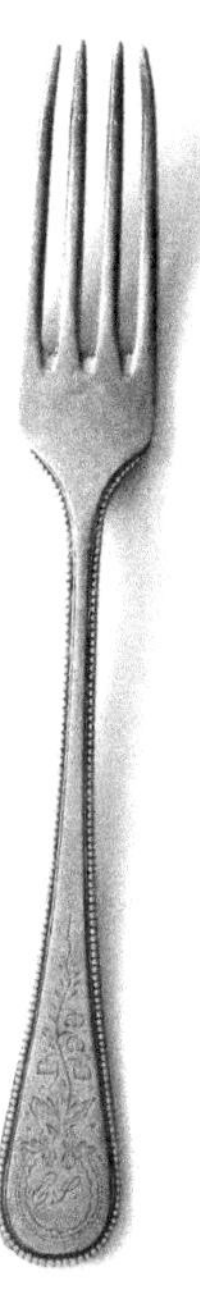

The Silence of the Chefs: Of Forks, Codfish, Edelweiss, and Marmots from the Avers

On February 2, 1545, at a banquet to celebrate the long-awaited birth of her first son Franz (1544-1560), who would later become the husband of Mary Stuart (1542-1587), Catherine de Medici insisted that a fork also be included as cutlery. This became a sensation and a topic of conversation for months and in turn led to the introduction of the fork into royal cutlery. Up until then the fork had been considered a bad tool that belonged only in the kitchen and with cooks. It was tolerated out of necessity but had no place at the dinner table. Since the fork had belonged to the table manners of the Arab world for quite some time, it was called a Moslem, and was considered the accoutrement of devils and witches. This curse of the fork, however, was broken at the banquet. Since that moment, Catherine de Medici has been regarded as the princess of forks as well as the princess of the woman's saddle, which she had similarly promoted and introduced; and also, and incorrectly, as the instigator of the Night of St. Bartholomew.

0.058g

The full breakthrough of the fork at European dining tables, however, took more time and did not occur until the late seventheenth century. The Catholic Church, as well as the Protestant, boycotted the fork as unwieldy, indecent, unmanly, mannerly, Venetian, or simply as the three-pronged tool of the devil ("God protect me from the little fork," wrote Martin Luther. "What is served, one must take with three fingers or with pieces of bread," wrote Erasmus of Rotterdam).

Catherine de Medici was a passionate gourmand, as her corpulence revealed, and listened attentively to her personal chef Tano Marotto, whom she had brought with her from her native Italy to France. In the late summer of the previous year Tano Marotto had joined a secret meeting with the royal and princely court chefs in the Avers.

There in the isolated, extraordinarily beautiful mountain valley, chefs from all over the world had been meeting since time immemorial to talk about new recipes and the tastes of their customers, their lords, and new trends, as well as to make binding agreements. The exact beginning of this meeting, which continues to this day, however, remains unknown.

Recent research on the colonization of Avers reveals that a settlement wave of free German-speaking Walsers reached the valley from the south in the middle of the thirteenth century and that the local population—which up until then had spoken Romansh—was slowly incorporated, adopted, and assimilated into the former's culture. And hence the many surviving Romansh place names such as Campsut, Cröt, Zacce Pürt, etc. Through the investigation of fireplaces and garbage dumps in Pürt, it was shown that two culinary cultures had become mixed—the food culture of the Romansh mountain people and the eating habits of the widely ramified, well-traveled, extravagant, pious and free Walsers.

In learning how to cook with the few things that the meager valley yielded, both cultures had become so creative that already in 1452 an "Avers Cook" was reported to be in the service of Pope Nicholas V (1447-1455). Whether this nameless cook—who remains anonymous—could be traced back to being the initiator of the meeting of influential European cooks cannot be verified, although it is assumed so. The first written account of the meeting of cooks in the mountains can be read in the *Manuscript of Chur* (found today in St. Gallen) from 1454 where the existence of "top chefs in the rear valley" is reported.

The next written reference comes from the notes of a cook from Ambras Castle in Innsbruck. This cook—whose name has not been recorded either—nevertheless wrote down many recipes and stated that heating and cooking times always had to be accompanied by Our Fathers and Hail Marys. This literate cook noted not only recipes, but also the many things that surrounded eating—table manners, drinking habits, eating rituals, and so forth. His notes are stored today at the Foundation for Historic Cookbooks, B.I.N.G. in Lugano. This cook, who represents a real treasure trove for gastro-historians, has also given us a short report in which he wrote about a meeting with five other cooks in the late summer of 1544 in a valley that lies to the north, but that is only accessible from the south. Aside from him, there was a cook from England, another from Spain, a Florentine, a Venetian, and one chef from the French court. Two other cooks who had announced their participation for some unknown reason did not attend. Those who did attend, however, were hosted by three farmers, and for only one gold Taler received the "very best treatment." The author mentions the names Juppa and Loretsch. After much discussion, going back and forth, weighing, dropping and then picking the subject up once again, the decision to introduce the fork was made and was presented by the Venetian cook to the table of the courts as an innovation. "The vow we made, as with any worldly oath, has bound us to keep our word, to connect the recipes to the prayers, to do everything in our power to keep silent and not to speak about this, and to hold further meetings." It was also decided that the young Roman cook Bartolomeo Scappi would be entrusted with collecting and writing a recipe book, which subsequently appeared in 1570 under the modest title *Opera* in Venice and is considered to be the first complete cookbook in Europe.

Another meeting must have taken place in 1597. From that year onward in all the European courts people suddenly began to speak about air-dried meat, which they referred to as *Averser* or *Bergalga* meat. Today it is known as "*Bündnerfleisch*" and is a popular delicacy. In the high valleys of the Alps it was a common method of preservation to rub the meat with local rock salt and allow it to dry in the air. Because of the *Averser* meat, which quickly became famous in Italy, there was a demand not only for dried meat, but for rock salt as well, the purity of which made it possible to produce today's Parmesan cheese. Thus, a lively salt trade developed with Italy, and an important trading-path led through the Avers. It should be noted, however, that the term "Bündnerfleisch" originated in the twentieth century and was introduced as a consistent and effective marketing tool.

That the meat was popular in seventeenth century Europe can also be seen in a letter of the Norwegian Duke Harald Blåtand (1617-1686) written in 1654: "…I am short of good *Gallischfleisch* [which was how *Bündnerfleisch* was known in Norway]. As the Danes have engaged in a trade embargo against our dried

0.058g

fish in order to aggravate Catholic fasting, a large part of the population—especially our fishermen—is starving, and I have no Gallischfleisch to eat. However, I am doing my best to make do without any meat at all. My cook, thank the Lord, brought back a large piece of meat from his trip." The reason for the fish boycott was that dry fish, a very important trading commodity of Norway, was at the time exported in large quantities to Catholic regions because the local population could not eat meat during times of fasting, which occurred twice a year, every year, for forty days as well as every Friday. This episode went down in history as the "Stock Fish Boycott" and lasted less than a year.

0.058g

Further evidence of the meeting of the cooks in the Avers is to be found in the documents of the Countess of Parma (1699-1779), a great edelweiss devotee and enthusiast. Her notes report that her cook—who is always referred to only as "Boy-o"—was absent for two weeks in 1724: "...he went up in the mountains somewhere, what he did there remains a complete mystery..." Upon his return, he began to serve edelweiss salad and later, on a regular basis, breaded edelweiss as dessert.

The culinary philosopher François Marie Daumart (1714-1798), the cousin of Voltaire (1694-1778), must have been at one of these meetings. In his seminal 1741 text *Pleasure and Thought*: "The art of cooking is one of the central arts of humanity—it stands above all others, it is angelic and related to music. In a secret place, high in the Alps, I ate the very best food, prepared by a handful of charming men." He goes on to say that, just as in music, where pleasure is lost in the moment of listening to the sound, the same is true in eating where taste appears only at the moment of "being-in-the-mouth," then unfolds and after chewing and swallowing irretrievably diminishes until it disappears. A life without music is imaginable, but a life without food is impossible, and therefore the art of cooking ranks highest among all arts and the cook the highest of all artists. François Marie Daumart was the first person to call the cook an artist and no longer regard them as mere makers of food.

In 1850 the cooks must have discussed marmot meat. A Piedmontese farmer reported that in winter many local farmers appeared in Nice with trained marmots and repeatedly claimed that they were human-like and that cooks should therefore keep their fingers away from the animals. In Saluzzo, after returning from a secret training trip for cooks in a hidden mountain valley, a cook offered up marmot meat. However, this was seen as a great evil, and he was pelted with stones and chased out of town. Both marmots and their meat were considered to be too similar to humans, and thus were not to be eaten.

In 1900, after a long struggle, the valley finally got a road connection to the Grisons, and the road to Juf was completed. The journalist Petri Höffner wrote in the *Neue Zürcher Zeitung* about a stagecoach ride to the Avers. He reports on a house in Juppa, standing near the road, down near the point where the Jufer Rhine River and Bergalga River merge together to form the Avers Rhine River. The stagecoach would stop there routinely and when he got out, Höffner looked through a window out of which wafted the most wonderful smell and saw a couple of men standing by a stove and gesticulating wildly. Intrigued, he watched how day after day the men would argue fiercely while never abandoning the stove, take down notes, speak in all manner of tongues and apparently understand each other. When he spoke to them, they presented themselves as members of an international geological society. In his article Petri Höffner called these men the cooking geologists of Avers.

It is astonishing to think that this meeting of top cooks, which, as we have stated, has been held for centuries, was and is known by so very few people.

The cooks have very serious professional ethics and are prepared, to this day, in spite of all the competition and envy, to strictly adhere to the agreements as well as to the vow of silence. For every cook knows where the other has his "dirty corner," or as they say in their jargon, "the cockroach nest," and it is not meant for the public. And this is precisely how cooking secrets have been kept through the centuries up until today.

Most of today's great cooks have some kind of attribute, a talisman from the Alps at their workplace—a small edelweiss, a picture of the Alps, a piece of stone. But just ask any one of them, ask Jamie Oliver, Lothar Eiermann, Karlos Arguiñano, Gaetano Trovato, or whatever their names are, whether they are familiar with the Avers; ask Sarah Wiener, Eckart Witzigmann, Harald Wohlfahrt and the others if they have heard of the meeting of the chefs that longago day. You are guaranteed to receive an immediate "no" for an answer—a "never heard of it," a "what's that?" "What's the name of the valley?" "It doesn't exist." All of these answers come just a little bit too quickly to be entirely true; in fact, they all sound as if they had been agreed upon in advance.

Literature:

François Marie Daumart, *Pleasure and Thought*, Frankfurt, 1978.

Alain Denis, *Barefoot through the Kitchen* (With a Foreword by Lévi-Strauss), Frankfurt, 1980.

Hannes Etzlstorfer (ed.), *Kitchen and Table Art Culture*, Vienna, 2006.

Bernhard Kathan, *Disappearances and Rare Guests of the Menu: A Cookbook*, Innsbruck, 2004.

Sándor Marai, *Die Gräfin von Parma*, Munich, 2002.

Gerd von Paczensky and Anna Dünnebier, *A Cultural History of Eating and Drinking*, Munich, 1999.

Moritz Schüber, *Salt of the Alps*, Zurich, 1954.

Johann Rudolf Stoffel, *The High Valley of Avers*, Zoffingen, 1948.

0.061g

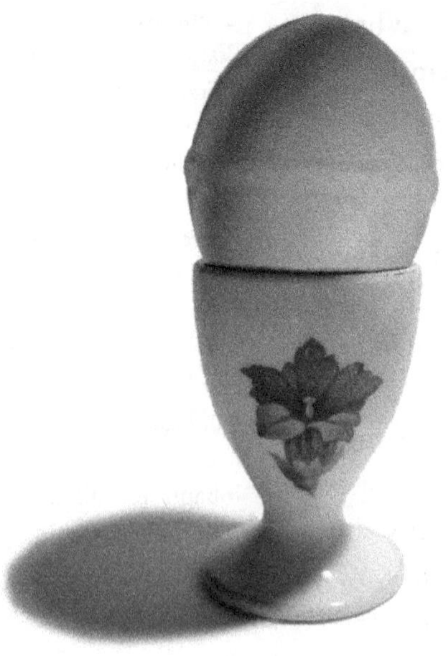

On the Impact of the Equator on the Inhabitants of Kröte (Wendland) or On the Earth-Ridge, Electron-Cord, Matterhorn and Africa

Kröte is an extraordinary place in the Northern German Lowlands, located roughly 120 kilometers southeast of Hamburg in the area known as Wendland. In the spring of 2008 this town organized a representative survey on the subject of where, other than Kröte, its residents longed to be. It found that a large part of the population felt a strong affinity to the equator, and quite literally felt close to it. This apparent identification with the equator was further confirmed through a subsequent in-depth survey published in *Pieces on Southern Yearnings* (Berlin, 2008), which revealed that a more than average number of residents of the small town actually had an equatorial or near-equatorial experience.

The local population's equatorial affiliation, which seems astonishing at first glance, can be understood when you consider that in spite of all signs and appearances—the 6000 kilometers between them—Kröte is closer to the equator than generally assumed.

The equator is where the globe is both at its thickest, and where it reaches its greatest extent. Here the centrifugal force of the rotating Earth is at its strongest, and the forces striving outwards at their highest. On this narrow strip with its spinning motion the Earth pushes the planet's mass 43 kilometers further out into space. The clustered mass of rocks, sand, water, etc., that you can find here is absent at the polar caps where the centrifugal forces tend toward zero. These enormous quantities of connected, outward-striving materials form an "Earth-Ridge" at the equator, which is also sometimes referred to as an "Earth-Cord."

This enormous centrifugal force not only produces the Earth-Cord at a visible level, but at this location this efficient force straddles the globe and, at the micro level, leaves traces on the smallest building blocks of matter. The electron shells, these charged clouds circling the nuclei, show the same variance as the Earth's crust in the equatorial regions. Similar changes to how the Earth bulges out at its ridge by 43 kilometers can be detected in the atoms and their coats in the form of the so-called "Electron-Cord." The deviations correspond to the exact same conditions as those of the equator in relation to the rest of the world.

This coincidence of phenomena in the macro and micro worlds is confirmed by chaos theory, which states that all phenomena that occur on a large scale will be repeated in miniature. Just as the African tectonic plate that collided into the European one near Zermatt in Switzerland formed the Matterhorn, the original continent had the same figurative phenomenon, only upside-down.

And so, just as part of Africa lies in Switzerland, one can find essential traces of the equator in Kröte. Using the highly differentiated C24 method, which also measures the smallest deviations of atoms, one discovers that many atoms here in Kröte have the same bulges and ridges as the atoms in the equator. This initially startling fact ceases to be so surprising when one considers that 150 million years ago Kröte was at the equator longer than any other place in the world.

The impact of the centrifugal forces at the equator is so strong and long lasting that it can be detected even after hundreds of millions of years. And these forces continue to

0.061g

impart their essential features even when they have been transformed into other forms of appearance. They have even rendered their properties onto rocks that only recently—that is, during the last Ice Age—immigrated from northern Sweden, and these rocks have already shown slight changes.

Therefore, one could rightly say—leaving out such superficial manifestations as average annual temperatures, the sun's path, precipitation amounts, etc.—that Kröte does in fact lie on the equator; in some ways even more so than countries like Ecuador, Kenya, or Sumatra, since, again, more than any other place, Kröte has sat longer and more intensively on the Earth-Ridge.

John Miller's Geo-Aesthetic theory, which has been gaining attention and growing in importance, also helps to explain why the people of Kröte feel and live their equator-existence. The theory states that everything surrounding a person influences him "through a pull" (Friedrich Nietzsche); that the environment, the reality of life, will become a part of one's self; and that "life is not determined by consciousness, but consciousness by life" (Karl Marx). We must therefore assume that the inhabitants of Kröte, being continuously exposed to strong forces of the equator's after-effects, have also developed a rather pronounced equatorial consciousness.

Recent studies have even demonstrated that by eating agricultural products from the area a piece of the equator will be taken in and added to the body. And so it comes as no surprise that even visitors to the place may develop short-term equatorial feelings.

0.061g

Literature:

Volker Artzt, *When Germany was at the Equator*, Berlin, 2001.

———, "Oceans and Continents," in *Scientific American*, Heidelberg, 1987.

Rüdiger Folker, *Lower Saxony Survey*, Hannover, 2008.

Haller/Müller, *Pieces on Southern Yearnings*, Berlin, 2008.

John Miller, *Fundamentals of Geo-Aesthetics*, Hamburg, 2002.

0.070g

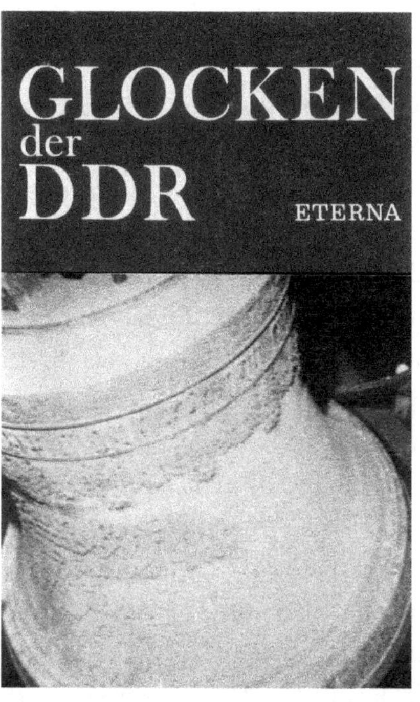

The Bells of the GDR: The Story of a Recording Containing the Bells of the German Democratic Republic Which Prepared the Fall of the Wall and Heralded Its Collapse

0.070 g

[*The tape was discovered by Stefan Tiedje and brought to the museum*]

If you ask Karl Lieberknecht about it, he always likes to tell the story of the bells. With a smile he'll tell you how the whole idea first came up at the Rostock Church Convention in July 1988. The convention was being held under the title "Building Bridges." Lieberknecht had registered himself for the work group "How old is the Old Testament? Is it old? It is the future!"

The discussion quickly turned to the trumpets of Jericho and how the walls of the city of palm trees had been shattered, the city captured, and one of the most fortified walls of that time conquered peacefully by the simple and incessant blowing of trumpets.

A man called Jan began to speak, "As the children of Israel stood before the gates of Jericho, God told their leader Joshua that he, God, had placed the destiny of the people of Jericho in his hands. Joshua was to conquer the city. He was, however, unsure of how to do so, as the city was a single fortress, and it was as difficult to get out of as it was to get in. Then God told him to walk around the city for seven days with numerous trumpets. The people were to be silent for the first six, but on the seventh were to begin shouting and to start a large demonstration. The walls would then collapse and the city would be conquerable. However, they were not to leave anything of the old at all. That's what the Bible says in any event." And then he added that everyone was to take the message seriously, as it was not just a metaphor, example, parable, or stale old thing.

Soon, however, the topic got too hot for everyone involved, for the parallels to the German division wall were just too strong. And yet, somehow the discussion always went back to the Wall and to the question of whether such a thing was conceivable.

A certain audiologist named Otto said that such thing was indeed possible through the use of overtones. "Overtones are something quite exciting. Without overtones, there is no music. It would sound very strange. What we hear, what triggers emotion within us, are always overtones—psychoacoustics are produced by overtones. The most exciting thing is that matter can be influenced by tones, by their oscillation. So the Biblical tale very well might have taken place as told. By simultaneously blowing hundreds of trumpets—which doubtless were metal shofars—extreme oscillations can indeed be created and those would have made the walls porous and fragile."

Then a quaint fellow from Annaberg named Georg entered the picture. Rumors surrounded him—that he had five children from five different women, two of which had been born at an interval of three days; that he lived in the forest; that he was a bona fide dropout. Be that as it may, he suddenly conjured a cassette out of his pocket and said, "How about we have a listen to all the bells of the Republic?" whereupon Otto proclaimed that bells had the richest overtones of all and would be even better than all the trumpets, trombones, and shofars combined.

The cassette tape had been made by Eterna, VEB German Records Berlin, and contained the bells of the GDR plus an announcement. The bells themselves had been recorded in

Frankfurt on the Oder, Meissen, Naumburg, Berlin, Marktneukirchen, and Leipzig—all the bells across the German Democratic Republic.

The whole circle listened intensely. Everyone was completely silent. They knew that something special had just occurred. There was a very strange atmosphere, something sacred had arisen, something awe-inspiring, something mysterious, and everyone present suddenly felt that the fate of GDR was in their hands.

After that everything happened rather quickly. All agreed that every Monday evening as many people as possible should hear the cassette, which also existed as a record. Everyone was to recommend it and invite everyone else they knew to hear the bells; and, once thousands had heard it, once the oscillation had been generated tens of thousands of times, it would indeed have an effect and would destroy the Wall.

By that time one year later, tens of thousands of people in the GDR had heard the cassette, which had been copied over and over again. Every Monday night in all corners of the former republic people listened to it. Bell parties were organized, and silent meetings were held just to listen to the bells.

How this continued on through the autumn can be read in any history book.

But then the Monday demonstrations began and no one listened to the bells anymore. People went to the demonstrations, and these in turn led to the fall of the already moribund and porous Wall. And, just as prophesized in the Bible, after that there was nothing left of the GDR.

Today no one speaks about the bells anymore or the meetings where people came together to listen to them. It has all been forgotten. But when with a chuckle Karl Lieberknecht mentions that not everything is in the books, that it was not all that bad, that many things that are not written there did in fact take place and you see his smile—you almost believe him.

Literature:

Joachim Gauck, *Winter in Summer/Spring in Autumn: Memories*, Munich, 2009.

Margot Hönleitner, *Changing History*, Cottbus, 2015.

Klaus Kaus, *The Power of Overtones*, Dresden, 2013.

Paul Schweigert, *The Other Story*, Berlin, 2015.

0.070 g

0.073g

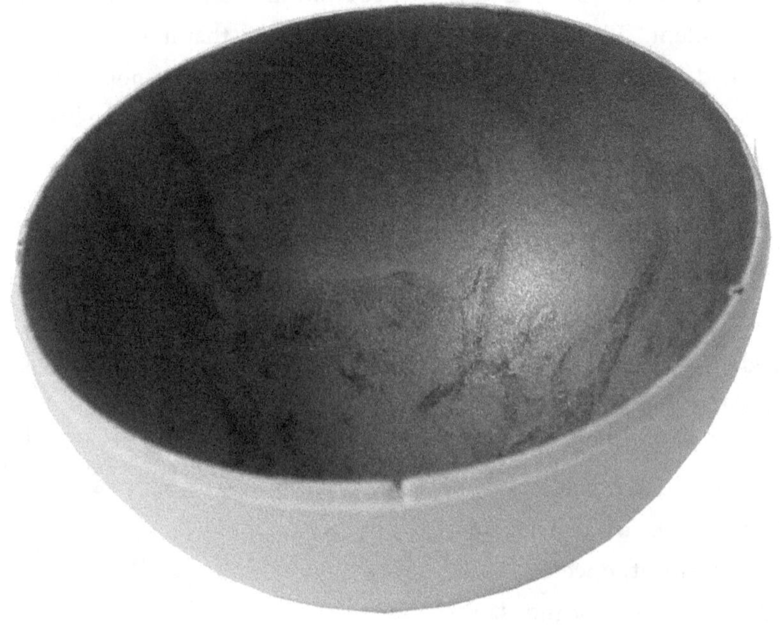

On the History of Early Recording Technology

or

The Word Bowls of Sanssouci and the Rediscovery of an Ancient Art

When the Berlin artist Carola Scheil presented her Word Bowls at Hans-Jürgen Sonkowski's Sound Gallery in the mid-1990s and referred to the long history of the art, she was showered with questions, for almost no one knew the method of preserving sound in lacquer.

When the first majolica (faience) came from the Arabic world to Italy through Mallorca—hence "majolica"—in the fifteenth century, people marveled not only at the material, but also at the technique of painting. The art of faience had been known in the Arab world for thousands of years (first evidence goes back to the fourth millennium BC). It had been highly developed in Persia and Mesopotamia, adopted by Islam, and was quickly imitated in Italy. These porous shards—which lent themselves to painting as well as to the creation of excellent sculptures, vases, jewelry, and bowls—were named "faience," through the Frenchification of "Faenza," the Italian city of ceramics. The formulas for both the tin glazes and the colors of the underglaze were borrowed from the Arabs and then varied, developed further, and kept hidden by individual manufacturers.

The preferred image motifs were those copied from imported Chinese or Japanese porcelain vases: pagodas became windmills and Geishas Baroque ladies. The city of Delft established world fame with its copies of blue, Japanese porcelain painting. Motifs from the Islamic world were not only disliked by the clergy, but subject to an unspoken ban.

None of the faience factories ever succeeded in producing products as thin as the almost transparent porcelain that came from China. Faience, in contrast, seemed clumsy and crude. What the manufacturers also failed to produce were bowls with a running pattern that never repeated itself. The hand-sized, extremely thin, semi-circular porcelain dishes from China were very rare and precious, and only a few of the European royal houses had the privilege of having some of these bowls to call their own.

The exterior of these so-called Word Bowls were mostly made of white glaze while their interiors were marbled by a uniquely beautiful and complex play of colors. Sometimes it seemed like one was looking at fireworks, sometimes a pattern of a map or the course of a starry sky. No one bowl ever looked like another.

They were known as "Word Bowls" because of an accompanying story which claimed that words were stored in the bowls as messages that only the knowledgeable could decipher. The size and wealth, as well as wisdom and protection, of the Chinese Empire was said to be based on such Word Bowls. The emperor of China would speak words into raw porcelain shells that then became fixed forever there when the bowl was subsequently baked. Such bowls, which were basically all the same size of 14 centimeters and exactly half of a circle, were sent out to all the provinces of the country so that the emperor's words could be announced directly out of them. Even in times of war many commands would be disseminated through these Word Bowls. The entire knowledge of the vast, almost mystically rich kingdom was recorded in such bowls, and then stored and kept in solitary mountain monasteries. The monks of these knowledge-monasteries were said to possess special warfare

0.073g

techniques that enabled them to defend the bowls from all enemies.

The knowledge of the great strategic significance of the words recorded in porcelain prompted the Saxon Elector Augustus "the Strong" (1670-1733) to vehemently conduct research on this "white gold." When in 1708 Johann Friedrich Böttger (1682-1719) finally succeeded in inventing porcelain in Meissen, with the utmost secrecy he immediately began to develop the necessary conditions to produce Word Bowls.

Ten years later the arcanist Samuel Stöltzel (1685-1737) fled to Vienna and brought the recipes with him, in the process creating Augärten-porcelain which managed to disrupt the monopoly of Meissen, and quickly spreading the knowledge of how to create it.

In 1751 in the Swabian town of Künersberg Jacob von Küner managed to create porcelain bowls with a glaze that transformed words into different patterns. One year later, Jakob von Küner handed his business over to his son who, however, was unable to either make a profit from it or even keep the composition of this glaze a secret. In 1765, a year after the death of his father, the factory was closed.

When the Prussian King Frederick the Great (1712-1786) bought the bankrupt porcelain manufactory of Johann Ernst Gotzkowsky (1710-1755) on September 19, 1763, he was not simply interested in the beauty of porcelain or the porcelain business, but in producing Word Bowls and evaluating their usefulness in war. He wrote, "It is to be determined whether messages can be sent back and forth via this route..."

Almost all porcelain manufacturers experimented with Word Bowls, and they succeeded more or less everywhere; however, the problem (which to this day has not been solved) was how to release the words from the bowls again. The bowls remained silent—no tone sounded, no sound intoned! Frederick the Great, who was obsessed with this technique, told his critics: "...one day, in a distant time, you will once again be able to hear me..." But even when at the suggestion of the job-seeking Giacomo Girolamo Casanova (1725-1798) Frederick the Great played an entire flute piece into a bowl and had it subsequently baked, the bowl did indeed turn out to have a beautiful pattern, but remained silent.

Over the years, many of his Word Bowls were accumulated in his palace of Sanssouci. It is said that there were hundreds, all of which were dismissed as simply "the old man's spleen." After his death they were forgotten or used as simple nut or candy bowls. Many others were lost in the renovations instituted by Frederick William IV (1795-1661). With the considerable destruction of the Charlottenburg Palace during the last war, the rest of the shells stored there were completely ruined.

The last time people spoke about this technology of word-conservation in fine porcelain bowls was during the Cold War when both sides experimented with the method in the hopes of to giving their intelligence services new techniques. When in 1967 the Western services believed that the Soviet Union had succeeded in making the baked-in words be read or heard again, they imposed a strict two-year ban on all porcelain bowls coming from socialist countries. Only after the 1969 Intelligence Conference in Tehran, where such absurd and ineffective accusations were openly discussed, was the ban lifted.

In 1985 a Lübeck company attempted to bring Word Bowls onto the market by offering bowls in which anyone could record their favorite word, and for a so-called "word fee" have this word fixed forever. However, this business idea quickly disappeared unnoticed from the market.

It was not until the mid-1990s that attention was once again brought to the art of the Word Bowls, thanks to the Berlin artist Carola Scheil. She no longer used porcelain, however, but ultra-modern, industrially produced half-bowls. She applies one of her secret, self developed varnish cocktails to the inner surfaces of the bowls, speaks to the varnish, and then has it dry out under high temperatures. Since then, many have tried to imitate her technique, but so far none has succeeded.

0.073g

At The Museum of Unheard (of) Things you can find bowls with the words "fish-scale soup," "apricot tree core cuttings," "creepy gram gray," "fresh lilac diligence," "watering-can birth principles," and "midwifery apron lace" on display.

Literature:

Hans-Wolfgang Bayer, *Muffled Fire and Sharp Fire*, Memmingen, 1995.

Ines Gessner, *Findelworte—On Finding Words*, Gießen, 1959.

Hans-Karl Hümmer, *Early Methods of Sound Recording*, Berlin, 1978.

Zhiyan Li, Cheng Wen, *Ceramic and Porcelain in China*, Beijing, 1996.

0.076g

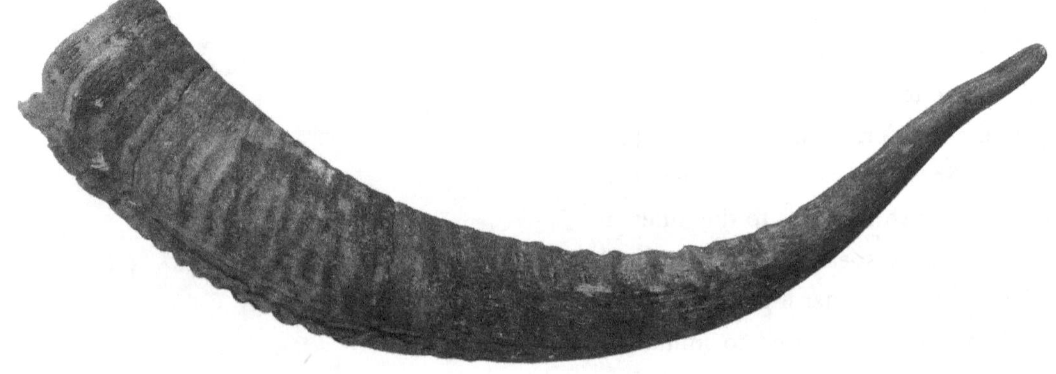

On Scapegoats and Their Descendants

[*Dedicated to SvK*]

The Expulsion

January 15, 1905. A group of German-speaking immigrants gathered to talk about their life in their new home. As of late conflicts had been accumulating in the community. The immigration department in Sydney had assigned them a dried steppe region between the Pacific Ocean and the Stur Desert, more in the direction of the latter than the former. They were assured that the region would be relatively free of indigenous people and that they should therefore not have any qualms about acquiring the allocated and rather large area. How they built their new existence was up to them as long as they demonstrated piousness, led a moral lifestyle, and were subordinate to the law and legislation.

Over one hundred people now had, and wanted, to find common rules of coexistence and a shared economy on this large expanse of barren land. Every one of them was dependent on the other, for alone they would not stand a chance.

They were a heterogeneous group—the only thing that bound them together was the fact that they all spoke German, albeit in very different forms. A large part of the group came from Hungary and Bukovina, and some from the Spiš country; others came from the Tyrol, from Swabia, and there were even some folks from Baden. The one thing they had in common was the fact that they all had compelling reasons to leave old Europe behind in order to begin a completely new life. The old world was not only to be left behind, but eradicated. Some had escaped bad economic situations while others had been driven by the desire for adventure; some had escaped punishment; several unmarried women had been cast out of their families and were trying to start over afresh with their children. A couple of young men did not talk about their past and a dark shadow passed over their faces whenever anyone inquired—something that, soon enough, people stopped doing.

The community had already lived together for one year, built housing, and elected a mayor to watch over their doings together with a group council assisting and checking him and making far-reaching decisions. Two clergymen were responsible for the group's spiritual welfare, one of the Jewish faith and one of the Christian. However, it always came back to disagreements within the group, to bickering, jealousy, insinuations, and physical violence.

Upon closer inspection, these mostly consisted of misunderstandings that had their basis in old Europe, in their different origins and hometowns, the local customs they still had, and the memories that each and every one of them carried within themselves. The clergy and authority's appeals for peace increasingly faded away into the background. So it was decided that they would hold a general meeting on Sunday, January 15, 1905. After a lot of going back and forth, it was determined that everyone was carrying far too much baggage, and that a new beginning could only take place when they were ready to get rid of all their emotionally-charged burdens from the past—the whole lot of it—they no longer wanted to remember. Only then would a real new beginning be possible, only then could

0.076g

the people be able to start over from scratch.

Consequently, it was unanimously decided that they would follow the clergy's suggestion and revive a proven tradition from the Old Testament: they would send a male goat laden with all their hardships into the desert. All had a week's time to anonymously write down on a piece of paper whatever they wanted to be rid of, their bad memories from the past, their hardships, the depressing issues, all those things they would never talk about, all those things that belonged far away, everything that they would rather not have anything to do with anymore. Thereafter all those slips of paper would be attached to the horns, tail, and beard of the chosen goat, and, with everyone's cooperation—truly everyone—it would be sent into the desert, taking with itself all that unwanted baggage and never coming back, forever exiled until simply passing away.

The following Sunday, January 29, was the hottest day of the summer, and the immigrants attached hundreds upon hundreds of paper slips to a powerful male goat. The slips dangled from its horns like a fluttering helmet, hung from its skin like a dress, from its tail to the ground; its beard was no longer visible, and they even stuck paper between its hooves. With loud shouts and insults the goat was chased into the desert, its terrified flight accompanied by a hail of stones.

And yet, ten days later, the goat was back again. It fondled its favorite doe with its horns. They captured it and drove it out once more. But, a few days later, it was back with its doe. Now they beat it and chased it away; it came back and was beaten even more. After the sixth time they wanted to kill it, but the clergy said no. In the end the goat was driven out twelve separate times; then, all of a sudden, it was never seen again. The doe had also vanished.

The Return

One hundred years later. For over ten years reports about the goats' return have become indispensable news in the Australian media, although the phenomenon has long been known. Complaints in the area about a disproportionate number of wild goats allegedly being on the loose have been on record for over seventy years and date back to the 1930s. All previous attempts at reducing the number of goats had failed. Rumor had it that more and more goats came from the not too distant desert and that that is where the home of the Sturgoats, the desert goats, was located. Again and again, hunters made stubborn attempts to find their home, the source from which the countless goats came, and to exterminate them. But all to no avail. And so the population suffered and has continued to suffer from the goats until this day.

The problem is not only the damage they cause to agriculture and gardens. There is also something else—namely, their bleating. It is perceived as accusatory, painful, and reproaching, and this is what tortures people the most, this is what robs them of rest and sleep. Some people's despair is so great that they have left the area to try their luck elsewhere; others have been more aggressive and have wildly shot off weapons after each bleat. Several people have tried to deal with it with love, giving the wild goats a new home, kissing them and hoping they would stop their derogatory, insulting and challenging bleating. This was attempted for quite a long time, but was recently abandoned out of desparation.

Since the first documentation and subsequent reports on the goat plague ten years ago, attempts at explaining the phenomenon as well as well-meaning suggestions have not ceased. Scientific studies on the goat population were made without explanatory results. A wild goat census found no excessive goat density that did not correspond to the Australian average. Sound experts discovered that these special goats had a rising "h" at the end of their bleating, which is perceived by humans as accusational. According to tone experts from the University of Brisbane, however, this was all nonsense. For their part, pietist preachers made repeated reference to the presence of goats as punishment for past sins, while psychologists interpreted the community's hatred of goats as a collective projection that could be blamed on their own untreated feelings of guilt.

A cooking show with special recipes for goat was broadcast in order to make goat meat popular and thereby decimate them through the public's power of appetite; this, however, only managed to benefit goat breeders who claimed that pure-bred goats alone—not wild ones—were pure and hygienic and thus suitable for consumption. The goats continue to bleat, annoying people but nourishing experts of all kinds.

The only positive result of all the media attention has been a tourist boom in the area; a "Hotel for Bleating Goats," complete with a petting zoo for children, opened its doors in 2010. These goats, however, were foreign goats from the west coast—from Perth to be precise. No one wanted to risk having the children be too frightened by the lascivious bleating of the natives.

Literature:

Z. Brummer, *Legends of the Desert*, Hamburg, 1974.

U. Geher, *The Great Story of Emigrants Overseas*, Volume 3, Bremen, 1986.

S. Von Kontz, *Life with Goats*, Melbourne, 2009.

R. Mucker, *The Guttural Sound of Some Goats in the Australian Desert*, Stuttgart, 1989.

0.076g

0.077g

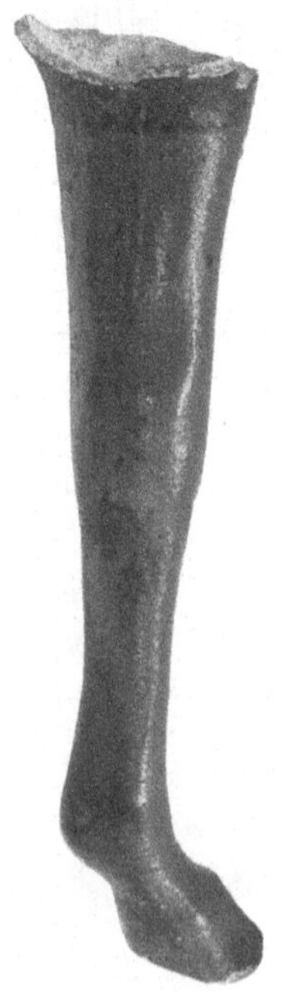

The Devil's Horse's Hoof

or

How the Devil Got His Foot

The Devil's problem is that when he wants to get in touch with us humans, he has to transform himself into an earthly form. Like all spiritual beings, he is, by nature, invisible. Nevertheless, spiritual beings do have different ways of getting in touch with us. They can appear to us by emerging as an inner image from within: they might stand in a cave, be seen in mines, or perceived in dreams. Sometimes they possess us, but they also take hold of other living things—not even stones or plants are safe. Usually, when one is possessed, thanks to an uncertainty of identity, symptoms of confusion can appear, as the possessed in question very often suddenly begin to doubt themselves. This is mostly perceivable from the environment, but the real intention—namely, the spiritual being's contact with a human—is not advanced.

For this reason a spiritual being also has the ability to take on the shape of an earthly being, to wrap itself in a visible shell, a cloak of invisibility in reverse, if you will. Whatever form the being decides to take it can thus interact with an earthly creature and as an apparent equal, undetected.

In this process, even though the hacked appearance may be perfect, when the spiritual being assumes human form attributes of its other existence remain visible. Some have wings, others have burning hearts, while still others suffer from being see-through, and so on.

The devil's problem is that, when he assumes a human shape, one of his feet turns into a horse's hoof. When he appears as a beast, as a speaking poodle, as a snake encircling an apple, or whatever else, no feature of any other being adheres to him.

In ancient times when he first decided to visit human beings in human form, he tried out a bird's foot, a crow's, and later borrowed a goat's from the god Pan. In fact, he learned a lot of things from watching Pan, the Greek god of the wild and the meadows: the flattering words, the triggering of panic, the casualness, and the temper tantrums, too.

During such fits of rage, the devil would impulsively stomp his feet on the ground in such a violent and powerful way that after his sudden disappearance only his footprint testified to his having been there at all.

The first horse's hoofprint attributed to the devil was recorded in the Bavarian city of Ingolstadt. There in 1040 the monk Albertus Peterus made an agreement with the devil (the content of which remains unknown), thereby managing to outwit the evil fellow. A scripture dating from the end of the nineteenth century mentions the time of the contract, which was signed in blood, as "twenty minutes before eleven." In 1050, after having confessed his pact with the devil and received the blessings of the Holy Communion, at seventy-one years of age, Petrus Albertus peacefully fell into eternal sleep in Winterthur.

This first hoofprint has, unfortunately, not been preserved. Ingolstadt was conquered several times throughout the ensuing period by the Hungarians and razed to the ground. It was not until around 1200 that the rebuilding of the once flourishing city began.

Over the next few centuries, the devil's horse's hoof seemed to disappear and be replaced by the male goat's foot. The appearance of a horse's hoof in Ingolstadt remained an early episode. Not until cities increasingly became important centers of human activity during the Renaissance and with the emergence of humanism did the devil once again appear with it. One can assume that by that time horses had a more important role than goats, which were seen more and more as poor people's animals and thus dismissed. Of course, a true devil is always hip to the times and therefore never has to limp after them with a goat's foot.

The first time the devil's particular foot was depicted was in a print by Albrecht Dürer. The engraving *Knight, Death, and the Devil* from 1513 is considered the first image of the devil's horse's hoof. After that, he appeared almost everywhere with one. People who met him remember his horse's hoof in particular, and in countless novels and plays he is described and illustrated in just such a way, with hundreds of prints of his horse's hoof documented throughout the country.

0.077g

One exception is the Alps. In the Tyrol, for instance, the devil has a goat's foot. This is likely due to very pragmatic reasons, for the goat is skilled in steep, rocky mountain areas, a better choice on scree slopes than an attractive and elegant horse.

Even today where the devil does not seem to appear so often, people still speak about a horse's hoof hiding in contracts, for a contract is often (or at least was) negotiated with the devil, and he always demands a soul in return for the assistance he provides. But if outwitted, betrayed, or cheated and denied his promised reward, if maliciously deceived and made a fool, the devil turns devilish indeed and will leave his mark! But the curious thing is that, in most cases, these are shod hoofprints; nontheless, there have never been any reports of a devil's blacksmith.

Beginning in the early twentieth century reports of the devil's appearance have become increasingly rare. It might be that the devil's desire for humans has decreased, or maybe he simply cannot be detected any longer. Some have also spoken about the possibility that the devil—who can adjust to all modes and manners—no longer demands souls in the wake of the general monetary economy, and instead wants money, investments, and holdings; and thus today he enjoys an international presence. With his profits, he can simply purchase the souls he desires. The benefit of these transactions, naturally, being that the flows through which money channels, the fingers it touches, are never seen.

Indeed, who in their right mind today would demand his or her business partner pull up their trouser leg at the conclusion of a contract so as to check their feet? And as in today's business contracts the benefits of both parties are taken into account and respected, no angry devil leaves behind any nasty footprints.

But sometimes, if you look closely and attentively enough, particularly in the snow, you will find more than enough things to pique your interest.

Literature:

P. Erept, *Deceived by Devils*, Mönchengladbach, 1967.

M. Frieberg, *On Horse's Hooves in Contracts*, Munich, 1958.

S. Meier, *Numbers in Their Significance*, Berlin, 2000.

G. Tielde, *From the Invisible to the Visible*, Freiburg, 1989.

0.085g

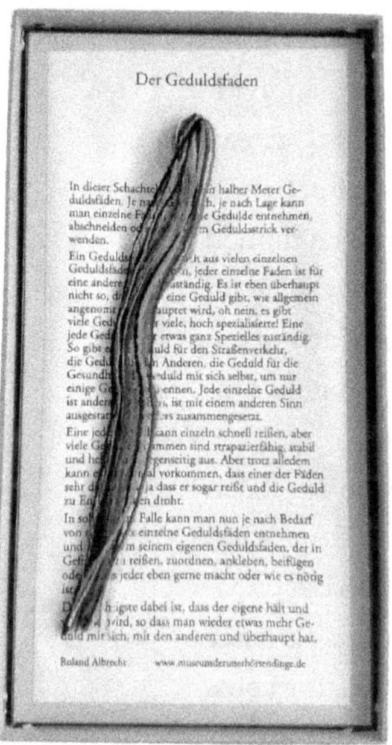

The Patience Thread

In this particular case we are dealing with approximately one meter of patience thread.

Depending on your need or location, you can remove or cut out an individual thread or simply make use of the entire patience knit. A patience knit is composed of many individual patience threads, each individual thread corresponding to a different kind of patience. It is not at all true, as is commonly assumed and claimed, that there is only one kind of patience—no, no, there are many kinds of patience, a great many, and they are highly specialized!

Each and every kind of patience is related to something very special. There is one kind of patience for road transport, one kind of patience for other people, one kind of patience for health, and one kind of patience for yourself, to name only a few. Each kind of patience is different in character, has a different feeling, and is composed differently.

Taken alone, each kind of patience can be destroyed with a fair amount of ease; taken together, however, they are durable, stable, and help each other out.

Nevertheless, sometimes one of the threads is too thin, and risks becoming split. This, in turn, threatens patience as a whole. In such cases, you can take individual threads from this box as required, and the particular kind of patience in danger of being broken can be repaired and glued in any way you like.

The most important thing is that the thread holds and reinforces a particular kind of patience, so that you may once again have a little more patience with yourself, with others, or just in general.

0.085g

Literature:

Michael Aufschub, *If It Has to Happen Quickly*, Hamburg, 1989.

Viktor Emerich, *When the Patience Reaches an End*, Berlin, 2008.

Rosemarie Redlich, *The Short Supply*, Munich, 1985.

0.085g

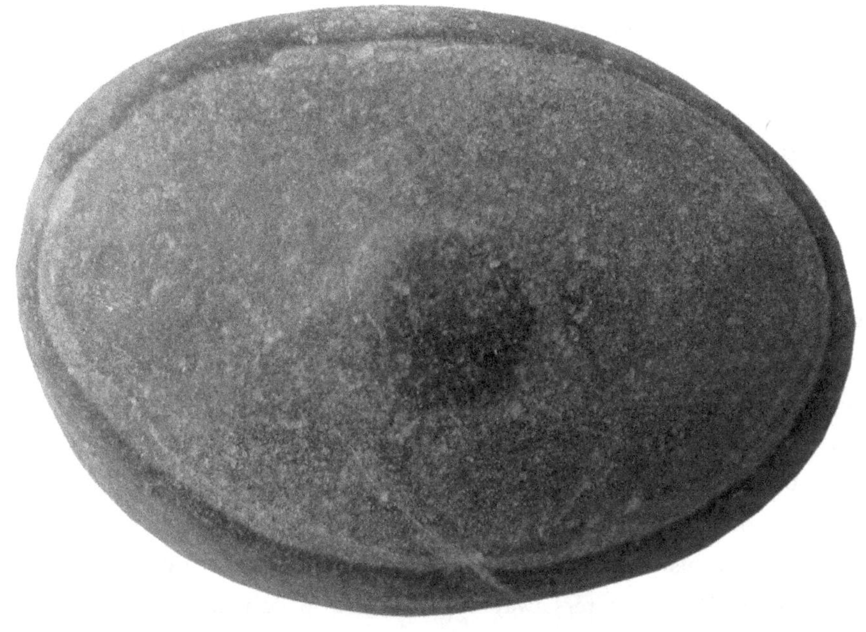

A Stone That Inspired Thomas Mann to Write About the Earth-Breast

[Courtesy of Dorle Döpping, Berlin]

Thomas Mann found this stone during his stay on the beach of Ahlbeck on Usedom in the summer of 1925. Since then it has lain on his various desks and accompanied him through the majority of the world's countries and books.

"Dear Gertrude…after finding a stone on the beach, taking it home with me, and rediscovering it in my pocket today, I am feeling better…" he wrote in a letter to Gertrude Rauf in the summer of 1925.

This stone must have been of great importance to Thomas Mann. It quite possibly may have functioned as an inspirational fetish, an ensoulment of the stone, a classic transitional object, and/or something similar. This stone found a place on all his writing desks, to his right, always about 20 centimeters away from the edge. Perhaps it was a muse's breast for him; and yet, it must have also caused him to suffer, had it not the following sentence he wrote in 1938 in a letter to Arnold Schoenberg would not make any sense—"I cannot separate myself from my stone…" It is a well-known fact that a transitional object generates satisfaction as well as despair through intense psychological attachment.

In his work we repeatedly see evidence of this stone: "Her breast was as round as a stone…", "the nourishing of a stone…" both from *Dr. Faustus*; "He covered her breast like a soft stone…" in *Krull*; "the nipples of the stone…" in the third volume of *Joseph*; "she made him think of his mother's hardness…" in *Buddenbrooks*. The greatest tribute to his stone, however, is found in his late work *The Holy Sinner* where a nourishing breast of stone is the central surviving object.

Before the prelate Liberius and Sextus Anicius Probus went chasing after their confusing, prophetic dreams of finding a new Pope with the name of Gregory and leading him to Rome, the latter lived on his own for seventeen years on a small, inhospitable sea cliff above a cone-shaped reef, chained, and doing penance. Gregory—who himself was the child of an incestuous relationship between a brother and sister—had married his own mother out of ignorance and then claimed his wife was doubly fertile. But once he discovered the double nature of his crime, he condemned himself as "God's greatest sinner" and exiled himself to the sea cliff. Grace, however, followed, for it was no ordinary cliff. It was located at one of the sources of the no-longer-believed nor used mammary glands of the Earth Mother who had once been the "nutritious source" of early man in ancient times. There on the deserted stone cliff was one of her last, small breast buds from which an almost dried-up, sweet, earth milk seeped out. For seventeen years Gregory lived on this heated mother's drink while castigating himself. That is, until he was appointed Pope.

In *The Holy Sinner* Mann dedicates a full three pages to the description of this Earth-breast, and it can be assumed that this dedication to a stone, this belief in its powers, and its inclusion in the essence of a novel could only have been implemented in a late work through the wisdom that comes with old age.

After the novel *The Holy Sinner* evidence of the stone does not turn up in any more

0.085g

of Thomas Mann's letters or other writings, though it continued to lay on his desk for a long time.

Literature:

Thomas Mann, *Collected Works*, Frankfurt, 1974.
——, *Letters 1889-1936*, Berlin and Weimar, 1976.
M. Zuber, *Fetish and Its Resolution*, Gelsenkirchen, 1991.

0.085g

0.091g

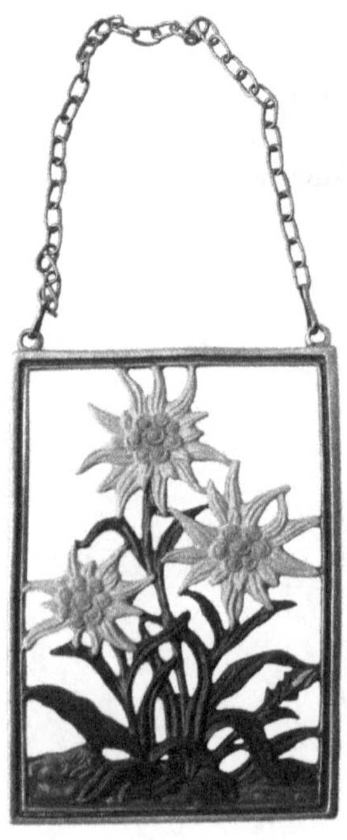

Why No Edelweiss Grows on Berlin's Kreuzberg

or

On the Young Gardener Mathias Kleiner's Misfortune

In announcing the result of the first public and anonymous park design competition awards on August 1, 1887, the scandal was perfectly set. Unexpectedly and unintentionally City Garden Director Hermann Mächtig (1837-1909) ended up in second place with his design for the southern slope of the National Monument commemorating the War of Liberation built by Karl Friedrich Schinkel in 1821.

Karl Friedrich Schinkel himself had wanted to design the area around his memorial—which had as its model the basic form of the iron cross and its tip in the form of a cathedral tower—but after the completion of the monument, there was no money left. And so the northern slope began to be used for sledding in the winter, and in the summer, to the horror of mothers, children could delightfully roll down its sandy slope. On the southern side, the Tivoli Amusement Park with the Schultheiß Brewery became a popular tourist destination. The city grew rapidly and the houses of the Tempelhof suburbs and the quarter of Luisenstadt expanded ever closer to the slope with its memorial, so that the general development plan finally incorporated a garden design for the northern slope. On the smaller, southern slope, the second extension of the Schultheiß Brewery had already been inaugurated in 1873.

As City Garden Director, Hermann Mächtig was asked to submit a design plan highlighting the hill as the highest elevation of Berlin's inner city. As not everyone in the office was friends with Herman Mächtig, voices were suddenly raised, saying, "Mächtig has already made enough: Pariser Platz, the Central Cemetery in Friedrichsfelde, the park of St. Elizabeth Church, Leopold Platz. Wherever you look you always see Mächtig's signature. Why don't they ever let any one else do it?" The voices were of course not said publicly or loudly, but they were disseminated and heard everywhere. To counter the muttering and murmuring Hermann Mächtig said, "Then others should also make proposals, and we shall see what comes out of it. An announcement should be made, and all proposals should be accompanied by a six-digit number. An independent committee under my chairmanship will then determine the best one. Then people will see what emerges out of social democratization." Mächtig saw the whole thing as simply an unserious game, and was convinced that there was no one but he himself who could win in the first place—if anyone dared to submit a different design at all, that is.

In March 1887 a little notice appeared in the Vossische Zeitung newspaper inviting people to submit their proposals for the design of Tempelhofer Hill until mid-May. To guarantee anonymity, each proposal would be given a six-digit number. By the deadline, six designs had been submitted. Hermann Mächtig, who chaired the commission just for fun, was not going to participate in the assessment of the submissions. Four proposals were immediately rejected without being seriously considered: one suggested the expansion of the amusement park, another envisioned a mountain cemetery, and the other two were simply jokes. The remaining two proposals, however, rather suddenly and unexpectedly ignited a real competition. Their numbers were 180837 and 231162.

Number 180837 proposed the building of a miniature replica of the Giant Mountains with Hainfall, a local waterfall. The Giant Mountains along with the waterfall were a popular tourist destination for wealthy Berliners, and their miniature versions would allow ordinary people to be able to experience their beauty.

Number 231162 proposed a park named "Kreuzberg Switzerland." "Kreuzberg," because people had been calling the hill the "Kreuzberg" for quite some time, and "Switzerland," because all beautiful areas are marked with the name Switzerland: there was the Saxon Switzerland, the Holstein Switzerland, and Mecklenburg Switzerland and now, Kreuzberg Switzerland. At the same time, the name "Switzerland" alluded to the fact that, up until 1806, the Canton of Neuenburg/Neuchâtel had been Prussian for one hundred years. This in turn addressed the national monument. The entire park was also to be designed as a mountain. Small waterfalls and cliffs, as well as miniatures of the Matterhorn and the Jungfrau, were to be built there. The highlight was to create an Alpine garden at the top of the memorial as a place for learning and enjoyment; and at its peak, at the pinnacle of the entire park, a magnificent collection of edelweiss. Mongolian Steppe Edelweiss was recommended, since it also thrived in low altitudes like Berlin, and only experts would be able to tell the difference from Alpine Edelweiss.

The commission quickly reached a consensus on Number 231162, thinking that such a sophisticated and well-thought out design encompassing so much vision and sensitivity for the mutual harmonization of educational as well as appreciative aspect could only be the design of the City Garden Director. The other Number 180837 design was also sophisticated, and, in particular, the big waterfall was praised appreciatively.

They sent City Garden Director Hermann Mächtig a messenger to congratulate him, complimenting his "Kreuzberg Switzerland" plan, and set about preparing a public announcement. Instead of returning the messenger, Hermann Mächtig came in person, screaming furiously: "What the devil is going on?" He had especially turned his birth date "08/18/37" into the proposal number so that it would be easier for the commission to figure out which one had been his; but whoever it was that had designed this Switzerland plan they had selected was not him. They opened the accompanying letter and read that it was by a twenty-two-year-old gardener, Mathias Kleiner (born November 23, 1862).

Through the hasty act of a certain confident commission member, however, the result had now been leaked. An official letter would not be enough to prevent the wider spread of the competition results.

In September 1887, the gardener Mathias Kleiner read the following article in the *Vossische Zeitung*:

> *The attempt to involve the people in the design of the Tempelhof Mountain has failed. The renaming of the mountain to Kreuzberg—something popular among lower-class citizens—has only proven to demonstrate the simplicity of the participant's mindset, and revealed the absence of any desire for something higher. The proposal to create an edelweiss garden is proof of*

> *the fact that the common people lack the ability to think in broader contexts. Last year, in 1886, the edelweiss was turned into a flower of so-called special protection by the Austrian emperor, and thus the flower is a symbol of the Austrian Empire. Edelweiss has long been the favorite flower of the double-headed eagle, since it was the Countess of Dornbirn who brought it back to Vienna after a visit to Matrei. How could Prussia tolerate the fact that edelweiss was going to be used to make a park in Berlin? Should the Austrian flower make the park a pilgrimage site for Prussia? Only a simpleton who can see the beauty of a flower, but not what lies behind it, its background and abyss, could make such a stupid proposal. This comical—rather than serious—competition has only proven to us yet again that the involvement of the people, that the rightfully forbidden worker's unions demand, is impossible even in the creation of a park.*

In the spring of 1888 the redesigning of the Tempelhof began according to Hermann Mächtig's plans, and today the waterfall with a water flow of 13,000 liters per minute runs for nine hours everyday.

In 1889 Mathias Kleiner—who was informed about the truth behind his rejection—immigrated to America, and there his tracks disappear.

In 1921 the newly built district came to be called "Kreuzberg." Since 2006 the park has been increasingly used by locals several days a week to practice Chinese physical exercises. Apparently, the Chi flows especially well there.

Literature:

Roland Albrecht, *How the Edelweiss Attained Its Fame*, Berlin, 2003.

Rainier Rieder, *The Long Road to Participation, Socialist Booklets No. 234*, Bad Godesberg, 1987.

Folkwin Wendland, *Berlin's Gardens and Parks from the City's Foundation Up to the Nineteenth Century*, Berlin, 1979.

0.101g - 0.170g

0.106g

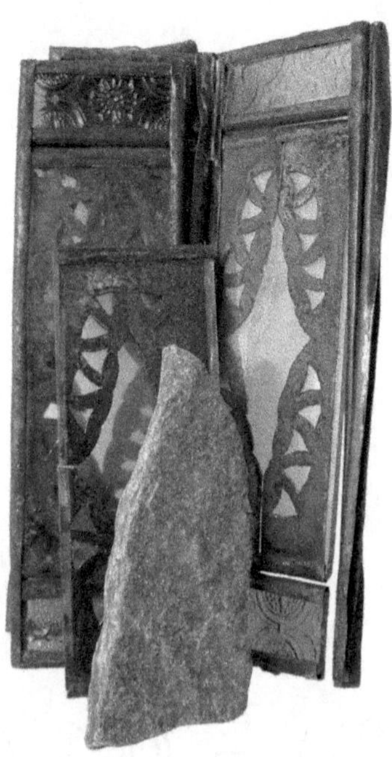

A St. Barbara Stone and Its Corresponding, Badly Damaged Shrine: The First Struck Stone of the Oldest Road Tunnel in the Alpine Region

This stone, seen here in the fragments of a shrine, was struck by a German miner on August 4, 1479, in a solemn stone-breaking ceremony attended by Duke Heinrich of Saluzzo and representatives from all the valleys and the Alps, such as the Po, Varaita, Maira, and Grana. The stone was subsequently consecrated to St. Barbara, the patron saint of miners, by Bishop Gino Bruscherie of Cuneo, and inserted into a specially prepared shrine in the form of a tower. This shrine was brought in procession to the nearest pilgrimage destination, San Chiaffredo, near Crissolo, and kept there on a side altar for general viewing.

There the stone was revered, not as a holy stone, but as the first-stone consecrated to St. Barbara. In intercessions addressed to the patron saint people prayed for the miners constructing the tunnel; and later, when it was complete, that all its users might come out in the same state that they had entered. Today people would say: the stone materialized the prayer that the entire tunnel was under the protection of St. Barabara and that everything in and around it would go well (patron saints in this respect are similar to government lobbyists—they represent entrusted interests with the rulers, in this case, God).

This tunnel was called the "Buco di Viso"—Viso's Hole—after the highest neighboring mountain of the Piedmont Alps, the 3,841-meter-high Mount Viso. In the course of four years, from 1479 to 1483, the tunnel was built 2,882 meters above sea level. It was 100 meters in length, between 2 to 2.5 meters in width, and was responsible for carrying animals of sufficient width and height such as mules and donkeys. The pass was also more or less accessible during the winter. Its construction at this unreal height was an engineering feat of the highest order; experienced miners from Germany had been specially hired for the construction.

The Buco de Viso tunnel opened up a new trade route to transport salt from the Rhône delta to Saluzzo because the other trade routes via the Tende Pass and the Roy Valley had been blocked by a coalition of Savoy and Piedmont. The salt from the Rhone Valley was an extremely important commercial product and formed the basis of the wealth of Saluzzo. The small marquisate was under great threat from the Piedmontese and so it made a pact with France (which is where the tunnel led to).

Due to the blockade of the traditional trade route, people thought of using the Colle delle Traversetta pass located at 2,980 meters above sea level. The Po River began 1,200 meters below it, and one would get into the plains by traveling just another 30 kilometers. This Colle della Traversetta was an easy walk right below the ridge, and was suitable for mules. The final 200 meters in altitude, however, were difficult, steep as they were and made up of exposed rock. All merchandise had to be unloaded, and carried on people's back, which was not without danger on the windy mountain pass. Several people had already lost their lives. People therefore kept trying to make the most dangerous places safer and more walkable by anchoring ropes and striking hairpin bends into the rocks, but extreme weather conditions and the strong winters destroyed every path built by human hands.

0.106g

When the blockade began, the people of Saluzzo came up with the idea of building a hole below the pass, where it begins to get difficult, in order to break a passage through the mountain.

After the successful construction of the Buco de Viso, a period of prosperity followed in the marquisate. The Piedmontese let up somewhat, even if always keeping an eye out for an opportunity to attack. Many churches were built, and old ones dating back to the twelfth century were newly painted. Culture flourished, and artists from all over Europe visited Saluzzo. In fact, the most magnificent building in the Western Alps is to be found in Elva (1,637 meters). An entire wall is blazoned with a crucifixion scene, which was attributed for a long time to the so-called "Maestro d'Elva." Today we know that it was created by the gifted Flemish painter Hans Clemer. In addition to Mary, kneeling and half-covered by her coat, one can see the shrine with the stone. Today the image has been freshly restored with money from the European Regional Development Fund and can be admired in all its glory. The shrine with the first-stone stands on the side altar in San Chiafredo in Crissolo, and forms an integral part of all the recited prayers.

Again and again, however, the Piedmontese and Savoys tried to attack the area of Saluzzo. From time immemorial the Marquisate of Saluzzo had given valley farmers special rights, such as freedom of law, elected representatives in the municipalities as well as in the valleys, and far-reaching self-government (the central Swiss farmers explicitly referred to the farmers' rights of Saluzzo in their legendary oath in Rütli in 1224). This was a poke in the other municipalities' eyes, as more and more farmers rebelled against their princes, and demanded similar rights.

In 1588, a hundred and five years after the completion of the tunnel, the Piedmontese, with the support of the Savoy, conquered the Marquisate of Saluzzo, though suffering heavy losses. Their first official acts were a cancellation of the farmers' rights, the closure of the Buco de Viso tunnel, and a directive to destroy the first-stone. The belief that the vandalization of something sanctified would bring great misfortune, however, prevented this latter decision from being enacted.

Over the following decades the French Calvinists grew ever more influential, and from time to time they greatly pestered the Catholics, sometimes murdering them, sometimes destroying many of their relics. The shrine with the first-stone of Buco de Viso was also affected. However, once the Catholics were back in power, they murdered the Calvinists in turn, and restored the churches. A cruel time swept through the valleys of the Saluzzo. Michel Montaigne, the famous French philosopher, commented in a footnote of one of his *Essays*:

> *Some argue that during big clashes, small things are overlooked, but I have repeatedly heard that a small stone in the Southern Alps has always held great importance for its residents. And thus I believe that great things often have little meaning, whilst, on the contrary, small, unnoticed things, great significance...*
> *(Book Two, notes to "16 'On Glory'")*

It is reported that, during the looting of the small twelfth century church of San Peye in 1657, where the stone was then located, loot-ers threw both the shrine and the stone into a mountain stream as neither was worth selling. Farmers, however, salvaged and held on to them. From generation to generation they have since been passed on but almost forgotten, in contrast to the tunnel itself. The Buco de Viso has always held a prominent place in the memory of the people of the region.

In 1970 the tunnel was once again uncovered through a collaborative endeavor by the Lions Club of France and Italy, and made accessible. Unfortunately, the French side of the tunnel has long been full of snow, making it very difficult to get through.

After an intensive amount of searching and many hints from friends of the museum, the stone, along with the badly damaged shrine, came into the possession of The Museum of Unheard (of) Things in 2002, and its original function—that of inspiring marvel and wonder—was returned.

Literature:

Reinhard Abeln, *Saint Barbara: Life, Legends*, Significance, Kevelaer, 2011.

Sabine Bade, Wolfram Mikuteit, *Giro del Monviso: Around and Criss-crossing the Region of Re di Pietra*, Roxheim, 2009.

Hubert Renner, *The Marquisate of Saluzzo*, Munich, 1987.

0.109g

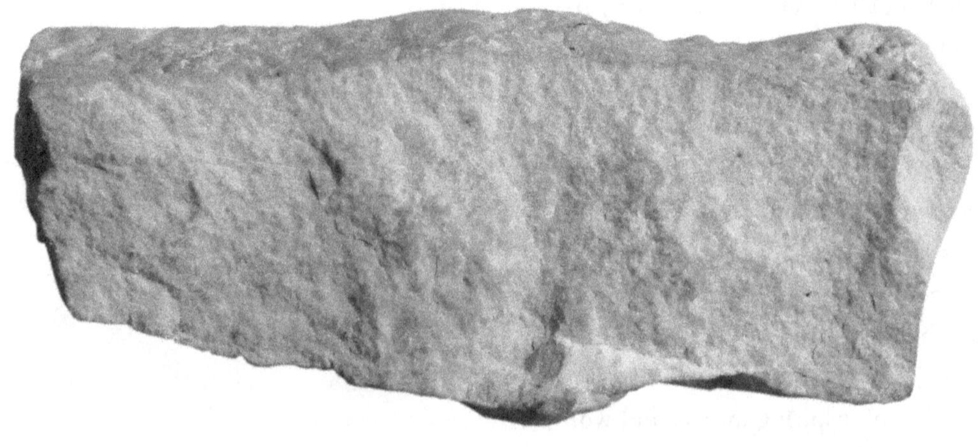

A Splinter of Rock from Mount Ventoux (1,912m) Where Francesco Petrarca Sat on April 26, 1336, During the First Mountain Climb in History

Since April 26, 1336, Francesco Petrarca, "the poet of all time," has also been known as "the father of mountain climbing" and April 26 as the birthday of alpinism.

> *Altissimum regionis guius montem, quem non immerito Ventosum vocant, hodierno the sola Vivendi insignem loci altidudinem cupiditate ductus, ascevdi. Multis annis hoc in animo fuerat...*
>
> [Yesterday I climbed the highest mountain in our area, which is not undeservedly called 'the windy one,' merely out of a desire to know the height of the well-known place...]

This was written by Petrarca and sent to François-Denis from Borgo Sepolcro on April 27, 1336—one day after the former became the first man in history to climb a mountain just for fun and to enjoy the view and then descend and describe the experience.

The poet sat on a rock on Mount Ventoux and reportedly read the Tenth Book of St. Augustine's *Confessions*. He was torn between the Holy Scriptures of the Spirit and the holy sight of the landscape opening up before him.

The rock that he sat upon, only slightly larger than a little stone, became known in later times as "The Poet's Rock." Later mountaineers first called it "Mons Ventosus," and later still "Pierre de Poète." Word quickly spread that a mountain could be climbed solely for the view alone.

Strangely enough this piece of large stone—continuing to be named and known by only a select few—survived the large-scale construction work conducted at the mountain's summit in the last century, as it was constantly pushed to the side and thrown around. It never became a sight of interest for tourists, or placed under any protection; it was neither a monument nor a natural phenomenon.

On April 8, 1995—almost 659 years after the epochal hike—a lightning bolt struck the stone during an electrical storm and blew it apart.

A Dutch guide from Vaison-la-Romaine who funnels tourist crowds through the Roman excavations of the area and is also a connoisseur of regional history, drew my attention to the stone and saw to it that I was able to salvage at least something of the soon no-longer-to-be recognized "Poet's Rock."

Literature:
German Alpine Association (ed.), *Early Evidence of Alpine Climbing*, Munich, 1986.
M. Karbe, *On Finding the Records*, Berlin, 1992.

0.109g

0.115g

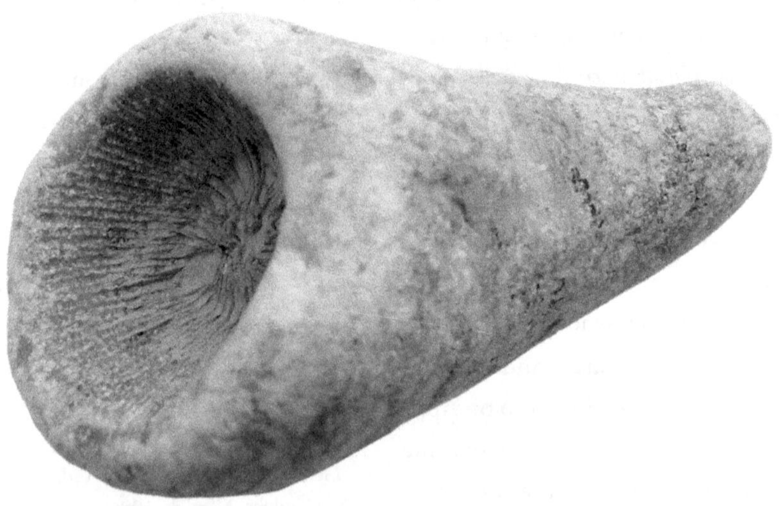

The Gender of Havlings

or

The Organization of Gendered Life

The Havlings genus populated the earth millions of years ago and has most frequently been detected in the northern part of the hemisphere, particularly on the southern tip of the island of Gotland. Near the fishing village of Havlingen, which is characterized by an inlet and is from where the Havling takes its name, new fossils of this primordial animal are constantly washed ashore. When the continental plates started to drift apart today's Baltic Sea was already quite stably formed so that only a relatively small turn toward the upper right took place, and the fossils which can be found there are very well preserved.

The Havlings, those animals forming the bridge between amphibians and reptiles, lived in the warm and humid water of swamps and/or on damp banks. According to our present conceptions the appearance of the Havlings was somewhat strange. They measured from 50 centimeters to 4 meters in size, depending on the kind (today approximately 200 kinds are counted in this genus). With an inattentive glance you might at first think these crawlers were birds. But, upon closer inspection, you would notice that they possessed refined, highly developed scales that surrounded their multi-colored, parrot-like feathers like a suit of armor.

We must imagine the Havlings' landscape as a colorful and rampant jungle. Ferns of the most diverse and glaring colors grew everywhere, and club moss shaded everything with its more than 30-meter high peaks. Diverse plants sprouted from all the cracks and corners and where that was impossible, the flowering moss did instead, oozing out from every crevice. There, in this colorful setting, well camouflaged by their colorful and scaly armor, the Havlings survived, feeding on the vegetation.

The entire genus had one thing in common: they were genuinely bisexual creatures that developed through self-fertilization. The Havlings were the last intermediary step before the emergence of the common and customary division of the sexes we know today. After allowing life to appear on Earth, evolution first designed amorphous beings that multiplied through asexual reproduction. A diploid cell would divide itself into two new identical parts. This life form would then multiply and multiply and multiply, forever resulting in the same identical cells. Billions upon billions of the same cells existed, and, in terms of evolution, it soon became clear that this was relatively simple and boring.

0.115g

Enter meiosis. This was a diploid cell that developed four haploid daughter cells and from the union of these daughter cells again produced a diploid cell, which nonetheless developed differently than the parent cell. This made it possible for different kinds of life forms and species in the form of plants, animals, etc., to arise. Proliferation was based on self-fertilization.

The mating of genera or species with one another was undesired, and therefore did not occur. Furthermore, it did not work. Within self-fertilization every existence was in harmony with itself. Seen from the standpoint of evolution, however, this did little to advance life. The development step was indeed harmonious, but advanced extremely slowly and arbitrarily since fertilization could be controlled by any lifeform itself. In other words, a form of auto-regulating birth control had increasingly become the norm. The population stagnated. To counter this trend, the division of fertilization came to prevail, and soon two separate beings were needed to achieve final fertilization. Thus the two genders were born.

The bi-sexual Havlings were of one gender for a time, and then became the other. These creatures could, depending on will, desire, and mood, be male or female, but never both at the same time. The Havling itself decided which gender it would assume at the moment of mating. In addition, it is one of the typical and most common of these bisexual creatures: an early gender-split genus. It had both sexes, and its sexual apparatus could either invaginate—taking on full-receptive capability—or assume the role of the producer through a protuberance. When two Havlings met to mate, they first had to decide which would take which part, and this regularly led to quarrels, misunderstandings, and conflicts. It must have been terribly confusing, and so, eventually, through evolution, that absolute gender division we know today was established. We will only know whether or not this is a satisfactory state in terms of evolution in a few million years.

0.115 g

Remarks:

Some researchers of sexual life in paradise assume that the very idea of paradise itself is an anthropological recollection of the era of bi-sexuality; whereby paradise here is not meant as a space of pure happiness, but rather, as the laboratory of a potentially satisfactory life.

For like-minded anthropologists the same applies to Plato's idea that people were formerly one and thus always long to return to that unity—a return to the time of the Havlings—where both genders were combined, were possible, and were available.

Another myth holds that a goddess and a god once argued about who felt more sexual pleasure, the male or the female. Unable to agree, they sought out the wise Hermaphroditos who was to decide. Many think that this myth, too, originates from recollection, believing, for example, that Hermaphroditos was a Havling. And so all these recollections are similar to the salty tears we shed that remind us we once emerged from out of the sea. Be that as it may, in the dispute between the gods Hermaphroditos opted for the female.

Literature:

Anton Unger, *The Neglected Gender*, Berlin, 2000.

Lars Wahlström, *The Dream of Genders*, Stockholm, 2003.

0.120 g

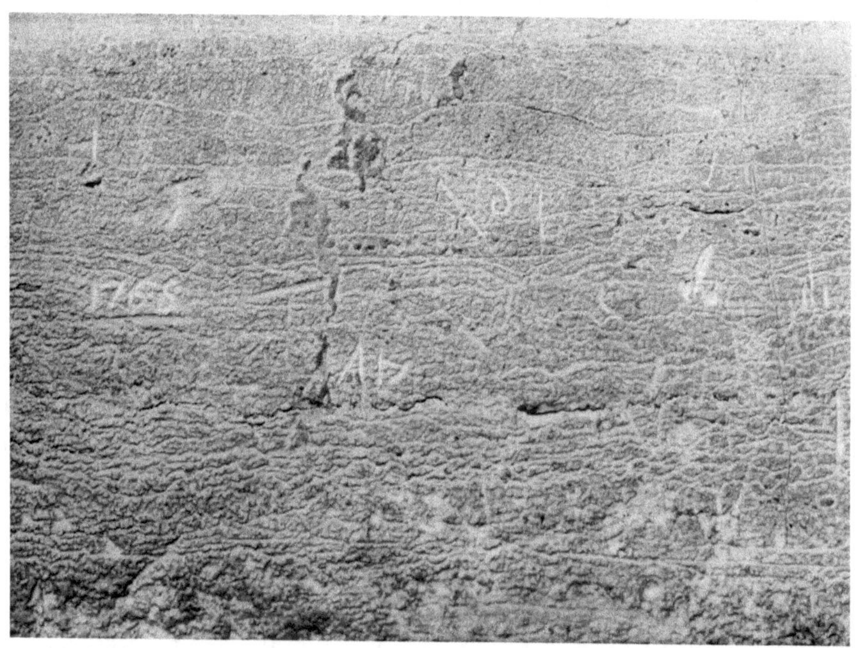

Casanova's Incision

When Casanova "was leaving at an early hour from Breslau," to his surprise the Lady Maton—whom, on a whim, he had asked the previous day to travel together with him to Dresden—also awoke. And his surprise was all the greater as he had already forgotten about her. And yet, as they boarded, he found the arrangement to be "excellent." "Once in Dresden I went into the best inn in the city and rented an entire floor." This inn was the Stadt Rom Hotel on the corner of Neumarkt and Moritzstraße, which remained in operation until 1931, and which was finally demolished in 1943. This was the hotel with the bay window that Casanova describes a number of times. During their joint stay, his partner, Maton, infected him with an "amorous disease with very nasty symptoms." Casanova reported his infection in detail and incidentally informed his brother Giovanni that such self-inflicted sickness was not something to be shouted from the rooftops, but to be cured in total privacy.

Casanova summed up the subsequent four months of his life in the fifteenth volume of his *Story of My Life* with a single sentence: "I subjected myself to strict treatment, and was fortunate to be healthy again by mid-August, as healthy as I had been before my departure from Warsaw." It is amazing and surprising for Casanova, this keen observer and accurate record-keeper of his life, to describe four months in only one sentence and with so few words—or, more accurately speaking, such reticence.

Casanova researchers of centuries past had always been suspicious of that fact. However, they found no explanation, other than that he wanted to ignore this "gallant" disease in a "gallant" manner—even though this did not really correspond to his style—because he was known precisely for his accuracy, honesty, and open rationality with all *noblesse* and self-referentiality.

The Togolese historian and expert on European erotomania, Georges Beta Husumu, through a comprehensive examination of the library Casanova built in Dux (near Chomutov, Bohemia) for Count Waldstein, which the former directed and expanded from 1785 to his death in 1798, found eighteen well-preserved and previously unknown pages, twelve of which describe the period of his convalescence in Casanova's own hand writing. These pages provide information about the previous blanked-out months of his life.

The description of this period begins with the exact same words as the authorized edition of the *Story of My Life* but from there follows a hitherto unknown account:

> *I subjected myself to strict treatment at Kuckuksbad on the Elbe River. Count Schwerin—whom I had helped out when he was in a similar situation a few years previously—was the only one I spoke to about my malheur, and he pointed out to me that, in recent years, there in Kuckuksbad the Brothers of Mercy had specialized in that disease. In 1708, Count Spork had founded these baths together with the asylum. Not so long ago this place survived a flood which had torn large parts of the residential buildings away. But what piqued my interest most was the allegorical cycle from the talented sculptor Matthias B. Braun, who wonderfully represented the twelve vices and twelve virtues. These statues give the current specialization of the asylum a distinctive and unique flavor.*

Casanova describes the constantly recurring daily routine of the health treatment center, the peace and the rushing of the Elbe, and the renunciation of bodily pleasures—with the exception of food—by all those present. He describes a large menu with freshly roasted larks, which were almost as good as the ones in Leipzig. In fact, they were considered the best in Europe. He sensed a slow recovery and a reduction in the swelling of the nodes in his groin. What he particularly liked was the privacy of the treatments: "The reason for being there was never mentioned, nor spoken about. Even when I arrived with my coach and auditioned for the first interview, the disease remained unmentioned. My stay was like an enjoyable healing spa visit similar to those advised in Franzensbad or Karlsbad, with the exception of treatments being of a specialized kind."

One evening Casanova got a telegram from Venice, his beloved hometown, with the order to appear immediately before the Doge police and to report on events in St. Petersburg, Warsaw, and Vienna. A meeting with the doge was promised him, as was an increase in his monthly allowance. He was also promised safe passage for his trip, but everything had to be done in secret. For centuries the doge of Venice had had the best news service and secret police in the world, and to oppose them was unwise, especially when one was involved with them more than simply through small bits of information.

The next morning Casanova signed off before his worried-looking doctors, saying that he had something urgent to do in Vienna, and boarded a coach. Over the next two days he often changed coaches as well as his name in order to cover his tracks. He covered the last part of his journey from Padua on a Burchielli (a large gondola) along the Brenta River. As he reminisced: "It was pleasant to sit in the Burchielli. Just like thirty-one years ago, when I was a twelve-year-old boy, I saw the shore glide pass me, and saw the trees move. Today, as a sick man, I do not know what awaits me in my home town that has failed me, and from which I fled."

Arriving in Venice, he immediately went to the Doge's Palace and demanded to speak to the inquisitor and doge of Venice, Ladovico Manin. After his "letter was suspiciously examined and checked," he underwent multiple searches and a long wait at the upstairs gallery before the Scala d'Oro, the grand staircase of the palace:

> *There I was, in front of the Bocca del Leone, the mailbox of denunciation, waiting, until they granted me admission. I had heard that the Doge Ladovico Manin—who was a year younger than I and whom I had often met as a child without ever having made friends with him—liked to increase the wait time, that subtle form of humiliation, into torture. There were now supposedly eight stages of waiting, four more than when I had last been in Venice. But I shall come back to the inglorious downfall of this system later.*
>
> *I tried to start a conversation with the two guards provided to me, but it appeared that they were either mute or forbidden to exchange any words, much less move at all. So I stood leaning against the balustrade and looking down into the courtyard of the palace, behind me the Bocca del Leone, which had plunged so*

> *many people into trouble with its ravenous lion's mouth. The nodes of my groin ached and I was afraid that my health, which was so important to me, could suffer from this trip, but what was in store was just too tempting not to undertake the journey.*
>
> *Absorbed in my wait I ruminated and thought about the death of the Emperor Franz I, which I had learned about at a reception at the court in Petersburg a year prior, and on which occasion Prince Lobkowitz consented me on how close death was to us all, but how surprised we nevertheless were when we too met him.*
>
> *In just such a state, deeply lost in thought, I scratched the year of the Austrian Emperor's death, 1765, into the marble handrail of the balustrade, and right above it, the reasons for the pain in my groin, in which indeed life, pleasure as well as desire, dwelled so near to destruction, mutilation, and even death. When I realized what I was doing, I was shocked because any damage to any part of the palace would be severely punished. My silent companions, however, neither saw nor suspected anything as I had been leaning forward and my body had concealed my actions.*

0.120 g

Casanova waited for another five hours only to find that he was not to be admitted. He had to leave the water city of Venice that same evening, and arrived four days later back in Kuckuksbad on the Elbe, where he completely recovered from the trip as well as from his illness. "...And I was fortunate to be healthy again by mid-August, as healthy as I had been before my departure from Warsaw." It can be assumed that Casanova was so humiliated by this trip that he removed it from his written record. What does remain of his journey are the carvings at the Doge's Palace, in the exact same spot as he described.

Literature:

Giacomo Casanova, *Story of My Life*, Fifteen-volume edition, Munich, 1960.

——, *Correspondence*, Munich, 1828.

W. F. Ilges, *Casanova in Dresden*, Dresden, 1931.

Inge Hanna Ahrens, *Kucks-Kuckuksbad: The Virtues of the Baroque*, Berlin, 2001.

0.123g

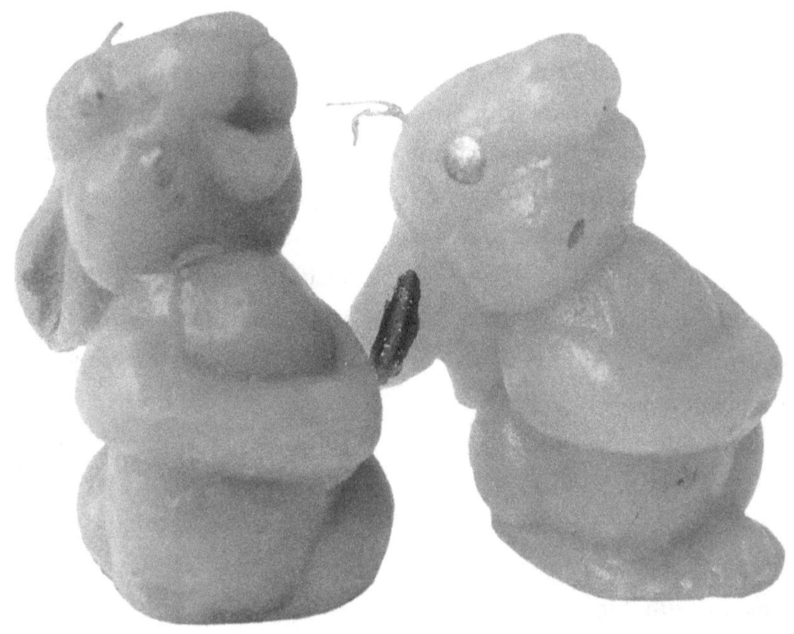

Beuys' Primordial-Rabbits

or

How Joseph Beuys Discovered Rabbits

Joseph Beuys, that primordial rock of the arts, refers again and again to rabbits throughout his vast and fascinating oeuvre. He identified with these animals to such a degree that he formulated sentences like: "I am not human, I am a rabbit," "I am a very sharp rabbit," "The rabbit that I am," etc.

The rabbit is an animal charged with symbolic power and ancient mythological meanings. In the Germanic world spring was a rabbit; the Egyptian goddess Unut wears a rabbit on her head; for the Chinese and the Aztecs the rabbit was a moon animal; the Tartars saw the rabbit as the creator of light; the Christian Middle Ages knew it as a symbol for the resurrection of Christ—to name just a few. Joseph Beuys called the rabbit an "organ of the people" and saw the animal as an "external organ." Beuys assumed that the rabbit had "…a direct relationship with birth...For me, the rabbit is a symbol of incarnation. Because the rabbit does in reality what man can only do in thought. He digs himself in, he digs himself a hollow. He incarnates himself in the earth, and that alone is important."

Joseph Beuys' work is often reduced to being only made of felt and fat. These two key materials certainly occupy an important place in his art. However, the equally important role that rabbits play is overlooked. Already in his first public action *Siberian Symphony* made in 1963, Beuys had used a rabbit as a reference point, as a partner, and as a central figure; and for the very same reasons he used felt and fat.

Flying a JU 87 in 1944, Beuys was hit by Russian anti-aircraft fire but managed to make it over the front line. Nevertheless, because of a terrible snowstorm he crashed in "a complete wasteland atop the bottle rim of the Crimea." The Tartars living there found the badly injured and unconscious man. The Khairetdinov family tended to Beuys as best they could. They rubbed his injured, wound-covered body with animal fat, wrapped the battered body in felt blankets, and put burning candles by his bed. These were the so-called rabbit candles, candles in rabbit-shape, that are widely used in Tartar settlement areas. From time immemorial the Tartars have considered rabbits to be both bearers as well as keepers of light. And thus, since earliest times, candles there have taken the form of rabbits. Even today one can find rabbit candles in every southern Russian grocery store. This rabbit candle, these light-giving rabbits, were the first, and for a long time only, things Joseph Beuys saw and perceived when awaking from out of unconsciousness.

The fact that not only the animal fat and felt blankets but the rabbit as well came from his experience with the Tartars is often overlooked and little described, even though Beuys himself made no secret of it.

Literature:
Joseph Beuys, *Self Credentials*, Darmstadt, 1972.
Henning Brandis, *Talks*, Berlin, 1989.
Philip Mason, *A Hare in the Manger*, Feiburg, 1992.
John Stüttgen, *The Whole Belt...*, Frankfurt, 2002.

0.124g

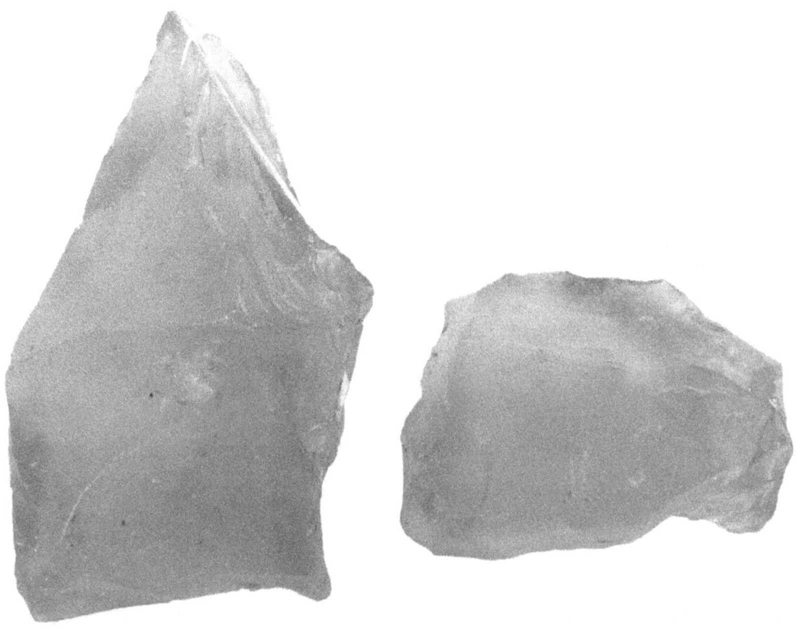

Petrified Ice:
An Extremely Rare Specimen of
the So-Called Pseudo-Stone

[*Found by Hanna Sjöberg and Klaus-Jürgen Liedtke*]

During the second glaciation of the Earth in the Mindel Stage of the Pleistocene Epoch, also referred to as the Second Ice Age, large glaciers in the north of present-day Sweden rolled over the dried Baltic Sea to Central Europe. This was the beginning of the history of geology. These massive glaciers plowed the earth, pushed huge compounds of soil, rocks, and debris in front of themselves, loaded mountains onto their backs and transported them southward to where they were unloaded, but not before they had leveled out a number of existing mountains. And this is precisely how today's rivers—the Oder, the Vistula, and the Elbe—were formed.

0.124g

At the front edge of the glacier, around its tongue as well as its lips, mountains of piled up earth, rocks, and chipped ice were formed. This collapsed mass was constantly washed away by outflowing glacier water only to come back together once again. Sometimes these earth movements dislodged pure, thick glacial ice that was covered and enclosed within a great mass of debris. When this mass consisted of a certain ratio of sand and mud, it enclosed the ice in an airtight grip, which then became increasingly compressed because of external pressure. The conditions for forming pseudo-stones were right, and the petrified ice could thus emerge.

Sand embedded the enclosed ice and masses of mud densified the whole thing so that a solid crust was formed and hardened, just like the bread that surrounds Prague ham. This airtight encapsulation created the classical clay pot effect with its own microclimate. When all of this came together, when the lump of sand and clay with its core of ice was covered up by huge masses of earth so that a tremendous weight was placed upon the metaphorical clay pot, the conditions were perfect for forming petrified ice. The baked ice cooled the firmly pressed, condensed mixture of mud and sand, which was externally warmed thanks to its large mass and pressure. In this tension between external pressure-heating and internal self-cooling, an ice concentration of highest density was formed. The ice could not melt, for to do so it would first have to be able to expand and there was no room for that because of the pressure and encapsulation. And, in any event, where could the melted water flow out to? So the ice became more and more condensed to the degree that, in the end, only a hyper-dense ice core remained. This in turn continued to be concentrated and prepped, until finally, only the ice-mineral, the ice-molecule as a mass, was left.

The petrified ice is comparable in some way to schnaps, which is the aroma concentrate of the original medium. That is also why the petrified ice is such an intense blue, a glacier blue. The ratio of the initial volume to the final volume is approximately 2,000:1 to 3,500:1, depending on the mineral density of the ice.

Three sites are known for having produced petrified ice: Molodga in Siberia, Sudbury in Canada, and Lower Lasatia in Germany. Only at these locations with their terminal moraines could the petrified ice, the pseudo-stone, be formed.

Petrified ice, however, is not to be confused with Bluedi, which is a type of a diamond found in the Kingsuit Mine in South Africa. Blue rock crystals found at Plaun la Greina in Switzerland have also often been confused with petrified ice.

Literature:
Richard Brumann, *The Phenomenon of the Moraines,* Frankfurt, 1955.
John Funk, *Related Stones,* Birmingham, 1954.
Hermann Rötzler, *The Gifts of the North,* Munich, 1937.

0.124g

0.135g

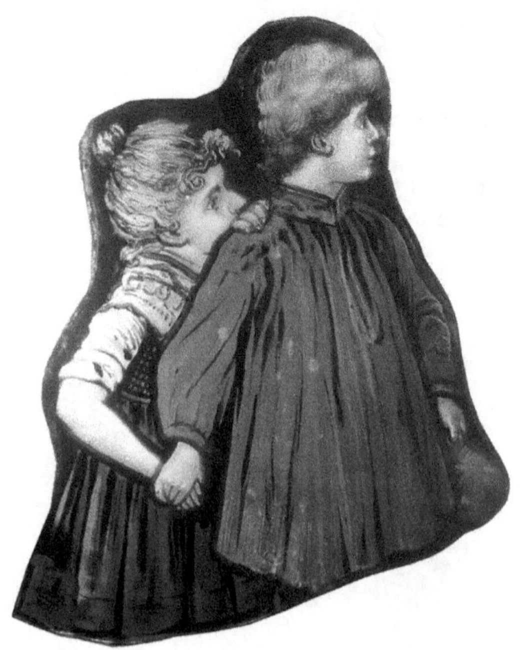

The Children of Greifswald

or

On the Whale in the Marketplace

For a long time art historians have wondered about the enigmatic stained glass fragment depicting two children found by a certain Sascha Löschner in Greifswald. Until recently neither the artist, the exact date, nor the circumstances that led to the creation of the image were known. The figure was attributed to the northern German region by the Baltic Sea and was found near Greifswald. The children's clothes, like their hairstyles, date back to the early/middle part of the sixteenth century. The general consensus was that it had to be a fragment of a larger picture, and the imagery provided evidence of having come from a southern German glass painter.

The boy's self-confident pose in the foreground, as if he were competing against someone or taking on a challenge, together with his large and curious eyes that seem to take in every detail, have repeatedly given rise to various interpretations. As for the girl, she is generally believed to be his sister and hiding behind her "brother" who is holding her right wrist as if to calm her down. Firmly protected by his broad shoulders, she almost seems to be hiding to his right, while looking wide-eyed at what we, the viewers, cannot see.

The secret hidden beyond the frame has, naturally, led to wild speculations and fantasies. In fact, the entire image has been interpreted almost exclusively through what is not to be seen, that is, through what is absent.

In his very interesting book, *Breathing in Painting*, published in 1998, Robert Rubens also deals with what we cannot see, what is concealed from us. In his treatise he cites a theory developed by the nineteenth century painter Arthur B. Davies; namely, that from Greek art up through the first century, people in painting were always depicted during inhalation, and that from the second century onward until today only during exhalation.* From this, Robert Rubens concludes that the master of the stained glass violated both the secret and the taboo concerning breathing, and depicted the children in respiratory arrest—in other words, as if they were holding their breath. Rubens suspects that the unknown artist noticed his far-reaching violation of the taboo right away, and retroactively justified having done so by claiming that the children were so impressed by what they saw that they had stopped breathing; that he had violated no taboo at all, but simply provided an appropriate and realistic depiction of the given scene.As to what exactly the children were looking at, however, Rubens has little to say, only that it must have been something enormous.

0.135g

Strangely enough, it was a historian of commercial fish that gave the decisive clue to solving the mystery. Very often a mystery, a puzzle, what we call the unknown, is sensed as being more beautiful than the actual, bare, simple, and mostly disappointing solution—an ignorance that stimulates the imagination. In this case, the solution, the disclosure of the mystery, was so intertwined with the mystery itself that the wonder was not washed away by mere facts.

Already in her 1991 book, *Fishing in the Late Middle Ages*, Dr. Gerda Schifferts had written about the custom of bringing over whales that had been stranded in Wiek, just outside the city, to the venerable old Hanseatic city of Greisfswald, and exhibiting them for learning purposes and entertainment in the market square. She cites sermons from the years 1423, 1535, and 1578 where the incomprehensible, miraculous power and greatness of God was explained in relation to whales. She quotes from an indictment and appeal sent to Duke Wartislaw IX in 1461 which complained that both the Christian and Jewish population's staging of the Biblical story of Jonah as a mystery play in the market square in Greifswald on account of the whale that had been placed there was unacceptable. In both the Christian as well as the Jewish Bible the story of Jonah is identical. The letter of indictment and denunciation asked for permission to hold an anti-Jewish pogrom in order to punish the Jews' impudence. In the surviving reply permission was refused and the exhibition of whales was praised highly.

In St. Mary's Church in Greifswald—"Hefty Mary" as the locals affectionately call it—a mural of a male Orca, 7.30 meters long and 3.50 meters high, has hung since the summer of 1545. This whale was stranded on March 30, 1545, in Wiek, brought into the city and immortalized in life size by a local painter. This painting was copied over and over again. A copy fell into the hands of the naturalist and illustrator Conrad Gesner and inspired him to depict an archetypal whale with two water-spouting horns in his 1555 work *Historia Animalium.*

During the 2015 renovations of St. Nicholas's Church and the cathedral in Greifswald, more unknown paintings of whales were found, thus confirming that there had indeed been this custom of hauling stranded whales into the city and putting them on display. It remains unknown whether the abandonment of this custom in the fifteenth century was connected to the silting of the port which began around that time, or whether the repeatedly documented complaints from the citizens, particularly the merchants, who felt the sickening stench of decaying fish to be abominable to health and damaging to business, were legally taken care of once and for all. The last mention of a whale exhibition in Greifswald dates from the year 1608.**

In the spring of 2015 Schifferts' book, *Fishing in the Late Middle Ages,* fell into the hands of art historian and fish-painting specialist Anna Witsch who was looking for early medieval illustrations of herring. The "catch," the discovery that she made in her reading, was a reference to a detailed description of the city of Greifswald in a Swedish travelogue written by Elias Jakobson in 1745. He mentions a highly acclaimed glass window in the Town Hall Apothecary. In it, a whale in the market of Greifswald is depicted in fifty-two, lead-framed, stained glass images.

Anna Witsch drove immediately to Stockholm and in the Royal Library gained direct insight into Elias Jakobson's original description of the town in the window. He describes festively dressed burghers being amazed by a large whale and continues with a description of the visibly proud mayor in his chain of office, together with his wife and eight children, looking at the whale while standing among the councilors. Numerous amazed residents; kids horsing around and being scolded. And there, in the center foreground, in a very refined, subtle manner precisely at the golden section, the glass painter has depicted a bourgeois boy with his sister. These two—alleged to be the children of the merchant Hermann Grisze—are gazing intensely at the whale and holding hands. The window is attributed to an unnamed glass painter from Mittelwald in present-day Austria.

Anna Witsch described her discovery in the art-historical journal *The Fish*, revealing that the children are in fact looking at a whale; however, she also stressed that the whole puzzle was not yet solved, as the question of what the boy was keeping in his left hand, remained open—is it a bag, and if so, what is in it?

Literature:

Gustav Eisen, *The Great Chalice of Antioch*, New York, 1923.

Rupert Halig, *The Secret Outside of the Picture*, Hamburg, 2012.

Robert Rubens, *Breathing in Painting*, Munich, 1998.

Gerda Schifferts, *Fishing in the late Middle Ages*, Lübeck, 1991.

Fredrik Sjöberg, *The King of Raisins*, Cologne, 2011.

Anna Witsch, "The Whale: The Answer," in *The Fish*, Kiel, 2015: 78 -122.

———, "A Detail of One of the Rare Glass Paintings in the Baltic Sea Region," in *Mare Baltikum*, Berlin, 2016: 125-187.

* Frederik Sjoberg writes in his book *The King of Raisins* (Cologne, 2011) about the collector and researcher Gustav Eisen who uses the inhale-exhale theory to support his discovery of a Grail Cup, as well as about the founder of respiratory theory, the painter and inspiration expert Artur B. Davies (1863-1928). In all likelihood the latter "stole" this theory from the dancer Edna Potter Owen, his model and lover. And Owen was in turn strongly influenced by the dancer and Greek dance expert Isadora Duncan. Without the breath, there is no dance. Should you want to delve further into the topic, the chapter "Legends of the Holy Grail" in *The King of Raisins* is highly recommended.

** Discussion is presently underway in Greifswald as to whether to revive the tradition of whale exhibitions, and to newly perform the so-called "Whale Games" in the form of a modern mystery play. At the center of these games, in which all are to participate, there would, of course, be two children.

0.135g

0.136g

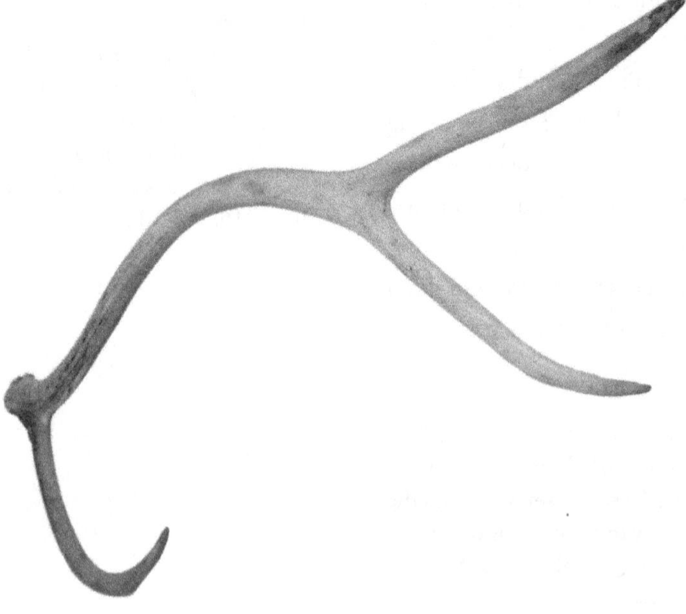

A Reindeer Went to Spain: A Rare Case of Neurological Events in a Reindeer

On July 17, 1913, in the Spanish village of Tharsis near the Portuguese border, an animal was spotted which frightened the inhabitants of the village very much. No one had ever seen such an animal before. The farmer Jesus Tellez shot it. When he saw its earmark, he realized that it had already had contact with humans and might even have been a breeding animal.

Señor Carlos Dávla, the vet who was called in, identified the animal as a reindeer and saw to it that the fur as well as the skull—antlers and all—were sent to the Zoological Institute in Madrid.

Prof. Dr. Eugenio Ruibérniz, who had just had the first zoo in Spain built, wondered about the animal and conducted research on where the reindeer had come from. He identified the owner of the animal as the reindeer herder Nils Virtanen from Kirkenes in the northernmost region of Finland known as Lapland.

Mr. Virtanen wrote to the professor that the animal had been behaving strangely for a year, always preferring to be in the vicinity of the fire as if it were cold, and that it had been missing now for the past six months. How it came to Spain, he did not know. Formerly it had indeed been a good breeding animal.

Through his research, Prof. Dr. Eugenio Ruibérniz found that the reindeer had come to Spain on its own initiative. In fact, he was able to quite accurately track its migration:

April 1: sighted in southern Sweden.
April 18: in Denmark as it grazed by the seaside.
May 6: in Germany as it swam across the Rhine.
May 29: in the vineyards of the Rhône valley.
June 1: in southern France.
June 12: hunted unsuccessfully in the Pyrenees.
June 29: spotted in Madrid.
July 17: shot at Tharsis.

Prof. Dr. Eugenio Ruibérniz examined the skull of the animal in detail and was able to determine that the right antler of the reindeer had, for an entire growth period, grown inward as opposed to outward, and had thereby pressed the temperature center. The antler thus formed an acute amount of cartilage inside, which compressed the specific part of the brain responsible for the sensation of heat. The temperature sensitivity of the reindeer had shifted so that it felt frozen almost continuously. In this state of constant shiver, it consequently headed for warmer regions and ended up in Tharsis in the south of Spain.

0.136g

Literature:

Pedro Sanchez, *The Story of a Reindeer and Its Pathologies: Changes in the Temperature Range of the Brain*, Madrid, 1916.

Lars Wahlström, *Physiology and Neurology of the Reindeer*, Stockholm, 1934.

0.141g

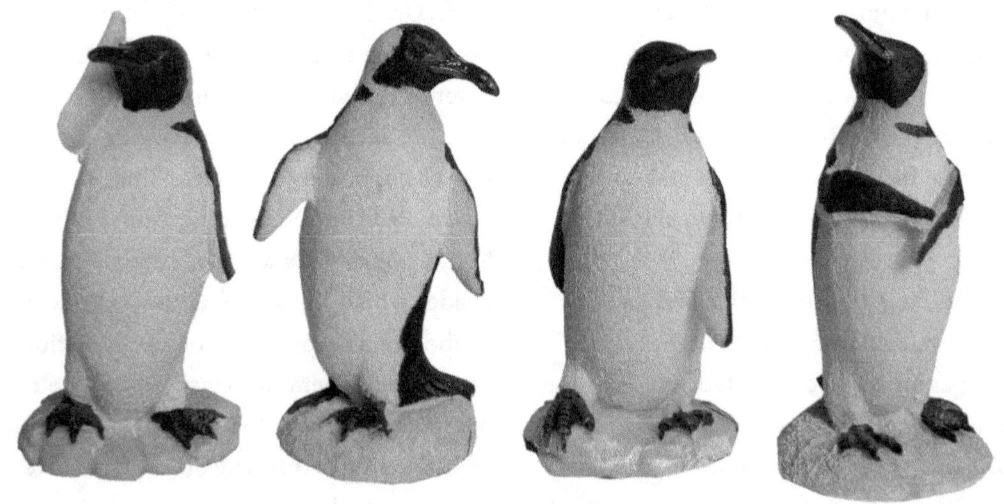

The Basic Forms of Penguin Qi Gong

or

Settling Yourself in the Ice

In 1896 the Norwegian polar explorer Aeki Kronilson observed and described the repetitive motions of emperor penguins. Reflecting his times, he interpreted the same recurring movement as the expression of a form of debilitation pertaining to animals that live in seclusion. In their extreme isolation, they only receive minimal stimulation from other species and, thus left on their own, are bound to repeat a single movement over and over again.

In 1921 the German/Argentine Joe Moeller devoted an entire chapter in his seminal work *Penguins in Their Everyday Lives* to the "ritualized movements of the penguins." He had observed the same recurring movements in almost all species of penguins. He notes that after long times of observation, it could be seen that these movements were not continuously taking place, but, instead, were executed about twice a day at different times. The movements were related to one another and were carried out individually or in small groups.

For a long time thereafter the study of the movements of the penguins remained quiet. It was only in 1984 when the Chinese intensified their own polar research that the zoologist Chie Sun Xie, who died far too early at the age of thirty-six, investigated these movements again and compared them with the basic form of Qi Gong, which at the time was despised in China. He described this observation and its interpretation as a cautionary tale of idealistic trends in wildlife observation. He went on to debunk such representations as examples of reactionary, superstitious, and pre-socialist science. Today these critical remarks are interpreted as having been the only way for him to skirt the strict censorship and report his actual research results.

The most recent observations of the American/Australian scientist Alex Grundwing and Hi Gong-Carl offer a new and more nuanced image. The interdisciplinary team around the two scientists systematized the penguins' repetitive movements. With the help of interpretation by experts from the Tai Qi Forum in Berlin and the assistance of a traditional Chinese medicine doctor Barbara Wagner, they published their research in 2008 under the title *Basic Forms of Qi Gong for Penguins: The Gathering of the Qi as Strategy for Life and Happiness*. In this acclaimed book they note how penguins use four basic forms which are repeated in turn over four varied processes. These four basic forms, just as the resulting four movement variations, correspond exactly to the rock paintings of Chin Chang, which date back to 500 BC and are deemed to be the first representation of today's Qi Gong. 0.141g

These earliest pictorial representations also relate to that of Mawangdui-grave No. 3 (168 BC) in Changsha City, Hunan Province, where methods of "Leading and Guiding the Qi" were found written on silk paper.

The immediate opinion proffered by Antarctica esoterics that the theory of Qi Gong basically descends from penguins is pure speculation. Recent research assumes that Qi Gong emerged as a guide to the omnipresent life force that works as an overarching principle in all living things using the four basic principles of Open-Close-Rise-Fall. Advanced botanists now believe that these four basic principles can even be found in plants.

Master Hi Xong of the University of Shanghai, who in his epoch-making book *Language as Expression of the Mental Conception of External Movement* demonstrated the importance of the linguistic and literary terms of Qi Gong exercises, has solved the movements of penguins and made them accessible to us.

Master Hi Xong, *Language as Expression of the Mental Conception of External Movement*, Freiburg, 2006.

The four basic forms are: "Find Your Center in All Horizons," "Harmonize the Top with the Bottom," "Submit Plenty to Accommodate," "Stand Still Within Yourself and Let Go."

The four processes: "The Safeguarded Egg is as Light as a Feather," "Greet the Krill and Welcome Him Warmly," "The Feather in the Storm Withstands the Forces," and "Assume the Wind and Reassure the Ice."

Since Master Hi Xong's having made the exercises of the penguins understandable to us, the popularity of these exercises has been on the rise. In many Qi Gong schools "Settling Yourself in the Ice: The Four Basic Exercises of the Penguins" has already become the most popular class.

0.141g

Literature:

Rudolf Ayax, *Movements in the Animal Kingdom and Their Interpretation*, Reutlingen, 2005.

Rainer Jakisch, *The Sages Show/White the Way*, Berlin, 2007.

Grundwing/Gong Karl, *Basic Forms of Chi Gong with Penguins*, Hamburg, 2007.

Aevi Kronilson, *Polar Lives in Constant Light and Constant Darkness*, Berlin, 1915.

Joe Moeller, *Penguins in Their Everyday Lives*, Basel, 1938.

Wilhelm Reich, *The Discovery of the Orgone*, Berlin, 1969.

Barbara Wagner, *The Power of Movement in Reduction*, Munich, 1997.

Chie Sun Xie, *Victim of Science in China*, Dresden, 2002.

0.142g

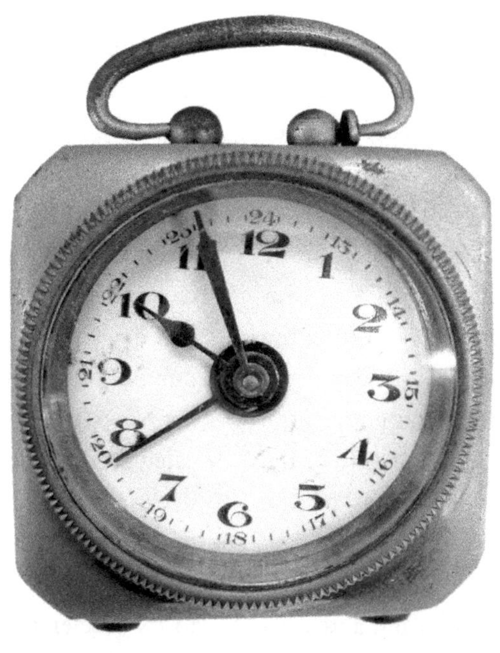

Marcel Rödiger, the Inventor of New Time

or

How the Authorities Did Not Like It At All When the Day Became Twenty Hours and the Hour Fifty Minutes

Marcel Rödiger, the firstborn who came into the world on August 25, 1833, in Saint-Imier, Canton of Jura, did not take over his parents' farm. Instead, from a very young age he was drawn to the village horologues. In 1851, he was designated a trained clockmaker's apprentice and, after two years' wandering through various workshops and with a master's certificate in his pocket, he went on to establish his own independent workshop in Saint-Imier. In the Canton of Jura many small workshops produced fine precision clocks that still form the reputation of Swiss analog clocks today.

In the nineteenth century the entire Jura, on the right as well as on the left side of the ridge, on the Swiss side as well as on the French side, was considered a stronghold of European anarchists. Pierre Joseph Proudhon, Victor Hugo, Charles Fourier, and Gustav Courbet were born there; Piotr Kropotkin and Bakunin visited the area several times. As clockmakers were considered just as well-educated and well-read as cigar rollers, they naturally came to the special attention of the police. They organized themselves into cultural groups and debate clubs, became engaged readers, and ran into conflict with the authorities again and again. When followed, they simply moved across the border and found shelter with their comrades.

It was in this intellectual and technically highly skilled milieu that the clockmaker Marcel Rödiger grew up. Even as a teenager he discussed models of society and, like many clockmakers, believed that social life should be organized just like a clock, one part merging with the other, each playing an important role, and no one wheel dominating any other. No man would be called useless, for there could be no superfluous, emptily spinning wheel. Every individual would be productive and equally involved in the community. Society would be structured in a clear and concise manner, and recognize neither masters nor servants.

With this in mind, he developed a new way of keeping time. In 1858, he presented a clock which worked according to the principles of the "New-Time" (as he called it). The day had only twenty hours, an hour fifty minutes, a minute fifty seconds. He justified his New-Time by saying that it was easier to calculate as it fit in the groundbreaking new decimal system. Another important reason for his New-Time, he stated, was his concern that any shortening of time would only lead to its acceleration. Confining oneself to less time units, on the other hand, would actually result in one's getting more time, which could in turn flow more meaningfully into collaborative tasks.

Rödiger's New-Time fell on extremely fertile soil. It was talked about everywhere, eagerly discussed, and more and more people began to adapt and live according to it. His clocks became so popular that, even though he had ten assistants, he could not produce enough of them in his available hours. He therefore quickly granted licenses to satisfy the demand. Soon this time bore the name of its inventor, and though it did not quite sit right with him there was nothing he could do to oppose the power of the masses. "Rödiger-Time" had been born.

Within a year almost the entire valley of St. Imier had adapted Rödiger-Time, and even in that important center of traditional clock-making, La Chaux-de-Fonds, many began to follow the ideas of New-Time as well.

In 1860 the army marched into the valley of St. Imier in order to confiscate and destroy all the clocks of New-Time. It was the sovereign's right to determine how to keep time and this whole idea of New-Time, this so-called Rödiger-Time, was an anarchist campaign that had to be eradicated. Marcel Rödiger himself was an anarchist who only wanted to cause confusion in order to sell his new clocks. Naturally, the authorities used these raids as a means to settle accounts with other unpleasant anarchists too.

Marcel Rödiger was arrested and imprisoned in Neuchâtel (Neuenburg). The possession of Rödiger Clocks became strictly forbidden as did mention of New-Time itself. Today, two beautifully preserved copies of Rödiger Clocks can be seen in the International Clock-making Museum of Neuchâtel. Marcel Rödiger was charged with Time Rebellion: he had no right to proclaim his own time just in order to have more of it. The division of time was sovereign law, and thus any attempt to re-articulate it was paramount to the crime of printing one's own money and disturbing the flow of currency.

After a very unfair show trial, Marcel Rödiger was sentenced to five years in prison.

One year later he was liberated by a so-called "Rödiger-Bunch," which consisted of like-minded people who had become political during the time of the time-ban and worshiped him as their leader.

After liberating Rödiger, the group hid in French region of Pontarlier and later in Besançon. In 1864 together they traveled to America and founded a Rödiger-community in Tennessee that still exists today and lives according to Marcel Rödiger's New-Time. Its network spans many countries.

In the former socialist countries Rödiger-Time became strictly forbidden beginning in 1972. All existing clocks had to be corrected and reset to normal, standard time.

The piece on display at The Museum of Unheard (of) Things is a retroactively built Polish Rödiger Clock, which was acquired in Poland in 1982.

Literature:

R. Tiemeyer, *Time and Consequences*, Zurich, 1975.

T. Tihmer, Rödiger: A Visionary? Berlin-Neukölln, 1978. Trans., "Time as a Lever,"

in: *Under the Cobblestones Lies the Beach*, Vol 21, Berlin-Neukölln, 1982.

W. Müller-Funk, The Clock as a Narrative Element, Vienna, 1999.

0.142g

0.143g

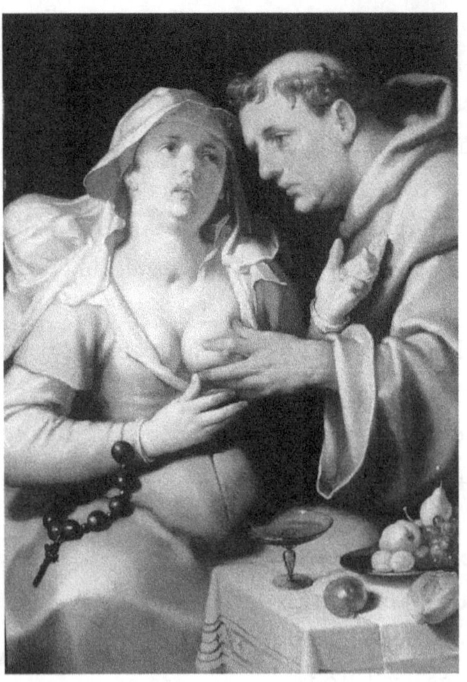

"The Beguine and the Monk":
A Painting by Cornelis Cornelisz van Haarlem
(1562-1638)

In the early thirteenth century the world was out of control. Christian values were slowly establishing themselves but had yet to become fully anchored. Purgatory was discovered and introduced in order to give light sinners one last chance. Women began to rise up, as they no longer wanted to unconditionally surrender to men or to Roman law, to which they absolutely refused to be subdued. The veneration of Mary spread more and more and empowered women in their rebellion.

Laws changed, and women were finally included in inheritance law, which had previously been denied them. They did not have to get married and could refuse marriages they did not agree with. More and more women joined together in Marian communities so as to lead independent lives and as a form of rebellion against the roles imposed on them. Many wealthy women, princesses, and societal widows bequeathed their fortunes to these associations and took them under their personal protection. In most cases, these women's groups settled in the vicinity of Dominican monasteries, since these were considered the most modern of all and had repeatedly rebelled against the ossified Church. These monasteries provided protection for "the Beguines," as they soon came to be called.

The term "Beguine" is of uncertain origin. It may be derived from St. Begga, founder of one of the associations but could also have been derived from the priest Lamberti di Beges ("The Stutterer"), who founded many of the women's convents. The name may have also come from the word "beige," after the gray-brown color of their robes.

The Beguines were no uniform movement, and the name was a generic term for any association that lived by its own rules. Some lived a monastic life, while others took the form of large residential communities that held up to 200 women. Some convents required women to join forever, others for only a certain time. All of these associations were financially independent and were active in trade, commerce, and nursing.

Each community had different rules. Some had almost none at all, while others were very strict. What all of these associations, communities, and monasteries did have in common was the fact they were withdrawn from male domination and violence, which in turn inspired and brought male imagination to bloom. The Beguines were accused of sexual savagery and of living a life contrary to nature. Daily orgies were suspected, and they were accused of enjoying freedoms of all kinds, of living a licentious life, and so on. Because of the protection of the Dominicans and the patronage of duchesses and other highly respected ladies, however, for a long time one did not dare to condemn these associations openly.

During the Reformation, when Mary worship became prohibited, the inheritance law was revised to the disadvantage of women, and male rights were put back in full force, most of the women's associations disbanded or became integrated into the Dominicam monasteries.

The painting by Cornelis Cornelisz van Haarlem, *The Beguine and the Monk*, depicts a Beguine's pregnancy test. A Dominican monk, trained especially for this purpose, is checking whether milk or wine is coming from out of

0.143g

her breast. If milk, the fetus was a fetus of sin, of the flesh; however, if what came out was wine, the fetus was spiritual, and the pregnant Beguine a wife of Jesus and therefore pure. As you can see, this painting shows a pure Beguine, because at the bottom right of the canvas we can see a drop of red wine disappearing into a wine glass.

Literature:

C. Chrutkov, *Early Medieval Women's Movements*, Dormagen, 2001.

O. Magnus, *The Dominican Order*, Ottobeuren, 1999.

0.143g

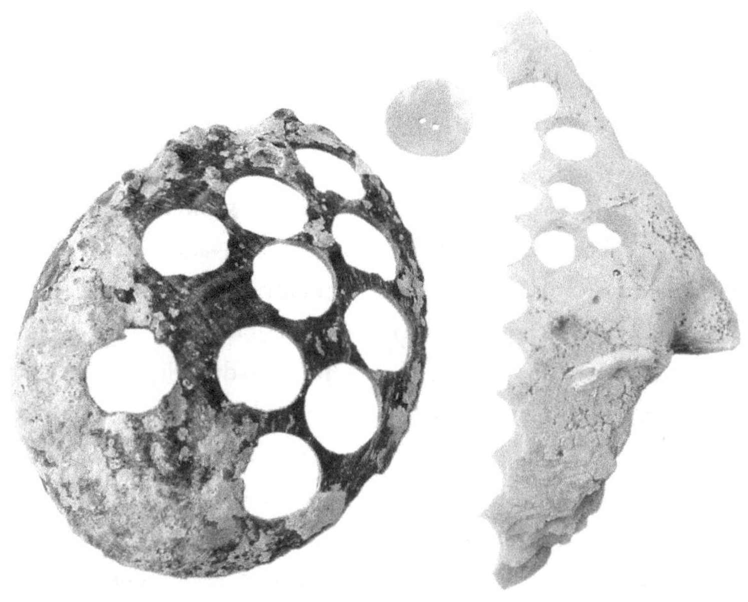

Mussels from Which the Mother of Pearl Buttons of the Soldiers of Empress Maria Theresa Were Produced and Why a Case of These Buttons Can Be Found at the Museum of Regional Studies in Mexico

In the spring of 1743 a lordly coach and elaborate retinue ascended to Riegersburg Castle. "We have arrived, Johann Joseph, your uncle Field Marshal Ludwig Andreas is here too. Now go on, Joseph, get out!" a resolute woman's voice could be heard. This was the great Maria Theresa, one of the most important women in history, who was making a stop here deep in the provinces to seek lodging.

Her visit was not entirely unexpected, but no one had suspected that she would be coming that day. The staff knelt down, listened to the Empress's moral exhortations, then got back to work only after she had made multiple requests.

Maria Theresa was traveling to Prague to negotiate peace between Bohemia and Moravia. Important discussions in Vienna had delayed her departure, but she had nonetheless decided to head off and lodge in Riegersburg Castle, which her consultant, the successful General Ludwig Andreas Khevenhüller, had often mentioned in conversation. The castle's owner and resident, Johann Josef Khevenhüller, the nephew of the General, was Lord Chamberlain of the Empress, but had never actually met her personally.

General Ludwig Andreas Khevenhüller had told Maria Theresa about a pearl button factory in Lord High Chamberlain Johann Josef Khevenhüller's district. Below the castle in Hardegg by the border-river of Thaya, hard-working folks collected mussels in order to make high quality and very durable buttons.

Maria Theresa, who was already preoccupied with her military reforms (the first phase of which she would initiate in 1749), or at the very least already thinking about them, was quite interested in buttons. Her military had to have a uniform appearance, for what would people think about her soldiers if each of them were to wear something different? She would later establish the first national army with 108,000 soldiers, all of whom were dressed sufficiently well, and the different military ranks consistently distinguishable by their clothing.

Her motto had always been: "In righteousness and gentleness" ("Justitia et clementia").

One of the first things to do, then, was to create a standarized uniform and one that had to shine—and what do people see most in a uniform? The buttons! And so she placed special importance on good buttons for good uniforms—durable, shiny buttons. The trousers and soldier's tails were not to simply be held together by cords, but also by buttons, and visible ones at that. But these could not be buttons that would fall of at the first skirmish or when things began to get serious. Her soldiers would never stand with their trousers down around their ankles on the battlefield; they could have homemade ones, but never ones that would fall down.

In the company of General Ludwig Andreas Khevenhüller and Lord High Chamberlain Johann Josef Khevenhüller, Maria Theresa and her husband Joseph observed the hard-working people who produced the buttons and had them show them what they produced.

She was so excited about the "clever people of Hardegg" and their buttons that for her the saying "like the hard-working folks of Hardegg" became a synonym for industrious, honest people.

She later ordered many buttons from Hardegg. A house production line was introduced and, as a result, the mussels in the Thaya River soon became extinct and mussels from other rivers had to be processed instead.

0.143g

Maria Theresa returned to Riegersburg Castle several times. Two of the dressers she brought as gifts can still be seen at the castle in one of the magnificient rooms, the China Salon. They were a gift for Johann Joseph Khevenhüller, whom she later ennobled as a prince.

One hundred and twenty-one years later, on November 10, 1864, Captain Johann Carl Graf Khevenhüller of the Khevenhüller family together with several loyal officers set sail from the Loire estuary in St. Nazaire in France, and stepped foot on the port of Veracruz in Mexico on December 7. After many days' train and wagon ride, they reached Mexico City where Emperor Maximilan of Mexico held his domicile. Emperor Maximilian, also known as "the Unfortunate," had traded his stunningly beautiful domicile at Trieste, Miramare Castle, for an emperor's chair loaded with dynamite. Captain Johann Carl Graf Khevenhüller followed his Emperor and led the 5th Squadron with sixty Hussars. These Red Hussars were soon to become notorious and feared by the enemy. Indeed, the mere presence of Red Hussars unnerved the enemy. Captain Johann Carl Graf Khevenhüller had brought a chest full of buttons that came from the Empress Maria Theresa. He handed over this chest under the roaring yells of "Viva!" from his Hussars to the new Emperor Maximilian of Mexico and swore eternal fidelity to him.

When the Emperor of Mexico was sentenced to death by court martial on July 19, 1867, and the sentence was immediately carried out, the imperial bequest passed into the possession of the state. General Diaz, who later became President of the Republic of Mexico and who had been against the execution, ordered that the bequest be preserved in its entirety. Thus the chest with the buttons of the "hard-working folks of Hardegg," buttons that had been intended for the army of Maria Theresa, ended up in the Ethnographic Museum in Mexico. They are still there today in basement room C-54 A along with other bequests of the Emperor Maximilian's. These rooms are not publicly accessible.

On July 22, 1867, Captain Johann Carl Graf Khevenhüller embarked again with his remaining Hussars, but this time to Europe. He retired to Riegersburg Castle, got married, engaged in astronomical measurements, cartography, geography, medicine, climbed Mount Sinai on November 24, 1869, made a seventeen-day trip to the wilderness with seventy men and 160 camels, traveled to Bombay, and came back again. King Ludwig II awarded him the George Medal and knighted him. Khevenhüller repeatedly visited the Pope and, being a great animal lover, buried his beloved dogs in a specially designed dog cemetery. This too can still be seen today.

The pearl button factory also remains there to this day. It is located halfway between Hardegg and Riegersburg Castle in a place called Felling, and is a family business. They still produce high-quality mother of pearl buttons.

Literature:

F. Müllner, *The Baroque Castle of Riegersburg*, Fronsburg, Undated.

———, Johann Carl Fürst Khevenhüller-Metsch, *A Fellow Soldier of Emperor Maximillian of Mexico*, Complemented by Francesca Filo della Torre, *Countess Pilati*, Riegersburg, 1990.

L. Nikolic, *The Language of the Court*, Vienna/Belgrade, 2003.

Inventory Catalog of the Museum of Regional Studies, Mexico City, 1995.

0.149g

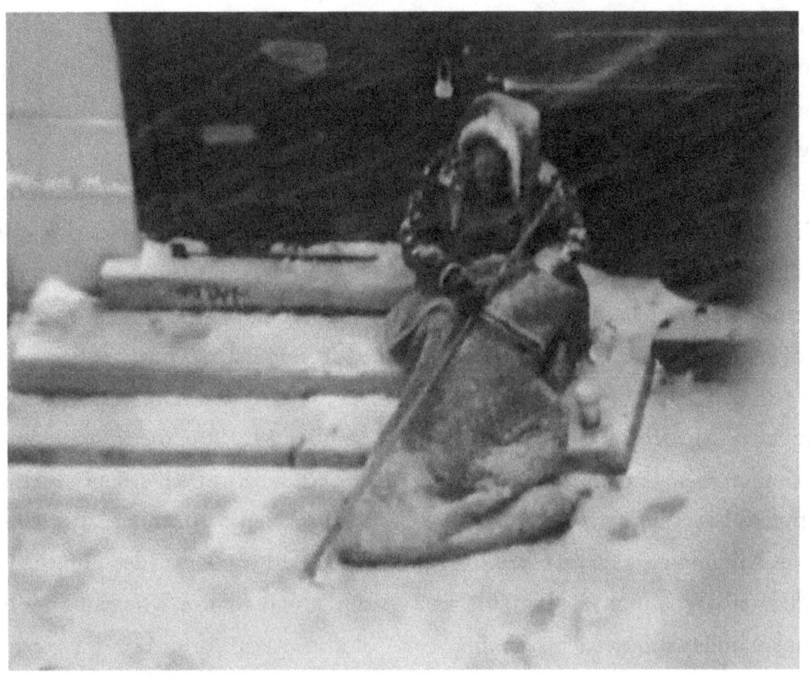

The Beggar on Hudson Street:
A Film by Günter Eisenhardt

After its very first broadcast on the afternoon of December 24, 1978, all the news stations in the country reported that New York television station NYN had aired some of the most shocking images the nation had ever seen—a film shot with a hidden camera by G. Eisenhardt.

The film—a twenty-minute clip without commentary, music, or any sound at all—was broadcast again several times during the Christmas holidays. The factual and cool introductory words of the presenter were only: "We will now show you images from New York."

The ratings were the highest in the history of the station, which was shut down in 1999 because of the disastrous mismanagement of the executive board. Advertising revenues immediately increased after the broadcast of these distressing images. There was probably not a single US television network that did not purchase the film.

The mayor of New York had already held a press conference on the problem of the homeless in New York City on December 27 in which he called on the people to take care of them as well as the socially excluded and even promised to host a homeless person for a week at his home. The President of the United States, Jimmy Carter, dedicated four sentences to the problem of the homeless in his re-written and re-recorded New Years' message of 1979, which was very heavily peppered with the idea of social justice. All the country's politicians reacted immediately; they wanted to prevent the already very strong liberal civil rights movement from getting even stronger through its engagement with the problem. Commentators compared the effect of the twenty-minute film with the great poverty report of the 1960s that had led to the emergence of the countless soup kitchens which are still in operation today.

As 1978 turned into 1979 homeless organizations were founded, homeless sponsorships offered, and homeless shelters opened all across the country.

Various, even reckless, offers of assistance were also made. One Mr. Blyrie, a Texas oil magnate, suggested flying homeless people down from the north to the warmer southern states during the winter months and then flying them back again in the spring along with homeless people from the south so that the issue would be distributed appropriately and socially across the entire country. He acted immediately and chartered a plane that waited for five days at New York's John F. Kennedy airport for homeless people who were ready to depart. The only two people who showed up were journalists in disguise hoping to land a big story.

0.149g

The activities triggered by this film continued for a long time, and included a nationwide association for helping the homeless that every year around Christmas gathered to take care of the homeless, providing support and supplying donated packages to them on Christmas Eve.

Despite various calls and search operations, the man in the film was never identified. Nobody recognized him, and he never reported himself voluntarily. The $7,335.67 he would have been entitled to from the film rights were donated to a homeless association in 1984.

Literature:

B. Kohler, *The Effect of Permanent Films*, Berlin, 2000.

L. Müller, *The Sociology of Madness*, Cologne, 1975.

0.152g

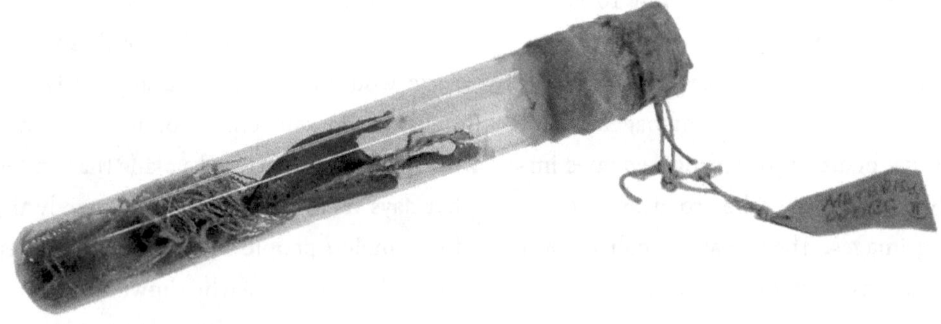

The Shoemaker, the Barber, and the Smells

[For Hans Schohl]

It used to be that a shoemaker not only manufactured and repaired shoes—shoes that made up people's standpoints and the durability of their convictions—but also had an important advisory role, as he was the keeper of the knowledge of human smells. Based on the specific odors that naturally concentrate in shoes, early shoemakers could detect and determine people's features, habits, and characteristics. Some shoemakers specialized in odor perception and the analysis of their subjects' physical health. For example, the art of plantar reflexology, which is still practiced today, developed out of this ability and was first described in 1738 by the French shoemaker Pièrre Lephot.

Most shoemakers, however, dealt with interpersonal issues, particularly with those areas in which people were expected or required to tolerate others; naturally, this led to their being involved in initiating marriages as well as issues of cohabitation and sex. Many still existant sayings bear witness to this. For example, "Smell the shoe, no worries for you!" [Franconian], which means that difficulties can be avoided by simply smelling your potential partner's shoe, or by having it smelled by a shoemaker; and, as for marriage procrastinaters, people would say "Once the shoemaker's smelled it, nothing's left in the way" [Alemannic]—both quite compelling opinions of the shoemaker's olfactory skills.

There were also those shoemakers who established original scent collections. A shoemaker named de Wiedemann from Landtuhl, Palitanate, is reported to have had a collection of 438 odors. He took these odors from shoes by putting a slightly oiled cloth in each one for two days. The oil would pick up the scent and the oil-coated cloth would then smell of it. In Grasse, the perfume capital in Southern France, scents were taken from naturally pleasant smelling products like vanilla, rose, and so on, by employing the same method. From then on, shoemakers would enclose these cloths in airtight containers and only take them out for comparison or study. People thought very highly of shoemakers, and maintained a thoroughly positive attitude towards them.

During the transition to the Baroque period, however, barbers became increasingly fashionable. They were no longer concerned with natural smells, but, instead, offered people new, foreign, and refined odors; smells behind which people could hide as well as deceive. Barbers considered themselves to be shoemakers' natural competitors and felt superior to them; for the latter, in their opinion, could only smell, whereas they themselves could produce odors.

This in turn led to an undeclared war between barbers and shoemakers. Shoemakers spread the rumor that barbers nebulized people with their scents, could only produce rumors from their "rumor mills," and, basically, simply "stood around in their smells." Barbers in turn spread the rumor that everything shoemakers did was only "cobbled together," that "shoemakers' nonsense" "stank to high heaven," and angrily wanted them to "stay at [their] cobbler's lasts!" The saying, "If the barber's got you in a bind, don't worry, the shoemaker'll make it fine," shows the people's

0.152g

attitude during that time of great upheaval. It is proof that, in moments of insecurity and danger, people still turned to the shoemaker and not the barber, whom they did not quite trust yet. The shoemakers' eventual displacement, however, could not be stopped.

More and more barbers forced themselves into the foreground. They conducted venesection, became lapidaries, and, later, modern-day doctors. However, they did not take over the original social advisory function of the shoemakers, which, instead, remained a vacant position until the appearance of modern psychologists. With the displacement of the shoemaker, the shoe was also ousted. As a result of this displacement, something which has become very common today can be read for the first time in Baroque novels and seen in the countless erotic images from the same period: shoes as an erotic fetish.

Today the shoemaker is a marginal phenomenon. One throws away broken shoes and switches shoes in accordance with the next trend. When something is wrong with the sole, you just go to a heel bar; fixed standpoints are similarly in short supply.

But sometimes you can indeed still find a shoemaker, a cobbler, and when you enter a local shop, it smells of leather, of metal nails and little donkeys, of fat and the tangy odor of people's shoes. And if you have a bit of luck and a lot of sympathy, you can understand the shoemaker as an initiate of smell, because, so it is rumored, the deeper, secret knowledge of smells continues to be passed on from one generation of shoemakers to the next up to this very day.

Literature:

Karl Redlich, *Social History of Odor*, Cologne, 1998.

Lutz Röhrich, *Encyclopedia of Proverbial Sayings*, Freiburg, 1991.

Hans Schohl, *The Barber and the Devil*, Anzefahr, 2003.

———, *The Barber's Shadow*, Anzefahr, 2012.

0.168g

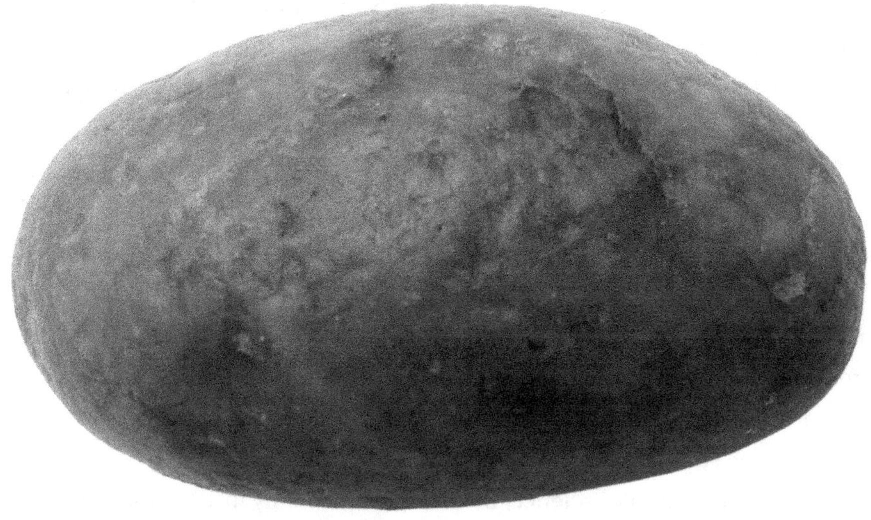

The Mystery of Petrified Potatoes

Among the Highland Indians of Peru they were called "Papalolilaa," which means something like "a potato fallen from heaven." On the one hand they served as cult objects, as good luck charms, and have frequently been discovered as grave items; on the other, these stones in potato form were used as projectiles in military conflicts. In 1687 the Spanish conqueror Carlos Moreno reported being attacked by a hail of stones that looked almost exactly like potatoes and which, in addition to being hard as rocks, caused substantial damage to his soldiers.

For a long time it was unclear how these stones came to be shaped like potatoes and belonged to the many mysteries of nature. As the world began to be increasingly explained and demystified in the early nineteenth century through the systematization of science, the petrified potatoes were at first dismissed as natural peculiarities. Indeed, E.F. Schlotheim's book *Description of Strange Herbal-Footprints and Plant-Fossils* from 1804 did not include them. But ten years later, Johann Mayersohn, in his *Tubers that Turned into Stones and Their Occurrence*, published a description of the petrified potatoes, noting that potato-shaped stones occured in all potato-growing areas and that these had to be considered fossilizations of the potato tuber.

0.168g

Later the petrification of potatoes was once again denied, as, it was argued, petrification only occured in geological times and, in any event, could not have occurred in Europe as potatoes had previously not existed there where the stones were being found. However, as the knowledge of plate tectonics came to growing prominence in the 1960s, the petrification theory once again became actual.

In his book *When the Continents Were One: The Supercontinent Gondwana*, Hartwig Müller-Frank describes the fact that, as petrified potatoes can be found in all continents, it is clear that all the continents once formed a single unity. That, as one of the earliest plants, it is possible to find the potato in petrified form on all continents. The question as to why, when the Earth's plates separated, potatoes were later only to be found in South America remains to be clarified. However, the fact that today they once again grow on every continent without difficulty, and indigenously, is a clear indication of their former global presence and their spread today is a kind of reconquest of the ancestral vegetation period.

It was only in 1999 that the German bio-geologist Brigitte Lembke succeeded in clarifying the secret of the stones in potato form. Under certain conditions unharvested potatoes can solidify and turn into stones. During the silicification process the potato's minerals are replaced through impregnation by means of silica. Thanks to ideal laboratory conditions Brigitte Lembke was able to document this process of the quick-silification of a potato in just two years. The high starch content of the potato is responsible for ensuring that it retains its color. The detection of such a fast silicification process led to a fierce debate among petrification experts as to whether quick-silicification exists in other plants as well; if so, it would have disastrous consequences for all current theories. To date, however, this process of such rapid silicification has been observed only in potatoes.

The silicification of potatoes can only take place when the soil is free from artificial fertilizers and over very different lengths of time; processes varying from five to hundred years have been reported.

The silicified potato on display in The Museum of Unheard (of) Things comes from Demeter Hof Flegel in Kröte, Wendland, and is an excellent specimen.

Literature:

B. Lembke, *On the Quick-Silicification of Potatoes*, Hirschhorn, 1999.

Johann Mayersohn, *Tubers that Turned into Stones and Their Occurence*, Heidelberg, 1814.

H. Müller-Frank, *When the Continents Were One: The Supercontinent Gondwana*, Berlin, 1969.

E.F. Schlotheim, *Description of Strange Herbal-Footprints and Plant-Fossils*, Gotha, 1804.

0.168g

0.169g

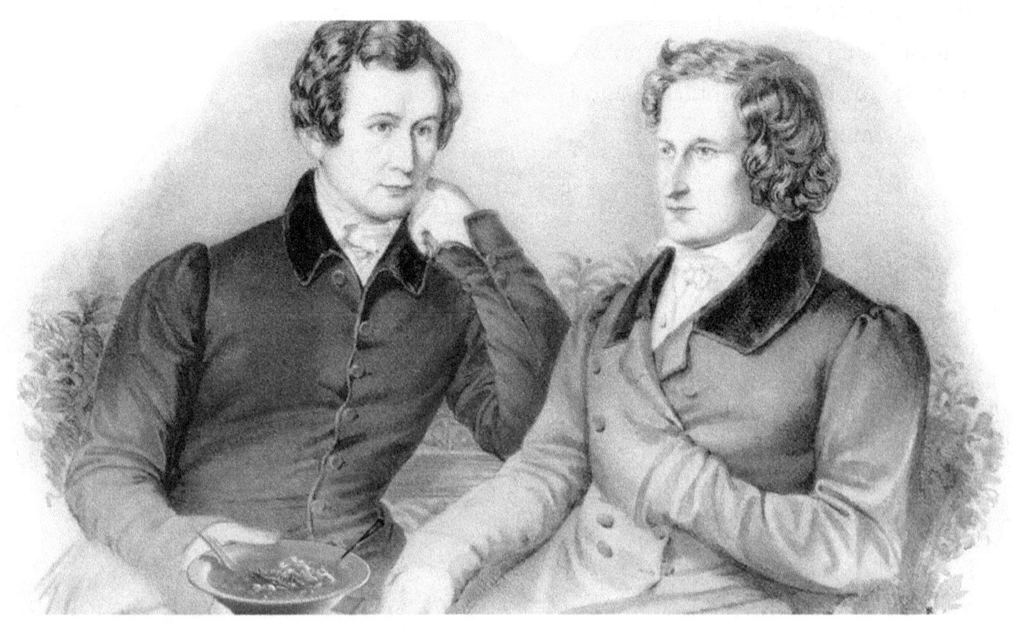

The Inventors of Alphabet Soup

or

How the Brothers Grimm Were Also Cooks

This was just too much. A general murmur ran through the room, one cough followed another, and some of the German-speaking scholars simply got up and left the conference hall. Many whispered to their neighbors: "Who invited that guy back again? This just isn't going to go well." The delegations from England and Slovenia had insisted on their right to choose the speaker for themselves and had thus invited Adam Algrim to be their keynote speaker. The International Conference of German Linguistics, organized in different German universities every four years, was being held in Marburg that year. As always, the list of those assembled read like a "Who's Who" of German Studies. Adam Algrim's invitation, however, ensured discord in the German delegation from the start. He was not popular within the field of German Studies in Germany whatsoever. His theories led him to being considered a traitor, a complainer, and an all around obstructionist. And yet, on the international stage, Algrim was considered an original, clever, and accurate scientist from whom new and unconventional views could always be expected. His book *The Words on the Couch,* based on Adolf Josef Storfer's *Words and Their Destiny* and *In the Jungle of Language*, gathered a lot of international attention but was dismissed by the Germans as being "unscientific," "too speculative," and "too poetic."

And now this Adam Algrim had just given a talk about the founding fathers of German linguistics, Jakob and Wilhelm Grimm. The title of his lecture "Of Eating and Speaking" was already enough to raise a few hackles.

Adam Algrim came straight to his point and after only five minutes managed to cause a scandal. According to Algrim, the Brothers Grimm were both the inventors of alphabet soup, and the authors of an alphabet soup cookbook. Alphabet soup, Algrim claimed, had decisively helped the Grimm Brothers understand the principles of vowel and consonant shifts and thus inspired them to investigate the origin of words and their components. And so we have alphabet soup to thank, so to speak, for modern etymology.

In his presentation Adam Algrim relied on a rather detailed little booklet he had found in 2003 in the town of Müncheberg, Brandenburg, in which the Brothers Grimm were described as the inventors of alphabet soup. The author of the book was a certain Arnold Liebreich from Berlin who had once been one of their neighbors. Liebreich had lived at Number 8 Linkstraße; the Grimm Brothers at Number 7 from 1847 until their deaths. In his diary-like booklet Liebreich describes many encounters with the Grimms and how they tenderly cared for his five children, read them their newfound fairy tales over and over again, and brought noodles in small letter form while urging the children to eat heartily. The idea was that, in order to better understand language, they were to incorporate letters at an early stage.

Liebreich reports how he was often invited by the Grimms to participate in scientific sessions, how he had to eat this kind of alphabet soup, and how he was then expected to talk with his mouth full. In the soup, letters had formed particular words, which Liebreich was requested to speak first with a full, then with a half-full, and, finally, an empty mouth. The Grimms wrote everything down and carefully examined the phonetic shifts they heard. They told Liebreich that with this method they were getting closer to the origin of words. That the speaking of words formed by precisely those letters found in the mouth was very useful for the accurate investigation on the origin of words. The placement of the letters of a word on the tongue would contribute significantly to determining its origin. Liebreich also mentions that the Grimm Brothers made fun of the phrase "One must never speak with a full mouth." In their opinion, the phrase reflected the fear one experienced before remembering a word's meaning, which was the same fear one had of getting words confused.

In his talk, Adam Algrim also spoke about the Brothers Grimm's cook, Martha Blaseitz, who worked closely with a blacksmith named Gotthelf Protschka. Gotthelf Protschka was responsible for making the small cookie cutters which were used to form the letter-shaped pasta. Martha Blaseitz then told him what he needed to improve in order for the forms to be ready for the kitchen.

It is said that Martha Blaseitz once complained to the author of the book, Arnold Liebreich, that the Grimms with their soup experiments had extracted a great toll on her table linen, seeing as that she constantly had to remove the alphabet pasta that fell from their mouths and stuck to the cloth by hand before it could then be washed.

The highpoint of Adam Algrim's presentation, however, came when he showed a cookbook for alphabet soup recipes dating from 1854, which was dedicated to Martha Blaseitz. In the book, the Grimms referred to her as being essential to their research before going on to describe sixty-seven recipes.

This cookbook was discovered in the Central Archives of German Cooking Literature in Darmstadt. The author is unknown. Yet on the basis of many details and in comparison with Mr. Arnold Liebreich's records, in addition to the writing style, the book can be clearly attributed to the Brothers Grimm. Thereafter, Adam Algrim presented five independent assessments from major experts certifying the book's authenticity.

Finally, from this cookbook attributed to the Grimms, *Lovely Martha's Soup Cookbook for the Incorporation of Alphabets, Words, Sentences, and Whole Fairy Tales,* he read the recipe for "The Preparation of a Clear Broth with Meat for the Purpose of Word-exploration":

> *Since preparing the soup and sauce with meat broth is the healthiest, most nutritious, and simply best thing to do, in addition to being the most important thing in the culinary arts, here we shall only concern ourselves with this matter and, above all, show the manner in which one produces a good, rich meat broth following the rules and principles of science in order to allow letters to float in an organized and clear way, and to make them a treat for the tongue in the name of linguistic research.*
>
> *Beef makes the best broth, so it must also be used in greater quantity than other types of meat because it contains the largest amount of nutrients or osmazone, which is the most important constituent of meat next to fibrin or fibrous material, gelatine or gelatinous material, fat and protein.*
>
> *You should therefore use the freshest, and not too fat, beef (for every 1 liter of water, 1/2 kilogram of meat), about half as much coarse veal, some chopped veal bones, and beef mar-*

0.169g

row bones. Do not wash the meat, but wipe it off with a clean cloth. Put it in cold water over a gentle flame, and let the water slowly come to a boil so that the protein contained in the meat is released first, congeals, and rises to the surface where it appears in the shape of foam, which must then be skimmed off thoroughly with a slotted spoon, because otherwise you will not obtain a clear broth, which is essential to the study of words on the tongue. Add the salt and root vegetables only after skimming, but avoid using onions or spices, since they will give too strong a flavor. In order to obtain a proper and strong broth, the meat must be covered up well and simmered for six to seven hours so that the nutrients are gradually extracted and nothing but the tough, leathery, juicy fibers next to the bone remain. At this point, gently skim off all the fat, sieve the broth through a cloth, and use it for the soup by adding the alphabet pasta. It is now time for you to turn your attention to how the words, lying upon your tongue, are pronounced.

0.169g

Literature:
Adam Algrim, *The Words on the Couch*, London, 2000.
Adolf Josef Storfer, *Words and Their Destiny*, Berlin, 2003.
——, *In the Jungle of Language*, Berlin, 2003.
Unknown, *Soup, Vegetables, and Meat: A Cookbook for Home Cooking*, Darmstadt, 1876.

0.171g - 0.250g

0.180g

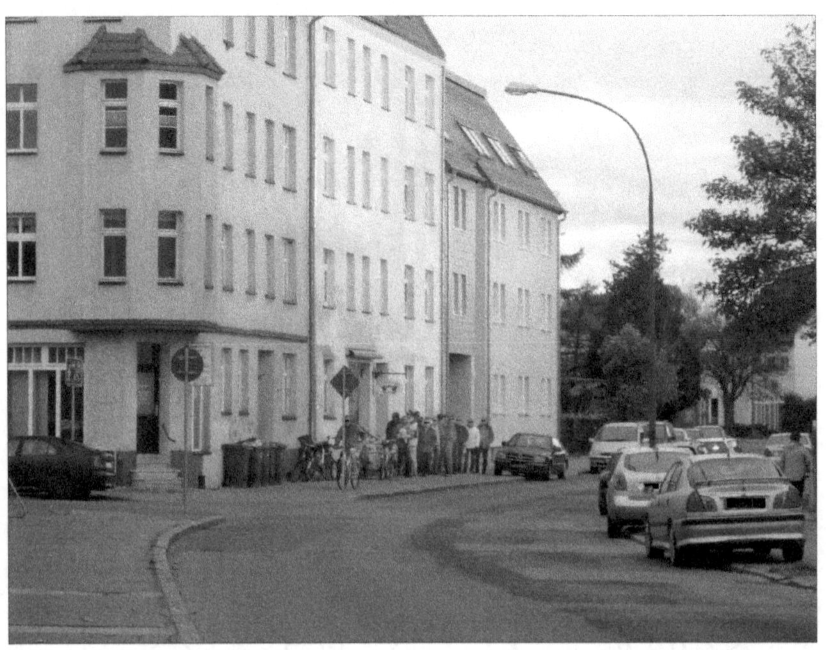

On the Essence and Significance of Time Agencies

Time Agencies are mostly located in small back streets, and, oftentimes, at first glance you won't even recognize them as time-agencies at all—there are no signs, no indication whatsoever of what they may be doing. In fact, often the sign of the former business is still hanging on the door: "Bakery," "Beverage Base," "Kiosk," "Household Goods," and so on. In these rooms, Time-Havers' extra-time is consumed and restructured so that they appear to be just like Time-Manglers, and therefore the former no longer have to suffer any embarrassing misunderstandings. Here time can be given away and/or consumed.

To have time, to simply have time, is something unusual, something offensive; it is not, so to speak, in keeping with the times. It is certainly something you want to avoid. Only those who have fallen out of time have a lot of it, standing around as they do on corners, sitting on park benches on sunny weekdays. Those who have time no longer belong and have to be watched: you have to be careful they don't steal your limited time or get in your way, for example, by walking too slowly or just standing around stupidly.

Just try asking on the phone "Can we meet up today around six p.m.?" You might think this is a simple question, but in response you'll most likely get "Oh, I don't know, I have to see if I have any appointments. I have so little time, you know."

Pensioners and children used to have all the time in the world. Those days are long gone. Pensioners in their third stage of life now hold honorary posts and keep themselves busy, they travel around within world history, go back to school, keep their bodies fit. And for children school is just one appointment among many others—ballet classes, private tutors, music, horseriding, therapy sessions, etc. Time is limited, and there is never enough of it.

Having time is considered a stigma. Beggars, those on unemployment, good-for-nothings—they all have time. The precarious class wastes time. Having time has become a social problem. Time-Havers are located apart from society; they eat poorly, do not exercise enough, are lazy, uneducated, have too many children, and are prone to committing violent acts, especially in the case of young Time-Havers. Other Time-Havers become depressed from having too much time to think and to brood and end up feeling that having so much time is a burden and that they themselves are outsiders. They become passive, sluggish creatures tormented by gloomy thoughts. Those who have time don't know what to do with it, because, were it otherwise, they wouldn't have time anymore.

The number of Time-Havers has grown worringly large. Unemployment is creating more and more Time-Havers and producing people who have more time than they can consume. This is the gap, the niche, within which Time Agencies operate. They are difficult to recognize—there are always long lines outside a good bakery, a butcher's shop, or a store with a sale going on, but it is impossible to see that people are lining up to get rid of time, to consume it, to unload their heavy Time-Ballast.

Every Time-Haver who is involved with a Time Agency has a schedule and must move

0.180g

accordingly. They are in constant movement and living life just like a Time-Mangler. They have to economize their time and regulate their Time-Consumption. In a time like the present, where mobility is the ultimate goal, the body must be in constant motion: we jog, cycle, climb mountains, are flexible and well-built, and every movement is filled with purpose.

One always has to adjust to the current understanding of time and be extremely flexibile so as not to miss any connections. New programs have to be learned; constant training adjusts one to this current time; lifelong learning is what is called for since we all know that what is learned today will be outdated tomorrow.

Time Agencies give Time-Havers meaning again by incorporating them back into time. They take away their available time in a meaningful and sophisticated manner. Critics of Time Agencies accuse them of being Time-Thieves who are simply interested in stealing others' time.

Time Agencies, on the other hand, see themselves as being at one with the times. They incorporate their members, subject them to Time-Management and a sophisticated Time-Economy, give them support, and guide them on to meaningful ways of Time-Planning and Time-Expenditure. Some truly dedicated Time-Havers even manage their Time-Deadlines through an organizer that is electronically synchronized with a computer on a daily basis.

Unnoticed by the majority of society, Time Agencies first spread throughout the states of the former East Germany but can now be found throughout all of Germany. They emerged from the initiative of Time-Havers. The first National Congress of Time Agencies was held in Essen in 2006, and that was where the coordination of Time Depositories was decided. Since the spring of 2007 there has been an International Association of Time Agencies, as word has spread the idea of Time Depositories to other countries where they have also been accepted and successfully implemented.

Literature:

Bernhard Kathan, *Herd Management and Queuing*, Innsbruck, 2008.

Friederike Thomas, *From Bakery to Time-Collector*, Stralsund, 2007.

0.197g

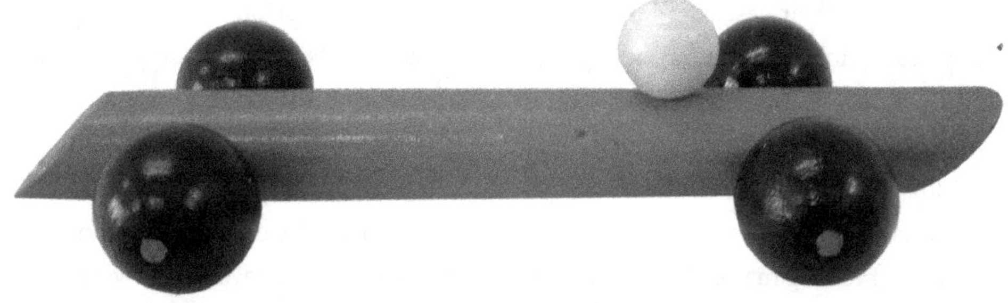

The Story of a Children's Race Car

By 1921 the Bolshevik government was fighting for its very survival. In the south the counter-revolutionary "whites"—supported by France, England, and the USA—continued to conquer ever more areas, while Japanese troops had landed in the east. But the worst thing was that the Bolsheviks had almost no support in their own country; the population simply watched their struggle with utter incomprehension.

Artists, who from the beginning had stood on the side of the revolution, were asked to dedicate themselves entirely to its service. They were to leave their easels and paint propaganda pictures instead. Actors were to go around the country visiting factories to spread the revolution's ideas. Agitprop trains were sent out into the countryside while ships and trucks were cheerfully decorated to win the people's support for the major changes underway. Never before or since have artists been so closely tied to politics. They gave the revolution everything they had. Leon Trotsky called for the entire artistic community to "cheer the popular imagination with actions and inextinguishably implant the idea of revolution into the memory of the people."

In the spring of 1922 at the 2nd Annual Congress of the State School for Art and Technical Studies (SATemas) founded in 1920, various artists' groups presented different works for the revolutionary transformation of everyday life. There was talk of revolutionary ceramics along with emblems for ministries and architectural designs (Tatlin's model of the monument to the Third International was also discussed). Again and again questions were raised as to what revolutionary daily life should look like and how revolutionary everyday objects were to be designed. Kazimir S. Malevich presented the first draft of his Suprematist Teapot (made in 1923 by the SPM). The central argument concerned the question as to whether new forms had to be functional, or if, on the contrary, revolutionary objects did not need to submit to functionality, in which case they would have to be stripped of it entirely so that one only paid attention to the interaction of the forms.

The strong group of supremacists around Malevich prevailed. From then on all objects without exception were to be made from the basic motifs of circle, square, rectangle, and triangle.

One work group, under Malevich's direction, collectively created a children's race car in which all the essences pertaining to the perspective of the revolution were to have been applied: simplicity of form, a reduction to the essential, to dynamics, and to the symbolism of colors.

The red of its body represented the power of the revolution and the black wheels, which were larger than the body, the force of the entire movement. The wheels' red centers showed that they simply followed the momentum of the revolutionary Volk, whereas the white head represented the infinity of the driver and the weightlessness in which future man would be able to move. The protests of those contributors who claimed that the colors were the exact same as the official ones of a southern German town were dismissed as suffering from petty-bourgeois anxiety.

Several copies of these racecars were made for the new experimental psychoanalytic kindergarten being opened in Moscow. The children's reactions to the new toy were observed and repeatedly reported back to the artists' committee for consideration. The racecar was praised as a successful example of the new form, was loved by the children, and recommended for production in large quantities.

But it never made it into series production. Late Stalinism banned almost all artistic ideas, including the racecar, and so it wandered, like so many other things, into a sealed archive in Moscow.

It was only in 1988, in the wake of perestroika and Glasnost under Gorbachev, that parts of the secret archives were opened, and the racing car discovered by art student Nataly Danko. Nataly was the granddaughter of Nataly Y. Danko who, along with her sister Elena Y. Danko, had participated in the Congress of 1922. In 1990 the racecar was finally put into production at the Toykombinat IV in Leningrad.

0.197g

Literature:

Nina Lobanov-Rostovsky, *Revolution Ceramics*, Basel, 1990.

Rosalda Nemilski, *The Function of Children's Toys*, Bremen, 1999.

0.198g

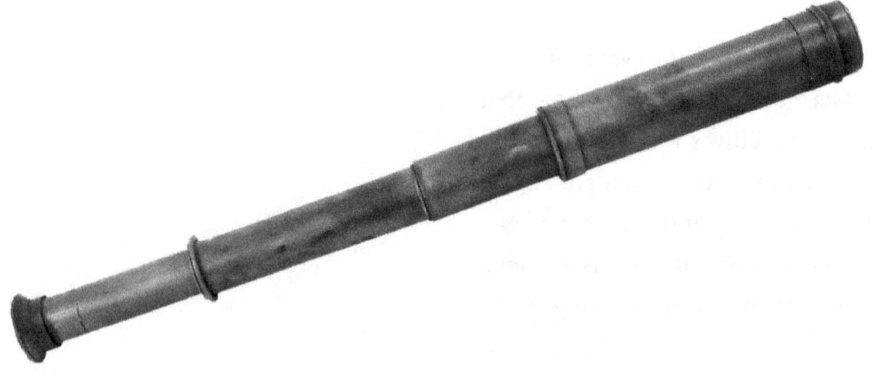

The Telescope of Columbus

or

How the First Exhibit in the Museum Came When the Museum Did Not Yet Exist

My father had given me five marks for the field trip, not a small amount of money at that time. My father was a concerned father who thought that his son should be well off, want for nothing, and, especially, never be hungry. It was the post-war era and, as in all post-war eras, the memory of hunger was still quite fresh in his mind. Whatever money I did not spend on food could be used to buy a souvenir or memento, a pendant or a miniature castle maybe, which later would remind me again and again of that beautiful and interesting excursion.

I was eleven years old and we were on a school trip to visit medieval castles. There were two parallel classes, each on one bus, accompanied by witty teachers concerned about both our discipline and that we not get lost. Our first destination was Teck Castle. Throughout the course of the day we stopped at other castles too, though I can't remember any of them.

Weeks earlier we had learned what knights were and how their castles were built; how defenders would pour down boiling pitch and sulfur on the attackers to drive them away, how the besiegers in turn would launch heavy stones and iron balls into the castle using catapults, how they would assault the gates with battering rams until they cracked and splintered and the castle could be conquered. In shop class we'd built just such an apparatus. With the help of my much more diligent father I built a battering ram with three chains; I was convinced that no gate, no matter how strong, could have withstood it, even if built by my father.

The buses stopped to let us children pee, eat, stretch our legs, and see the castle. Already from the first stop I'd had my eyes on a boy from the other bus who was continuously looking through a four-part, extendible telescope made of brass—a beautiful, old, and well-worn object. I saw how he handled it, how he'd show it off only to draw attention to himself, as if he were more important than the object itself. I noticed how carelessly and dishonorably he treated it.

How was I going to speak to him? I had no friends at school. All of my friends diappeared after the last school year of elementary school when, instead of advancing to the Gymnasium, I was kept back since my grades were not good enough and because I was to take over my father's retail business—and what a merchant needed was the ability to count, not Latin or Greek. I felt isolated and alone, and was afraid of the others, those bullies who shoved, pinched, and hit me—most often between my legs. How could I talk to the boy, how could I get closer to his telescope?

I felt that he didn't deserve it, or worse still, that he was putting it in danger. How could I set the telescope free? How could I save it from such unworthy treatment?

At one of the next stops I managed to get closer. I stood quietly and let all the others past me. When the boy showed up, I simply began to walk along next to him. The telescope was just two meters away from me. Up this close, my thought about the importance of the telescope was confirmed.

Using the five marks my father gave me I bought it from the unsuspecting, unworthy braggart. Today I no longer know how I managed to do it, but it was all so exciting. It was probably the courage of the desperate that gave me the strength to speak and to strike a deal with my five marks, the hard cash, for the ragged, old, chafed telescope. He got the money, I got the telescope. I remember not looking through it—that was not necessary, I knew what I had.

I turned it upside down, wrapped it in my barely used handkerchief, and put it carefully into my pocket. I remember how guiltly I felt, for the same feeling still arises whenever I see the telescope today. I felt like an impostor, for the boy did not know, indeed could not have known—being too ignorant—what he had just sold me for a measly five marks; what had been taken out of his hand, what I had wrangled out of him.

It was nothing less than the telescope Christopher Columbus had used to see America for the first time. I knew this for a fact, just as if I had been there when Columbus stood on the starboard railing on October 12, 1492, and heard the call from high up in the mast: "Land in sight!" I could see the slight smile that crossed his face. He could not express anything more than that, for the sailors would have interpreted it as a sign of weakness, and the danger of mutiny was omnipresent. But this one time, his smile, even if only a quick one, fit the occasion. He gave the order to keep ahead. Then he leaned slightly over the railing, took out his telescope—the one now located in my pocket—from his captain's jacket, pulled it gently, emotionally even, apart, focused it on his right eye, and looked. What he saw was America and America looked back. Then he took his sextant, calculated the longitude and latitude, went to the captain's cabin below deck, and wrote everything down. Captains always write everything down. He wrote that they had reached their destination—his destination—of India. Columbus did not know he had discovered America, of course; he thought that he had glimpsed India, but that doesn't matter, that can happen to anyone.

Only later, much later, back at home, did I look through the telescope. I didn't see America either, or India for that matter, just our neighbor's garden. But that was to be expected too.

Many decades later I founded The Museum of Unheard (of) Things and, when I set up the depository, the first item I hung on the wall was "The Telescope of Columbus."

When I came back from the field trip, I proudly showed the telescope to my father the merchant. I presented him my great, precious treasure that I had bought with his five marks. He shook his head, both concerned and perplexed, and said, "Every day a fool stands up and one has to do business with them." Then he turned around and left. It took a long time for me to understand what he meant, but what I understood at once was that he and I just could not understand each other, and that if that was the way a merchant thought, I would never become one myself.

Literature:

BWL, *Bavarian Economics*, Munich, 1966.
Hans Eberle, *A Distant Land*, Memmingen, 1952.

0.206g

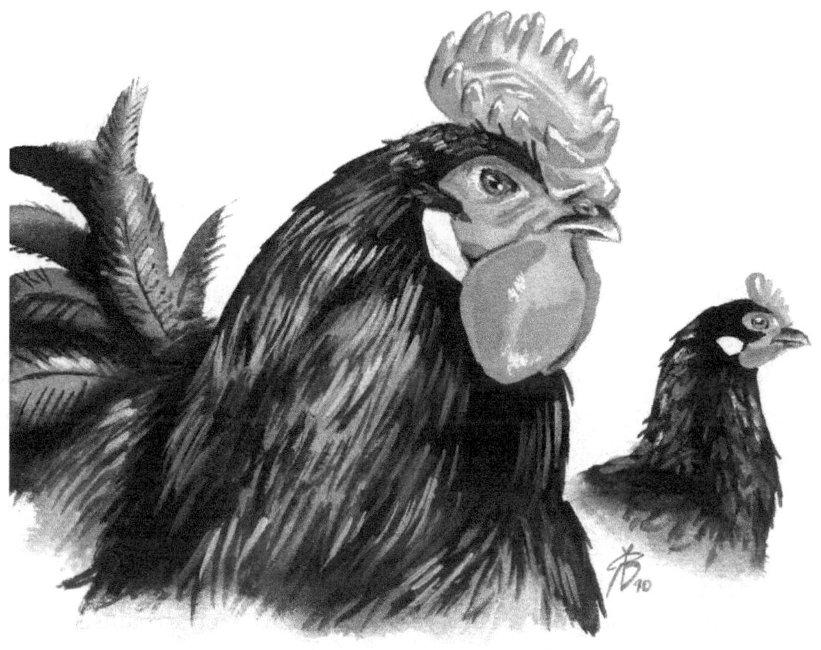

The Augsburg Chicken

In the summer of 2004 art-biologist Gunda Rose Sprengel discovered an uncatalogued plant during a survey of local fauna in northeastern Mongolia. This plant—a rampant, green, ground-covering plant that massively repressed any competing ones—was not welcomed by the local population, for it was a weed that greatly hindered garden farming. In her survey of the population about how they dealt with this annoying plant, G. R. Sprengel was repeatedly told about black chickens that eagerly pecked away at the plants thus creating a "clean" soil in which the locals could then plant their gardens. G. R. Sprengel was then shown the chickens: they had dusty blue, black-rimmed feathers, and a head crowned by large, beautifully red, beaker-shaped combs.

0.206g

She interrupted her return trip several times in order to stop at villages along the Trans-Siberian Railroad to investigate bio-ethnographic viewpoints. She repeatedly encountered these black chickens with red beaker-shaped combs. In the city of Karsnouralsk at the western end of the Ural Mountains the appearance of this type of chicken ceased abruptly. However, in the late autumn of 2004, Gunda Rose Sprengel found this very same chicken at a chicken breed show in Berlin. In front of the chicken-cage was a red sign with a yellow exclamation mark:

! The Augsburg Chicken !
Category I (extreme risk of extinction)
Society for the Preservation of Old and Rare Breeds

In 1880 Julius Mayer, a chicken farmer from Augsburg-Haustetten, crossbred a La-Flèche rooster with a Lamotte hen. The result was a medium-weight chicken with a broad chest and a more edible and tender meat; in addition, it was between 2.3 to 3 kilograms heavier, produced up to 180 white eggs, and had a weak breeding instinct. The chicken was quite robust and had dark, dusty blue feathers lined with black. The leg-ring size was 18 milimeters for the rooster and 16 milimeters for the hen. What was special about this chicken was that the red horn-like crest of the La-Flèche rooster had evolved into a large, beautiful, proud, beaker-shaped comb. Both the French La-Flèche rooster, together with the Italian-bred Lamotte, originally stemmed from the Spanish Minorca chicken that comes from the area of Santo Domingo de la Calzada.

When thinking of a name for his new chicken breed Julius Mayer first considered "Mayer Chicken," then "Haunstetten Chicken," but eventually settled on nearby Augsburg and so called it the "Augsburg Chicken." (Haunstetten was later incorporated into Augsburg on July 1, 1972).

At the third annual Swabian Chicken Breed Show of 1882 in Günzburg, the Augsburg Chicken aroused great interest. Julius Mayer sold six strains of 1-3 each (one rooster, three hens), and went home happily with twenty-five preorders. Subsequently, the chicken spread rapidly throughout the Bavarian-Swabian region.

The farmer Joseph Schnaiter from Uterkirnach in the Black Forest had dropped by the chicken breed show in 1882 while visiting his cousin Gertraud in Ulm and taken home a strain of the Augsburg Chickens. Thanks to him, thereafter the Black Forest became the second most important center for the dissemination of the Augsburg Chicken.

In the Black Forest at that time the style of traditional clothing was beginning to change: the once-colorful costumes were being replaced by plain black vestments and, of the former, only the colorful headdresses, Chappi ribbons, and tuft remained. Many Black Forest residents saw a resemblance between their black clothes and big, red hats and the Augsburg Chickens (which, as previously mentioned, also had black gowns and red headdresses) and therefore happily welcomed the latter.

Over the following decades the Augsburg Chicken spread throughout Germany. In terms of regional centers, farm-animal historians talk about the so-called "Lower Saxony Bars." These are the villages of Natendorf, Dörmte, Polau, Zarenthien, and the Wendland villages of Waddeweitz and Küsten. Each of these towns had Augsburg Chickens and together they formed a kind of a strip through the Low German Plain. Other centers were Rochwitz in Dresden, Martinsbuch in Lower Bavaria, and Braunsberda in Leipzig.

The chicken was highly valued as a livestock and show chicken. What is today considered as a special defect or as the primary problem of breeding—which was precisely why the Augsburg Chicken was placed in Category I of endangered breeds of domestic animals—was then seen as a positive characteristic: the beaker-shaped comb is a split trait!

Statistically, in the mating of two Augsburg Chickens, there is a 25% chance for horn-shaped combs and a 25% chance for single combs; only 50% will develop beaker-shaped combs. Many of the beaker-shaped combs are not closed at the rear, others are non-uniform, and some are just too high so that they fall to the side and thus do not satisfy the strict competition requirements.

At one time this only bothered a few chicken farmers, as there was not yet a breed serving double duty as both farm and beauty chicken. While a particularly successful hen or a handsome and proud rooster could excel at breed shows, the others could be used as livestock without any special considerations or concerns; meaning, in this case, turned into food.

The Augsburg Chicken experienced its greatest dissemination a few years after the end of the devastating Nazi era. Under the leadership of the first Bavarian Prime Minister, Dr. Hans Ehard, the newly established Bavarian State Government quickly realized that the Augsburg Chicken was the only Bavarian chicken breed that corresponded to the new Federal German standard of chickens. By promoting this Bavarian race, the Bavarian State Government was able to strengthen its position in the newly combined Federal Republic as well as demonstrate its independence as a Free State, thus emphasizing Bavaria's uniqueness.

The Bavarian government awarded generous subsidies, organized competitions with rich rewards, and offered grants to all the owners of Augsburg Chickens, so that this race of chickens flourished throughout Bavaria. Soon there was no Bavarian village, no matter how small, where at least one farmer did not have a few Augusburg Chickens. Indeed, in some contemporary caricatures one can see the black hen cuddling with the Bavarian lion. In

0.206g

southern Germany, on April 1, 1958, newspapers printed an April Fools message stating that Bavaria intended to replace the lion in their emblem with the chicken, and that the Free State would soon begin negotiations with France in the hopes of becoming part of that country.

In the mid-to-late 1960s, the situation changed rapidly. Up until then the chickens had pecked through kitchen waste, searched the ground for roots and insects, and in the spring been given extra treats. In those years the children happily gathered junebugs, which they would throw to the chickens who in turn would greedily crack and swallow them down. Their eggs were taken every day, which they did not seem to mind, and every now and then one of them disappeared under the ax; not a few just before the holidays.

However, at some point in the 1960s, anonymous and cold chickens wrapped up in plastic suddenly began to appear in the supermarkets. At first, people were quite skeptical about these cold, hard chickens. Many families organized tastings comparing the cheap, cold, and shrinkwrapped chickens to the ones which had been freshly slaughtered, finding the difference to be rather slight; the former were cold but much cheaper than the latter. Thus, the anonymously packaged chicken quickly began to become more popular.

Augsburg Chickens were not suitable for pure chicken meat production, since they were too stubborn and claimed more space than was available in the cages. There were more amenable breeds for the narrower cages and these proved easier to pluck by machines, they laid more eggs to be taken by conveyor belts, and were satisfied with simple fishmeal. This meant that fully commercial chicken farmers could not use the Augsburg Chicken. The beautiful chicken's genetic trait now had a negative effect—indeed, what was one to do with a whole flock of chickens that did not have the beautiful, red, beaker-shaped comb? Furthermore, government subsidies were removed, though Bavaria was able to maintain its independence as free state. Funding now flowed into those chicken farms that produced industrially and innovative chickens for the rapidly developing grill market. The conditions of existence for the Augsburg Chickens rapidly melted away.

In the German Democratic Republic caged chickens were used on a large scale to fulfill demand, but some agricultural cooperatives bred Augsburg Chickens for political reasons. These chickens were of a particularly beautiful blue so that today they exist in two color variations and at shows are evaluated at double the price. The eastern Augsburg Chicken regularly won prizes at international shows and repeatedly made the western chicken look miserable and withered. In addition to the mass keeping of caged chickens, the "Pure Joy" cooperative in Leipzig specialized in the breeding of black chickens. Most of the international prizes they scooped up showed the East's clear superiority over the West, even in such a marginal seeming sector like the breeding of the Augsburg Chicken.

In 1972 the "Pure Joy" cooperative presented their Augsburg Chickens at the agricultural All-Unions-Exhibition of socialist countries held in Kiev. Juri Chechi from a collective farm near the district town Krasnouralsk—a temporary stop on the Trans-Siberian Railroad route located in the foothills of the Western Urals—acquired twenty-five chickens, five male and twenty female. This was the great leap for Julius Mayer's Augsburg Chickens into the deep east where they would embark upon an unexpected, and occult, career.

After German reunification, the chicken species in the German Democratic Republic were almost completely destroyed; people were interested in the "Golden West" and the German mark, and not in the old regime whatsoever. The agricultural cooperatives were passed over, or had to start over from scratch; nothing helped them, for cooperatives were now unpopular, painful, and unnecessary ruins, which was also true of the former "Pure Joy." Still, despite the rapid expansion of privately owned chicken farms, some of the old collectives managed to hold out, though their number decreased every year.

Thus, there are only a few remaining specimens. In fact, they are so rare that afficianados have taken to searching for them on the internet. One or two strains can still be found in some "Ark" farms, which specialize in endangered domestic animal species. Until recently, a Farm Museum in Illerbeuren in the Allgäu region had a strain of Augsburg Chickens. These chickens were the pride of the museum; but early one evening, they were unfortunately caught by a hungry fox.

However, a variation of the GDR chickens had spread completely unnoticed throughout Russia. Starting from Krasnouralsk, the Augsburg Chickens had wandered east through the small, private, village-to-village trade along with the regional transport of Trans-Siberian Railroad. Some of them mingled with indigenous chickens, but the dominant Augsburg genotype always prevailed, with the result that the Augsburg Chicken can now be observed as far away as Mongolia.

At the instigation of Gunda Rose Sprengel, a research team under the leadership of Professor Inge Licht of Humboldt University in Berlin examined the spread of domestic animal breeds along railway lines. The title of the DFG-funded project was "Interdisciplinary research on the spread of livestock from trainstation to trainstation, on the basis of evidence of the spread of the Central European minimized moth with the help of the railway network."

0.206g

Literature:

P. Hammer, *The Way of the Chicken as a Civilizing Process*, Dissertation Press, Göttingen, 2004.

O. Ott, *The Chicken as a Mirror of Agriculture*, Illerbeuren, 2002.

N. Platzbecker, *The Great Poultry Standard in Color* (3 Volumes), Reutlingen, 2000.

T. Sperl/W. Schwarz, *Raising Chickens for Anyone*, Reutlingen, 1999.

D. Sprengel, "Surprises on Field Trips," in: *Contributions to Excursion Research*, Berlin, 2005.

E. Verdoef/A. Rijs, *Chicken Encyclopedia*, Utting am Amersee, 2002.

0.207g

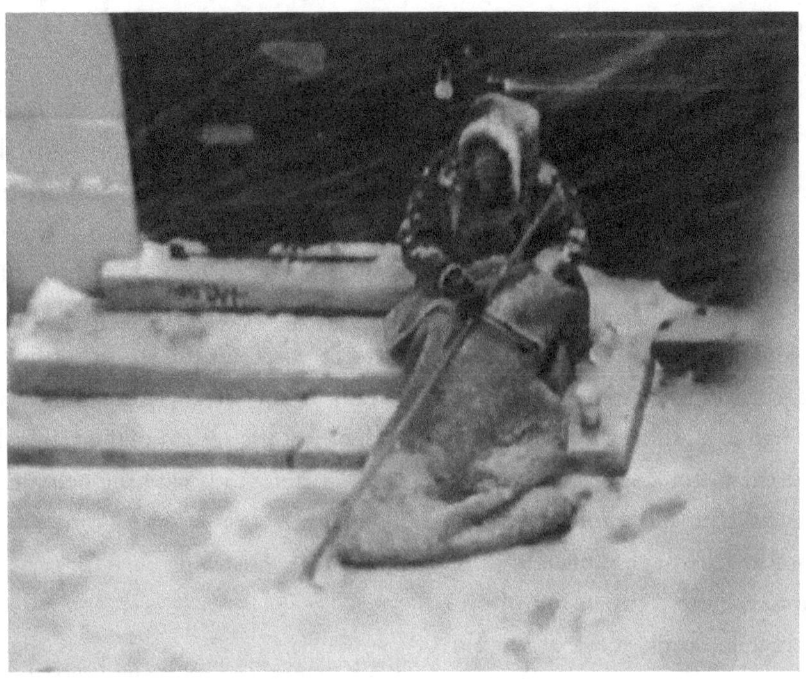

Training Seminar at Klein & Young, New York: A Film by Günter Eisenhardt

0.207g

Klein & Young is a highly sought-after, international agency for creative management. Their slogan simply reads: "Shape Your Mind and You Shape the World." At Klein & Young not only can one book a seven-day long creative survival training course in the wilderness in order to explore, learn, and strengthen the limits of one's being, but one can also live for five days as a beggar in New York City in a training course entitled "Service is Power in Indignity."

Based on the practices of the Buddhist Fun Kno Luh Monastery school where monks are required to become beggars for long periods of time in order to acquire power over themselves and their needs, course participants must perform exercises of subordination, humility, and "non-existence."

These classes are usually fully booked for years in advance and are among the most expensive, as well as being regarded as the most effective, classes in the entire program at Klein & Young.

The experience of going through five days of non-active acts usually makes top-class executives conscious of their ever-present, inevitable finitude. Furthermore, the subsequent four-day evaluation of the experience leads the vast majority of participants to highly effective action and thought. In particular, an increase in the ability to assert things has been reported. G. Eisenhardt filmed all the participants with a hidden camera.

The five days spent sitting at the roadside, begging for alms, being exposed to the weather, driving away dogs, and being ignored leaves its mark on each and every participant. This experience of "existing-no-more" troubles and disturbs all participants, especially during the first few days.

This unrest is the basis of learning—to learn that power lies in indignity, to awaken it, and to recognize its validity. Through this humiliating non-attention, attention is reclaimed, force is applied, and learning is accomplished. This passive sitting, this non-behaving and acting, the act of letting people pass back and forth—and thereby becoming the true master of events—is the very aim of the course. The person crouching at the roadside becomes the master of a guilty conscience. He controls the shame of the passers-by and can thus operate very actively indeed. The act of sitting on the roadside in the dust—that helplessness teaches him that he who humbles himself controls others' conscience, occupies their morals, and from that position of power has more influence on them than mere superficial, formal action. Precisely when these anonymous others pass by without paying any attention at all to any of these students, or even confront them aggressively, they above all show themselves to be on the defensive and, similarly, subjected to the person sitting there. The goal of the course is to learn this power to control one's conscience as well as the feelings of others and to act upon them.

After learning about these manager courses, the Fun Kno Luh Monastery wanted to have a court order issued that would prohibit their exercise. They explained their concern saying that their techniques were not dedicated to efficiency, or to the increase of wealth and other worldly goods, but only to serve inner illumination and recognition of the Buddha. Klein & Young for their part argued that their courses were also only for people's internal illumination, and that the goal was in the attainment of the participant's inner freedom. Whatever these people went on to do later, however, was not Klein & Young's responsibility.

Klein & Young won.

Literature:
A. Kran, *Managers and Their Responsibility*, Frankfurt, 2001.

0.212g

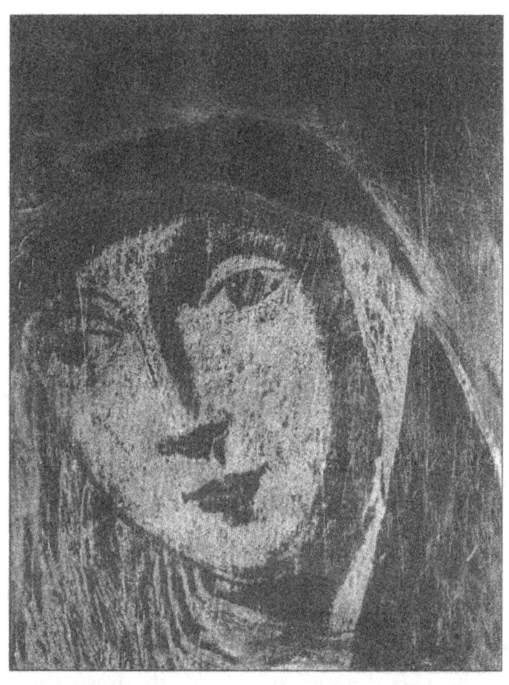

How a Photographic Image Venerated to This Day Was Created Thirty Years before the Invention of Photography

or

How Two Lovers Were Unable to Find Each Other

There are many accounts in literature concerning two lovers who simply do not come together. Some are not allowed (Romeo and Juliet), while others have been affected by magic (Orlando Furioso and Angelica). There are those whose love is so intense that the beloved may not even exist (Petrarch and Laura), or will only be met in paradise (Dante and Beatrice). And then there are still others who are joined in death out of sheer affection (Heinrich von Kleist and Henriette Vogel), or those for whom the object of love is simply too difficult to reach, being, in the end, his or her own ego (Narcissus).

And then, sometimes, what is described in literature is more harmless than what actually happens in reality.

At the end of the eighteenth century in Tyrol there lived two young people who loved each other, but who were forever to remain apart. The boy was from the wealthy city of Innsbruck, and the girl resided just a short walk away from the village of Absam. Georg Johannes Stebenbauer, the son of the painter Johannes Friedhelm Stebenbauer, was nineteen years old when he first saw eighteen-year-old Rosina Bucher at a well during a trip to Absam with his father.

Father and son had been taking a hike to indulge in picturesque nature studies, as, at the time, it was fashionable to draw and paint from nature. Rulers were demanding more and more landscapes so as to be able to recognize their surroundings, while at the same time augment their perspectives with a bit of Italian flair. And so, father and son were busy honing their skills to meet just such a demand.

The two were sitting near the well and looking at the mountains of the northern ridge that stood between the farmhouses when Georg Johannes suddenly saw a stunningly beautiful girl. He could see a long brown skirt and a dark green stole, a piece of white blouse sticking out at the top of her neck, and a glimpse of hair (which actually could only be imagined, as it was covered by a modest headscarf that framed her petite, but still peasant, face) as she went to the well to scoop up some water.

She noticed the young stranger's gaze, tilted her head, formed a slight smile, and turned away before a blush crossed her face. "Who are these two men? No doubt they must be from Innsbruck. Recently town folk have been coming to our village ever more often. What are they doing with paper across their legs? Are they drawing? How handsome the younger one is! How properly he turned his eyes away from me when they met mine." With these thoughts in mind she drew her two jugs of water from the well, and then went back, blushing more and more, towards her home. She briefly looked back at them one last time before turning to the path that led to her house. She saw the beautiful boy look away again and knew that he had been looking at her. Indeed, he was sitting in a place that conveniently allowed his eyes to accompany her all the way up to her house.

Once back in Innsbruck Georg Johannes tried to revive the phenomenon at the well by creating many drawings from memory.

His longing to see her again grew stronger and stronger, and so a few days later he went back to Absam. He walked in circles three times, and the fourth time he positioned himself very close to the well. He began to draw the path where she had last gone, and as he looked up to get perspective with his pen, saw her coming down the road.

At first she hesitated. "There he is again, just as I anticipated. But now I do not want to go—will it be chaste to appear before him? And what is he doing there? I just want to fetch some water. Will I manage to ignore him?"

Once there, he stood beside her and she him. He spoke to her so decently and in such a mannered way that she was indeed able to remain chaste and nevertheless exchange a few words with him.

She usually came when the sun had reached the rear of the church, she told him. Now he knew how to meet her, and so began to thoroughly exploit the opportunity.

It was only on his fifth or sixth visit that he dared to ask if he could make a painting of her. "Well, it would be inappropriate, but you can so long as I do not notice." He paused for a moment to think, and then asked if he could indeed capture her reflection. He would hold a reflective paper against her window; all she would have to do was look at it without moving, just as she so often did when looking dreamily out of the same window. The image, reflected there on the paper, could then be claimed as his own.

Together with a friend, Georg Johannes had long been making experiments with chemical liquids that reacted to light. This time, however, he wanted to try something new. They had already managed to capture small images using light on paper. But could they create a mirror image on a piece of paper?

On the afternoon of January 17, 1797, when no one was at home as had been planned, he stood in front of her window with a strong piece of paper that had been soaked in refined and caustic substances. He attached the paper to the fourth upper part of the right panel of the 7 x 5" crown glass window and smoothed it out. Then he waited.

For a long time, sewing needles in hand as always, she looked dreamily into her own reflection. A quarter of an hour, a half an hour, or a whole? He took the nearly dried paper away, wiped the glass meticulously clean, and looked at her one last time through the window. Then he hurried home, washed the paper with various materials, rubbed it with an acrid fixing paste, and hung it up to dry, waiting for the moment when her face would appear. But nothing happened.

After a week of waiting in which he did nothing but try in different ways to wrest the image from the paper, his courage finally failed him. Rubbed away from all the treatments it had undergone, the paper grew thinner. There was nothing left to do. He decided to go upon his way to Absam to confess his failure.

0.212g

The village was atremble. Religious people hurried back and forth, talking excitedly. Georg asked a nun of Perpetual Adoration from a nearby cloister what was going on. She looked at him in surprise and asked how he could not know. Here, on the seventeenth day of the month, just over a week ago, the Virgin Mary, our dearest Virgin, Mother of the Lord Jesus, had appeared in the house of the Buchers late in the afternoon, around four o' clock. The highly gifted Rosina was now on everyone's lips. Rosina, the chosen one, at first had not believed it and had tried to wipe the image off of the window, but before it was barely gone, it reappeared. Passing peasants saw her attempts and immediately realized that it was Mary who had appeared there. The priest they summoned confirmed that this was indeed the pure image of the Blessed Virgin and knelt down before it. The ever-so-modest Rosina could not believe it and denied it. Again and again she repeated "It cannot be—no, it is not so." She simply could not believe the Holy Virgin had appeared to her. Everyone understood her confusion and expressed great compassion; after all, she was the one to whom the sacred image had appeared.

The agitated nun wanted to move on, but Georg Johannes kept her a bit longer and breathlessly asked what was going to happen to the girl. She told him how at the convent there was much debate as to who should get her. Five claims had been sent to the bishop, all requesting to receive the chosen one, for each convent wanted to adorn itself with the one who had been chosen to see the mother of God. Then the nun pulled herself away and hurried off.

Georg Johannes went back to Innsbruck in despair. What was he supposed to do? If he recounted what had really happened, no one would believe him and he would be accused of heresy, pride, and deception. How would he ever see her again? The guilt of having condemned her to being immured behind the high monastery walls through his actions tormented him. How could he ever be happy again? A gnawing pain began to eat away at him.

Six months later, Georg Johannes left Innsbruck. Evidence suggests that he went to Augsburg, but that he did not stay there for long. Then his path becomes difficult to follow. It is said that he appeared in St. Petersburg, but it is also reported that he set sail for America from Nantes. In any event, after Augsburg, all traces of him disapppear.

The glass with the etched image, however, was brought to Innsbruck for examination. It was inspected by the high clergy, analyzed by enlightened scientists, washed, scraped, and treated with alkali. And yet, nothing happened. The image remained. No one had ever experienced such a thing, and it was decided that, depending on one's belief, it could be seen as either a curiosity or a wondrous appearance. After much discussion they decided that it should not be made into a big deal, but simply recognized as a regional miracle.

In a solemn procession, the image of Rosina was taken into the Baroque village church in Absam. Today the village church is a sanctuary where the image can be seen to the right side of the altar and worshipped or simply admired.

At first there was no tear in the Venerable Maria's eye. This only appeared three years later. On the day Rosina was married to Jesus, they took away her worldly name and after a perpetual vow she assumed the name Maria Walburga and renounced the world. And upon that very day a tear appeared in her image, and it was immediately considered to be the sign of yet another great miracle.

Literature:

The Miraculous Image of Our Lady of Absam in Tyrol, Prayer Cards, Unspecified.

R. Hinrichsen, *Pilgrimages: An Adventure*, Innsbruck, 1999.

Th. Neulicher, *What's Behind It?*, Munich, 1967.

P. Neufer, *What's Behind the Walls?*, Vienna, 1939.

0.214g

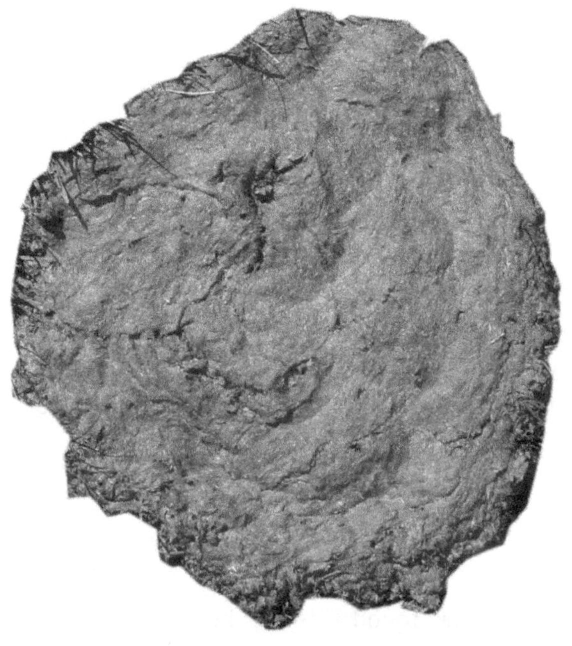

The Power and Mystery of the Cow Pie: On a Cow-Pie-Worshipping Community That Withdrew to the Engadine Valley, In Order to Establish a Cow Pie Cult but Failed

It all began when a group of three men commenced building a hut far back in the valley at 1,800 meters above sea level. Or rather, with the building of a cattle shed that they could live in from the materials they had there at hand. The three had come up from Monte Verità, the "Mountain of Truth," which at that time attracted many intellectuals, dissidents, anarchists, mystics and reformers to the area of Ascona in the Swiss Ticino. Up on that mountain with its magnificent view of the Lake Maggiore a new, different style of life was being attempted. Vegetarianism, naked dancing, love that transcended the division of genders, the worshiping of new gods…everything was possible up there and captivated many who wanted to be different than the rest of the evil, boring, and unjust world around them.

Most of their contemporaries found this public reform of lifestyles shocking and were rather hostile towards it, considering it the work of the devil. And yet, for others like Hans Gerd Schuber, Peter van Hungen, and Lydia Labser, life there was too slack, too populist, and not consistent enough. And so they split off and formed their own commune far away in the upper valley of Chöglias, just below the Fimber Pass. The way they saw it, the pass, that ancient, prehistoric conjunction between the Engadine and the Paznaun, would carry their thoughts and their love for the cows, and for cow pies, out into the world.

Cows had already been considered sacred in ancient Egypt. Hathor, the goddess of love, peace, beauty, art and music, was a cow and sheltered the sun through the night. And the great Hindu god Krishna had spent his childhood among cows. The cow was the embodiment of earth, of nourishment. In all ancient mythologies one ultimately encounters a cow. Even in old Norse mythology the cow was at the top of everything. She was known as Audumla, the creation cow, and she lived when nothing else did, at a time when even the gods did not exist. She was the beginning and from her four teats rivers of milk flowed to feed the giant Ymir and his sons. In the absence of anything else, she even licked an ice block made of salt for nourishment.

The three called themselves "Audumlaists," and survived—freezing and shivering—the first winter of 1910-11 up there in the rear valley. They kept their feet warm by stuffing them into cow dung, stuffed the windy cracks in the hut with half-dried cow dung, smeared cow dung on the walls to insolate them, and heated their oven with dried cow dung. In this fashion they became more and more intimate with the cow dung, and realized that the cow was not only an animal that nourished all of creation through her milk, but that her shit was also beneficial, not only for humans, but also for the meadows, where, thanks to the cow, more things were growing than before. The cow gave more than she took. They were increasingly certain that it was the dung of the primeval cow Audumla that enabled life. From her dung sprang life. Her manure was the beginning.

Soon thereafter they realized that the shape of cow pies corresponded to the Indian mandala, and henceforth began to worship the cow for her droppings in the form of cow pies too.

The following summer Julie von der Mühlen, Jakob and Peter Grülen, and Peter

Machig joined the group. They built another cow shed to live in. During that summer over a hundred pilgrims came to visit and experience the new doctrine. Outside, beyond the valley, word spread and articles were published in the relevant journals stating that, far back in the Engadin Valley, an association had been formed which had discovered the true mythology of all mythologies, the singular point from which everything flowed, the very source of all things. Every search for the meaning of life ended in cow dung. Therein lay the core of all mythologies: Being originates in cow pies.

The next winter was particularly mild, but once again the Audumlaists spent it with cow pies on the walls, across their feet, and drying out in the oven.

During the summer of 1912 almost 300 pilgrims came to the rear valley, and many of them sought the cow pie as a devotional object. Down where the valley began Jakob Grülen and Julie von der Mühlen constructed a hay hut as a devotional-object store where they sold cow pies, cow-pie water, cow-pie elixir, and watercolor pictures of cow pies. A palmist from Munich often stayed with them and pointed out auspicious shapes and smells within the pies. He maintained that every man and every woman had a pie that uniquely corresponded to them.

One day, however, a terrible quarrel broke out in the commune. Some wanted the pure doctrine to be developed further in peace, claiming that it was still in its infancy, while others wanted to financialize the process and go on selling. This led to the emergence of fractions, exclusion requests, various schemes, etc. The following winter came, and they agreed to overwinter together. The winter of 1912-13 was a very hard and cold one. On December 28, five communards, emaciated and frozen blue, came down from the valley to Sent and asked for accommodation. They reported avalanches, terrible cold, too little fuel, further arguments among the groups, and that the two main contending parties were eager to stay there in order to not leave the place to the other.

Only in early April did it become possible to reach the rear valley. A group of experienced mountain farmers set out on the road. When they returned, with them in their carriage they had two bodies that had been frozen together. They said that they had found these famished, conjoined bodies one on top of the other in a hut, and that they had not been able to separate them. In the heated farmhouse room, the bodies were defrosted and released from each other. The police took on the case and handed over the bodies to the families, which were then transferred to respective cities to Germany.

Rumors about the whole tragedy quickly spread throughout the reform movement, and soon no one talked about the power of cow pies anymore. The beginning of World War I then obliterated every other concern so that, today, almost no one knows anything about the mystique and power of the cow pie at all.

0.214g

Literature:

Bernhard Liebkirchen, *The Cow and Its Droppings*, Munich, 1973.

Tilo Tom, *Oh, Beautiful Engadine*, Chur, 1987.

Renate Zumriß, *Ways, Wrong Ways, Ways Out: On the History of the Reform Movement*, Zurich, 1984.

0.248g

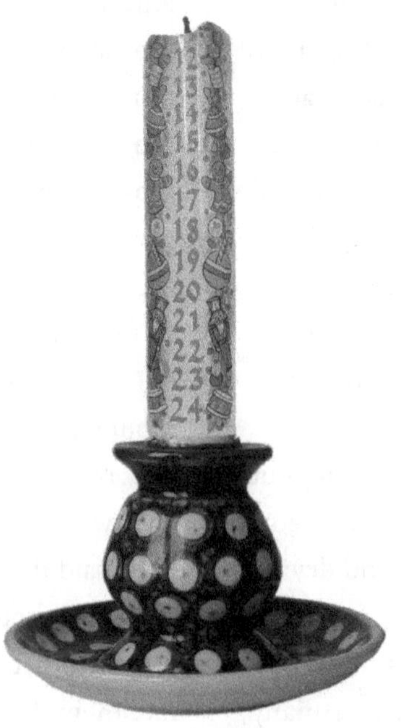

The Watchmaker Johannes Meiner's Twenty-Four Hour Candle

or

On the Struggle for the Right Time

At 11:16 on May 13, 1997, the candle on his bedside table was blown out. He had wanted it that way. A request which his son, who had accompanied him throughout this, his final hour, granted. He had wanted at least to place a sign within time. A sign like the period that ends a great novel.

The extinguishing of his candle, the last of what were known as his time-candles, was to coincide with the very point, the very moment, his earthly existence ended.

Johannes Meiner was born in the Swabian town of Überlingen on March 5, 1908. His father was a watchmaker, and his mother Christa worked in a laundry. Johannes was his parents' third and last child, but the first boy. He became an orphan at the age of eight when his father did not return from the war. Whether a gas mask leak or a shot in the heart, what felled him was to remain forever unclear.

Johannes's father Helmut, Master Watchmaker, had been a follower of the banned Reform-era Swiss watchmaker Marcel Rödiger, who had escaped prosecution by entering into exile in America.Johannes Meiner learned how his father made clocks and, guided by his mother's stories about him, at an early stage began to concern himself with the essence of time, its sense, and its meaning.

For Johannes, time was something faint and flowing and could not be represented by a stroke. It was not something that passed rhythmically, noisily and hard, but without any ticking, softly, quietly. And so from already quite an early age he sought a time opposed to that which simply jumped from one point to the next.

He began to work on a linear concept of time. He did not desire any New Time, nor any re-articulation of it as many of his colleagues did. What he wanted was a different representation of time altogether. Again and again he called for a different conception of time, for it not to be understood by the clock, but to be thought of completely anew. Johannes preached that time was only a human conception and, as such, tied to life, but that outside of human life there was no time. Man as a creature needed time, and indeed he lived within it.

In many cultures life was symbolized by light and rightfully so, for light was responsible for life. Without light there can be no life—eternal darkness is the same as death. Thus, these cultures also believed that time stood still at night, and feared that if the sun were to rise no more, darkness and death would be victorious.

0.248g

On the basis of such considerations, Johannes said to himself that only light could truly represent our lives—that is, time. Thereafter he strove to find a Light Time, a representation of time through light.

Since ancient times candles had been the dispellers of darkness. For Johannes they were therefore ideal for representing time: in their tapering time would be both converted to light and simultaneously represented in a flowing, quiet, and warm manner, which would no longer be measurable because of the basis of its very nature.

Johannes retired from watchmaking in 1970. His wife, who until then had run the store selling watches, no longer wanted to stand behind the counter. Arthritis had made it impossible for her to continue, and orders had begun to dwindle in the face of digital watches that required no master watchmakers. Indeed, Johannes's son chose an entirely different path altogether, and became an elementary school teacher.

Now, as a retiree, however, Johannes Meiner finally had time to completely devote himself to his own time. He found an understanding partner in the similarly retired candlemaker, five years his senior, Hubertus Treuherz, to develop candles that represented time.

Among people who concerned themselves with time, the watchmaker Johannes Meiner and the candlemaker Hubertus Treuherz soon became known as competent time-researchers with a not uninteresting approach.

0.248g

In 1978 the two appeared with great success at the Time-Congress in the Dutch city of Groningen and presented their candles. They now possessed the following types: day-candles, month-candles, week-candles, even tiny minute-candles and immense year-candles. The wax was precisely dosed and equipped with a newly developed wick that allowed for their accurate and controlled burning. Numbers were attached to the candles, which they called Time-Figures, and corresponded to the appropriate time designation. Most of the candles were decorated and therefore pretty as well as decorative.

For quite some time, however, the Time-Candles caused consternation in Catholic circles as people wondered, "Did not the eternal flame, that ever-burning oil flame, also mean eternal life?"

In 1985 Johannes's wife Martha died unexpectedly. His colleague and fellow researcher Hubertus also became increasingly curmudgeonly and forgetful and in 1987 had to be placed in a nursing home. Soon thereafter he could no longer recognize either Johannes or his own wife, and a little while after that forgot about time altogether. He thus found himself in a timeless state to which no other man had access.

In the years to come Johannes Meiner's life became ever quieter. He had only a few time-candles left, and he used them sparingly.

When at eighty-nine years of age, by that time bedridden, he finally began to grow weaker—breathing had already become a struggle—he asked for his remaining candles to be lit. He simply wanted to see how those last candles of his would burn, how the light—that is, his life—would slowly begin to take leave.

As the flame began to consume the eleven of that twenty-four-hour candle—his final one—Johannes slowly turned his head to the side and closed his eyes forever. Then, as promised, his son blew the candle out.

Literature:

Congress Logs, Gronigen, 1978

M. Ketzing, *The Changing Time*, Munich, 1998.

W. Müller-Funk (Eds.), *Time, Myth, Phantom, Reality*, Vienna/New York, 2000.

0.251g - 1.000g

0.265g

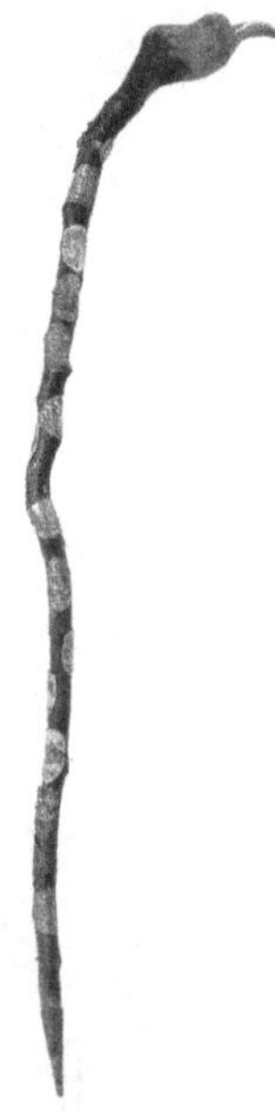

On Jakob Wachter's Missing Stick Badge

or

On Love

In the spring of 2012 a young woman brought an old hiking stick to the museum in order to donate it to our collection. I almost never accept things from "outside," since they do not typically fit in with the concept of my literary cabinet of curiosities. Therefore at first I balked at exhibiting the old hiking stick with its many stick badges. However, the young woman then told me its curious story, which I shall relate here.

The stick is missing one stick badge, one of those little, tin souvenirs that are the pride and joy of so many hikers, demonstrating that they have indeed traveled to a place, a fact testified by the image on the nailed souvenirs. The missing stick badge had never been nailed to the hiking stick—it had been a burial gift for the young woman's grandmother who had passed away two years before at the age of ninety-four.

Her grandmother, the young woman continued, had first met Jakob Wachter of Oldenburg in the spring of 1984 during a hike through the Emsland. In fact, though she had been a girl at the time, the young woman could still remember something about the man. He had been small but strong.

Rosi Piller, her grandmother, and Jakob Wachter were both passionate hikers. Both had lost their partners quite early on, and so in order not to have to walk alone, they took advantage of guided walking tours for nature lovers. And it was on just such a hike that they met. Every day they walked side by side, the entire time discovering that they had more and more things in common, so much so that by the end of all the walks they had become lovers. The entire hiking group, who had only rumored about it at first, now flapped their mouths about it nonstop.

The next few months saw a lot of letters sent back and forth between Oldenburg and Hannover, where Rosi lived. Then the two began to visit each other and got to know each other better and better and, starting in the summer of 1985, began to hike together several times a year as a couple, yet still remaining connected to the Friends of Nature Club.

They repeatedly discussed living together, but as they both had children and grandchildren in their respective cities, they would not and could not bring themselves to abandon those bonds. And so they shuttled to and fro, and carried out a fairly happy long-distance relationship, with all the respective advantages and disadvantages such a relationship entails.

Every trip Jakob Wachter would buy a badge and hammer it into his hiking stick. He already had quite a collection of lovely bebadged sticks at home. To the degree that he could, however, Jakob Wachter tried to conceal his increasingly serious heart problems from his girlfriend. When she asked whether he could still hike so often, he replied that his doctor had simply recommended that he not overexert himself, and that over 1,500 meters of altitude in the mountains would not be such a good idea.

In the summer of 1988 they again went on a hike, the third time that year. He said that he felt everything would go quite well, and that they should therefore go to the beautiful region of Tyrol, a region they had never visited together. Again, he would be just fine so long as they abstained from long distances and high altitudes.

They decided to stay in Jerzens, in the Pitz Valley, and take little day trips.

On August 18, they took the chairlift to the Hochzeigerhaus. It was a beautiful day—the white clouds in beautiful contrast to the deep blue of the sky. They hiked to the Alpine meadows, rested often, and hand in hand confirmed how happy they were with each other. He did not want to let go.

At noon they sat down under a Swiss pine, opened up their bags, and ate what they had brought along. They were tired and fell asleep in each other's arms. But then Jakob Wachter suddenly woke up with an unpleasant, oppressive feeling. Something tightened in his chest, and it became difficult to breathe. Clinging to Rosi Piller he whispered to her to hold on to him tightly, that he was so happy to be with her, and that he would never be without her.

She could feel what he meant. Later, she would repeatedly mention the tranquility he had emanated and how she had responded to this in turn with an astonishing serenity, as well as the quiet and satisfying conversations they had. As he grew weaker and his breathing heavier, she snuggled even more closely into him and whispered in his ear. It did not take long before he died.

She asked a passing hiker to tell the mountain station to send a doctor, as her husband was not feeling too well. She did not want to scare the man by speaking about the dead.

For three quarters of an hour she held her lover in her arms, quite content and happy, until the doctor noted and determined the time of death. He then alerted the mountain rescue, which came and took the body away.

Rosi Piller took the chair lift back down into the valley, where she suffered a fainting spell and was treated by the paramedics who were already waiting for her. The stick badge of Jerzens that Jakob had had in the pocket of his knickerbockers was returned to her once back in Jerzens.

She kept it with her always, and her children had to promise her that they would lay the stick badge on her urn. They were not to put it inside the coffin, as it would then be burnt along with her. No, they were to put it in the ground together with the urn. And they didn't have to worry about whether it was possible—it was, she'd seen it at a funeral herself.

Two years ago they managed to fulfill her final wish.

After clearing out of the apartment, the grandchild saved the stick with its many badges, and its single missing one, before it could be disposed of.

Literature:

Marianna Ludwig, *The Walking Stick Badge, The Hat Pin*, Munich, 2001.

Ingrid Thurner, "Souvenir as Symbol and Need," *Viennese Ethnographic Journal, NF*, Vol. 36/37, 1994-95.

Karl Wimmer, *Beautiful Pitztal*, Innsbruck, 1967.

Gerhard Zummer, *Death in the Heights*, Bregenz, 1972.

0.268g

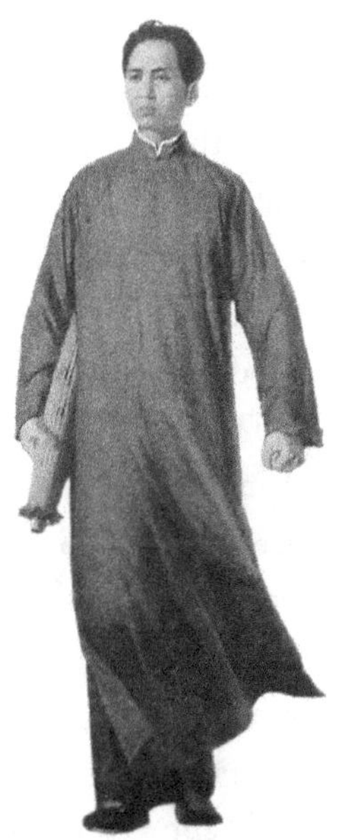

How Mao Tse-tung Turned into St. Anthony of Padua

or

On the Pious Peasants of Xi Mu Lan in Fujian Province

The Christianization of China has always been associated with the shadow of an oppressive, violent religion. The Western conquerors came with priests and gunboats. Among the few exceptions were the Benedictine missionaries who at end of the nineteenth century were successful in widely evangelizing the coastal regions opposite the island of Formosa, Fujian Province. But after Christian monks lured young Chinese boys to Europe with false promises during the First World War only to use them as cannon fodder, many Christianized Chinese returned to their Buddhist traditions and turned their back on Christianity in disgust. In many places the priests were driven out and expelled from the country.

Xi Mu Lan, a village of rice farmers almost at the geographical center of the province of Fujian, considered itself Roman Catholic and kept to its faith even as all the other neighboring villages were turning away from Christianity.

Why should they have to change yet again and once more adopt Buddhist teachings? The people of Xi Mu Lan had grown accustomed to Christianity and gathered regularly in their small chapel dedicated to St. Anthony of Padua to pray and to celebrate Mass together with their priest. They were a pious and respectable people and, though often somewhat ridiculed and seen as eccentric, were for the most part considered harmless by the people of other villages.

The tremors of the long march, the revolution, the abolition of all values, the establishment of the Communist People's Republic, mostly passed them by without causing any problems, almost without leaving any mark at all, as, for the time being, nobody cared about their insignificant, remote village.

When in 1966 Mao Tse-tung proclaimed the Great Cultural Revolution and crowds of mostly fanatical and incensed young people became inspired to enact it, the inhabitants of Xi Mu Lan finally received a visit from the Red Guards. They heard about the pious villagers and, under the campaign slogan "War on All Tradition," set themselves the goal of making the place religion-free in order to set an example, to establish a tribunal against all religion for the sake of scientific and clear socialism. The Catholics had to be shown what the Red Guards were capable of. The Buddhist villages were to think it over once more, and then smash their Buddhas by themselves without waiting for the guards to come and take over.

Under the leadership of Zhuo She, twenty-two Red Guards stormed into the village and found almost all the population praying on their knees in the completely overcrowded Anthony Chapel.

As the Red Guards roared into the chapel with the Bible of Mao in their hands, glowing, swearing, shouting out their slogans, a corridor opened up and room was made for them so that they found themselves suddenly looking at the ceremoniously venerated image on the small altar.

They stopped. Right there in front of them stood an image of the young revolutionary Mao Tse-tung crying out in full revolutionary fervor at the viewer. One hand clenched into a fist, the other holding a shield, the mountains of China behind him.

The Red Guards froze and looked at the bystanders humbly standing around them, their backs gently bent, fingers pointing to the picture with a welcoming gesture as if inviting the Guards to join them in prayer.

The Guards silently left the chapel. The image of Mao Tse-tung remained on the altar where they had found it.

What had happened: The young, illegal priest, Tung Tsedu, had remembered the icon discussion and told the farmers that, in any case, it was not appropriate to worship images, and, furthermore, that images were only representatives of other things. That being so, why couldn't one honor St. Anthony in just such a beautiful picture which, in the end, looked more like him than any other depiction they'd ever seen? That others might see the Communist Mao Tse-tung there—well, there was nothing they could do about that. But for them, it really could be St. Anthony. It certainly would be more pleasing to God for St. Anthony to be worshipped in this form than for them to be tortured and humiliated and forced to deny the true faith.

The Red Guards took credit for the fact that the population was committed to the leader of the revolution—and even if it was in a somewhat naïve form, their dedication nonetheless was exemplary. A few weeks later, the village was awarded for its special contribution to the revolution. Many other awards followed, and in no time at all it became a model village.

The real story behind the image was often whispered about, but the revolutionary forces had no time for such quibbles. Their revolutionary strength required unambiguity and clarity.

Ten years later, the Cultural Revolution was declared to be over. In the meantime, the residents of Xi Mu Lan had grown accustomed to their beautiful Anthony of Padua, and so they left him standing there. The image of Mao Tse-tung remains in the sanctuary even today, and St. Anthony of Padua continues to be worshiped in him, with him, and through him.

Literature:

M. Charlotus, *Pictures of Saints with History*, Regensburg, 1990.

L. Hummel, *The Dedication in Faith Processes*, Ottobeuren, 1957.

Mao Tse-tung, *The Words of the Chairman*, Beijing, 1978.

0.276g

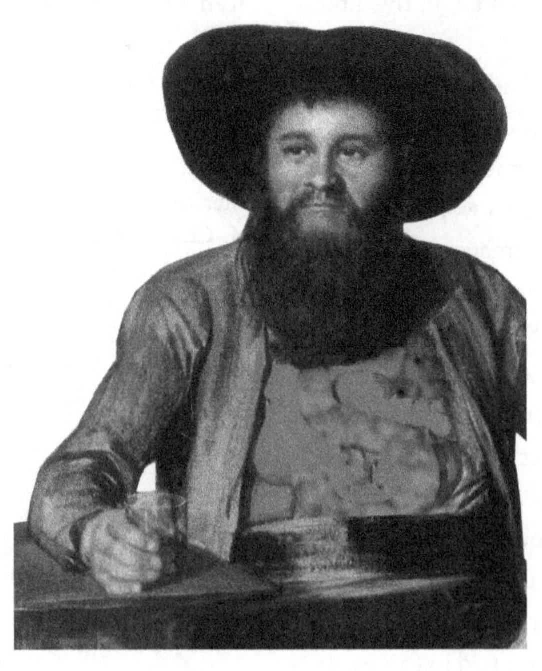

Andreas Hofer: The Shot, or How the First Conserved Sound of the Shot of Andreas Hofer's Execution Disappeared but Was Recently Rediscovered and Made Audible by a US-China Research Team After 200 Years of Silence

[On the bicentennial of his death]

When after two years of work the wax template was once again circular and the wax preserved and newly hardened, all awaited the solemn moment when the recently developed laser needle would reveal the sound which had been preserved in the small, barely visible grooves. Through the latest advances in technology, the electronics had been calibrated to preserve everything.

It took a tremendous effort to coax sounds from the almost melted wax, which, in reality, was really more of a roll than a lump. Indeed, it proved a major challenge to the newly formed research team under the direction of the Cantonese Chi Yu Xong to extract a previously unknown, perhaps even unheard, sound from this wax, to tickle out and explore the background history, and the very reason for the sound recording's existence at all in a verifiable and comprehensible manner. The political pressure on obtaining a result was immense.

And it was for political reasons that the team had been assembled on an egalitarian basis: to set an example of how American and Chinese scientists were now working together and to show that other similar projects could thereafter be realized. However, it was not to include or affect any primary areas of existing research. It had to be politically neutral and characterized as scientific, and yet cover multiple interdisciplinary areas at the same time. Therefore, a project could only come from an uncontroversial area of history.

It was agreed that large gaps still remained to be filled within the field of historical sound recordings. The Scientific Councils of both countries assembled a team under the leadership of the aforementioned thirty-five-year-old Chinese sound engineer Chi Yu Xong. His proxy was John McLoerry, an acoustic-historian. The first item to be investigated was a mass of wax from the Alva Edison Museum in Beaumont, Texas.

An old wax template was reputed to be at the museum but, in truth, it was more of a spherical lump of cracked wax than a cylindrical mass. Furthermore, this mass of bonded wax was alleged to be one of the first sound recordings in existence and thus the forerunner of today's CDs and mp3 players.

In 2007 the team convened for the first time. They agreed on a two-pronged approach. A separate, independent team of historians would find out from whence the wax had originated, to whom it belonged, and what sound was to be expected. The second independent team, consisting of technicians, would deal with the reconstruction of the roll itself as well as the nearly impossible attempt of bringing it to "speak" again. Every other month there would be a comparison of results, and every six months a face-to-face meeting. Each team went to work.

On May 5, 1821, the former emperor of France, Napoleon Bonaparte, died on the island of St. Helena which is located in the Atlantic Ocean on the southern side of the globe. It was immediately decided that none of his remaining belongings were to be returned to Europe. Everything was to remain in St. Helena or to be incinerated. But the power of the objects, their ensoulment if you will, grew feet (so to speak), so that later some, indeed many, things that had belonged or allegedly

0.276g

belonged to Napoleon began to appear. One soldier took his buttons; another took Napoleon's boots; others still his letters. The doctor Francesco Antomarchi, who carried out the arranged autopsy, supposedly took the emperor's penis, which is today supposedly mummified and kept in an American museum owned by the American urologist John K. Lattimer. But here opinions differ.

In any event, since the date of his death, things that belonged to Napoleon have often emerged. In 1852 the American horse trader Hubert Schwächlinger acquired a part of Napoleon's estate. The reason why the horse trader bought the estate is unknown, since he died shortly after its purchase in 1854 at the young age of forty-eight. His relatives immediately parted themselves from the objects as they suspected a link between the purchase and Schwächlinger's sudden death.

The estate was sold and moved into different hands. A small wooden casket upon which the handwritten words "Je veux la reprendre, vengeance!" (I want her back, revenge!) were to be found, had moved through five different owners until 1895. In 1899 the casket was acquired by Thomas Alva Edison (1847-1931). He repeatedly wrapped the box with pages of The New York Times from September 12 1895, laced it with pack string and wrote: "A predecessor, incredible!"

After the death of the great inventor in 1931, all his belongings as well as his estate were incorporated into a foundation, and are now managed by the Alva Edison Museum.

Chi Yu Xong and his team received the still sealed original box. It contained a wax template; or rather, the remains of a wax template such as had been used in the early days of the phonograph. The French inscription written directly on the casket troubled the researchers. Why was something French inscribed on an Edison-template? A close examination of the wax using both the radiocarbon method (C14) as well as isochron dating (usually only applied to Stone Age pieces but which is amazingly accurate with wax analysis) showed that the wax dated from the year 1807. Furthermore, by using a refined propolis determination process, the wax's origin could also be fixed: it was a marram grass beeswax from the bitterly poor southern Brittany island of Ile d'Arx, located 60 kilometers north of the rich port city of Nantes.

Font experts identified the French handwriting as clearly belonging to Napoleon Bonaparte. A graphological expert concluded that the words "Je veux la reprendre, vengeance!" had been written in anger and unrestrained wrath. Other writings of Napoleon had already proven to be written in anger, wrath, and great excitement, and clear similarities in the position of the letters and in the pressure of the ink pen became apparent.

But how was it possible that Napoleon owned a sound wax template when the first functioning phonograph was only presented seventy years later, in 1877, to an astonished and perplexed audience by Thomas Alva Edison? Ten years earlier, in 1867, the French poet and philosopher Charles Cros (1842-1888) had demonstrated the first automatic telegraph and also described the basic structures of a phonograph and a gramophone at the World's Fair in Paris, but he had failed to construct one.

These questions suddenly created tension within Chi Yu Xong's team as the Americans wanted to prevent the discovery of sound recordings from moving back yet again to Europe, the "old world" from which they were constantly trying to distance themselves. Further research was approved by the highest level of the authorities, albeit with the caveat that the official history of technology could not be altered. Any new discoveries would have to be presented only as curious footnotes, as anecdotes to the research of technology.

Napoleon, that great destroyer and reorganizer of traditional European political formation, was not only a fanatical politician, warrior, and workaholic who wanted to immediately put into practice everything that came to his mind, he also demanded the same attitude and mindset from his subordinates. If something did not turn out the way he imagined, the little man could make a great amount of noise: he would rage, scream, condemn, banish, and let heads roll, and not only metaphorically. He tolerated no argument. Napoleon, who not only had Paris built and rebuilt in ever larger dimensions according to his whims, but also regarded the whole of Europe as a playground for his imagination, was also very interested in technical innovation and development. In this regard Napoleon, and therefore France, was to take the lead.

In 1807 Pièrre-Simon Marquis de Laplace (1749-1827) came on the scene. He had given Napoleon the decisive vote in the Senate to become emperor, and was therefore knighted in 1806 by that new emperor, i.e. Napoleon. Laplace reported that documents from England had been leaked to him showing that local scientist and genius Thomas Young (1773-1829) had invented, as well as described in detail, an apparatus that could record sounds as well as store and preserve speech. Napoleon immediately recognized the potentials of this machine and said, "Develop this machine immediately. We must make this happen before the odious English. And when the device is ready, no sounds other than my orders shall be recorded. Pierre, get to work."

Pièrre-Simon Marquis de Laplace, who loyally served the All-mighty without a single criticism to the point of self-denial as well as to his own benefit, confronted the scientists of his Société d'Arceuil with Napoleon's orders to immediately construct a sound machine according to Thomas Young's plans. The chemist Claude-Louis Berthollet, Jean-Baptiste Biot, and Alexander von Humboldt, who also was part of the Société d'Arceuil, asked if all other works were to be suspended. Marquis de Laplace replied with a curt "Yes" before adding: "Not entirely, but take it easy, each according to his powers and abilities—though soon we should be able to hear Napoleon's voice here."

Now everyone began to study the secret writings that had been leaked, developing theories, giving orders to precision mechanics, constructing devices, conducting experiments, rejecting them over and over again, and pursuing the possibilities. Everything had to be done with the strictest secrecy for the English were never to learn anything—and, as everyone knew, secret agents from that boycotted and isolated island were everywhere.

Thanks to the sheer amount of confidentiality and secrecy, very little had been documented, and this presented the research team

0.276g

of Chi Yu Xong with great difficulties. Most of the things they found were trivialities like shopping lists or private letters; however, they did manage to discover instructions for equipment parts, which proved that research on a sound machine had actually taken place. Nevertheless, a functioning apparatus was never found; either it still awaits discovery or was destroyed in complete secrecy.

On January 25, 1810, Napoleon learned about the hiding place and the imminent arrest of Andreas Hofer (1767-1810), whom he detested. That dull cattle trader from the mountains had interfered with his affairs and had almost become the subject of negotiations at the Treaty of Schönbrunn with the Habsburgs. "Haaaaa!" Napoleon screamed and stamped his feet. Even later at his ceremonial marriage by proxy on March 11, 1810, just as at the belated wedding with Marie-Louise von Habsburg on April 1, which was supposed to have given him his long awaited child, Napoleon had the feeling that that innkeeper, that cattle handler, was still present, even though by then everything had long been over.

In South Tyrol everybody knows who Andreas Hofer was. Every year many young Tyrolean men and women still proclaim the native oath in his honor—the soil oath, liberty oath, protective oath, heart of Jesus oath, and all the rest. Several times a year on special holy days Andreas Hofer is dehumanized and mystified by his followers; he is turned into a superman, a super-hero, and a saint, and then disfigured. He is present in every souvenir shop, he can be seen on watches, and he peers up from the bottom of emptied beer mugs.

In the southern parts of southern Germany almost everybody knows him, but elsewhere in the world he is nonexistent. He passes by unknown and unnoticed: "Andreas Hofer? Never heard of him!" He is no more than a small footnote for dedicated Alpine historians, Napoleon specialists, and war historians. Andreas Hofer and his rebellion stopped nothing and achieved nothing. He later became a hero when German chauvinism turned him into a national hero in South Tyrol. A folk hero now, a saint in the deep valleys of the German Catholic Central Alps, sung in countless songs, represented in many plays, immortalized in monuments, protected by legislation until this day, Hofer continues to live on in the hearts of the people. Ridiculed by historians, however, his very name can also still trigger anachronistic scandals of vilification and disparagement.

Andreas Hofer, Tyrol, circa 1808. After Austria's defeat, Napoleon placed Tyrol under the rule of Bavaria and moved his troops into the area. The occupying Bavarian forces introduced radical reforms, which were intended to create a modern, enlightened state. The power of the clergy was radically abolished, priests' influence was forbidden, and public representations such as processions, rosaries, etc., were banned. The Catholic clergy rebelled against its loss of power, even refusing health care reforms and denouncing them as interference in the work of God, an arrogant presumption on the part of man against divine creation. The simple people whose priests were now called into question were confused and no longer knew whether they were coming or going. Were the old traditions and religious rule, according to which the priest was always right, to be abolished? Who would be in charge of the soul? To whom could one turn, who believe? Why had Austria bartered away their Tyrol? What were the unpopular Bavarians doing in their land? Why was everything suddenly different from how it had always been?

In the remote valleys of the Alps they rumbled against the Bavarian occupation. The city intellectuals, the enlightened people, looked contemptuously down on the rural people who had never been beyond their valley and who did not understand what they were in for, what modernity was. And, for their part, from the valleys insecure but proud farmers looked back contemptuously.

The mountains rumbled too. Fierce talks arose in the inns along the mountain roads. There was talk of riots, and people spoke about the right to defend their own land, which was protected by the Heart of Jesus. Andreas Hofer, a simple drover from the Passiria Valley who frequently came around for work and also ran the Am Sand Inn in St. Leonhard (which was also his birthplace), became the mouthpiece for the farmers' discontent. Hofer could hold his drink and was an affable and very pious man who suffered greatly in the new era in which all sense of direction had been lost. As an upstanding man, he felt obliged to the government authorities, as well as to the words of the priests. The government authority, Emperor Franz I, was in Vienna, but no longer ruled Tyrol. Listening to the priest had been forbidden. The confusion was therefore complete. Who could one rely upon now? "The people are right: they can only rely on themselves, on the Tyroleans, on the sharpshooters, on the oath of 1796, on the Heart of Jesus. Our country has to be defended against the madness of renewal, against the New Age. Priests have to get back their say and Emperor Franz I has to get his Tyrol back again." This thought permeated Andreas Hofer's mind, and he began to speak about this at all times and in all places, at every meeting, with every farmer. People liked to listen to him, and talked about him and his speeches a lot.

Bavaria's decision to begin conscription for their army in 1809 was the straw that broke the proverbial camel's back. How could a Tyrolean serve in the foreign Bavarian army? The proud Tyrolean doing service for the occupying forces? They, who were vested in their own right to self-defense? They, who had to defend their own country and nothing else? Never! That could never happen!

On April 9, 1809, a riot broke out in Innsbruck and two days later the first armed confrontation took place between the Bavarian police force and Tyrolean sharpshooters under the command of Andreas Hofer. On April 12 there was a decisive battle at Bergisel, the so-called First Battle of Bergisel. The Tyrolean riflemen won this first battle overwhelmingly. Other successful battles followed. The sharpshooters took advantage of the steep terrain to which they were accustomed, and lured the enemy repeatedly into the small ravines, narrow paths, or canyons, where they were cut off from the rest of the troops and annihilated. These were well-fortified men who emerged from hunting associations and non-paramilitary groups, and were anchored in the region with excellent knowledge of the area. Every year since 1796 they had made an oath to the Heart of Jesus for a free, self-defending Tyrol.

After the first battle was won, the Austrians, who viewed the activities of the marksmen favorably, reclaimed control and the old law was reinstated.

Napoleon was outraged. He issued the order that under no circumstances was Tyrol to become another Spain. There the French army had been dragged into a grueling, devastating guerilla war. Napoleon ordered all forces to take Tyrol back again. Troops were to get ready immediately.

On May 16, 1809, Napoleon learned that the banner of the 2nd French Line Infantry Regiment had been missing since April 13, and that one had to assume that the most important symbol of the army had fallen into the hands of the enemy, the Tyrolean sharpshooters. Indeed, it had not been seen since the battle of Wilten. The standard bearer was in strict detention, and could only give confused information. The usual negotiations with the enemy for exchange of prisoners and captured flags could not be made here. The Tyrolean shooters were considered terrorists and were always to be shot immediately and promptly without question.

This time Napoleon did not scream, but remained silent. In a pale and half-whispering, half-pleading voice he mumbled, "Je veux la reprendre, vengeance!" The messenger left the room silently.

The Tyrolean Hans Lang, a marksman from Inzing, had captured the banner. He hit the French Standard Bearer with his rifle, and had managed to snatch the flag without killing him. Hans Lang hid it in a blanket and took it home. The heap of Inzing riflemen celebrated the loot and swore exuberantly in all kinds of oaths that this banner would never ever be returned.

The banner remained concealed by the people in Inzing for decades. The Musée de l'Armée in the Esplanade des Invalides in Paris exhibits all the standards of the line infantry regiments, except for the one captured by Hans Lang. To this day a visit to the Esplanade des Invalides can still stir a feeling of shame in many French people. The approximately 82 x 85 centimeter silk banner bears the inscription "L'EMPEREUR / DES FRANCAIS / AU 2ME REGIMENT / D'INFANTRY / DE LIGNE" on her square box, and can be seen under the inventory code "MA 1976 164" in the department of national defense in the armory of the Innsbruck Tyrlolean Provincial Museum on loan from the shooters of Inzing.

The struggle for the freedom of Tyrol continued. The Austrians retreated once again. Bavaria came with the French, lost battles, and won battles. Over the course of the year the sharpshooters had some big successes, so that Andreas Hofer became the Innsbruck Regent of Tyrol for two months, from August to mid-October 1809. But Hofer always saw himself as only a placeholder for Emperor Franz I. By then the latter had already begun negotiations with Napoleon and was naturally willing to give up Tyrol. Tyrol for him was nothing more than a bargaining chip.

At the Treaty of Schönbrunn, Austria again ceded Tyrol to France and, off the table, the marriage of Marie-Louise von Habsburg, the eldest daughter of the Austrian Emperor Franz I, was also discussed. It was to take place the following year.

Andreas Hofer, who did not understand the mechanizations of politics, was more upset about the world than ever and was only a puppet to the whisperings of the radical clergy. He prayed a lot, wrestled with himself, and drank more and more. He felt hopelessly overwhelmed by the situation.

On January 11, 1809, he attempted yet another armed conflict with a group of faithful followers and was beaten mercilessly. The population turned away from the "oddball" and a further, personally signed call for uprising had no effect. In the valleys people no longer spoke well of him. Hofer had to flee and was arrested in a hut in the mountains in the Passeiertal on January 28, after having been betrayed.

He was transferred to Mantua and tried before a military tribunal. The interrogations to follow had only one goal, and had been ordered from the very top: Andres Hofer was to return the banner. The only problem was that, he, Andreas Hofer, knew absolutely nothing about it. He repeatedly asked where it was, begged his former comrades to surrender it so that his life could be saved. There was no reply. Copies of these letters are secretly kept in the Military Museum in Paris. The originals have been lost. Many historians believe that due to the subsequent glorification and mystification of Andreas Hofer, these letters were destroyed to prevent a negative light of misery from falling on the hero. Perhaps the very last words Andreas wrote—"Farewell, cruel world, dying seems so easy that my eyes are not even wet"—should be understood within the context of his pleading letters having been ignored by his riflemen.

The verdict of the military court was death by firing squad. The Viceroy of Italy, Napoleon's stepson, Eugene Beauharnais, and his brother, Crown Prince Ludwig of Bavaria, intervened against the death penalty: "we believe him when he says that he does not know where it is," the latter wrote to Napoleon.

Just one day before Andreas Hofer's arrest, Napoleon summoned Pièrre-Simon Marquis de Laplace and asked if the development of the sound recording apparatus had already been completed. When Marquis de Laplace told him that recordings could be made in no time, Napoleon ordered him to get everything ready, as there would soon be an opportunity for something he would like to hear, but could not do so in person. Because Napoleon immediately was thinking about listening to the execution after the fact, it is assumed that even if Andreas Hofer had managed to persuade his former followers to return the banner, his life would not have been spared.

0.276g

In the early morning of February 20, 1810, a small group of precision engineers and scientists, still tired from the long journey they had undergone from Paris, set up a peculiar device on the lawn under a wall on the left side of the Porta Maggiore in the Mantua fortress. Admired by passing soldirers, this device had a large funnel and a hand crank, small gears and braided wires. All this stood upon a mysterious box on which a wax roll with a small pointed pen attaced was mounted.

At ten o' clock the fusilier commander received the notice that everything was ready. At 10:30 twelve soldiers from the 2nd Battalion of the 13th French Grenadier Regiment marched on, and ten minutes later brought out Andreas Hofer, accompanied by a priest, and stood him before the wall.

The fine gentlemen in their suits from Paris stood by their strange device, nodded their heads in agreement, and turned the crank. The commander gave the orders to load, aim, and shoot, and when the shot trailed off, to repeat.

Andreas Hofer was executed, the shot was recorded, and therefore Napoleon could hear it in distant Paris. It is not known, however, whether Napoleon ever in fact heard this sound, since there is no indication as to whether there was a device that could play the sounds back. The only thing that exists today is the wax template with Napoleon's handwriting and Alva Edison's wrapping paper.

Chi Yu Xong's team of researchers nevertheless managed the almost unimaginable task of successfully making audible a sound recorded almost fifty years before the first official sound recording existed—the sound of Andreas Hofer's execution. But Andreas Hofer's famous final words, "Ah, you French, you shoot poorly," cannot be heard in the recording, and so it remains unconfirmed whether they were actually spoken by him or not.

0.276g

Literature:

Erich Egg/Wolfgang Pfaundler, *The Great Tyrolean Sharpshooters Book*, Vienna/Munich/Zurich, 1976.

Humbert Fink, *To Mantua in Gangs*, Dusseldorf, 1992.

Franz Herre, *Napoleon Bonaparte: A Biography*, Munich, 2006.

Hans Kiel, *From Clay Bowls to MP3*, Berlin, 2008.

Hans Kramer, *Andreas Hofer*, Brixen, 2004.

Hans Magenschab, *Andreas Hofer: Between Napoleon and Emperor Franz*, Graz and Regensburg, 1994.

Gunther Rothenberg, *The Napoleonic Wars*, Berlin, 2000.

Bernhard Sandbichler, *Andreas Hofer 1809: A Story of Loyalty and Betrayal*, Innsbruck, 2002.

Siegfried Steinlechner, *Hofer's New Clothes*, Vienna/Munich, 2000.

Volker Ullrich, *Napoleon*, Hamburg, 2006.

0.277g

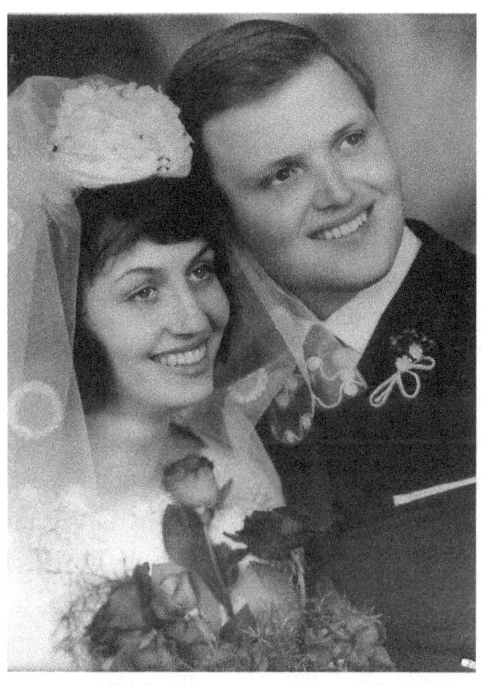

The Life Story of
Gertraud Pachulke and Lena Tribukeit
or
The First Lesbian Wedding of 1950

On August 15, 1950, the Feast of the Assumption, Lena Pachulke, née Tribukeit, and Gerd Pachulke were married in the registry office of Berlin's Charlottenburg district, which was at that time still provisional and marked by damage from the war. The mandatory after-marriage wedding photo was taken in Sailer's Photo Studio in the Zillestraße, and then a lunch for sixteen people was hosted at the nearby traditional guest house Hög. The two had chosen the date of August 15 as it fell right in between their birthdays.

Gerd Pachulke was born Gertraud Pachulke on May 10, 1925, in Abschwangen in East Prussia, about 40 kilometers southeast of Königsberg. In 1943 she left home and went to Königsberg where she worked as a waitress at the bourgeois Café Adler, which was located at the corner of the Steindamm in Heumarkt.

A month after she started working, she met Lena Tribukeit, whom, as she learned, had been born on November 21, 1925, in Uderwangen, which was just 10 kilometers east of her home.

Five months later, they moved together into a small apartment at 7 Michaelsstraße.

Lena Tribukeit worked as a housemaid for the Noldenkothen family, which ran a relatively well-known shoe store in Königsberg. The Noldenkothen family was fine with Lena moving out, as a new child had just arrived and the eldest daughter Mathilde could use the room previously inhabited by the housemaid.

Since the 1920s Königsberg had been known as a stronghold of tribades and uranians. Even in the times of the delusional, racist campaigns against otherness and homosexuality, small, hidden niches could be established. Women met in places that were hardly recognizable to outsiders, like the Café Adler, for example; men, however, enjoyed almost no public spaces whatsoever and thus withdrew almost completely into private life in order to escape persecution.

Only a small circle of the initiated knew that Ms. Tribukeit and Ms. Pachulke had become an inseparable pair. At that time, two young women living together in the same house as server and domestic help was not considered strange, so no one had any further thoughts about it.

In the autumn of 1944 as the Russians were rapidly approaching Königsberg and the first refugee trains had already left for the west, the two joined 2,000 others on a train headed for Danzig (Gdansk). On the evening of April 15, 1945, they were some of the last passengers to board the completely overcrowded hospital ship *Pretoria,* which, though severely damaged, set sail from the Baltic Sea port of Hela. The 16,662 GRT ship *Pretoria* is today a pilgrim ship and sails under the name of *Gunung Djati* and under the Indonesian flag. On April 16 they both arrived safely, if one can use the word in such a context, in Copenhagen and were admitted to a refugee camp in the southern part of the city, in today's Amager district. While fleeing Gertraud Pachulke had lost all of her papers—at one point the *Pretoria* had leapt and her bag slipped away and fallen into the Baltic Sea. Lena Tribukeit, however, was able to prove her own identity and then vouch for that of her friend.

But now the confusion of the post-war period began. In the early summer of 1945 both of them arrived in Lübeck, then in a camp in Cologne, and finally in Sindelfingen where they remained working as assistants at the local hospital until 1949. Gertrud Pachulke still had a tentative ID card, for an official one could only be issued once definite identification of the person had been obtained.

In 1949 the two managed to come to Berlin where they hoped to start over. Even to this day, Mrs. Gerd Pachulke, with a smile on her face, tells the story of how they accidentally obtained a passport with the name of Gerd Pachulke in Cologne. Because this other Gerd Pachulke also wore his hair short the officials did not look very closely. Gerd and Lena laughed, and at the same time, independently thought of the momentous idea.

In Berlin they looked for an apartment in Charlottenburg and tried to get by with various jobs. However, the "Cologne idea," as they called it, would not let them go. They fell into newly formed artists' groups and circles. Many gay men began to once again appear in "private" public spaces and contact bars emerged where survivors were able to meet, as did new places for women. Everything in Berlin was nestled within a large circle of other survivors, artists, gays and lesbians. It was from out of this milieu that, for example, the legendary Leierkasten Pub at Zossener Straße in Kreuzberg arose.

In any event, the two obtained all the necessary papers to get married from Oskar Huth, who during the period of Nazism had meticulously forged identity cards that were more real than the real ones, and now, in the postwar, was engaged in manufacturing very realistic looking food stamps. Gertraud Pachulke's was issued to Gerd Pachulke, and she even received a certificate saying that Gerd Pachulke had been indispensable in Königsberg and therefore did not need to be sent to the front.

"Why we wanted to get married, I really do not know," Mrs. Gerd Pachulke says today. "But somehow we were fed up with wandering and wanted to have at least some sense of security. It also became a kind of idée fixe. We have never regretted it."

Oskar Huth was present at the happy ceremony and was impressed with the good work he had done. "It was a dream wedding, and we really just had to have a genuine wedding picture of us," Gerd Pachulke reminisces.

The freshly married pair acquired a newspaper kiosk in Wilmersdorf in 1954, which they ran together until 1984. For their birthdays they often met up with friends to eat their native Zodder meatballs with potato wedges in the East Prussian pub of Marjellchen at 9 Mommsenstraße.

0.277g

As to the question of whether they were ever afraid of being discovered and having everything brought to light, Mrs. Pachulke responds with a curt "No."

On the evening of their 52nd wedding anniversary, seventy-eight-year-old Ms. Lena Pachulke passed away in the arms of her friend. She found her final resting place in the cemetery in Wilmersdorf.

Mrs. Gerd Pachulke, who lives by herself in a nearby retirement home, visits the grave two to three times a week. On the gravestone it says:

Lena Pachulke - Gertraud Pachulke, born Gerd Tribukeit.

* 5.10. 1925. † 14. 8. 2002 / *11. 5. 1925

Rest in peace, for in peace you have lived

Literature:

Pierre André, *The Other Berlin*, Berlin 2010.

K. Kalemir, *The Story of the 16.662 GRT Ship Pretoria*, Kiel, 1988.

Magdalena Otto, *Tribades and Urninden*, Berlin, 2001.

0.292g

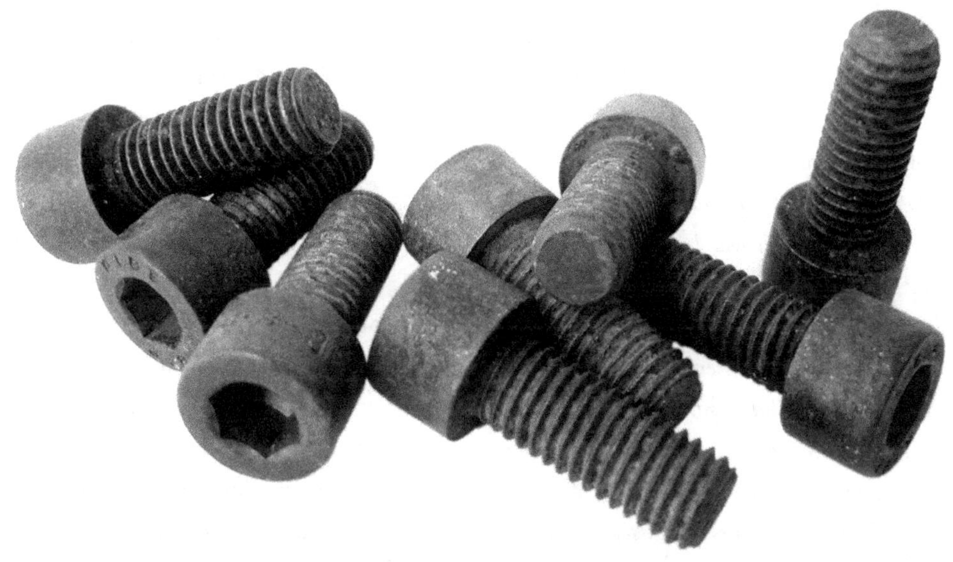

Freed from Eternal Ice:
Screws from a 1939 Plane Crash in Peru
Where the Only Survivor, Gary Dlugos,
Survived Thanks to Singing a Bartók Melody

On May 15, 1939, during a flight over the Andes in dense fog a plane crashed into the massive glacier located below the 6,394-meter-high mountain known as Avzaogare. Except for Gary Dlugos, all thirty-four passengers and crew perished.

Dlugos, a music teacher from Salina, Kansas, miraculously survived the crash unhurt and was, by a second miracle, able to save himself.

He later reported:

> *After I saw what had happened, I put on a parachute suit that was lying on the ground, and wrapped a couple of blankets around my body. It was very cold, even though the sun was shining. I had never seen a glacier, let alone stood on one. What I saw here was gigantic and overwhelmingly beautiful. Everything was white and blue. I just went downward, downhill. When I saw the first crevasse, I looked for a way around it. It took a very, very long time, because there were crevasses everywhere, and I had to avoid them all. Only later, in the hospital, I learned how dangerous my evasive maneuvers had been. I spent the nights in self-built snow caves, which I remembered reading about in a children's book on Eskimos.*

After four days on the glacier and twelve days of trekking—during which he subsisted on roots and pods—in search of people, Gary Dlugos came upon an Indian settlement. The Indians were initially suspicious of this bewildered, starving man who constantly hummed and softly sang strange sounding melodies. They called him "The Singing Man from the Mountain." When he had somewhat recovered, they took him to a missionary station. From there he was moved to the provincial town of Parur, then to Cuzco, and finally to Lima, where he was released after three weeks of hospitalization.

When asked how he had survived the period of anxiety and disorientation, Dlugos said:

> *I just continued to hum the melodies of Béla Bartók to myself. They saved my life. In particular, I arranged the melodies of Mikrokosmos to local conditions. I assigned the crevasses a major, other places a minor. The hillside was Allegro and everything else Andante. Later, while wandering around for days, I heard the landscape more than saw it. Through this music I was never alone, and never felt abandoned.*

The only complication was that thereafter he could no longer hear Bartók without falling into up to four hours of continuous catalepsy.

Gary Dlugos died in 1978.

Neither the plane nor the bodies were ever recovered, because the winter came and covered everything with snow. The aircraft, like the victims, was glaciated.

It was only in 1991 that the glacier freed up the first parts of the aircraft.

Literature:

Lima Times, June 3/4/7, 1935.

Patrick F. Jackson, *The Miracle with Bartók*, Dallas, 1942.

Paul S. Oz, *The Viewing of Music*, San Francisco, 1958.

0.350g

Dr. Almut H. Mayer
Traumabgabestelle

Rückgabe, Zwischenlagerung, Depot, Umtausch, Archivierung, Sortierungen, Revision, Endlager, Entsorgungen, Sammlungen, Stornierungen, wie eine zweistündlich geleerte Traumklappe

Mo., Di., Do., 8 -16 Uhr / Mi., Fr., 8 -13 Uhr

Bei Notfällen oder Anonymitätsbedürfnis: Bitte Klappe benützen

Keine Bewertungen und Deutungen von Träumen

On Dream Depositories

After many months of going back and forth and many discussions with her friends, Maria K. decided to drop-off her persistently recurring dream. She had been having the same dream again and again, and every time it made her terribly confused. Going to visit one of these Dream Depositories for advice on what she should do with herself and her strange, debilitating dream was not an easy step to make, however. She therefore sought out a woman, Dr. Gerda H. Mayer, an experienced Dream Collector and member of the DTAS. Maria K. appeared at the agreed upon appointment time punctually and very nervous.

At this first rather long meeting her options were explained to her, as was how she could deposit her dream and what could thereafter be done with it. The dream could be dropped off forever, or only temporarily stored; she could share it with others, for example, who did not dream and were looking for some and might just like to dream the dream she had been having; or she could exchange her dream and get another one in return. She could also offer the dream with a right-of-return policy, or assign it an expiration date; or, if she brought it to the attention of the Dream Caretaker, there was even the possibility of Dream-Elimination.

At the end of their fifty-minute conversation, Maria K. decided to set up a Dream Depository where she could store her dream. Gerda H. Mayer mentioned that the way they now dispensed dreams was such that Maria's original dream would very likely be replaced by a new and different, but still quite similar, one. A Dream Depository where she could leave her ongoing dreams would have the advantage of allowing Dream-Comparisons, or Dream-Overviews, and she could later decide which of her dreams she wanted eliminated and which she would like to have back.

Particular importance and clairvoyant powers have always been attributed to dreaming. From the Pharaoh's dreams, Joseph prophesied seven years of abundant harvest and seven years of famine, thereby helping Egypt's rise to becoming a major economic power. Many mystics like Hildegard von Bingen recognized and explained the world and relationships with God through their dreams. We find books on dream interpretation not only in Babylon and ancient Egypt but in all cultures that have been known to humankind. Humans have consistently tried to catalog dream images and give them personal meanings. They have aimed to curb the arbitrariness of the dream and to make sense of its seeming nonsensicality. Borders were set to wild dreams, as man assigned them to a second world where laws were certain. In this fabricated space dreams were both understood and contained as prophecies, as profound insights, and as being connected to the gods. Anxiety was thus eliminated and turned into something positive.

By the beginning of the last century, the time had finally come to establish the first Dream Depository. These people saw the dream for what it was: the dreamer's possession. The dream was understood as a completely individual event, as something that had only to do with the dreamer. Every individual dreams his or her very own, singular, and corporeal dream, and it says nothing about anyone other than the dreamer. Even the most utterly foreign individual dreams his own dreams. Every individual is responsible for their own dream in that it cannot be passed on to others, nor shared with others, nor seen as something imposed.

There are of course Dream Objectors, of which there are two kinds. The first are the Dream Deniers who want nothing to do with their dreams. They attach no value to their dreams, distrust them, find them annoying, or are so scared of them that they don't want anything to do with them or admit that they have anything in common with them. The other category of Dream Objectors is the Dream Concealers who dream very much indeed, but who refuse to tell others about their dreams because they do not want to reveal their deep particularities. They believe that when you talk about your dreams you abandon your individuality and expose yourself to Dream Interferences, an expropriation of your primordial dream. "What do my dreams have to do with anyone else?"

Naturally, there are also Dream Masters. These are people who constantly talk about their dreams; they are sometimes referred to as the Dream Proud. If you happen to meet two Dream Masters together it can feel as if you were attending a dream world championship: there are so many dreams tumbling out from their memories, they are so weird, and so many sheer impossibilities are reported that the normal, average dreamer will only shake their head in disbelief. If lucky, you might at some point gain enough courage to throw in one of your own dreams during one of the short breaks.

The Dream Depositories are responsible for all of these dreams. Soon after their creation they spread to all the major cities of the world, and are now connected through various national and international associations that hold Dream Meetings and publish Dream Periodicals which report the latest research on dreams, their sorting, and classification. Specialized publishers sell books with titles like *Whither with Coerced Dreams?*, *Concerning Dream Oblivion*, *Life in Seemingly Foreign Dreams*, *Do Daydreams Require a Separate Archive?*, *The Dream-Valve: On the Anonymous Depositing of Dreams*, *The Dream Informer*, *The Problem of Borrowed Dreams*, and so forth.

In Dream Depositories dreams are generally not distinguished as good or bad, important or unimportant, significant or insignificant. They are simply accepted in accordance with the wishes of the Dream Dropper—dropped off, temporarily stored, and collected according to what it is the dreamer wants. Under no circumstances are the dreams ever judged.

As the Dream Depositories are spaces of the highest individuality, and as this indiviuality is taken very seriously indeed, they are suspicious to totalitarian and authoritarian systems. What exactly happens in these Dream Depositories? What goals do they have? What do they actually do with their stock of dreams? What kind of efficiency tests could these places be subjected to? How and by what criteria could they be evaluated? Some regard the view of the dream as the guardian of the individual to be the very myth of the modern age. Dream Deniers mostly.

Maria K. now regularly dropped her dreams off with Dr. Gerda H. Mayer at the Dream Depository and, over time, amassed a considerable number of them. Very slowly she came to realize that her dreams always revolved around a more or less similar problem. And, with time, she learned not to fear bewildering dreams and instead to find them amicable, and sometimes even fun. After much consideration, she ultimately dissolved her Dream Depository and took back all of her deposited dreams. She would not let them simply lie there, for they now truly belonged to her.

Many dreamers visit the Dream Depositories. Most of them first come in order to get rid of their dreams, never wanting to see them ever again. But then, after looking at their own dream collection, after examining it closely, sorting it out, re-estimating it, most of them decide to reclaim their collected dreams. Their utter elimination is rarely requested. And why should they be when one can both handle and live with them quite happily?

Literature:

S. Freud, *The Interpretation of Dreams,* Vienna, 1900.

T. Gellert, *The History of Dream Depositories,* Hamburg, 1997.

R. Möchlig, *Dream Pride,* Stuttgart, 1967.

Z. Muller, *The Overflowing Dream Depository,* Heidelberg, 1996.

P. Puder, *The Search for the Right Dream,* Berlin, 1999.

M. Reich, *From the Dream: The Elimination,* Lucerne, 1934.

0.425g

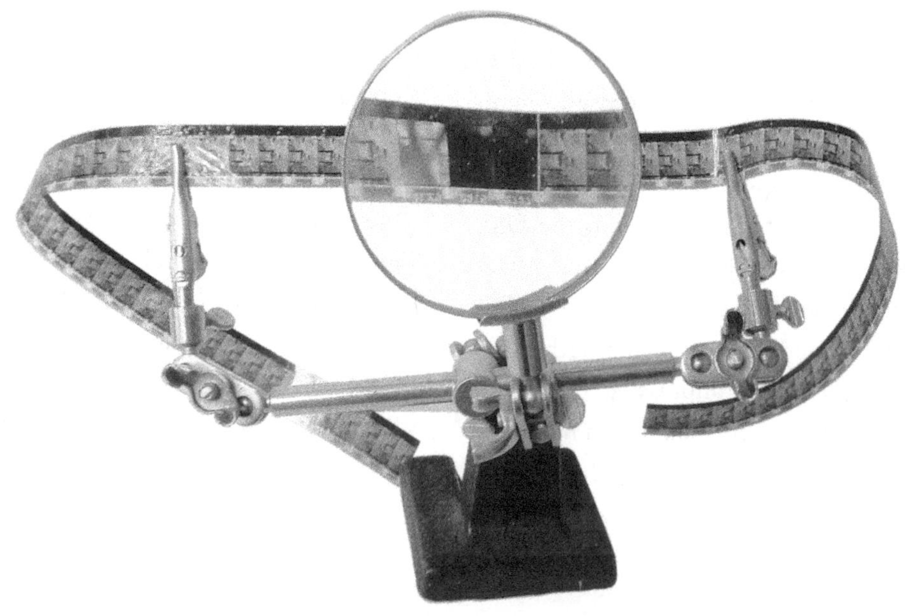

Film Snippets of Subfilms

Subfilms were films in which images imperceptible to the human eye had been spliced in so as to have a subtle, unnoticeable influence on the subconscious minds of viewers in order to affect their minds and manipulate them.

In the spring of 1951 the Republican Joseph McCarthy, who led the Senate Committee on Un-American Activities from 1950 to 1954 and was responsible for spreading anti-communist hysteria throughout the USA, commissioned Bob Spencer, a native of Germany, to develop and produce patriotic films. These films were meant to strengthen the American public by impressing them with images of a free America bathed in happiness while at the same time enabling them to recognize the looming dangers of whatever was un-American, which they were to confront with vigilance.

Bob Spencer's team immediately set out to work, and in the summer of the same year the first films were shown to a select audience. In these films a happy and beautiful America was portrayed—an America of nature, work, family, an America of a constitutionally guaranteed happiness. The viewer was supposed to feel happy and grateful to be living, to be allowed to live, in the most beautiful, most free, and best country in the world. But there was also the need to create the subliminal feeling that such happiness was constantly under threat by the enemies of good so that every US citizen would always be on guard against evil. They had to be prepared to recognize evil within themselves and fight it, because there, inside every one of them, the enemy might have already anchored his very seed of destruction.

What they did not know was that these patriotic films, full of good and happiness as they were, full of sunshine and brightness, had been edited with hidden images imperceptible to the human eye, images of prostitution, of people starving for bread, images of sexually transmitted diseases, symbols of the hammer and sickle, images of darkness and evil.

On the one hand these films existed to make their viewers feel happy and light; on the other hand, they were to make them feel uncomfortable, to make them sense a threat that could not be localized. The great difficulty in making these films was in finding the right balance between happiness and threat. Bob Spencer's team researched in detail how many images of danger could be accommodated, with what frequency, whether regularly or irregularly, and whether to insert only one image or up to three images. Experiments were conducted with 16 milimeter material.

When in 1954 anti-communist hysteria subsided and McCarthy was reprimanded and deposed for his actions, Bob Spencer's team was dissolved and research discontinued before any of the films could be shown to a wide audience.

In the 1960s the advertising industry experimented again with this method, but without much success.

In 1965 the Swedish director Ingmar Bergman—increasingly upset about the censorship of alleged obscenity in his films—decided to give the censors something to consider in the third epilogue of his film *Persona* by inserting an imperceptible image of an erect penis.

Literature:
Tobias Diddman, *Travels of the Movie "R.C.A"*, London, 1974.
Sabine Nessel, *The Image Event that One Cannot See*, Berlin, 2001.
Steve Ollyconn, *The Image between the Image*, London, 1963.
Winfried Paulleit, *Standing and Moving Images*, Berlin, 1994.

0.425g

0.489g

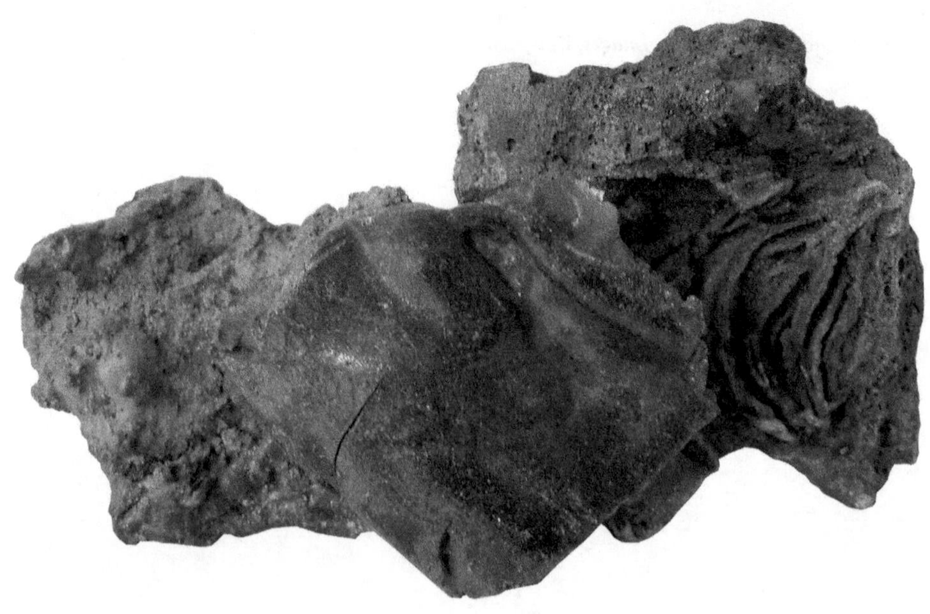

Jan Eliasson's Revenge: Stones that Became Ceramic from a Burning Furnace in Gnarp, Sweden

Jan Eliasson worked in Johansson's Ironworks in Gnarp, central Sweden, for thirteen years. He discharged ships with iron ore, loaded up others with recovered cast iron, and stoked the furnaces until the cinder separated from the iron. He was employed in all kinds of work: in summer, when the days never come to an end, as well as in winter, when the days were lit with torches and the glow of the burning blast furnace. In 1752, the year of the disaster, Jan Eliasson was in charge of the combustion cells.

In 1734, when he was just sixteen years old, Jan Eliasson began working at the Johansson's ore smelter. He was the second son of four from a family of forest farmers. As a child he had learned how to collect branches and wood and how to cut down trees. His parents had two scrawny cows that they milked on the barren glades, they had planted some wheat, and now and again hunted an animal. In short, a life full of privation.

Jan Eliasson wanted more.

When he was twelve years old, he accompanied his father to distant Gnarp by the sea to deliver wood and brushwood, as well as a few pieces of fur, to one of the Johansson's Ironworks' purchasing centers. With the little money he received, Jan Elizason's father got a new axe and, with what he had left, purchased some clothes for his wife. For the first time in his life, in Gnarp Jan Eliasson saw the sea as well as people who were not dressed like peasants or marked by heavy physical work. He saw written words, and wanted to learn how to decipher them. He was fascinated by the life he encountered there.

At home in the woods he spent the long evenings carving wooden figures—most of which were later sold in Gnarp—and dreamed of living and working there among all the other people.

At sixteen, a full-grown giant of a man, he walked away from the forest to work in Gnarp at Johansson's Ironworks. Initially hired as an assistant, thanks to his skills he was soon employed in other activities. As a wage he received free food, accommodation with nine other men, and eight Reichstaler every six months. Jan Eliasson liked life in Gnarp. Life among nearly 400 people, as well as the constant comings and goings, fit his style. There were always itinerant people busy delivering tons of wood as the blast furnaces swallowed wood twenty-four hours a day. Iron ore arrived on barges, and ships transported raw iron. He had to work a lot, but he had plenty of time, apart from going to the market now and then. It was precisely the life he had dreamed of in his solitude back at home in the woods.

From 1745 onwards, however, Johansson & Sons' business went from bad to worse. Competitors tried out novel iron melting techniques and new and very abundant deposits of iron ore were opened up. Gnarp became increasingly unprofitable and thus Johansson & Sons began to invest less and less in Gnarp before pulling out from the general production of iron completely and becoming increasingly involved in its refining, which is why they built a new factory using the latest methods 550 kilometers away to the south. They appointed a new administrator to Gnarp, and he was expected to squeeze out whatever was still economically feasible from the ailing and no longer

0.489g

lucrative furnace. To say that he ruled with an iron hand would be putting it mildly.

As a result, Jan Eliasson grew more and more resentful. He had to work faster, heat the ovens faster, which, naturally, also had to be punctured sooner. He knew that this produced poor quality iron, as, in order to obtain a good flow of iron, the ore had to be allowed sufficient time and boil slowly so that the slag could be separated from the clean iron.

At the beginning of July 1752, all in one day, he had to operate two ovens, climb up another one, and, on top of that, light a further one. He did it, but his silent resentment began to solidify.

On the night of July 28 to 29, he saw the furnace getting hotter, the fire clay beginning to glow at some points, and knew that it would not be long until the oven exploded. All the same, Jan Eliasson put even more wood inside. Though alone, he was doing the work of several people at once. Throughout the evening he continued to feed the furnace with tons and tons of wood. He opened all the shafts and shoved the largest pieces of timber into the combustion chambers, thereby using up a week's worth of wood. In the morning, just as the next shift was getting up, the industrial town of Gnarp was rocked by a loud explosion. The oven blew apart, splashing hot iron everywhere, which then solidified into bizarre shapes in the water, while the coke melted into liquid ceramic. There was a flow of boiling material and the solidifying of what had boiled. It was as if the Earth had suddenly started to growl and the torments of hell allowed to roam unfettered. The people ran and hid. It was only in the afternoon that the workers began to extinguish the fire. It took them two days.

A week later a committee from Stockholm came to investigate the fire and the explosion but could not find any cause. Their intensive questioning of Jan Eliasson, who was still under shock, revealed nothing about how he managed to survive the explosion save by some miracle. The final report stated that the outdated technology must have been the cause of the accident.

Iron was never again melted in Gnarp, and it consequently shrank into becoming just another small town in central Sweden. Only the remains of the furnace can still be seen.

Jan Eliasson survived because, seeing that the explosion was imminent, he quickly added a couple of tree trunks, smeared his face in black soot, and disappeared from the factory using a previously explored escape route. By the time the explosion occurred, he was standing safe and sound on a hill to enjoy the spectacle he had himself produced.

Literature:

Jörg-Peter Findeisen, *Sweden: From the Beginnings to the Present*, Regensburg, 2005.

Lars Wahlström, *On Gnarp*, Stralsund, 1984.

——, *On Revenge*, Stralsund, 1991.

——, *Satisfaction*, Stralsund, 1979.

>1.001g

1.159g

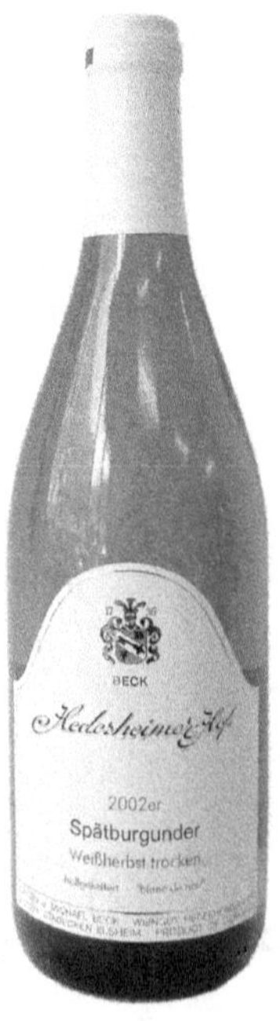

On White Red Wine

or

How Sacramental Wine Lost Its Red Color

Until the second half of the fifteenth century red wine alone was used as sacramental wine. The first time white wine was used as sacramental wine was in 1478. In a letter to Pope Sixtus IV, who was busy with the construction of a new papal chapel, Bishop Clemens Bruno of Cuneo humbly asked for permission to use a Pinot Noir, which was then to be vinified into a white, to be the sacramental wine for the celebration of the Holy Eucharist. A barrel of this white vinified red was sent to his excellency in Rome so that he could also learn—through firsthand sensual experience—what it was all about, how much it might cost, and whether the wine would truly be to the greater glory of God. The response letter, dated October 8, 1478, allowed the use of this white vinified Pinot Noir and carried an additional note mentioning how much his Excellency had enjoyed the wine and asking whether it would be possible to send another barrel to the Holy City but, if possible, a slightly larger one than the first.

Pinot Noir was the most popular sacramental wine, and the one most widely used for liturgical purposes. There are many legends surrounding Burgundy wine; for example, the vinegar that was passed to Jesus on the cross with a sponge attached to the tip of a lance is said to have been vinegar from Burgundy. It is also said that Noir vines grew on the hillside of the vineyard where Jesus foresaw his death during Holy Week and that their sweet scent offered a small consolation to his great pain. Another legend reports that at the Marriage at Cana the second wine produced by Christ was a Burgundy.

What is historically verifiable, however, is that this type of wine was first mentioned in 1226, though it is widely assumed to have already begun to be cultivated and grown two thousand years ago. The Pinot Noir (Pino Nero, It.) was cultivated in the fifteenth century in large lands in the region of Piedmont but today has almost entirely disappeared from the region. People appreciated the reddish purple of the wine, as it stood in contrast to the white altar cloths and the colors of the liturgical vestments of the priests.

In the middle of the fifteenth century in the small Piedmontese town of Saluzzo there lived a priest named Gino Dante (of no relation to the other Dante). This priest was very popular because of his thrilling sermons. People came to Saluzzo from all around just to hear them and returned home filled with new power and energy. Father Dante himself experienced his own sermons in a very intense way, working as he did with his entire body, pulling himself up again and again and waving his spread hands so that the Lord's words could be represented clearly and intensely. The only problem was that, in so doing, he regularly spilled the red sacramental wine on himself.

1.159g

As a result, the heavily stained altar cloth had to be replaced after almost every mass. That would have been fine, but in his great bodily exertion for the annunciation of the Lord, Gino Dante repeatedly poured red wine onto his chasuble too. These vestments were exquisitely decorated and accordingly expensive, and this was therefore rather annoying for the citizens of Saluzzo. They could not continue buying new mass vestments simply because Monsignor Gino Dante was so clumsy. On the other hand, they could not do without the popular priest. If they could just send him off to a monastery, they thought, or to a rural community, his cleanliness would not be an issue. But here in the city where so many foreigners came to hear him speak it just would not do—the priest could not be sent to the altar wearing stained mass vestments. This priest brought a large audience through his immensely popular and emphatic sermons, and all these people also left behind a lot of money in town.

Using all the necessary means for bleaching—from the most common to the most secret methods passed down from mothers to daughters—the women of Saluzzo tried to figure out a way to deal with the red wine stains. But their attempts mostly failed, and even when they did to some extent succeed, everything was nullified by the next celebration of mass at the latest. Furthermore, there were constant discussions about whether it was permitted to deal with these stains in any way at all; for as the stains were caused by the Holy Consecration, by extension they had been caused by the blood of Christ, and it would not be possible to simply remove them with the profane abrasive cleaners one usually applied to the body. Again and again the citizens were forced to take up extra chores because new vestments and new altar cloths repeatedly had to be bought.

Eventually the exhausted citizens of Saluzzo asked the competent bishop Clemens Bruno of Cuneo whether it would be possible to make a special case for the priest and allow him to use white wine as an exception. The immediate answer was no. Sacramental wine had to be red as it was the blood of Christ and not his sweat, and blood happens to be red and not white. They would therefore have to decide whether to exile Father Gino and thus live without him, or to converse with him further and penitently accept their fate of having to constantly do the laundry (the bishop gave them special permission to allow already transfigured wine to be washed, but only carefully) and to occasionally buy a new chasuble. At that time, the Nuns of the Holy Blood's vestments were the most beautiful and reasonably priced, and the convent was in Clemens Bruno's immediate jurisdiction.

The request that Gino Dante dilute the Burgundy with more water in the future was of no use as he poured very little water into the wine the way it was. He reasoned that the less water there was in the wine, the more intensely Jesus would be present in the Holy Communion.

A wine grower from nearby Revelo, located directly at the first slopes of the Southern Alps, liked to listen to Father Gino preach and knew all about the problem from his many conversations with the townspeople. He thought to himself: if they had to continuously clean the crazy priest's mass vestments and even replace them with new ones just because all that discoloration made them unattractive, then they should just deal with the problem beforehand by making the discoloration fail to happen in the first place. The wine grower was not a man of theory but of action. He thus set to work at once by treating a part of his Blue Burgandy from the following grape harvest as white wine. During pressing he separated the grape skins from juice in the mash, thereby keeping the wine from having a chance for extraction and preventing the red wine from becoming red.

The result was a classic red wine made from the Burgundy grape, but one that was not red. When fermentation was complete and the winemaker drew the first sample, he was amazed by what a good, and truly exclusive, white wine he had produced.

He sent the first sample bottle to Father Dante. Dante was very excited and sent a package to the bishop, who in turn sent a barrel to the Pope. In the autumn of 1478 permission to use the white red Pinot Noir as sacramental wine was announced.

In the first session of the epoch-making Council of Trent, it was decided that all wines of any color that were vinified conscientiously and without the addition of foreign substances would in the future be allowed to be used as sacramental wine.

1.159g

Literature:

R. Grosslindner, *The Pure Sacramental Wine*, St. Pölten, 1959.

J. Priewa, *Wine*, Munich, 2000.

G. Schmid/A. Schulz, *The Vintage: Methods, Regions, People*, Berlin, 2002.

1.207g

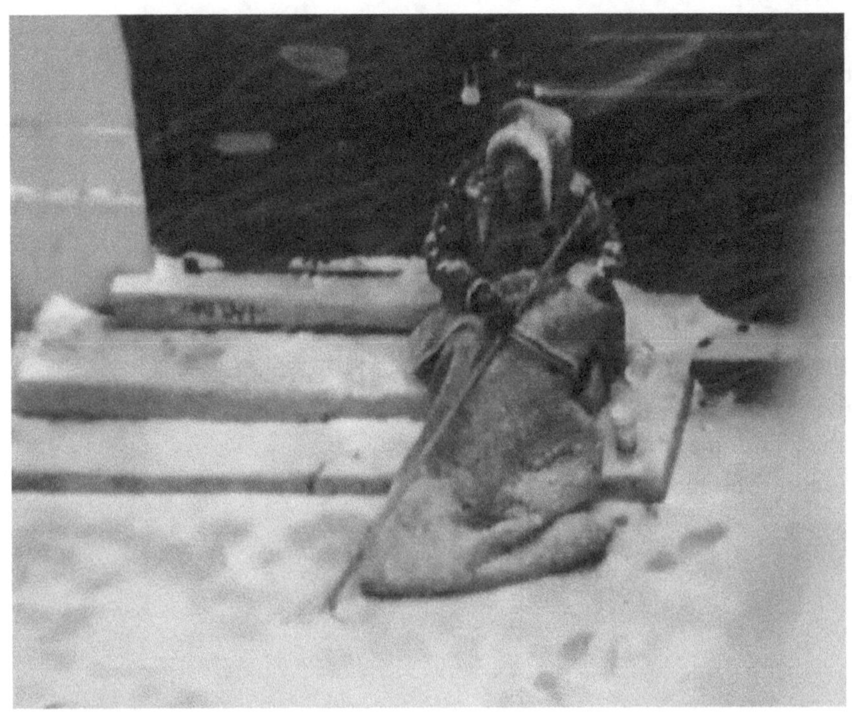

A Performance by Jack McNeil
in Honor of Joseph Beuys:
A Film by Günter Eisenhardt

In order to commemorate and honor the 10th anniversary of Joseph Beuys' death on January 23, 1996, the performance artist Jack McNeil sat on the curbside on Hudson Street in New York City from January 22 to 24 in the style of an archaic shepherd with a long staff. With this "Action" he reflected upon Beuys' famous 1974 coyote performance *I Like America and America Likes Me* at the René Block Gallery in New York. In regard to his action, Beuys had said: "I used an animal that plays a major role in the American psyche: the coyote. It represents the unresolved past of the murder of the Indians, and is therefore despised by Americans to this day."

It was in response to this statement that Jack McNeil named his action *The Coyote is Free, America Hates the Coyote, It is the Coyote.* McNeil explained: "All I see in American society are coyotes. Everything that passes by me is a coyote. All human beings are coyotes—they roam around continuously looking for prey, looking to eat. They produce consumption and a life dedicated to consumption. In its hatred of coyotes, the American psyche has become the very thing it detests."

On April 26, 1996, the art magazine *Art One* wrote:

> *The most touching moment was when the human sculpture, Jack McNeil, lying down on a large felt blanket, began to spread it out with almost frozen, stiff hands—hands which from time to time were obscured by the falling snow. Within this imagery the words of Joseph Beuys appeared: "The purpose of the action was to reestablish the dialogue of human beings with the natural kingdom." Reenacted in the most impressive way, this phrase was given a new, highly actualized image with McNeil's action.*

On December 5, 1996, the magazine *Art of The World* wrote:

> *No one who has seen this film will ever forget the sequence in which Jack McNeil moves out of the frame, leaving his harrowing tracks behind in the snow, then reappears to assume his place again before the traces disappear. Precisely because of its minimalism, this performance is one the most impressive events we have seen in a long time.*

The Parisian journal of philosophy *Posthistoire est Historique* stated in the summer of 1996:

> The Coyote is Free, America Hates the Coyote, It is the Coyote *is impressive, if only because Jack McNeil sits there quietly, forever writing some characters on the snow with his staff. These are primordial patterns. These characters take us to the beginnings of cave paintings and confront us with a new code. They raise the question of runes; one wants to know what they have to communicate. But they disappear as quickly as these very thoughts. They are covered, obscured by the same volatile snow from which they originated. This volatility of dialogue in public that is not performed—because they simply go unnoticed, for they cannot be perceived—opens a new chapter in the debate on the understanding of misunderstood discourse.*

The entire action *The Coyote is Free, America Hates the Coyote, It is the Coyote* was filmed by G. Eisenhardt. The original version exists as a sixty-two-hour film in two copies. The movie premiered in its full length on May 12, 1997, on the 76th anniversary of Joseph Beuys' birth and was projected on the outer walls of PS 1. After this performance, the former school became so well known and so popular that it was acquired by the Museum of Modern Art in 1997.

Literature:
Art One, New York, 1996.
Art of The World, London, 1996.
Posthistoire est Historique, Paris, 1996.

1.215 g

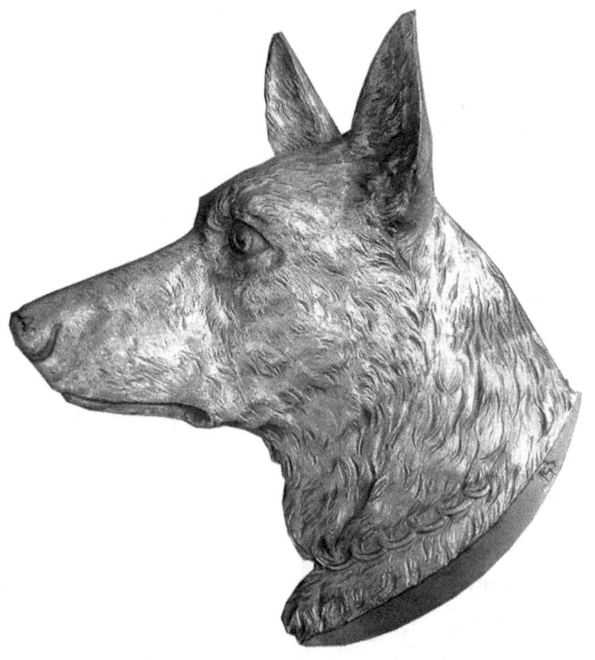

The Model of a 22-Meter-High Relief of the Space Dog Laika

1.215 g

November 3, 1957: The 40th anniversary of the great October Revolution is celebrated. For the second time in just two weeks the USSR has demonstrated its superiority over western capitalism. On this occasion a 508-kilogram capsule—a man-made artificial star—was shot into space to orbit the earth. Onboard *Sputnik 2* was the first terrestrial being to travel in space: a female dog named Laika.

Only four weeks before, on October 4, 1957, the glorious Soviet Union had paralyzed and shocked the entire free western world by launching into orbit its first satellite. *Sputnik 1*, weighing in at 83 kilograms and constantly emitting a repeating clear beep tone with its four antenna for all of humankind to hear, was the first spacecraft to ever orbit around our blue planet every ninety-six minutes at a speed of 28,000-kilometers per hour.

Four weeks later the dog Laika, artificially fed for ten days, went around the Earth every 104 minutes, documenting and sending back to Earth the sounds of a beating heart in orbit. Then she was euthanized peacefully through a cannula. Edward Teller, the American inventor of the hydrogen bomb, spoke of a battle lost that was "more significant than Pearl Harbor."

Sputnik 2 orbited the earth another 155 days as a sign of the superiority and triumph of the socialist nation against the exploitative and individualistic countries on the western side of the planet, only to burn up as it made its entry back into the atmosphere on April 14, 1958.

The West's horror and silence was termed "Sputnik Shock."

Nikita Khrushchev, First Secretary General of the Communist Party, in his much-publicized speech to the Central Committee of CPSU on November 5, 1957, claimed, "The Socialist Collective has advanced humanity, and life itself. The socialist people have overcome capitalism. And though we will continue to see American dogs on TV, who could possibly be interested in a dog like Lassie today when our Laika has orbited the Earth a hundred times? And thus, in honor of this dog, we shall create the largest relief humanity has ever seen..."

Immediately "The Committee in Honor of Socialist Achievements in Orbit" was established. The task of the committee was to give the collective achievements in space their deserved expression on Earth. And the first thing to be established was a relief of Laika.

Angelina Zikanowa, the reknowned socialist sculptor, was commissioned to make the relief in February 1958. After the first draft had been submitted to many authorities and committees, passed through many evaluations and assessments, and then gone through even more changes and corrections, a 1:10 scale model was produced. The original was to be 22-meters high and mounted on a wall near the Kremlin at just such an angle that Nikita Khrushchev would be able to see Laika from his window.

The work of the "Committee in Honor of Socialist Achievements in Orbit", however, did not proceed so smoothly. There were too many directions, tastes, and considerations. The problem was that dissenters, resfuseniks, the disreputable, and the unpopular were pushed into the committee, who were then shut out and finally exiled, and this naturally made life difficult for everyone else.

And so the project dragged on. Input was slow or not processed at all; decisions were never made. Mutual denunciations and slander became commonplace.

Meanwhile, Laika stamps already existed in Romania, Albania, and Poland. Ulan Bator wanted to erect a Laika statue, but this met with opposition from Moscow precisely from the aforementioned committee because the 22-meter relief of Laika had to be unveiled in Moscow first.

The only thing that "The Committee in Honor of Socialist Achievements in Orbit" actually achieved was to give John F. Kennedy the puppy Strelkas—the first dog to safely came back from outer space in the fifth Sputnik—in 1960.

When Khrushchev was discharged in 1962 after the Cuban Missile Crisis and subsequently forced out of the office of General Secretary of the CPSU in 1964, the great Laika relief remained unrealized, with the exception of the 1:10 scale model.

After Khrushchev's fall, no one wanted to talk about the relief, and the model was returned to Angelina Zikanowa. In 1975 Zikanowa had only the following bitter remarks to say about her efforts to realize the Laika relief: "They want nothing." She passed away in 1982, was given high honors, and was buried in the artists' cemetery known as "The Glowing Star" with magnificent pomp.

In 1995 a part of the artist's estate came to Germany.

On December 16, 1999, Wolfgang Hak donated the unknown relief of a dog to *The Museum of Unheard (of) Things*. The result of the museum's own two-year research showed this relief to in fact be the model of the space dog Laika originally sculpted by Angelina Zikanowa.

A special thanks to Ms. Sersisa Celbn-Hentger without whose tireless persistence the solution to the mystery of the relief would not have come to light.

Literature:

Peggy Ämdler, *Laika's Dance*, Berlin, 1999.
Mikel Bures, *A Case Study of Statecraft 1959-1965*, New York, 1973.
Inge Lümers, *The Animal in Orbit*, London, 1974.
Ruth Kümmerle, *Caught in the Net of the Dog Laika*, Berlin, 2001.
Vasily Lunin, *The Footsteps of the Successful*, Moscow, 1972.

1.215g

1.217g

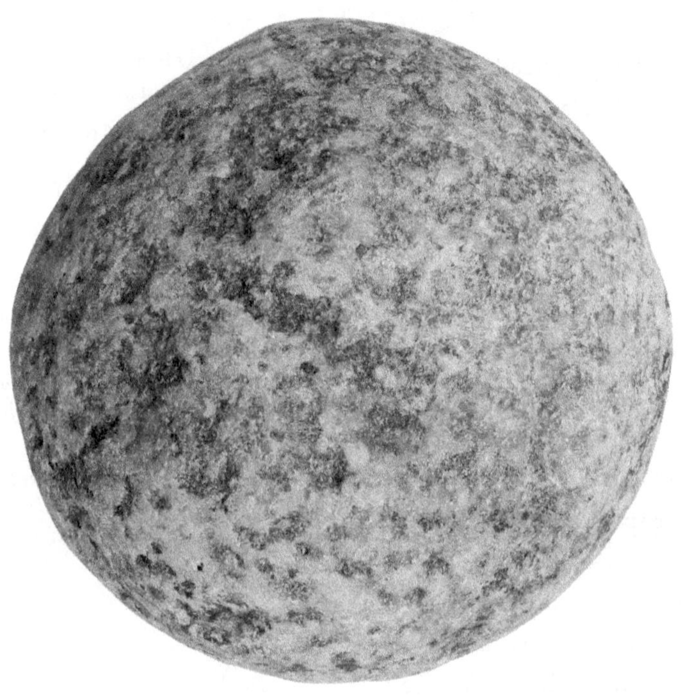

On the History of Interpretations of Nature Based on a Cobblestone from the Natural History Museum in Vienna

In Eggenburg, Austria, about 80 kilometers west of Vienna, where the great plain ends, the landscape rises, and the Austrian Waldviertel region begins, there at one of the first mountainsides lies the Limberg quarry. This quarry is also sometimes referred to as the "Book of Geological History" because the displacements, sediments, and residue of more than 20 million years can be sorted, delineated, and read there, almost down to the exact year.

Johann Karahuletz (1848-1928) of Eggenburg was an avid collector who, unchallenged by criticism or hostility, carried out his research and developed an archaeological museum with his collection. In fact, he was the first person in modern times to recognize the uniqueness of this quarry. One of its special features is the smooth, perfectly round stones that can be found in different sizes. Today these stones are known as cobblestones and are made from Maissauer Granite, a very strong and robust rock. However, these round stones are not only interesting as stones; the diversity of interpretations and applications surrounding them allows for a reading of how history, and history's usage, as well as perspectives, change over time.

These round stones have been popular as long as humans have been around and have always attracted attention. In many flexed-burial graves and burial mounds from the Bronze Age and even more remote times—for example, the early Iron Age—it is common to find these round stones as funerary objects. Among the objects found in early historic settlements of Kagran and Aspern, located where Vienna is today, one sees these round stones, though their significance is still unclear. Soon after the Romans established their military camp Carnuntum in the area of present-day Vienna in AD 15, the first spherical stones began to appear in Rome. Once the Legion X Gemina Pia Fidelis settled their headquarters in Vindobona (as the camp was now known) in AD 114, a brisk cobblestone trade flourished until the Romans retreated in AD 500. In ancient Rome it was considered very fashionable to own and display such round stones. Thus, some historians attribute ceremonial properties to them.

Be that as it may, the first mention of these stones in writing appears in 1213. In a letter—preserved only in fragments—from Bishop Clemens to the newly elected Pope Benedictus VIII, the bishop writes about a hamlet called Luftritz (about 20 kilometers from present-day Eggenburg), and reports that people were talking about a landing site for "aeronauts" who were coming there in order to collect the uniformly round, spherical stones as ballast. The existence of aeronauts was a widespread belief in Europe at that time, and reports about them came from just about everywhere. One center for aeronautic landing was in southern France, in the area around Lyon, but the aeronauts' presence and activities had also been reported from as far afield as England, Spain, Northern Germany, and even Austria. The existence of aeronauts stemmed from the belief that the space above the clouds, the blue of the sky, heaven itself, was lively and populated. The people living there—these so-called aeronauts—sometimes came down to earth to collect the aforementioned ballast, which was necessary for their airships to maintain altitude and to be able to navigate. It was assumed that each weight slowly evaporated in the high altitudes of the sky, and therefore, from time to time, had to be renewed.

But ballast was not the only thing the aeronauts were after; for, seeing as that they were already here, they also carried off harvests, emptied wine barrels, stole freshly baked bread, etc. One just accepted them as a given, and had a rather mischievous relationship with them. For example, taxes hidden from the authorities were explained as having been stolen by visits from the aeronauts.

Things, however, were different with the church in Rome. The church authorities vehemently fought the belief in aeronauts, seeing them as rivals to God and his angelic hosts. The sky was not intended for a species demanding tribute. In fact, the letter from Bishop Clemens to Pope Benedictus VIII deals with the issue of fighting this belief in aeronauts. He asked how it was possible for him to compete with this fixed delusion and how to explain the presence of these beautiful, unique, round stone balls in other ways. Unfortunately, no reply has been recorded.

In 1318 the by now lost but repeatedly cited and richly illustrated book *God's Creatures of the Heavenly Paradise* mentioned and depicted a unicorn playing with a ball with his horn. According to numerous reports, this ball was in reality a round stone. The unicorn stands in a suggestive plain before a golden, brocade-like background. To the right and left one can see a hill ascending from the plain, which is very similar to the quarry in Eggenburg. Mention of unicorns playing with stone balls appear again and again in transcripts from the Benedictine monasteries of Reichenau, now kept in the library at St. Gallen. It should be noted, however, that these reports have no images or any detailed information of place. The unicorn playing with a round stone symbolizes the power of virginity. If one stands within the power of undisputed virginity, that is, the virginity of Mary, one can move the heaviest stones without any effort, just like the unicorns. Unsurprisingly perhaps these round stones had a relic-like status in Europe for some time. In fact, they are still kept in the treasuries of many cathedrals.

In 1475 Leonardo da Vinci sketched a windmill in which the entire mill house turned with the wind. In precise drawings he impressively depicted the house standing on many, similarly sized, round stones, which were held up and down by a U-shaped ring. Pitted and partially crushed olives can be seen being used as a lubricant. This drawing is considered to be the first depiction of a modern, well-conceived ball-wheel. In his distinct, laterally reversed writing, da Vinci wrote a note saying that the most appropriate balls for this kind of construction were "Viennese Balls."

These "Viennese Balls" from Eggenburg were at the time very popular in Italy and were displayed in many households as such. It was the Renaissance, and in the return to the old traditional values of the Greeks and Romans, the latter's stone balls were rediscovered and highly revered. They now symbolized the power and beauty of antiquity but also the symmetry of God, the harmony of ancient culture, and the uniformity of God's creation. This interpretation persisted, however, for only a short time. Just fifty years later, the same balls were used as a secret sign for those clinging to the forbidden Copernican worldview which held that the world and the universe were spherical.

In 1529 under Sultan Suleiman the 100,000-strong, richly dressed, and impressively bejewlled Turkish army stood before the gates of Vienna. Niklas Graf Salm let the suburbs burn down and led the city's defense. On September 22, 1529, the Turkish siege was completed. Sultan Suleiman organized a sort of shuttle with hundreds of oxcarts to the Limberg quarry in Eggersburg, and mined the round stone balls in large quantities. Together with catapults they were used to bring down the gates of Vienna and to overcome the defense system. Many people were hit by the stones and many roofs were shattered. After a particularly heavy attack, children were employed to roll the stones aside so that street traffic would not be affected too greatly. And yet, the very early winter that year forced the Turks to abandon their siege by October 14, 1529, and withdraw without having achieved anything. However, in just twenty-two days more than 15,000 stone balls had rained down on Vienna.

Between 1713 and 1728, Ludwig Graf von Schowiks used the debris to make his first ballistic trajectory calculations. In particular, he preferred rather round stones for his experiments. Promised extra income, the population of Eggenburg was thus inspired to search for good examples. Von Schowiks could not get enough of them. For him, these stones were particularly suitable because they were regarded as ones with a centered sealing core. This theory states that certain stones—"core stones" as they were known—grew from the inside out, that they possessed a high-density core, and that they had developed their present spherical shapes around these so-called watchtower cores over thousands of years, similar to the rings of trees. At the quarry in Eggenburg the conditions for such round stone growth had been ideal, as the stones were able to develop free from any external influences; and these stones proved most suitable to Graf von Schowiks' ballistic research, for they had the same weight from the core on all sides—in other words, there was no elliptical side weighting to pull the balls from out of their predetermined path.

In 1855 an eccentric party from Great Britain visited the Eggenburg quarry. Together with thirty-five others, Sir George Watt settled down for two months in Eggenburg to investigate. Five years previously Sir George had been on an expedition to the Hoggar Mountains and since then had only worn the clothing given to him by the Tuareg people. Seven of his staff members were brought from the Sahara and granted the party an air of authenticity. In 1841 Sir George Watt had heard Anthony Richard Owens' lecture in the UK, which for the first time mentioned the fossilized remains of reptiles from Great Britain and employed the previously unknown term of "dinosaur" to describe them. Ever since Sir George had been travelling around the world to find dinosaur fossils—just one of the many "dinosaur hunters" not uncommon in those days. He was convinced that the stones from Eggenburg were dinosaur eggs. He took twenty-three samples back with him and held a lecture on August 5, 1856, in a private scholarly academy in London entitled "On the Evidence of Dinosaurs in Large Quantities, Discovered and Evaluated by Sir George Watt Himself." After his lecture, he donated his dinosaur eggs to the Natural History Museum, which was still under construction at the time. They can still be seen there today.

Today, of course, the spherical stones can be explained by the presence of the ancient sea of Paratethy that existed 20 million years ago. Where the quarry is now was once the seaside and an immense, stony beach; the rolling and roiling of the sea ground the rock down into the round stones that we know today.

My thanks to Reinhard Golebiowski from the Natural History Museum in Vienna for drawing my attention to the existence of the cobblestones and for leaving me one.

1.217 g

Literature:
T. Frunka, *The Unicorn's Game*, Leipzig, 1912.
P. Mayer, *On the Development of Ballistic Parabola*, Nuremberg, 1986.
F. Römer, *1000 Years of Austria*, Vienna, 1996.

1.405g

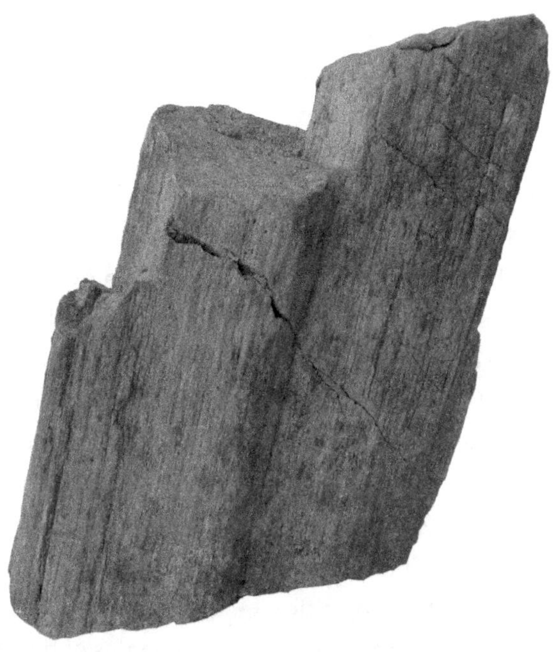

The Last Tree
in One of the Finest Prehistoric Forests
of the Late Paleozoic Era
in the Area of Present-Day Central Europe

Three hundred sixty-two million years ago the Earth was inhabited by only a few creatures. There were just several species of reptiles, amphibians, insects, and cyclostomes during a time period that is now known as the "late Paleozoic." Back then the Earth did not have many continents, as it consisted of the great mega-continent Pangaea, and this Carboniferous Period saw the growth of large forests of club moss, horsetail, and ferns, which later became coal forests.

Around the area of today's Moravian-Austrian border, more or less between the idyllic town of Drossendorf and the famous wine-town of Retz in Austria, one of the most beautiful and diverse forests of this type could be found. For 1,503 years it grew without major disruptions, fertilized by its own diversity and differentiating various species. It was the healthiest, most wonderful, and most magnificent forest far and wide until a gigantic storm came and destroyed it. Storms were not uncommon, but that devastating a storm was something which occurred only once every thousand years and always left irreparable damages behind. And this was the case here. This storm not only snapped the trees in two (which would have been harmless), but uprooted and tore everything down that stood in its path, dismembering the bark, and shredding the wood. For six and a half weeks it ran its game of destruction until there was nothing left to resist. Apart from one tree, a giant club moss 35 meters in height, everything was razed to the ground. This particular club moss even stood on a small hill, and four separate times was bent flat on the ground by the storm, but managed to stand up again every time. It watched as the storm finished off its destructive work—certainly more than a bit ruffled, in addition to missing most of its leaves and being uprooted—but stood there and recovered.

The demolished and dismembered trees around it choked all life beneath them, rotted, and acidified the ground. A sticky liquid was created that poisoned all the soil and made any kind of vegetation impossible. Then rains came and washed away the slime while continuously eroding the earth until only bare rocks remained.

In the middle of this major ecological disaster, in the area of what is today's Central Europe, the 35-meter-high club moss stood upright and alone in the resulting stone desert. 228 years later, it finally snapped, fell, and turned to stone.

Near the village of Hadeck, at a bend of the Taya River, the attentive observer can still see the remains of this tree today.

Literature:

Siegfried Schmuttermaier, *The Petrified Tree Outside of the Forest Area*, Vienna, 1967.

Alois Wammerl, *Early Ecological Disasters*, Vienna, 1985.

1.489g

The Biceps Trainer of the First Telephone Operators

or

How the Telephone Lost Its Weight until It Was Almost Unbearable

1.489g

By November of 1877, one year after the telephone became patented in America, the Berlin company Siemens & Halske was already producing 200 phones a day.

Quickly trained telephone operators manually connected callers through telephone switchboards. The Switchboard Operator Lady had been born. Initially development engineers doubted whether women could adequately deal with such technology. However, with their higher frequency, women's voices proved indispensable, as they could be transmitted significantly better and more intelligibly than men's voices could.

Telephony, however, first had to be learned by the callers, as no one was used to the abstraction of a disembodied voice. At the beginning of a conversation people usually said, "Hello, Hello" to test the volume of transmission, after which they kept their voice as low as possible throughout the subsequent conversation. When the transmission was particularly distorted, one talked about being on "long lines," or "getting the wires crossed."

The phone revolutionized the business world—suddenly, you could talk with business partners without being physically present. Negotiations with different locations could now be conducted without leaving the room. A businessman could respond quickly and directly.

In larger enterprises, small switch centers were established with friendly young ladies sitting and wiring incoming and outgoing calls. In addition to using the recently introduced typewriter, these women were also responsible for mediating conversations.

Such constant lifting and dropping of the at-that-time heavy handsets strained some of the ladies to the extent that complaints of nightly muscle soreness and upper-arm fatigue began to be aired in the newly founded "Association for Efficient Women in Office Work."

One of the first schools for secretaries, "Gerda Kaiser's School for the Preparation of Well-trained Young Ladies for Professional Life, Since 1892," had offered free classes on typewriting and telephone conversation from its inception. In the spring of 1905, they introduced an obligatory intensive course on telephony.

These young ladies were initiated into the finer details of how the various models functioned—complete with their idiosyncrasies and flaws—as well as how to fix things themselves. In these courses, the young ladies were also briefed on the anatomical structure of the hand (for the typewriter) and the upper arms (for the handset). In the name of worker's protection, they were also taught finger exercises and encouraged to use telephone bicep trainers on a regular basis.

Weights in handset form had been especially developed for long-distance-call secretaries and these telephone biceps trainers were now being promoted. They were to be used every day, for a quarter of an hour, in accordance with the attached instructions.

The company that produced these special telephone bicep dumbbells, Henke & Maurer, advertised them together with a certificate from "Father Jahn's United Gym."

Henke & Maurer's telephone bicep dumbbell was on offer up until the end of the 1950s.

Later on, the company began to produce only sports equipment, and over the last twenty years—under a different name—have become one of the leading sport club outfitting companies.

Over time, the telephone handset has gotten lighter. Since the proliferation of telephony throughout the private sphere in the 1960s, many people's communication behavior has changed. Hour-long phone calls, the habit of saying "just call me," made the person's absence sometimes more important than personally and physically being able to meet them.

And then, later on, the handset was emancipated from the cable and went wireless. After that, the mobile phone was introduced and remote verbal contact was everywhere and possible at any time.

The hand, which was once essential to making phone calls, has since become superfluous. Today a single, tiny plug is inserted into the ear and a small device in your pocket then transmits the eagerly awaited calls directly into your ear via Bluetooth. The typical telephone posture—head inclined slightly to the side in a sign of respect to the other party—has become outdated and unnecessary. Talks are now held with an upright, unobtrusive head posture.

1.489g

Literature:

H. Hortmann, *Occupational Safety Release Measures: Past and Present*, Stuttgart, 2002.

R. Kümmerle, *Secretaries in the Mirror of Time*, Berlin, 1978.

T. Morel, *From the Crank to Bluetooth*, Berlin, 2008.

2.305g

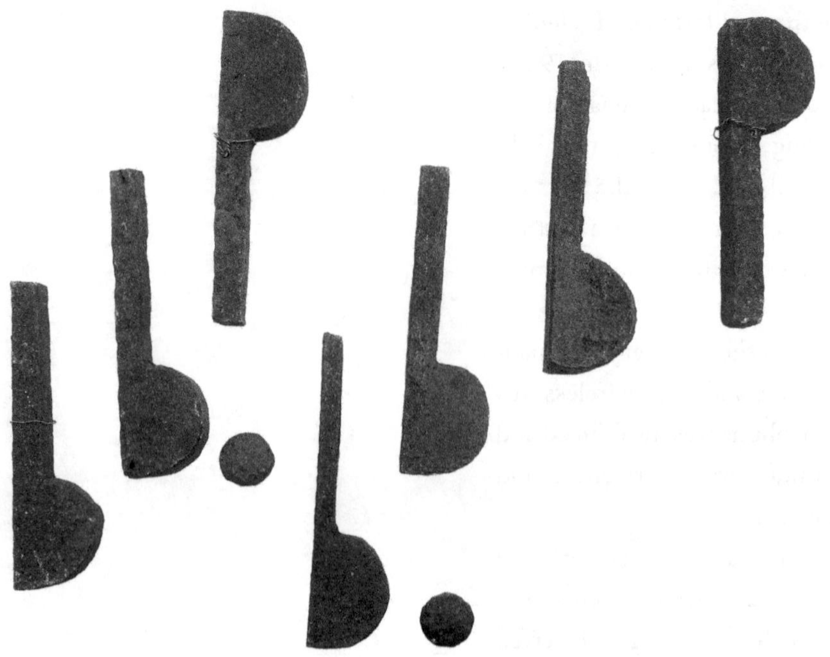

Iron Notes

A gift from the revolutionary workers of the Red Star Shipyard in Leningrad to the revolutionary workers of Rickmers Shipyard in Bremerhaven on the occasion of the performance of the great *Symphony of Factory Sirens* in Leningrad on August 20, 1920. The gift consists of the punched iron notes from the opening bars of the symphony.

During the Leningrad performance of the great *Symphony of Factory Sirens* on August 20, 1920, a machine punched, to the beat of the music, notes from a 18-milimeter-thick steel plate and thus transferred the music from the outside to the inside.

The gift was handed over by a worker of the Red Star Shipyard, Uri Kslovikil, to a worker of the Rickmers Shipyard, Hubert Jolcka, on May 5, 1922, during a clandestine meeting in Kremmen, where an arrangement for an international agreement of shipyard workers was to have taken place. There were great difficulties with language at the meeting, for the entry of the interpreter traveling from Leningrad had been refused, and the negotiations had to thus be postponed.

The notes were kept by the worker Hubert Jolcka in the false bottom of his toolbox, which stood in the pressroom in Rickmers Shipyard. Seventy-five years later during demolition of the factory building, the toolbox was destroyed by a depalletizing vehicle and removed. The only thing to remain was the bottom of the box with its contents—the now rusted notes. A year or so thereafter they were found under a birch tree on the by-now empty land.

Literature:

Arseni Avraamov, "The Symphony of Sirens," in Douglas Kahn and Gregory Whitehead (eds.), *Wireless Imagination*, London, 1992.

——, "Klin-Klinom (A wedge drives the other)," in *Muzykalnaja Kultura*, Moscow I, 1924.

P. Gorsen and E. Knödler-Bunte, *Proletcult: System of a Proletarian Culture*, Stuttgart, 1974.

Melita Palika, *Bremen and the Avant-garde*, Bremen, 1992.

2.305g

3.800g

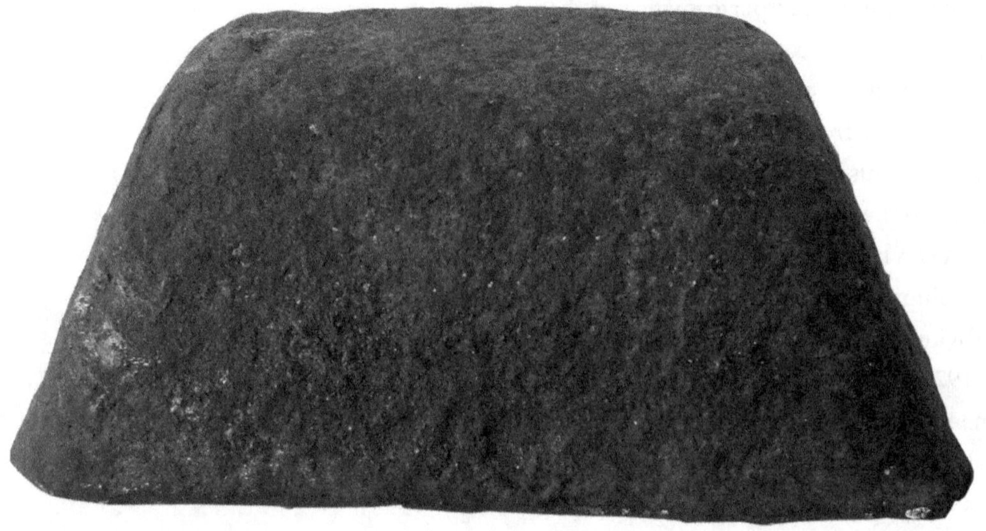

The Story of a Piece of Iron

Dimitri Ivanovich Nechyugov was part of the fourth shift employed in the cleanup of Block 3 of the nuclear power plant at Chernobyl in April 1987. Dimitri Ivanovich Nechyugov went into the nuclear reactors a total of twenty-four times and received the medal of bravery for his actions half a year later.

What no one knew was that Dimitri Ivanovich Nechyugov had smuggled a piece of metal out of the barriers of the damaged nuclear power plant as a personal souvenir of his mission. It was a piece of molten iron that had been dropped into a dent of the cool-down tank and there become solidified.

Dimitri Ivanovich Nechyugov smuggled the 3.5-kilogram piece of iron from the enclosed area by putting it into a bulge of the concrete bulk tube with which helicopters laid the mantle of the sarcophagus that covered the nuclear power plant All Dimitri Ivanovich Nechyugov had to do was to then pick up his piece of iron at the provisional helicopter airport. He brought it back home with pride, and there it stood behind a glass in the living room closet until 1997.

In the spring of 1990 Dimitri Ivanovich Nechyugov became ill. He was diagnosed with exhaustion and general weakness. He was sent to Sochi for rest in 1992 and began to receive his pension in the summer of 1993. His questions as to whether his illness was linked to his employment in the nuclear power plant were ignored.

Dimitri Ivanovich Nechyugov died in the winter of 1995.

Literature:
Theo Mangel, *The Forgotten History*, Berlin, 2010.
Ivan Staloy, *The Liquidators*, Dresden, 2000.

3.800g

>21.311g

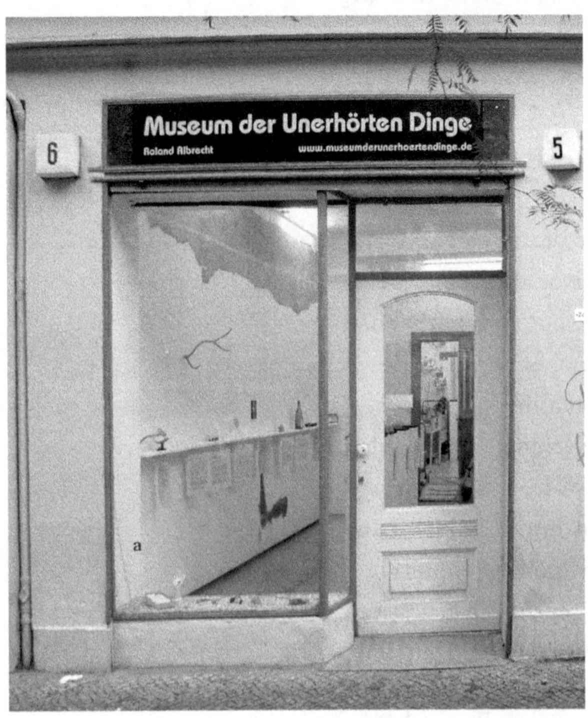

The Museum of Unheard (of) Things

The very first thing, the very first object, something like the very first exhibition piece of a museum to come (albeit one I was not yet aware of), was a telescope. We—the telescope and I— first met on a class trip to a medieval castle in Württemberg. I was just eleven years old, and my father had given me five marks for food and drink. On the bus ride to Teck Castle I watched a schoolmate from another class as he kept looking through a four-part, extendable telescope made of brass. Observing him I noticed that he did not treat the telescope in a very loving manner: rather than appreciating it for its own sake, he simply used it to brag and to draw attention to himself. I knew that I had to free this telescope from such unpleasant, undignified treatment by its owner who did not understand, or worse, did not appreciate, just what it was that he possessed. I, however, had recognized it immediately: it was the very telescope through which Christopher Columbus had seen America for the first time on October 12, 1492. I saw Christopher Columbus standing at the bow of the Santa Maria, his upper body slightly bent over the railing, both hands on the telescope. I could see the satisfied smile that slid across his face as he saw his America and his America looked back.

The other boy did not know all this of course. Later in the day when he lost interest in the telescope, I bought it from him with my five marks then hid it in my bag so that it would be safe and so that no one would mistreat it any longer. Without knowing it, that telescope was to be the first object of the future The Museum of Unheard (of) Things founded many decades later.

Over the course of time, I found more and more things—an Auroch's horn upon which Stone Age hunters blew; coins that could be used as pay in foreign countries; glassbeads which never made it to Africa. All the things I found were placed in a shoebox, and when that became too small, wandered into a larger box, a treasure chest of sorts.

All of the things gathered in this box were of immense value. Every piece told me its own unique story connected to that one thing and that one thing only. The pieces have no monetary value—their value exists only in the imagination and therefore remains inviolable while making them more precious than anything you could ever buy.

Very soon, however, I learned that not every piece told the truth; that some were, and are, capable of lying, of exaggerating, that the things too can be consumed by vanity. There were eloquent chatterboxes as well as rather silent things—just as there were also stubborn or timid things. And so I realized that every single thing, without exception, had a story, and that, often, things which had lost their meaning, whose functions and names I did not know, were in reality extremely eloquent.

All of this I learned over the course of the following several decades, and it all began with buying the telescope on the school trip.

Today more than 400 things have been archived, numbered, measured, photographed, and sorted according to their weight in the depository of The Museum of Unheard (of) Things. And so Christopher Columbus's telescope now hangs in the weight category "140g-200g" next to an artificial hip joint that, when struck, emits a beautiful, high, and

›21.311g

long-lasting tone, and in the vicinity of a ship in a bottle and a reel with a 100-meter-long yarn of hemp.

All these completely different things—like the wooden boat with a mechanical weaving loom; a military chaplain's pen with the inscription "God Protect You"; a potato masher from a commercial kitchen that hangs beside simple, practical, and fast replacement pockets for ironing and across from a fire-breathing deer or a cookie cutter in the shape of a rabbit—have not been arbitrarily juxtaposed; their proximity to one another results from their weight and complementarity. This variety has one thing in common: every single thing has a story, something it has shared with me, and over the years we have developed a very personal relationship, the things and I.

>21.311g

In reality, it is not all that dissimilar from a shell you bring back home from a vacation you spent at the seashore that allows the experience to resurface, however briefly, and bring those emotions back to life every time you look at it. But I am not the only one who has a relationship with all the things—the things themselves also have relationships with and to one another, and it is the associations of the things to me and with each other that produce this intertwining "depository-entanglement."

But, again, within this entanglement there is a precise order. Every thing hangs in its chosen place and has been catalogued and labeled so that in the immediate vicinity of a living mouse trap that has never caught a single mouse there is a box of school chalk with which nobody knew what to write; and next to that, a porcelain heart filled with medicine and a small red sign protruding from above that reads "7 РАДИОУЗЕЛ."

I suspect that the things of the depository visit each other, at night for instance, that they have their flings or arguments according to their unique forms and their thingly nature and ways.

The mission of the museum is to listen to these things, these entities, without prejudice, to take them seriously and to write down their stories. In a way, the things of the museum are on a psychoanalytic couch and I dedicate my "evenly-suspended attention" to them.

It is not, however, about holding the seashell to your ear to hear the conserved sounds of the ocean, to regard the shell as a container of sounds, as an archive of the sea. The issue, rather, is of finding out the precise, innate story of the shell, to listen to it tell its own story. It is a thoughtful hearing of the as-of-yet unheard. It is about the shell and not the sea.

Only the hearing and its contextualization give a thing an aura that makes it relevant to the museum and turns it into a museum piece. The story told inflates the thing, makes it stand out from other profane things, differentiates it, and turns it into a narrative; that which is special, chosen, and individual, protected by glass, lying in showcases, placed on stage under the spotlight, located in the public exhibition space to meet the high expectations of museum visitors; that which is sought after with grace, never to disappoint.

These things now on display in the museum tell unheard of stories—of petrified ice whose occurrence has been witnessed at only three places on Earth; of how the Chinese art of Qi Gong was copied from penguins; of a breast stone that belonged to the writer

Thomas Mann; of a piece of the typewriter on which Walter Benjamin wrote "The Work of Art in the Age of Mechanical Reproduction"; but also of dream depositories, the impact of thought flashes, and the red threads that run through life.

Through the stories appended to the things the museum becomes a kind of literary *Wunderkammer* where the haptic meets and complements the literary. These pieces—whose calls have been heard with their unheard (of) stories—have not been subordinated to any ordering system such as natural science, humanities, engineering, or geology. The Museum of Unheard (of) Things is therefore closer to the princely cabinet of curiosities of the Renaissance and Baroque than to today's systematized and specialized collectors' museum.

Visitors to The Museum of Unheard (of) Things, located on Crellestraße in the Schöneberg district of Berlin, see objects and read the accompanying texts attached to them; for example, the one on a "Patience Thread" which is not made up of one but rather a number of patiences, or the story about the remaining screw from a plane crash in 1937 in which the music of Béla Bartók plays a central role, or the one about the lifelong love between Lena and Getraud Pachulke and their wedding in 1950s Berlin. And, furthermore, whoever enters the museum plays their own part in contributing to its record of being the most visited museum in Berlin—if one offsets the number of visitors to the square meters of the exhibition space, that is.

"It is, however, also fascinating to witness the other spellbound visitors who sometimes stay for hours reading. One is then dwelling in a secular, personal recess of reading which may develop into a reading group experience: a worldly devotion involving a switching between smiles and amazement that condenses into a tangible atmosphere and transfers from one visitor to another"—writes Winfried Pauleit about The Museum of Unheard (of) Things.

The museum was founded in Dresden at the Raskolnikov Gallery in 1998. It settled in the internet in 1999 and in 2000 moved to its permanent location here in the Crellestraße between house numbers 5 and 6. The museum presents temporary exhibitions of related artists, and holds regular events—concerts, film screenings, and discussions. It also takes part in the "Long Night of Museums," presented throughout the city at other museums and art exhibitions.

>21.311g

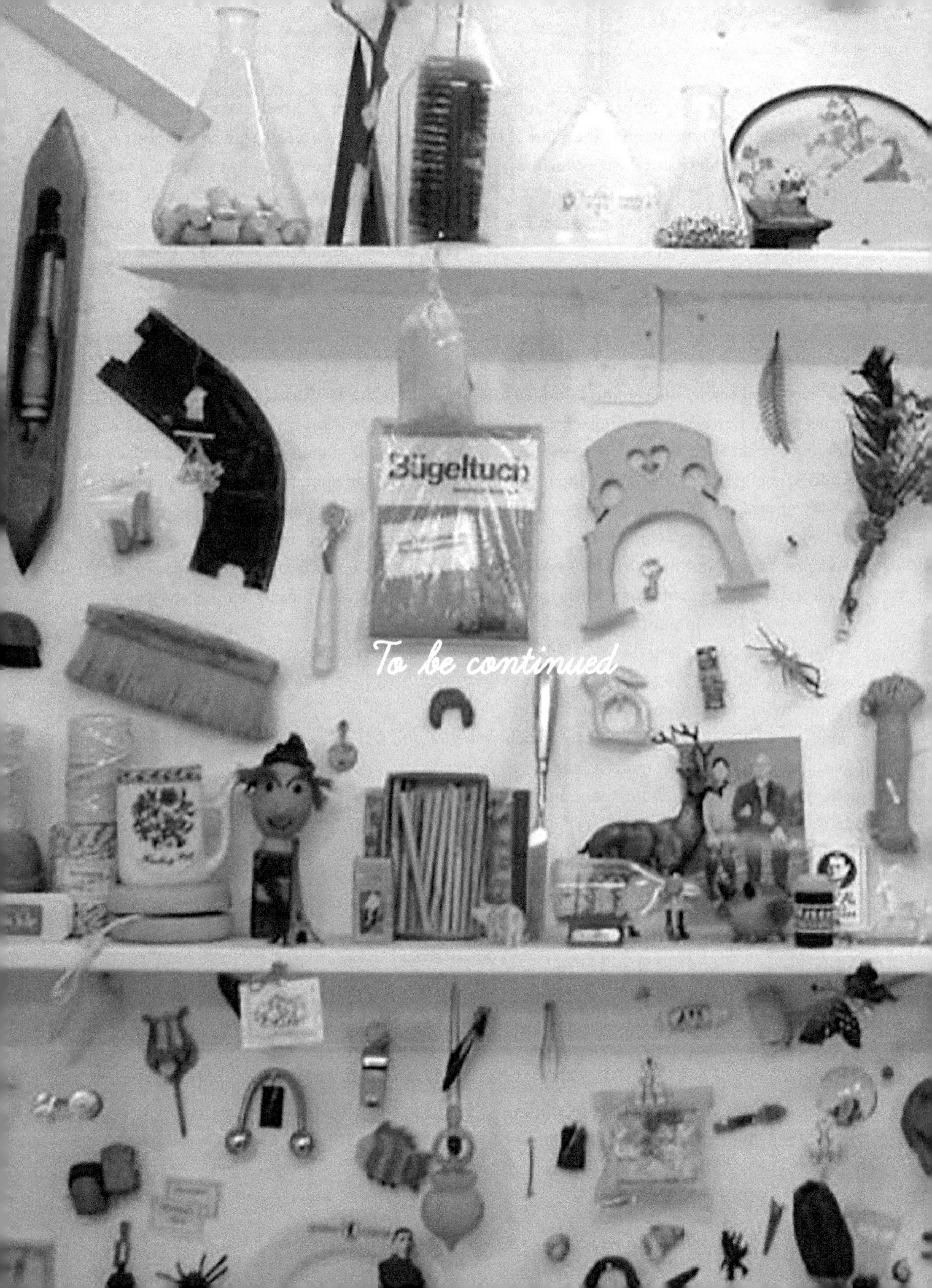
Bügeltuch
To be continued

AUTHOR

Roland Albrecht was born in 1950 in the town of Memmingen in the Allgäu (Southern Germany). He lives in Berlin and has worked in various medical professions. He is a photographer, artist, and writer who has published and exhibited widely with pieces that mainly focus on text and object. His work includes collages, short radio plays, short films, soundscapes and audiovisual portraits. He has been curating The Museum of Unheard (of) Things since its inception in 1997.

TRANSLATORS

Alexander Booth is a writer and translator. His work has appeared in numerous international print and online journals. He lives in Germany.

You Nakai either makes music, dance, haunted houses and other works as part of No Collective (http://nocollective.com), or publishes books and other paraphernalia as part of Already Not Yet, or does research on music and other curiosities and writes about his findings in the form of academic papers.

ALREADY NOT YET http://alreadynotyet.org

is a publisher based in Brooklyn, New York, run by members of No Collective, dedicated to consummating the age to come by making available unprecedented texts that question and/or traverse the boundaries of art, theory, fiction, and other curiosities, primarily via the medium of language.

ANY 01 | May 2014 | 180 PP (Full Color)

Ellen C. Covito: Works After Weather

Edited and compiled by No Collective

Argentinian composer/choreographer Ellen C. Covito has been gaining wide recognition in the recent years for her Composed Improvisation *and* Improvised Composition *series. This book brings together for the first time all her major works, along with theoretical essays that analyze her approach in depth and an exclusive interview with Covito herself. Edited and compiled by No Collective, the group that has organized four concerts of Covito's music and dance in New York, Tokyo, and Berlin, this is the definitive overview of one of the most radical artists working today.*

ANY 02 | November 2015 | 262 PP

Museum of Unheard (of) Things

by Roland Albrecht | Translated by Alexander Booth and You Nakai

ANY 03 [*Works on Progress* series Book 1] | December 2016 | 112 PP (Full Color)

Are We Here Yet?: Questions and Answers and Drawings by Aevi

Here are answers to everything you always wanted to know but never thought of asking (a four-and-a-half-year-old). Why is your hair stuck into your brain? Why do chickens want to fly a bit? What is the last number? Why do I have a shadow? What happens when you die? Why do you have books? These and many more age-old conundrums answered and illustrated for the very first time!

ANY 04 | January 2017 | 220 PP (Full Color)

MATT ERS OF ACT: A Journal of Ideas [A]

Edited and Compiled by No Collective

The first issue of a periodical which probes and fabricates the density of various unrealities. Features a detailed report on the large-scale earthwork project "Robert Smithson without Robert Smithson," a compilation of somewhat odd proposals sent to Movement Research in 2013, reviews of philosophy books written by children, interview with a reclusive poet who makes his works by reshelving books in a library and is upset about conceptual poetry not being conceptual enough, and more.

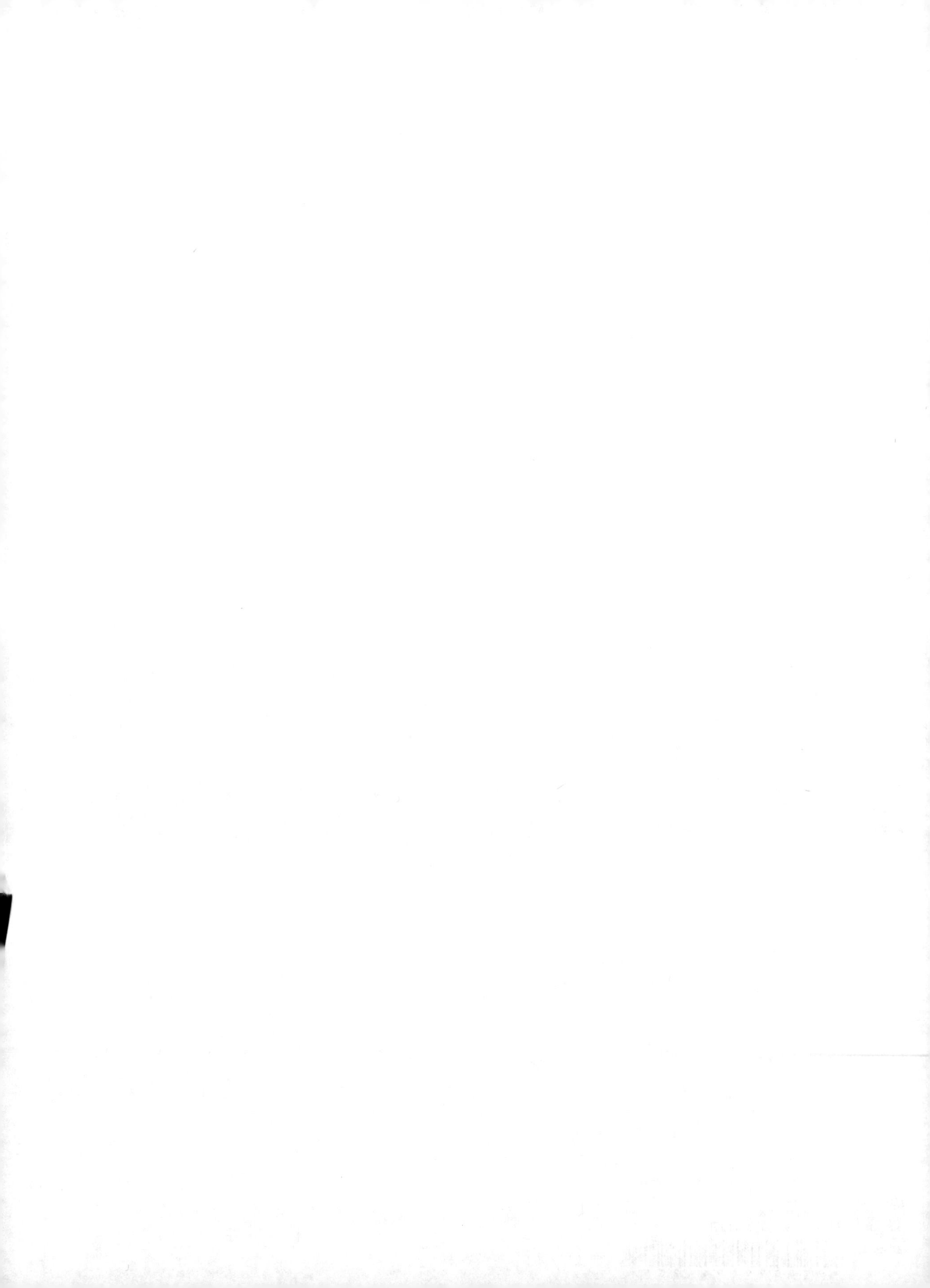

www.ingramcontent.com/pod-product-compliance
Lightning Source LLC
LaVergne TN
LVHW081322110826
845149LV00007B/1570

* 9 7 8 0 9 9 6 9 4 4 2 0 5 *